"Why did you destroy the Tov [...] "I don't want—" Ward [...]

"No," Ker said. He seemed like a different person, his charm shed like a winter coat. "We bet. You lost. Answer truth."

"I was angry," Ward shouted, feeling like Ker had been interrogating him on the subject for hours. "They took everyone from me. Everyone. That company, agency, whatever the fuck you want to call it, they did it. I don't give a shit about your beliefs or theirs. It all kills people. All of it." The words kept coming. "I wanted answers, I wanted my brother back, but I didn't go in to destroy it. I didn't do it to be your symbol. I went in for answers, but the only truth in there was that they killed my brother in that Labor Camp."

"You did it because they took your brother from you. You went in ready to do it. That's not anger. That's planning."

"I wasn't going..." Ward couldn't finish. He'd told himself a hundred times he hadn't gone in to do it. To kill all those people. He'd repeated the lie over and over: when he'd logged into the REC mainframe and saw the files, the details about the fire, about the slaughter, he'd lost his mind. He'd taken down the whole thing.

He'd let himself believe the rage did it, but that was a lie. Ker was right. He'd gone into that building for revenge right from the start.

"What makes your family worth killing for?" Ker asked. "What makes other families worth dying for yours?"

The silence around the table was like smoke, choking and blinding.

"Truth," Ker said. He shrugged and walked away.

THE LONG OBLIVION

RAFAEL WARD BOOK TWO

BY MICHAEL POGACH

For Olga

ACKNOWLEDGMENTS

There is a mythic image of the solitary writer, a romantic dissident tortured by genius and depression. Feel free to conjure images of fedoras, cigarette smoke, coffee, whiskey, and Lord Byron.

I am not that author.

Yes, writing is often a singular endeavor, lonely and maddening. But writing is only half the job (and maybe even not that much). This novel, like all my work, grew out of solitary writing and collaborative rewriting. It grew out of casual conversations about mythology and movies and books, and it grew out of notes I scribbled furiously while reading articles and blogs and essays on writing. It grew because I grew as an author, as a husband, as a father, as a teacher, and as a person.

While I couldn't possibly list here everyone who had a hand in helping (nudging, cheering, begging, threatening) me to complete this book, I'll do my best and hope that if I forget anyone they'll know they're appreciated just as much. So, here goes:

David and David at Crossroad Press; second homes are sometimes better than first homes, and I'm thrilled to be working with you guys.

Dan Schall and Michelle Tooker, and all current and former members of the AG Writers Group, for helping shape not only this world and these characters, but me as well; and for keeping me on target when life threatens to get in the way.

Stephen Mazzeo for leading me to Lethe.

Amara Royce for your weekly check-in emails, as well as your almost always dead-on suggestions.

Abigail Michelini for volunteering your time, your eyes, and your valuable insights.

Alfonso Boix Jovaní for delivering me Spain, and for letting me torture you.

Tobias Götz for helping with the German.

Sandra Del Cueto for helping with the Spanish.

Shannon Peitzer for your glorious insults.

Alana Abbott for your edits and your encouragement.

Gwen Nix for never going easy on me with your critique (and for your insistence I research every little detail, like the difference between bobcats, cougars, and mountain lions). This series is the best it can be because of you.

Shawn King at STK-Creations for making the most badass book covers around.

Mommom, Gigi, and Trish for the hours you give me to write.

Colleen and Coraline, my wife and daughter, what else can I say but thank you.

Last, to everyone who's read what I've written over the years and (even still!) asked for more, your encouragement keeps the words flowing and the doubt demons at bay. Thank you!

PART 1: CITIZENSHIP

A wrong is unredressed...when the avenger fails to make himself felt as such to him who has done the wrong.
— "The Cask of Amontillado," by Edgar Allan Poe, 1846

Find out just what any people will quietly submit to and you have found out the exact measure of injustice and wrong which will be imposed upon them.
—Fredrick Douglass, 1857

Today, in the aftermath of this terrible tragedy, this horrific attack on our freedom and our sovereignty, I declare to you, my fellow Americans, that our Republic will not flinch, will not falter, and will not rest until the perpetrators of this crime—the ones behind the Tower Terrorist, who died in his own inferno—are punished. The Tower may have fallen but our resolve has not. Make no mistake, every resident of this Republic has a choice to make. Either you are a loyal Citizen, or you are with them, the terrorist Believers.
—Clayton Barclay, 6th President of the Citizens Republic of America, 20 March 2054

CHAPTER 1

She ran the full way, a little over a mile, to the Quick Price Convenience Store & Truck Stop. She didn't have to. There'd be ten minutes or so to spare before Curfew if she walked, but Samantha Vasquez wasn't taking any chances.

Ten minutes would barely be enough time to switch out the register, roll over the codes from Mia—who'd stayed the extra hour to cover the shift until Sam could get there—and run the lockdown protocols. No time to find out who she'd missed. No chance to catch Dragon Lady before she skittered off. No shot at winning the contest.

So she ran, her apron bundled under her arm, her Port wrapped in the apron, her legs churning harder than they had since the end of track season. Despite how cool it was for early June in Arizona, she was sweating hard and breathing harder when she arrived at the Quick Price with twenty-five minutes to spare.

The always-too-slow automatic doors dinged as she pushed through. Mia stood behind the checkout kiosk to the left, helping a hunched old woman in a green-brown trench coat: Dragon Lady, so named by the Quick Price employees for her fearsome breath and rasping voice.

"Thought I mightn't had enough," Dragon Lady said, more to the pile of coins she'd dumped on the counter than to Mia. "But there it is, alright. Thank God."

Sam winced, as much due to the stabbing ache in her side as the language Dragon Lady used. Mia, her eyes rounder than coffee lids, looked to the ceiling. To the security cam above the register. Sam could tell what she was thinking: *They can hear her, can't they? They'll be coming for her.*

Fear gripped Sam deep in her stomach. Edict 7, the guiding principal of the Republic's faithless perfection, was not to be played around with. Curfew could be broken by a few minutes and you might be okay, if you were in high school like Sam and Mia. Maybe a fine and a night in jail to scare the shit out of you and your parents. Maybe get put on a list if the cops who caught you were in a bad mood. But get caught speaking out against the government after the terrorism in the Atlantic District a couple years back, after the rise of the Seer and his fanatics, and there could be a black bag in your future.

Get caught praying or saying the word "God" and, sure as lizards creep around in the desert, you would disappear forever.

Sam's fingertips tingled. She needed a prod of Lito, but she didn't dig into her pocket for the injector. She'd already taken her daily half-dose with breakfast, and she didn't like the way a second dose made her feel, no matter how many people told her it was perfectly normally and safe. Forget that everyone at school prodded halves and three-quarters for each quiz or presentation. Forget that her teachers, her doctor, her mom, and the news feeds preached how Lito was the cure-all for every high-schooler's anxiety. A second prod, even a quarter-dose, made her feel slow.

Not Mia. She was fitting her injector over her left ring finger as Dragon Lady gathered her bounty—a couple rolls of toilet paper and a bottle of wine—and waddled to the door, the smell of gin and urine trailing her.

Ding.

"We didn't stop her," Mia said, calmer but not fully serene. She must have been incredibly frightened. "Are we in trouble? Will they come for us too?"

The question made Sam's heartbeat drive up into her throat. Mia was right. They hadn't stopped Dragon Lady. They were accessories.

"No," Sam said. "No, no, no."

Then her injector was in her hand. All her fingertips tingled. She couldn't remember which one she'd prodded this morning. She shoved the injector over her left thumb. There was the faintest hiss. A sharper, more energetic tingle in her thumb. Her pulse slowed. The danger became less immediate. They hadn't done anything wrong. Dragon Lady was the criminal, not them.

She skirted the kiosk and put her arm around Mia's shoulder. "It's okay," she said, believing the words as she spoke them, as if their sound made them real and true. "They'll take just her if they heard. Only her."

"Of course they heard. They're always listening. That's the point of the whole thing, right? Unity for Peace. Witness-Report. You can't not report. It'll all fall apart."

"It's fine," Sam said, seeing things more clearly now. "We're fine. Remember the guy with the cowboy hat, the night Junot dumped the dog food all over the floor? He said it was a good thing, you know, what happened in Philadelphia." She wouldn't allow herself to name the event, the destruction of the Tower by the man the Republic now referred to as simply the Tower Terrorist. "He left that night and that was it. Gone. They never came in here."

"I don't want them to come in here," Mia said.

Neither did Sam. The thought of REC Agents walking through the door was enough to make her legs tremble. The castigating hands of the Republic, Agents had the authority to black-bag anyone, Citizen or not, minor or not, for crimes against Edict 7. Black-bags didn't go to the local Kingman jail. They didn't get a jury trial. There was no bail to be paid. There was only a transgression and a disappearance. Sometimes the family of the black-bagged never even found out what happened.

Stop it, she told herself.

She looked up, right at the cam's eye, and said, "No, it's okay. We're fine. She's on the cams, right? That's as good as calling the hotline ourselves."

"It is, isn't it?" Mia asked, less frantic now, then answered her own question. "Yeah, it is."

"Exactly. If the cams aren't working, Mr. Gomez is the one in trouble, not us," Sam said, not happy with the idea of the store manager Mr. Gomez being black-bagged. He was a nice man, but any head other than hers in a black bag was better. Any conversation other than this one was better. "So, Dragon

Lady? You didn't get her, did you? She hasn't been in for weeks. Junot thought she died."

Mia perked up. "I know, right? But then in she comes tonight, like right when you should have been here. You're going to love this," Mia said. "And hate me."

"Oh, Mia, no." Sam stood back.

"Yes ma'am. I got it."

Mia held up her Port, a slightly blurry photo of Dragon Lady's face centered on the screen. Sam wondered, with the old woman's severe hunch, if Mia had to lie on the ground to get such a straight on shot. But there it was. Seven months into the contest and freaking Mia, who only staked in because Sam needled her to, got the first photo of Dragon Lady.

"Did you get an ID?" Because if she had, Sam was out of luck.

"No," Mia said, "This building, you know the uplinks don't work on anything older than a Five."

It was true. Any Citizen's Port model older than a CP5 was as useful as a camera and a doorstop inside the Quick Price. Sam's own CP2—her father's, actually, not that he used it anymore—sometimes wouldn't even power on in the store. All the more reason Sam needed to win this contest. Her future Citizenship was on the line. And with Citizenship came a brand new CP8, or maybe a CP9 if they were out by then.

"I'll trade you three shifts for it," Sam said.

"Oh right, your little...thing there. I forgot. I don't understand why you don't make Lucas pay for it."

Bullshit, Sam thought. *You made sure to message me that Dragon Lady was here on MY shift even though you knew I was late because of Dad. Just so you could squeeze me for what? Five shifts? Eight? And Lucas, well, you know the answer to that, too.*

She did her best to let none of this show. Mia was her best friend since elementary school. Since Sam had rescued Mia's pigtails from Anthony Montez during one particular autumn recess period. Best friends or not, however, they were competitive. Grades. Salary at the Quick Price. Boys, like Lucas.

"Come on. It's not worth shit to you," Sam said, refusing to get into the Lucas issue again. "You could catch Beard Man tomorrow and you'd still have no chance to beat Junot. I'm the only one who's close."

"Not close enough. It's over on graduation night, remember? You're going to need Beard Man *and* Hoodie Guy, plus Dragon Lady."

Mia was almost right. The contest was simple. Each of the homeless regulars who lived under the I-40 off ramp was known to the Quick Price employees by an alias. Dragon Lady. Squishy Boots. Captain Farts A Lot. And so on. The goal was to get an ID scan on each. Find out their real names. Ten points apiece. Another ten for any warrants that were flagged.

Then there were the tough ones. Three who the employees in the contest—Sam, Mia, shift manager Junot, Julian, and Chuck—agreed would be the most difficult, maybe impossible, to get. These were fifty points apiece.

Dragon Lady because of her posture and infrequent visits.

Beard Man, the one who'd inspired the contest when an impromptu attempt to photograph his ridiculously overgrown beard had resulted in an inconclusive ID scan. There'd been at least five photos taken of him since, all returning the same inconclusive scan.

And Hoodie Guy. He was the star of the show. Coming in every few days, buying nearly the same thing each time, and never letting anyone get a good look at his face. It was like he knew about the contest and was actively working against them, keeping his head turned always the other way, hood always up, ducking behind displays. No two employees could give similar descriptions of him, other than the ratty leather jacket and the zip-up hoodie beneath.

There was an extra fifty points in it for whoever guessed Hoodie Guy's story. Serial killer on the run. Burnout stalking his ex-wife. Former soldier who'd lost his mind. Sam put in for a blathering drunk fugitive—the guy swayed and stumbled almost as good as Dad—from the whole mess up north when the prison burned down at the start of her junior year. Maybe even the one who started the fire.

Whatever his story, if Sam could get Dragon Lady from Mia, she'd be fifty points behind Junot. Beard Man was a lost cause. That meant she would need Hoodie Guy to tie Junot. If she could add a ten-point warrant or nail her guess about his past, she would win the five-hundred-dollar pot outright. That, along with her last two paychecks, would be enough to pay for her "little thing."

She wants more than three shifts is all, Sam told herself. *Probably going for seven or eight. But maybe I can get her with...*

"Five shifts," Sam offered.

"I pick?"

"Yes. No. Not school nights."

"Samantha," Mia prompted, carrying the last syllable until she ran out of breath.

"Fine. You pick. Tap it to me."

Sam unbundled her Port—it powered on!—and held it out, almost letting it slip from her fingers. *Come on, Lito,* she thought. She couldn't afford to drop it again.

Mia tapped the corner with her own Port. The photo transferred. In the morning, Sam would uplink it on her walk home. Then maybe her luck would turn. Maybe Hoodie Guy would come in and give her a chance to swipe victory from Junot's stupid, cocky smirk.

"One condition," Mia said a few minutes later as they were transferring the codes for the night.

"You can't negotiate a done deal."

"I want dinner."

"I'm working tonight."

"Not tonight, silly. This weekend. O'Grady's. Burgers and a milkshake."

"Deal," Sam said.

Mia made it out the door and into her car with six minutes to spare before Curfew. Sam brought out the stool the day shifters weren't allowed to use from the stockroom. She set it behind the kiosk and sat, imagining Junot transferring the full winnings from the escrow they'd set up for the contest. Imagining her and Mia driving out to Las Vegas to take care of her "little thing." Imagining never having to tell her mother or beg the doctor on Enrollment Day to break the law and take care of it so she could enter her Citizen's Duty, the compulsory requirement for all Americans to earn their full Citizenship rights.

The register screen flashed yellow then red, drawing Sam from her thoughts. The Curfew announcement then came over the store's feedback-laden speaker system. Sixty seconds later the front door locks clacked, locking down the Quick Price for the night. Sam spent most of the next eight hours doing what offline homework she could on her Port and fighting the panic each time a trucker came through.

Curfew, like all rules, had exceptions. While the rest of the nation stayed safe and vigilant in their own homes, the shipping industry had to keep moving. Commerce had to be kept alive, so the truckers kept driving, stopping in at registered truck stops like the Quick Price for fuel, snacks, and sometimes showers and naps in the adjacent Truck Center. Each time one of them logged into the Quick Price, Sam jumped a little on her stool thinking it was the REC coming for her.

At exactly one minute to six in the morning, the register flashed yellow then green. The Curfew Release announcement played over the speakers, and sixty seconds later the front doors clacked, the locks disengaging.

No more than a minute later, while Sam was on the floor cleaning up some crumbs from the granola bar she'd just finished, the doors dinged.

"That was fast," she muttered. She stood and saw a dark shape—a person—disappear down the chip aisle.

Oh shit, no, she thought, her eyes going up to the cam on the ceiling. *Agents. They're really coming for me.*

CHAPTER 2

Sam watched the chip aisle, waiting for the Agent who would black-bag her to emerge. Would he believe she wasn't the employee on the clock when that withered old bitch said *that* word? Would he care that she was only eighteen and so looking forward to serving the Republic?

She was suddenly aware of needing to pee.

The sound of bottles clinking came from the liquor aisle. This was exactly like all the stories Sam had heard about the REC. They didn't come right at you through the doors. They caught you from the side while you were looking the other way, like a monster from the closet soon after you've outgrown the fear in such things.

Her hand was halfway to her pocket for her Lito injector when he came out of the liquor aisle. Disheveled, bearded, dirty. A bottle of green-label bourbon in each hand.

She faced Hoodie Guy at just after six in the morning.

For the briefest of moments, her fear lifted. As if she'd conjured him, here was the man she needed. The key to winning the contest. Then she remembered her narrative for him. The prison. The fire. The convicts. The dead. What if it were true?

Panic set her hands trembling. Whatever the truth might be, in that moment, for Sam, Hoodie Guy was the fugitive she'd imagined. A killer and an enemy of the Republic. A sadist alone in the store with her. Alone *together* for almost an hour before Chuck and Mr. Gomez would arrive for the day shift. What kind of horrors could he inflict on her in an hour?

He lumbered toward the register, slow and purposeful, his right leg dragging a little.

He's going to kill me and rob the store, Sam thought.

She tried to say something. To announce she had a gun beneath the counter. Or some other lie that might save her life. But all she could manage was, "Sir," her voice sounding like someone else's from very far away.

With the hood up, his face was little more than shadow, beard, and mouth, but she felt him watching her as if scanning her brain. As if his hidden eyes were tearing her down to the very cells which defined her. She thought she might cry if he didn't look away.

He took both bourbon bottles in his left hand. His right hand went into his jeans pocket. Sam remembered the alarm button beneath the register. Her brain calculated the movements it would take to press that button then run to the back storeroom and out the loading doors.

Too many movements to make before Hoodie Guy murdered her.

He withdrew his hand from his pocket. Sam flinched. He held a wad of cash, turning the rumpled bills over in his hand. He grunted as if agreeing with the cash. Then, instead of continuing to the counter, he went up the medicine aisle.

Sam exhaled, only then realizing she'd been holding her breath. She blinked hard and flexed her suddenly tight back.

I can win the contest, she thought. The next thing she knew, her injector was sliding onto her left index finger. She felt the hard tingle of the prod. The injector chimed to let her know it was empty. Her pulse slowed, but she could still feel the adrenaline kicking through her veins. She withdrew her Port from her apron's kangaroo pouch and slid her finger across its screen, opening its camera function. She positioned it on the counter beside the product scanner.

When she looked up, he was coming back to the register, a bag of chips and a box of pain pills added to his haul. There was a sway in his walk, in addition to the limp, she hadn't noticed earlier. A familiar stagger she knew all too well from her father. The sway of a drunk.

He placed his items on the counter in front of Sam's Port. She couldn't help but think that the way he did so was the depiction of a beaten man. She reconsidered his worn, though clearly once cared for, jacket. His splotched and dusty jeans. His backpack over his shoulders, the left strap held together by a few pieces of gummy twine. His beard, scraggly and full. They all spoke of a man who had given up.

Not my problem, Sam thought. *He had his chance at being a good Citizen. I need this.*

She forced her hand to steady over the Port's screen as he dug his money out of his pocket. All he had to do was lean forward a bit.

As if on cue, he swayed over the counter. The hood's shadow receded just enough.

Sam hit the camera icon on the Port's screen. It flashed and *click-clicked.*

"What the fuck," Hoodie Guy said, reeling back and knocking into a rack of condoms. Prophylactic boxes scattered but the rack didn't hit the floor. Almost quicker than Sam could see, his hand shot out and caught the display, then pulled it back to standing without losing his footing or his grip on his cash.

Drunks didn't do that.

He looked at Sam and grunted.

"I'm sorry," she blurted.

He threw a handful of bills at the counter and stormed to the door. His stagger and limp, maybe due to his anger, or maybe due to Sam's fear, seemed somehow diminished as he stomped out.

It took a moment for Sam to collect herself. It was just a photo, but he'd acted like she'd threatened to turn him in for having contraband or something.

Homeless paranoia, she told herself. *Or maybe he really is from the prison. Or some other fugitive. Which means he's my winner!*

She spun her Port around to see the photo she'd taken.

Uplink failed, popped on the screen.

"No shit," she said. She pressed the *YES* button to have the uplink begin automatically when a signal was found and then slid the progress window to the bottom of the screen.

She picked up Hoodie Guy's money from the counter and the floor, stacking the bills in the register drawer. That done, she examined the photo again. For the circumstance, it wasn't bad. Its contrast was off, as was the aim. But she'd gotten most of his face, including his eyes, in addition to a great shot of the oatmeal-colored Quick Price ceiling tiles.

Turned out Hoodie Guy was somewhat handsome, or could be if he wiped a wet washcloth through the layer of grime that coated his face and gave himself a good shave. What really caught her attention, though, was his eyes. They reminded Sam of her father's eyes—the shine of Dad's architect mind occasionally sparkling through the rheumy wall of his alcoholic disconnect.

Hoodie Guy's eyes had that same glint. No, not exactly the same. Brighter. Stronger. As evidenced when he'd caught himself from destroying the cupcake display, he wasn't completely lost to the alcohol yet.

"Good for him," she mumbled, a little shocked at how callous the words sounded. She didn't wish alcoholism on anyone, but her own troubles had to come before a homeless guy and his whiskey.

She settled in for the remainder of her shift, generally a boring time on a Saturday morning. As expected, the doors didn't *ding* again until Mr. Gomez arrived a little before seven, followed by Chuck a few minutes later. Mr. Gomez went through his usual eye-roll-inducing "How are things, Miss Vasquez?" routine. It wasn't that she doubted he cared. He struck her as a genuine man, the kind of fatherly-type who didn't cuss. It was just that he sounded like one of the guidance counselors in school when he asked it.

Mr. Gomez spent the next few minutes straightening up the displays that Sam hadn't gotten quite right, though he never chided his employees for not living up to his compulsive standards. When Chuck *dinged* through the doors, Sam made a get-over-here face and dragged him behind the register.

"Bullshit," he said when Sam told her about the photos of Dragon Lady and Hoodie Guy.

"You want to see it, Chuckie?" Sam said, keeping her voice low and an eye on Mr. Gomez. It wasn't that Mr. Gomez had outlawed the contest. He just didn't approve and preferred a don't-let-me-hear-about-it approach to monitoring such things.

"You know I do," Chuck said.

Chuck was in third place in the contest. More important, he'd had a crush on both Sam and Mia since middle school. Sam had always thought it was more like a crush on any girl who would give the slightly overweight and very shy boy the time of day. And while he'd been made well aware that he stood no chance with either of them, his enthusiasm for being involved in their escapades never waned.

"Then you've got to promise to back me up when Junot tries to wiggle out of paying me."

"He's a dick. You know he tried to grab Mia's ass the other night?" Chuck could always be counted on to make a point that he was the one nice guy in Kingman.

"He was trying to look down my shirt again yesterday."

Chuck's cheeks reddened. He stared hard at Sam's eyes, as if trying to prove a point by not looking at her chest.

Sam disguised a poor-Chuck smile as an atta-boy one and swiped on her Port.

The doors *dinged*. A man and woman in similar blue business suits entered and then split up, the man going to the breakfast sandwiches and the woman for coffee.

"Ahem," Mr. Gomez said from somewhere in the bread aisle, his forced cough announcing that social time was over. There were customers to help.

Sam dropped her Port into her apron's kangaroo-pocket. "I think you have a customer," she said to Chuck.

"Sure do," he said with a cheeriness that would be obviously fake from anyone else.

They switched out the register then Sam went in the back to log the cash and remove her codes from the system for the day. When she came back out on the floor, Mr. Gomez materialized from the right as if he'd been waiting for her. She nearly screamed.

"Be careful on your way home," he said.

It was a simple enough statement, but it seemed to Sam like it was laced with something else. An accusation, perhaps. Did he know about Dragon Lady? Her illegal exclamation? Was this a test?

No, he was just a nice guy who wanted to make sure she got home okay. The cams had done their job. If Dragon Lady was in trouble, that trouble had already begun.

"I will," Sam said, and trotted to the front door as quickly as she could without breaking into a jog.

Home free, she thought as the doors *dinged* behind her. When she'd turned the corner and the Quick Price was lost from view, she took her Port from the kangaroo-pocket and opened the screen. A message waited from her mom reminding her to pick up beer. She must have not heard it after Mr. Gomez came in. She shook her head and decided to tell Mom that she didn't get the message until she was practically home.

She swiped the message away and opened her photos. She clicked on Dragon Lady. Across the old woman's face a text window stated: *To confirm uplink press YES.*

"Yes," Sam said as she pushed the button.

The response earned Sam the points she needed to get within distance of victory: *Gertrude Alhambra. No Warrants. No Living Relatives.*

Feeling good, Sam enjoyed the sun on her even if it was quite chilly for June. Between the north-south runs of homes that lined the street, the desert stretched like a model asking an artist to paint it. Simple. Flat. With browns and tans and points of green. All of it crisp and fresh. Though she wouldn't miss Kingman when she entered Citizen's Duty, she would miss the desert.

A pickup drove by, whipping Sam's hair around in its wake. She abandoned her reverie and cut up Bond Street, where a Republic Motors dealership gobbled up the view and half the block. The Kingman North Casino, one of the generic state-owned facilities that were ubiquitous throughout the Republic, filled the rest of the street. Her mom had grown up on this street before the dealership arrived. Then, Mom had told her more than once, it was a neighborhood of small ranch homes and double-wides. That was before the big earthquake almost ten years ago. Now, two and three-story rowhomes sprawled across this portion of North Kingman—the rebuild financed in part by the two casinos in town—hiding the desert views behind apathetic cinderblock and neon structures.

Sam swiped to the next photo. Across Hoodie Guy's neck, in capital white letters, were three words: *NO MATCH FOUND.*

"Oh, come on," Sam wailed. She felt it all slipping away. Citizen's Duty. The CP8. Getting away from here. It was all evaporating faster than she could think.

Then she felt something else. Someone following her. She clutched the Port to her chest and quickened her pace. A dozen steps later she stopped, feeling foolish. It had to be Mr. Gomez. She must have miscounted the cash or left a report open in the computer in the back.

Or he'd found out about the old woman's religious profanity. About Sam and Mia not reporting it. He'd chased her down, almost all the way home, to confront her. Her stomach felt like a fist of ice. She steadied her breathing and prepared for her punishment. She turned.

It wasn't Mr. Gomez.

It was a shape. A blur. It was on her.

CHAPTER 3

Rough hands grabbed Sam's shoulders and spun her around. Shoved her against the wall. Her hair flung across her eyes. She threw out an open hand in an awkward attempt to slap her attacker away. It was a weak countermove her Safety & Defense teacher, Mr. Washington, would have mocked.

You call that a parry, Vasquez? she could hear her Mr. Washington say. *You'd be lucky to survive a mugging by an angry prairie dog.*

Where were those endless drills now? The rote muscle recall? Dodges? Parries? She couldn't even remember how to throw a punch.

Her attacker slammed her into the wall again. Her lungs compressed, squeezing out the air. She wheezed. Gagged. Tried not to cry.

Her attacker, definitely a man, moved again. He was larger than her but not a giant. No bigger than Mr. Washington, who she'd practiced flipping over her shoulder at least a dozen times. The man's hand went for a fistful of her shirt by the collarbone. This time Sam's muscle memory kicked in. Her knees flexed. The hand went high. She punched upwards into his ribs beneath his armpit. Her second jab went for his throat.

He caught her fist the way she imagined her father might have caught hers if she'd been a boy and they'd played like that.

"Quit squirming," the man said.

Sam went for his groin with her knee. He blocked with his own knee. She was off balance. Vulnerable. His next attack would put her on the ground. She looked up. The sky was blue and empty. She wondered why no one was rescuing her beneath such a bright sky. She braced for the blow.

It didn't come.

"Why'd you do that?" the man said. His voice was low. Grating.

Sam's breath returned. She leaned against the wall to regain her balance, then stood as tall as she could. She was eye-level with her attacker's scraggly beard. Hoodie Guy. The sight of him so close, along with the question he'd asked, disarmed her. The bourbon on his breath, combined with a stench of sweat and body odor, made her eyes water.

Over his shoulder, she saw only the empty street. No pedestrians. No cars. No help coming.

Mr. Washington's voice rolled through Sam's mind: "Show no fear. Ever."

"You attacked me, asshole," she screamed. "What's your problem?"

Hoodie Guy's eyes shifted down and to the right as if searching the sidewalk.

No, Sam thought. *He's listening for something.* Down and to the right indicated accessing auditory memory, she remembered from psych class when they'd talked about catching friends or neighbors in a lie during their weekly Witness-Report seminars.

Hoodie Guy's eyes came back up, clouded by disappointment. Not alcohol. Not rage. Clear and explicit disappointment. Then something seemed to click in his mind. His eyes narrowed, now angry. Dangerous. He looked up and down the street then reached for Sam's arm. She pulled back. He grabbed her elbow.

"We need to talk. Right now," he said. He half-led, half-pulled her around to the front of the dealership. Through the parking lot, empty but for the cars—the dealership wouldn't open for business until eight—to the auto-charge station at the far corner of the lot.

"I'll call the cops," Sam yelled more than once, hoping someone would hear her.

Hoodie Guy never broke stride. "I'm not worried about cops," he said as they passed between the first pair of charging pylons.

The way he spoke, with both fear and confidence in his voice, horrified and compelled her.

He pulled her through the standard five row pylon layout of the station to behind the final pair, where they'd be virtually invisible to any potential rescuers happening by on the street. He watched her but didn't speak.

"What?" Sam demanded. She pulled her arm free, doing her best to keep her fear hidden.

"Why'd you take a photo of me?"

"Seriously? You're kidnapping me over that?"

"You can't," Hoodie Guy started, then stopped. He watched her, his eyes clearing with each second that passed. Finally, he said, "You're *not* with them, are you?"

"With who?"

Hoodie Guy broke his stare and looked to his boots, a move that once again reminded Sam of her father. It was the way he looked when he woke up, half-sober, and saw the window he'd broken the night before, or the bruise on Mom's arm. A fading moment of clarity, of self-loathing, that would be erased as quickly as possible with another drink.

"You should delete that photo," he said. "It's going to get you into trouble."

"What kind of trouble?" Sam asked, control once more hers. If she could get him to admit being a fugitive, that might be enough to earn the points for the contest. She probably should get a hundred point bonus for the way he assaulted her. In any case, she softened her voice, trying to sound empathetic. "Who is 'them?' Are they..."

But Hoodie Guy wasn't listening to her. He'd dropped into a crouch, shooting glances in every direction but hers. A police car drove by the dealership then turn east. She watched it go without shouting for help. Without running into the street to catch their attention. If she lost Hoodie Guy to the cops before finding out who he was, her chances at winning the contest were over. It was awful logic, yet it somehow seemed right. So she watched the police car drive by without a word. When it had passed, Hoodie Guy seemed to relax but remained in his crouch.

"Hey, man," Sam said. "Let me buy you some breakfast or coffee."

He shook his head and stared in the direction the police car had gone. "It's too late," he said. "We're blown. Not my fault. It's on you. Get out of town but don't follow me. You need to run."

"Run? Blown? What are you talking about?"

But Hoodie Guy had finished with the conversation. He took off like an injured mountain lion darting across the freeway. Sam stood there alone, watching him go, for a long time before she began to shake from the adrenaline and the fear. She set her back to the pylon and slid to the ground, not bothering to fight the coming tears. She felt like a little girl crying over nothing. She was stronger than this. She'd had to learn how to be, with a drunk father and an enabling mother. With no one to pick her up when she fell or to help fill out her Citizen's Duty forms. Of course, she usually had some Lito to help keep these little girl hysterics in check. Now, with her injector empty, she could only let the moment pass.

When she regained control, she began passing her hands over her body, feeling for injuries. Other than a sore neck and a bruise on her arm, she was unhurt. But she'd lost her Port. Angry at herself for letting Hoodie Guy get away, as well as for losing her Port, she stomped back around the dealership to where he'd first grabbed her. The Port was there, face down against the wall, its screen a spider web of fractures radiating out from the top-right corner. When she switched it on, her wallpaper image of the sunset over the desert looked more like a tie-dye kaleidoscope. The Port was useless.

Dad's going to be pissed, she thought. Then she laughed. Dad hadn't been more than a beached whale on the couch for months. A few years ago, he'd have hit her for destroying the hand-me-down device. Wouldn't that be nice now?

"Not like I was winning the money, anyway," Sam said to the empty street.

She headed home, squinting into the morning sun. Wanting another Lito prod. Debating whether to tell her mom about the ruined Port and her "little thing."

Rafael Ward stopped running in the back yard of a sprawling ranch home with impressive desert-themed landscaping. A large shed in the corner of the yard offered some shade and some cover. He squatted on the boulders that bordered the shed and rubbed his bad leg. It hurt worse in the mornings. Much worse after walking a while. Running made it feel like it was on fire. A fair punishment, he'd told himself enough times, considering whatever damage he'd done to it occurred while trying to escape the Tower that morning two years ago.

The past, however, wasn't what mattered right now. He flexed his leg and reflected on how bad things had gone in the span of an hour this morning.

He liked that they called him Hoodie Guy. He'd first overheard it a month or so ago, some chunky boy and one of the brunette girls talking about him at the register, their voices not as hushed as they should be.

More than a year on the run without being caught wasn't enough to convince him that he'd truly made himself anonymous. Not a pedestrian walked by without him tensing. Not a car passed the ruined old high school he called home without his fight-or-flight instincts kicking in. But a simple moniker applied by teenagers working at a convenient store told him they had no clue who he really was.

He'd relaxed a bit since then. Allowed himself to enjoy the bourbons and whiskeys he bought on his trips to the Quick Price. Allowed himself to truly engage in the books he read in the cellar of the high school, sometimes getting lost for hours, putting the book down and having to concentrate to remember exactly where he was.

Then some kid took a photo of him.

Why? For who?

It didn't matter.

He bent over, hands on his knees, breathing hard. Had anyone seen him, they would have thought him preparing to pass out or possibly vomit. In another town, they might have sneered or yelled at him to get a job and get off the streets, but in Kingman, Arizona, where the homeless lived under the freeway overpass like ants around a dropped ice cream cone, no one paid attention. No one saw them.

It was good thing, too, the man knew. He sucked air, trying

to slow his heart and calm the stabbing in his side. Not to mention the throbbing in his bad leg. It wasn't that long ago that a mile or two sprint would have been no problem. This morning, two blocks felt like a marathon.

Stupid fucking girl. Why bother trying to help her? To warn her? What had it gotten him? Within fifty feet of a passing police car, that's what. He opened his backpack and helped himself to a long slug of his new bourbon. There was too much adrenaline pumping through him to taste it, but he liked the burning in his throat. Like drinking desert air. Like drinking clarity.

Why didn't the police car stop? he asked himself.

Because they're not interested in you anymore.

No, she took the photo over an hour ago, and I sat there waiting for her rather than leaving town. They should have come for me by now. They should have killed me by now.

The back-and-forth with himself felt good, like role playing the voice that used to whisper in his head. The sentinel that used to show him things his conscious mind missed. Used to keep him safe.

That voice, however, was long gone. And the silence was excruciating.

The solution, he'd discovered, was alcohol to dissolve the silence. A drink or two and lucidity clicked into place. Good enough during the day. At night it took more, many more, drinks to erase faces and dreams.

He looked up and down the street, a habit impossible to break. Not that he expected to see her. The redhead. Not here. Not after more than two years.

"Cheers," he muttered to the empty street, and took another swallow. Then another, hoping it might erase the stupid girl and her stupid photo from his mind. Maybe from existence altogether. It didn't work.

Her photo was the end. He needed to leave town. Find a new homeless shithole for disappearing. But the fucking girl...she was walking right into the slavering maw of the Republic. He tried to ignore it, but when he blinked, he saw a hundred faces begin to melt. Two hundred bodies incinerated. Three hundred lives crushed beneath steel and concrete and rage.

He heard a voice, not with his ears. From a memory. Or maybe the fiction of a memory.

If you want redemption, the French-accented voice said, *start small.*

He closed his eyes and tried to think of a reason not to help the girl. Thought about drinking one of the handful of two-ounce sample bottles of whiskeys—quality whiskeys not the cheap bourbon he drank most nights—he kept in his backpack.

No, those were for a better day than this.

He refocused on the girl and considered making a pros and cons list like he used to make his students do when judging the actions of historical figures. Why did Richard I go to the virtually useless castle Châlus-Chabrol in 1199, a choice that would lead to his death? Why did Margery Kempe visit mystic and recluse Julian of Norwich, adding to her already growing reputation as an outcast?

He started digging through his backpack for the small notebook and pen he kept, an old teacher's habit, but he stopped before he found them. The list, he knew, wasn't necessary. The only con was his own death.

How did it come to this? he asked himself, but he received no bantering response. His mind had gone silent again. It was his life or hers. He tried to think of himself as a reluctant hero, like Gawain who had to accept the Green Knight's beheading challenge when the older Knights of the Round Table refused, but he ended up only hating himself more.

It was with that hate fueling him that he retraced his sprint from the auto-charge station and went in search of the girl.

CHAPTER 4

I should tell mom, Sam thought, looking at her father's broken Port. She turned north onto her street, staying on the west side to avoid the shade, and the chill, cast by the neighborhood's two-story twin homes.

But she wouldn't tell her. That pattern was established long ago. Mom was as wasted away as Dad at this point. Not catatonic like him, but in such denial of the family's dysfunction that she just smiled and drank her coffee, stole the occasional quarter-dose of Lito from Sam's supply vial in the bathroom, and talked about tomorrow like that would be the day Dad got off his ass and got a job. Sam couldn't remember the last time Mom tried to get him to the dinner table, let alone show him a list of "For Hires" on the Port.

Then again, the last time Dad ate his dinner rather than drank it was before the earthquake. Before the North Mine shut down. Before Sam had graduated from elementary school.

Sam passed the Huxleys' house at the midpoint of the block and thought of the old photos she'd seen in school from before the big quake. Back then, the double-wides framed lawns of desert and brown grass. A dozen or so houses on the whole block. Not like the landscaped and irrigated lawns of the twenty-six homes that now lined North Roosevelt Street.

Recalling the barrenness of those photos made her feel like she was dragging her family backwards, from the nice homes of today to the squalor of a couple generations ago. She thought of everything she'd cost her family in the last month or so. A broken Port meant disconnect. It meant losing access to money, news, job openings, doctor appointments. It might even mean losing Dad's disability payments, which would mean the house being foreclosed on.

A broken Port meant no ID on Hoodie Guy, which meant no prize money. No trip to Vegas for her "little thing." No Citizen's Duty Enrollment. Then what? After the foreclosure, all she'd have left would be a life with the homeless under I-40.

"This sucks," she mumbled, looking up to make sure she could cross the street without getting run over.

Her front door was open.

"Come on, Mom," she said, as if her mother could hear her from this distance. While leaving the door open might keep the house cool, it let lizards and bugs and who knew what else into the house. It also let her dog Reina out. Not that Reina would ever run away, but you couldn't trust drivers in Kingman to care about a dog in the road more than a coyote. She started across the street, wondering with each step if she should go back to work and try to pretend like the entire morning hadn't happened.

She noticed the police cars as if they'd just materialized on the curb. Two of them flanking her house. Had her father finally succumbed to his addiction? The thought should have scared her, but it didn't. What she saw next did.

Two police officers marched out of the house, Sam's mother between them, hands behind her back. Her head slumped, her black hair hung like a veil. Her legs seemed to barely hold her weight. Fear, a different kind than she'd experienced with Hoodie Guy, spread from her chest to her limbs.

Her mother moaned, the sound growing into a horrible wailing.

She ran to the officers, to her mother, making it into the street before noticing the front door hadn't been opened—it had been smashed off its hinges. Her feet stopped moving halfway across the street, scenarios tumbling through her head.

Dad died and mom had a breakdown.

Dad finally woke up and hit Mom. She fought back and stabbed him with a steak knife or scissors.

Mom got fed up and tried to put him out of his misery. It didn't work. He called the cops.

A third police officer, this one a woman, filled the doorway. "Get her in the car. I'll take care of in here," the officer said. "Then go find—there she is, right in front of you."

The police woman—tall, broad shouldered, her hair pulled back tight as if demonstrating her power—pointed right at Sam. The officers who had her mom glanced at each other as if unsure which one should let go.

"Forget it," the female officer said. "Get that one to the station. I'll take care of the girl."

The officers shoved Sam's mother into a police car and sped off while Sam watched, her gut twisting over itself, still unable to move.

Say something, Sam's mind shouted, but the only word she could find was *Lito*.

The police woman came down from the doorway then stopped. She stared beyond Sam. Tensed into a half-crouch, a gun appearing in her hand. A gun pointed right at Sam's head.

Sam's Port clattered to the sidewalk for the second time that morning.

In the slowest motion Sam had ever experienced, she registered the blinding explosion of the gunpowder igniting in the chamber. Next came the smoke and the spent cartridge billowing from the exhaust vents on the sides of the weapon. In less time than the first intake of a sudden breath, the feeling of something too small and too fast cut through the air close enough to brush the hair back from Sam's left ear. The almost cartoon whistle of the bullet reached its screaming peak as that breath completed its inhale.

The street exploded behind her like a car accident. Her legs wobbled. She fell to her knees.

As if time had skipped, the police woman stood over Sam, her gun pointing across the street.

The cop fired again and again. Sam's hands clenched over her ears and she curled in on herself trying to keep the horribly loud explosions from detonating her brain. Her eyes sought, found, locked on the figure up the street.

Hoodie Guy.

He leaped from behind the front of one car to the back of

another. He slid over a hood. Darted across the street and back again. He moved like a fly trapped in a house, maddeningly chaotic yet with a desperate purpose. With each hole ripped into a car's fender, with each shattering of glass, Hoodie Guy got closer.

He's coming to kill me, Sam thought, barely aware that she was holding onto the hem of the officer's pants like a toddler.

Eight shots before it stopped. Maybe ten. A few seconds of silence, of stillness, broken only by the sound of Sam's weeping. She gathered herself as best as she could, swallowing her sobs.

The cop reached down and grabbed Sam's shoulder. "Let's go," she said, pulling Sam to her feet.

"He tried to steal my Port," Sam said.

"He's dead," the woman said, a pride in her voice Sam found disturbing. There was no time to dwell on it, however, as the cop dragged her to the remaining police car. "Get in," she said.

"I think there's been a mistake," Sam said, sounding to herself like a Quick Price customer who didn't understand the math of *buy one get one free.*

"Give me your Port," the officer demanded.

Sam stared, confused. Something was wrong. She realized she'd been thinking this since she first saw her mother flanked by the two cops. Since Hoodie Guy accosted her behind the car dealership. Since he'd walked in the Quick Price doors too soon after Curfew lifted. Only now, the idea was beating in her mind like a drumline in a song.

The police woman glared with a blankness that was almost inhuman. There was no concern in her entire being. No empathy for the scared girl in her custody, or her parents. The only glint of anything was in her eyes, like hunger. Or greed.

"Your Port," the officer said again, squeezing Sam's arm and pressing her against the car door.

"It was Hoodie Guy," Sam said, as if someone else—someone who didn't understand the severity of the violence around her— was speaking for her. "He's mad I took his picture."

There was a hand on the back of Sam's head. For a second, she thought the woman was comforting her. Then the hand shoved her face forward into the police car door. It was all Sam could do to turn her head enough not to take the impact straight on. The world blazed the brightest white.

She hit the ground, her vision blurring through a kaleidoscope of shapes and shadows all hazed in red.

Above her, Hoodie Guy blocked a punch from the police woman. He launched a flash of punches to her chest and abdomen. She swung her gun toward him. He grabbed her wrist, spun her, smashed her face through the police car's windshield. Glittering shards of crimson brilliance, glass and blood, danced through the air. The blue uniformed police woman slumped to the ground like an over-worn pillow.

"Let's go," Hoodie Guy said.

Sam's vision blurred again. She tried to hold onto consciousness. The red faded to a darkening contrast. She clawed at the macadam as if it would keep her awake. Darkness was coming. She barely had time to be afraid before it arrived.

CHAPTER 5

The knock on the Temple's door came a few minutes after eight in the morning.

"General," a voice said through the door. "He is back."

Neither MacKenzie nor the Seer responded. The soldier who knocked wouldn't wait for an answer. Task completed, he'd already be double-timing it back to the training hall.

The Seer, sitting on the floor opposite MacKenzie in the center of the Temple, nodded to his general as if to say, *You shouldn't have doubted me.*

Of course, she hadn't doubted him. It had been fourteen months since he'd recruited her to build him an army, and every claim he'd made had been accurate. Every instinct, interpretation, and tactic he'd offered had led to success. She had absolute faith in the Seer, as did her growing army.

But she did not trust Ker, the man who had returned.

"You're sure I need him for this?" MacKenzie asked.

"My doubt has always been whether I need you for this."

"If it's a legit lead, then you need me there. He won't come in for Ker. He won't come in alive at all if you send soldiers to retrieve him."

The Seer's large tattooed hand massaged his shaved head. He wore a multi-colored robe similar to one he'd shown her in an old film about the Exodus. "I believe you," he said. "I trust you. I just do not enjoy risking you like this."

He stood, a single, graceful motion, his robes billowing around him as if a fan had switched on. Someone meeting the Seer for the first time would notice he was a large man. But men of charisma, men of importance, always seemed large. The Seer *was* large. A few inches over six feet tall, with a powerful build, he reminded MacKenzie more of a laborer than a prophet. She'd almost asked him once about his background, but he'd glared at her as if he'd known the question was coming. Like his eyes were ordering her not to go there. Not yet.

"The Tower Terrorist is the key," she said, repeating the words everyone in Horeb—the underground headquarters for their army of Believers—had heard the Seer say over and over. "He's the symbol we need to embolden the people. To start the revolution."

The Seer turned to face the marble altar at the back of the Temple. Upon its plush covering sat a number of religious texts, all ancient. He passed his hand over them. MacKenzie, the only person other than the Seer allowed in the Temple, had never been closer to the altar than where she now sat: the center point of the square, austere room. She'd seen the Seer hold his hands over the texts like this before, but she'd never seen him touch one. She didn't even know which texts were on the altar, let alone which one he sought most often for guidance.

It didn't matter. Whether it was the Bible or Quran or some other text, the One God was the One God, regardless of what that crazy priest had told her and Rafe. Regional interpretations held no sway over Truth. Differences of opinion could be sorted out later. False gods dealt with after the revolution. After the atheistic tyranny of the Republic had been burned away like a farmer's field after harvest.

"He'll meet you outside the Temple in five minutes," the Seer said.

At first, MacKenzie thought he meant the Tower Terrorist, but she quickly understood he meant Ker, the army's Intelligence Tech Officer. An impressive title for the guy in charge of comms and keeping the army off the Republic's radar. The computer guy.

"It'll go quicker—smoother—if I go alone," MacKenzie said. "I don't need him."

"God has a plan. Do you doubt he speaks through me?"

"Of course not. I didn't mean—"

"He is the virtual-world insurgent we need. The gatekeeper

for our knowledge and beliefs in the after of the coming war."

"This isn't a virtual op, and we're not in the after." She knew she shouldn't argue. If she heard a soldier contradicting the Seer like this, she'd have that person lashed in front of the others. But her relationship with the Seer was different.

Still, there were limits.

The Seer smiled. He had many smiles, some she still hadn't deciphered. This one meant the conversation was over.

"Thank you, Sir," she said, and got up to leave.

"Hannah," the Seer said when she reached for the door. "Be careful. This one is public. It's dangerous."

"I'll be fine," she said, not unkindly. She liked when he used her first name. She'd been just MacKenzie for so long, a choice she'd made when she'd left the military and gone off grid, that hearing her first name with the type of concern he offered was warming. It was as close as she'd get to hearing her father say *ma cherie* one more time. "Be back in a couple days. That'll be good, yes?"

She didn't wait for an answer. He wasn't going to give one. She exited the Temple and took up position against the wall to the right of the door. From her right, two soldiers—Awasi and Owens, both privates in urban camo—marched in time, shoulder to shoulder. Eyes ahead, mouths set in straight lines, they didn't speed up or slow down when they saw their general standing in the narrow hallway. They simply maneuvered into single file as they passed her, each saluting, then back into two-by formation. Smooth and practiced like they'd been taught for the narrow corridors of Horeb.

Of course, the General would have preferred spending more time on martial drills, but the restrictions of their subterranean command center—a collapsed underground parking structure rebuilt as a labyrinth designed to best defend a ground assault—required pragmatism. If they couldn't maneuver out of their own way, her troops were worse than useless. So every new squad of recruits spent their first two weeks, before rudimentary weapons training, learning how to operate in the narrow, anti-thermal plated and painted halls of Horeb. Skills that would translate into urban assault scenarios.

MacKenzie returned their salutes, pride adding to the brief moment of familial warmth she'd felt from the Seer in the Temple. There were over four hundred soldiers in Horeb, men and women ranging in age from sixteen to sixty-one. Believers all. And thousands more stationed throughout the Republic, with the expectation of tens of thousands more rallying to the Seer when the war began. Watching Awasi and Owens, recruits who'd come to Horeb with no more aptitude than the childish training they'd received in Citizen's Duty, added to her confidence MacKenzie always felt after meeting with the Seer.

At the end of the hallway the soldiers parted.

"To Canaan," Awasi said to Owens.

"To Canaan."

Of this salutation, a battle-cry-in-waiting, MacKenzie was not fond. One of her few dissatisfactions. The Seer didn't agree with her dissatisfaction. He'd insisted she not interfere with its popularity.

"Let them march with the purpose of the Israelite army crossing the Jordan. Let them follow you, their Joshua, to Jericho and beyond," he'd told her.

What she'd thought but not said was that the Seer could be Moses all day long, but she had no interest in playing Joshua. Her part was the General. When the war was won, in the after, as he put it, she wanted no part of leadership, of politics.

The clunk of Ker's boots, large things for a guy in tech, announced him before he turned the corner from her left. She started that direction, meeting him at the corner.

"Breakfast yet?" he said, a tall, lanky man with a half-eaten cheeseburger in his hand.

He smiled, that easy, likeable smile that drove MacKenzie's distrust.

The problem with Ker was that she liked him. Everyone did. His likeability was somehow innate, nonchalant, as if he knew he knew he could grin his way to anything, even victory. When he walked into a room, you couldn't help but notice him, and want to be noticed by him. That was what bothered her. He distracted people, if only for a moment, and distractions were never good.

The Seer, however, insisted he was a Believer and an asset to the cause and to the army. On this point, MacKenzie had to agree. Ker's eyes, wolfish and intense, left no doubt about his desire for the coming war. For the return of Belief to the Republic.

"No?" he said when she didn't answer. "Bite?"

"Report," MacKenzie said, not interested in the small talk or the burger.

"You first."

MacKenzie glowered at him, threatening strangulation with his own boot laces. She did not tolerate insubordination.

"Relax," he said, and took a bit of the cheeseburger. "I got a hit on the Tower Terrorist."

"I know that part. Is the intel clean this time?" She was tired of chasing false positives and urban legends.

Ker popped the last bit of the burger into his mouth as if that confirmed the intel.

"Location?"

"Western Arizona," Ker said between chews.

They could make it in twelve to thirteen hours, MacKenzie figured. Quicker if that thing Ker did changing a car's registry got them through the Southwest District border smoothly. If her past attempts to find the Tower Terrorist were any indication, however, twelve hours would be far too long. He'd be gone when they got there.

"How'd you find him?" she asked.

"I'm good."

"Don't test me."

"He was flagged an hour ago."

"It took an hour to notify me?"

"No," Ker said. "It took an hour for the runner to get me, for me to go topside and verify the flag, then send notice to the Seer. That's what you asked for when you made Horeb go dark. No comm lines. No intel in or out without your authorization. Then the Seer had to call you into the Temple to tell you to bring me along even though you don't want to. Sound right?"

It all sounded exactly right, but she wasn't going to give him the satisfaction of saying so. Her attention was already on the op, planning the contingencies. This was by far the freshest intel on the Tower Terrorist. Their previous best had been nineteen hours. That was a year ago. If there was a chance he'd be there when they arrived, she needed to be ready.

"Flagged how? An attack?" she asked.

"Some guy."

"What does that mean?"

"Some private Citizen took a photo of him. The ID went through channels, got diverted to the REC, and our tags lit up."

"Shit. They'll be on site long before us," she said. But standard REC on site wasn't what worried her. She'd dealt with enough Agents to know their base tactics, know how to deal with them. What had her concerned was the Agent she'd encountered in Oklahoma City. Smarter. Stronger. Better trained. Militarized. Not an incident she wanted to recall or repeat.

"Could be worse," Ker said.

"How?"

"Be happy it's not some twenty-one-year-old college girl taking nudes of your boyfriend."

He was joking, needling her for a response, but suddenly the conversation became real. It was no longer just an op. No longer about the Tower Terrorist. It was about Rafe. The man she'd abandoned on an island in the Mediterranean. The man she couldn't forget when the small hours of the night dragged her to sleep. The man she'd been looking for since he'd walked into the Tower with a backpack full of explosives and brought that godforsaken fortress to the ground in a hellfire of murder and destruction. The man the Republic insisted was dead, killed in his suicidal Tower attack.

"We leave in thirty," she said. "Do you need anything from tactical?"

"You're the guns. I'm just tech."

"Just tech," she repeated.

"At your service," he said, the accent she sometimes detected strong in that phrase. Maybe it was the "v." Albanian? Greek? Definitely Mediterranean, she thought, though she could never put a finger on it.

"Be ready."

He left the way he'd come.

Maybe I can try once more to change the Seer's mind about Ker, she thought, though she knew it was an unwinnable battle. He was their prophet. She, their general. God's orders flowed one direction. Now wasn't the time for questioning. It was the time for action. Time to get out of Horeb and up into the sun. Time to find Rafe. Time to hope he didn't hate her.

CHAPTER 6

He knew it was a dream, but there was nothing he could do about it. In a moment, he'd be trapped in that video game split screen horror. Half of him watching from Center Square, the smoke so thick he couldn't help but choke on it. Half of him within the maelstrom, watching the bodies melt.

It was the eyes that terrified him. The eyes that made him want to die. Within the frenzied sounds of smelting steel and scorching bone, there was the endless symphony of boiling, popping eyes. Then the half-empty sockets staring at him as smoldering jelly ran down melting cheeks.

Where is he? they would ask. *Where is the one who did this us?*

I'm here, he would say, unable to not answer. *The coward is here, across the street, watching.*

We shall not perish this night unavenged, they would say, quoting the Roman epic poem the *Aeneid*, a line he remembered though he hadn't read it since grad school. Then they would come for him and he would wake in fear and sweat and tears.

This was the dream he knew. The dream the bourbon sometimes kept at bay.

Then it wasn't that dream at all. The Tower, built of burning skulls in the nightmare, was gone.

He stands in a child's bedroom. Bunk beds. Toy cars. A blue shirt crumpled on the floor.

"Raffi?" a voice asks.

The room grows. No, he shrinks. Becomes a boy. The part

of him that knows it's a dream has only a moment to recognize its own childhood before the dream takes over. Before he can no longer wonder why he is being visited by this ghost he reconciled more than two years ago.

"Mommy?" *the boy, Raffi, asks of the ghost.*

The room is only the bed, cars, and shirt. The rest is silhouette. Even Mommy. Just shapes and shadows.

"What do we do when we hurt someone?"

The boy looks at his feet, somehow not curious about the way his sneakers fade into the silhouette.

"Say sorry."

"Don't mumble, Raffi."

He raises his eyes and says to his silhouette-Mommy, "I say I'm sorry."

Mommy smiles. The boy can't see it, of course. Silhouettes have no mouths. But he can feel it. The room is warmer when Mommy smiles.

"Well?"

"But Mommy, they're all dead."

"They have friends," *Mommy says.* "They have families."

The boy groans. This is beginning to sound like work.

"Don't take that tone with me, Raffi. You were given a chance and choice. How many of each do you think you get?"

The boy's vision tinges red. He tries to blink it away only to find it's the silhouette of the room. From blackness to burgundy to crimson. Getting brighter. Hotter.

"Maybe only one more, baby."

Sweat beads the boy's hairline. His feet begin to hurt. He smells burning rubber.

"Am I going to Hell, Mommy?"

"Language, Raffi. And yes, in a manner, but only for a visit."

Mommy's silhouette changes. Begins to dissipate, like smoke when the wind picks up.

The boy is scared. "I don't want to go to Hell. I want to go to Heaven with you and Daddy and Daniel."

The boy's mind grows, for the briefest of instants, into the adult he'll one day be. "But Daniel isn't in..."

The smoke interrupts. "No more fires, baby. Okay? You don't set any more fires, and one day you can see Daddy and me again for real. Maybe even Daniel. Won't that be nice?"

The adult mind is gone. The boy tries to say yes but he chokes on the smoke that had been his mother. The bunk beds burst into a column of flame. The toy cars explode one by one. The blue shirt is the only thing not ablaze. The only thing the boy won't kill once he's old enough to destroy the Tower.

He is alone in darkness. Then he isn't. A shade approaches. No shape. No face. Human in the most generalized sense only. He recognizes it. Aeneas, the hero of Virgil's great epic about the aftermath of Troy and its consumption in fire.

"He's not who you think," Aeneas says.

"Who?" Raffi asks.

"The one who hunts you. The one you will hunt."

He is back in the bedroom. He calls out for the shade, but it is gone. Viscous eyeballs appear and boil into explosions all around him. He lunges for the shirt, the ocular napalm scalding his flesh. His fingers touch the cotton. It's cool. Like water. Like....

Rafael Ward fell. Spasmed awake. Panic receded, replaced by recognition that he'd been sleeping. He forced his eyes, gummy and tight, to open. The cracked and stained plaster of the basement ceiling greeted him with its usual lack of interest. He was home.

His neck and shoulder cracked as he stretched on the cold, hard floor, his right foot colliding with a stack of books. The sounds of the paperbacks and hardcovers slapping the concrete, echoing in the cellar, made Ward wince. The stack had been his *To-Read* pile. At last count it was seventeen books, barely a fraction of the number that were piled up the four walls of the old high school's basement.

The earthquake that had decimated Kingman a decade earlier had left these thousands of books, each cover stamped or labeled *Censure*, relatively unharmed and apparently forgotten. Ward had many theories about why they never made it to the censor fires. The most likely was informed by the fact that none of them appeared to have been published after the Reclamation. He guessed that the war came faster than the bureaucrats planned, and this hoard was simply forgotten.

Thinking of forgotten treasures brought Ward's hand to his jacket. To the small lump in his inside breast pocket opposite his heart. One of Childeric's Bees. The only relic he'd been able to rescue from the Tower before he'd set off the charges. The only remnant of former Commandant Gaustad's stash of contraband artifacts. A single millennium-and-a-half old hunk of gold and ruby, and some imperfection beneath the blood-red stone, in the shape of a honey bee. Together with the counterfeit Spear of Destiny he still kept in his backpack, the pair of relics represented how little remained from his old life.

The feel of the bee, thinking about the books, the dream—they all kicked off a thirst for nostalgia as Ward lay in the near-dark, the light from the small desk lamp he'd rigged to a lantern battery highlighting the imperfections of the ceiling. He cupped his hands behind his head and let his mind wander to his first night in Kingman. He'd trekked in from the desert to the north thinking only of whiskey and oblivion. Lucky enough the first convenience store he'd tried was stocked quite nicely with the former, which allowed the promise of the latter.

On his way out of the store, backpack full of bottles and beef jerky, he'd bumped into a homeless man on his way in. The old man, who smelled of body odor and cookies—an odd combination to be sure—grabbed his elbow and said something like, "Reading opens doors."

"What?" Ward had asked. It was the first word he'd said in days. He could still remember the way his throat felt, as if he were coughing up cactus needles.

"The old high school." The old man, his multiple layers of shirts flowing around him like robes, pointed east and coughed. "That's where we stay when we need a home."

"Who?"

"Homeless. Find a book; find an escape. Go on."

The old man had gone in through the store's dinging entrance before Ward could say anything else. But the man's face, old and wrinkled and familiar in that way an elusive word won't let your tongue speak it, kept flashing before Ward's eyes. He'd felt like he had no choice but to go in the direction the old man had pointed. Eventually, he found the ruined high school. It looked as if a giant had given it a good kick. Many of the walls leaned at Pisa-like angles. The gymnasium, a separate structure behind the main building, featured a partially collapsed roof.

A sign posted outside what was once the main entrance told the depressing story of the earthquake, a titanic disaster that resulted in the rebuilding of over half the town. The school, however, was left alone, a monument to the more than four hundred students and faculty who'd been killed in the mid-morning quake.

At first, Ward had been hesitant to enter. What was left appeared so unsteady he was worried a breeze might bring it all down on top of him. There weren't even signs of teenagers breaking in to drink or fool around. Yet the old man had seemed so sure. Ward gave it a try, entering through what had once been a second-floor window, now brought almost to ground level. Inside, the floor had led up like a ramp before dipping him back to the first floor along a central hallway.

The inside was worse than the exterior. Most of the classrooms couldn't be entered, what was left of their doors blocked by debris fallen in from the floors above. Lockers, blue and yellow, that once lined the hallways now lay like corpses on the broken tiles of the floors. There was evidence of fire, charred door jambs and half-consumed bookshelves tossed across hallways or through windows at unnatural angles.

Plus the dust. Far more than he would have expected for a place the city's homeless used regularly, as the old man had said.

In the whole building, as much of it as he could get through, the only intact door he found was the one to the stairs that led to the cellar. A hard kick opened that door and the path to a playground of imagination and education. Books everywhere, some stacked, most littering the floor knee-high or deeper. Some showed water damage. Some had rotted. More than a lifetime's worth of reading remained. Everything from How-To books about cleaning sink drains to classic adventures like *The Count of Monte Cristo* to twentieth century fantasies like *American Gods*. Everything but Bibles, Qurans, and the like, which would have been handed directly to the REC, not stored for future evaluation and possible burning.

It was a place Ward could cease to be himself. A place he could be more himself than anywhere he'd ever been. So he'd straightened up the mess, piling the books against the walls, reading each title as he stacked them according to subject, occasionally wondering if the school was left standing as a monument to the dead like the sign said, or if the Republic encouraged this kind of display. *Look upon me*, the devastated school seemed to say. *I am the result of science and nature, not some angry deity.*

In any case, as Ward lay on the hard floor of the cellar, his back cramped and his leg pulsing, he felt in no better shape than the school. He sat up and reached for what was left of his *To-Read* pile and grabbed the first book his fingers found. He brought it to his face and read the title in the dull glow of the desk lamp.

The Aeneid.

Of course. The dream. The shade.

His head spun like he'd sat up too quickly.

"Coincidence," he muttered.

The books beside Ward groaned.

He sprung to his knees, twisting away from the sound, *The Aeneid* in hand like an awkward sword. His other hand went to his still-spinning head.

A few feet away sprawled a girl.

The whole of the morning came back to Ward like the buffeting wake of a passing tractor trailer. The girl. The photo. The police. The fight. Throwing the girl over his shoulder like a box of textbooks. Carrying her from backyard to backyard, pausing each time before stepping into the open. Arriving, finally, exhaustedly, at the school. Into the cellar. Dropping her on the floor, injured and unconscious. Deciding to drink half a bottle of bourbon to join her.

His mind circled back to the photo. A photo of him taken on a Port. Forget the rest. The REC was probably already here in Kingman.

The anger that came with the memory of the photo surprised him. He had to fight the urge to grab the girl by the arms and throw her against a book-wall. Fight the wish that he could go back in time and let her be taken by the police, interrogated and executed. Fight to regain himself.

A vision of the police woman from this morning came to him, her face mashed in where he'd slammed her against the car. It reminded him of Agent Compano, his former REC trainer, on the train in Italy. Bullets had torn half her face away. What remained had been blackened and oozing. Barely human.

No one deserved that. Certainly not this girl. No more blood, he'd told himself after the Tower. He'd murdered, or caused to be murdered, enough. Far more than bourbon could ever wash away.

No more fires, his mother had said in the dream.

The girl twitched and rolled onto her side. She rubbed her forehead then her eyes before sitting up. Her new position left her facing the stairs, with Ward to her right.

He cleared his throat.

She yelped and scrambled away from him, losing her balance more than once on the books that littered the floor, eventually backing up to the far book-wall. Ward winced at the sight of the apple-sized bruise over her right eye and the cut on her cheek, now pasted over in dried blood.

She could have been any resident of Kingman, with the dark hair, dark eyes, and golden-brown skin that said her family had been here since long before The Wall went up between the Republic and Old Mexico. She reminded Ward of his mother. Young. Pretty. Bedraggled from the day's ordeal but with fight in her eyes behind the fear.

"You," she said, part recognition, part accusation.

"You shouldn't have taken that photo," Ward said. It was a cold thing to say. Almost mean considering the circumstances and what was most certainly happening to the girl's family in interrogation.

Happened, Ward corrected. It must have been hours since the altercation this morning. Interrogation was likely over by now. Her parents were dead. For no other reason than this girl had taken a photo of a homeless man.

"You kidnapped me because I took your picture?"

"Whoa," Ward cut her off. "I didn't kidnap you. I saved your ass this morning." He wanted to say more. He wanted to shout at her until he saw tears, making sure she knew how much she'd fucked up his life, but he belched instead, a hard, burning one that left him without further words on the matter.

The girl made a face.

Ward waved at her like shooing a fly and tried to say more, but his voice caught in his chest. He thought he might vomit. Exhaled slowly. Then plopped from his knees onto his ass.

"You're drunk," the girl said.

Ward almost laughed.

"Take me home," she said.

"Listen, girl," Ward began.

"My name's Sam. I don't need to be condescended to by some homeless asshole who tried to steal my Port."

"You're really something, kid," Ward said, finding it difficult not to grab her by the throat, an impulse so wrong—to want to hurt her, a kid—that it only made him angrier. "I saved your fucking life this morning. I don't give a rat's ass about your Port."

"It's not mine. It's my...shit, my dad!" she shouted. "My mom. They took her."

The girl's voice got louder, going on about her parents, but Ward's head hurt. The louder she got, the more he wanted her to go away. The more he realized that by bringing her here, he'd put them both in a bind. Underground. Wouldn't Agent Compano be disappointed?

"Shut up," he said. "Your parents are dead, and right now there's probably a squad of REC Agents kicking down doors in this shithole town looking for you and me. They don't care if you're my friend or not. You've seen me. That's why they took your parents. You'll be dead before dinner if they get you, so until I figure out how we're getting out of here sit still and shut up."

There was a defiance in the girl's face that reminded Ward of MacKenzie, but she quieted, speaking barely above a whisper, "They're not dead."

"Whatever time it is, it's too late for them."

"My mom. They took my mom. Not my dad."

Ward shut down the part of him that remembered what it was like to have parents. Flipped it off like a switch.

"Why'd you take my photo?"

"I need..."

"Hey," Ward said, louder. "Why'd you take my photo?"

The girl dropped her face into her knees. "We had a bet. Figure out who you are and win some money."

"You don't know who I am?" He couldn't believe it. In passing, with the beard, sure, just a homeless guy. But after this morning, even with the low light in the cellar, how could she not recognize him? What he'd done was unthinkable. He was surely painted as the greatest villain in the Republic's history. He'd single-handedly destroyed the REC's biggest stronghold. He'd murdered hundreds, many of them REC Agents. He'd exposed weakness in the Republic's seemingly indestructible façade. And he'd gotten away with it.

He watched her staring at him, searching but finding nothing.

Then it came to him the way it had in Paris when he'd understood the truth of the Republic propaganda machine. He could see it now. The lies interlaced upon lies. He'd died in the Tower. That was the only report the news outlets would be allowed to run. The only one that wouldn't make the Republic appear weak and incompetent. A lone terrorist killed in the act.

What else could they say? An escaped terrorist and murderer of hundreds? Destroyer of the great symbol of REC power on the loose? No, that couldn't be allowed.

He scratched at his beard, wondering if she'd recognize him even if he hadn't been declared dead. It was almost funny. A beard and a lie erasing him from existence. He decided to explain it all to the girl, the truth of who he was. He tried to stand, but as he got to his feet it was his own head spinning. He put out his hand to steady himself but there was nothing there.

The fall felt like flying.

The landing hurt.

When he opened his eyes, he was lying next to his backpack and jacket. The girl was standing over him.

"How much do you drink?"

Ward shook his head. The concern in her voice, not knowing who she was worried about, sounded like a line from a mid-twentieth century film. A mistaken identity comedy caper.

He contorted into a sitting position and repeated his earlier observation, "You really don't know who I am."

The girl's attitude changed. "I don't care if you're the District Admin. I'm going home."

She reminded Ward again of MacKenzie, her determination and force of will, but he didn't allow himself to dwell on it.

"My name," he said, "is Rafael Ward."

"Rafael...um..." She staggered a bit.

"You can call me Rafe."

Ward watched her eyes go wide. Pure fear this time. Now she understood.

"But," she stammered. "But."

Ward got to his feet, slowly this time. "Yeah," he said.

"You're dead," she finally said, her face twisted in disbelief in such a way that reminded him of Compano's non-face.

He laughed. He couldn't help it.

Panic morphed the girl's face. Ward thought she might run off screaming for help. He grabbed her arms.

"No," she shouted. "They killed the Tower Terrorist. He's dead. You're dead."

"Listen to me," Ward said. "Whatever you think you know is bullshit. I don't want to hurt you, but taking that photo puts you on the run. Your parents are gone. Nobody comes back from interrogation. You must know this. You and me, we have to get out of Kingman. We need a car."

"I have to go home," she mumbled, spinning her head this way and that as if expecting an escape path to light up and show her the way.

He could have let her go. Should have. He'd find a car. Get out of town. He'd make it.

But she wouldn't. They'd find her. They'd interrogate her. Worse than her parents. She was strong. She might last an hour, but that would only extend the suffering. Pain. Blood. Then the Crematorium. The thought twisted his stomach.

No more fires, baby, he again heard his mother say in the dream.

"Fine," he said. "I'll take you back to your house. My way. If your parents are there, we get them to go with us. Agreed?"

"Not with you," the girl said. "You're dead."

He was losing her. And he was in no shape to take care of a girl in mid-breakdown.

"Look at me." He shook her. "Look at my face. Not the beard. Not the dirt. My face. My eyes. I'm a monster, right? You've seen me on the news, right? Look at me."

She looked. Her eyes widened.

"They lied to you," he said.

"If you're not dead," she said, control returning to her voice.

"Exactly. They lie. They've lied to you about everything."

"You didn't do it?"

Ward let go of her arms. "No. I did it." He expected her to run at the admission, but she remained, examining his face. "I did it because they killed my family like they did yours."

"Mom is alive. I saw her getting in the police car."

"Fine. Then we go find out. Truth, right? But you've got to do what I say or we'll both end up in interrogation. Good?"

She squeezed her hands as if punishing them for not preventing all this and then said, "Fine."

Ward could tell it was a just-till-we-get-there pact. That was fine. Her house would be empty. He'd get her out of town. Somewhere far enough to be safe. Then she was on her own. He could find a new hole to crawl into. Find a bigger bottle of stronger whiskey and let it end him.

He reached for the girl, ready to tell her to keep her mouth shut and follow him, but she had backed away.

"Do you hear that?" she asked.

He didn't. Then, a second later, he did. The muffled sound of sirens from outside. He grabbed his backpack and looked around his books, floor to ceiling, one last time. The books that had been his solace for a year. The books that could have offered countless years more of reading, if only the girl hadn't taken his photo.

He offered a silent thank-you to the old man who'd pointed him here. If this had been the best his life had left to offer, so be it. It was more than he deserved.

As good a place as any for a dead man to die, he thought and started up the stairs.

CHAPTER 7

The sirens grew louder as Ward and the girl charged up the stairs. It was definitely not a single police car.

"Which way?" the girl asked as they pushed through the door at the top of the stairs.

Ward directed her left into a hallway of downed lockers and splintered classroom doors. The girl—*Did she tell me her name? I can't remember*—stopped and stared at the first locker blocking their path.

"Are we in the old high school?" she asked.

"Yes."

She didn't move. "We're not allowed in here."

"I think we're way past that, don't you?"

"My cousin died in here," the girl said, as if reading a cue card.

Ward understood how she felt, facing the ghosts of her dead family, but there was no time. He pushed her into a trot, then took the lead past the cafeteria, a haunting traffic jam of tables and chairs the way you might expect a freeway to look a decade after a nearby city got nuked. Through the missing cafeteria doors, he could see the windows at the back and the gymnasium beyond, looming like an impotent guardian over the campus.

A few more turns brought them to the school's north entrance, a massive set of double doors facing the parking lot. Only the right window pane remained. The left door housed a plank of plywood. To the right outside the doors was the gymnasium. Beyond that, a stretch of desert before the homes of East Kingman stuck up from the dirt and sand like shrubbery.

"Wait," Ward ordered, needing to yell to be heard over the sirens, at least four distinct whines.

The girl kept on toward the door, though whether by stubbornness or uncomprehending innocence he couldn't tell. Either way, anger frothed inside him, making him grab her arm and sling her to the side.

"Ow," she complained.

"Not until I know what's out there." He let go of her, knowing he would regret the way he'd grabbed her later, if they survived.

"Maybe they brought Mom," she said, "you know, to explain all this. The mistake."

"There's no mistake. They're not here for a family reunion."

She seemed to consider this a moment then said, "You're wrong. Mom will explain."

She reached around Ward for the door but didn't fight when he grabbed her arm again. Her wide eyes told Ward she knew the truth, even if she wasn't ready to let herself believe it.

"Don't move," he said.

He approached the window from the side, wondering if he might not discover the girl was actually right and her mother was standing out there waving like moms do. Then, he wondered if this was the moment some sniper put a bullet through his brain.

Not so long ago the voice in his head would have told him when to duck to avoid a sniper's bullet. He missed that voice. It would have helped him escape. Helped him find somewhere dark and cool to hide. The girl, too. She was just a kid. A fool taking a photo because kids do foolish things.

He shuffled to the window. The first thing he noticed was it was already evening.

How long were we asleep down there?

He shoved the question aside and took stock of the situation. The parking lot was filled with police cars and a cigar-shaped, bright red fire truck. He understood what was coming immediately. Before he pulled back from the window to tell the girl they were likely going to die, a black sedan across the street caught his eye, its front end visible as if peeking around the chaos in the parking lot the same way Ward was peering out the window. What stood in front of the black sedan scared him the way children are afraid of monsters in the closet.

A person. More like a shadow. A shade like in his dream.

No, a soldier.

He stretched forward more, putting his whole head in the window, to see the soldier better. He wore some kind of body armor covering him from head to toe. He wasn't moving. He didn't appear to be communicating with the police on scene. Yet danger emanated from him like ominous music from a speaker.

"Is that a fire truck?"

Ward pulled back. "I told you stay put."

"I don't smell smoke."

Ward ignored her. He needed to figure out how they'd found him. Knowing that would determine their best route of escape. Had they been followed? Seen entering the school? No, even drunk he wouldn't have been that careless. They must have been tracked another way to bring this type of fully committed response. Something like...

"You and your fucking Port."

"What?" she said, backing up.

"Your Port. Give it to me."

"I told you it's broken. You broke it."

"Give it to me."

She dug the Port from her pocket and handed it over. The screen was shattered, the casing cracked. It didn't power on. None of that meant it was truly broken, however. He pulled a folding knife from his pocket and pried the back cover off the device.

"What are you doing?" she asked.

He didn't answer, instead ripping the battery from its internal dock. Waiting in the shallow cavity beneath was the IC Chip. The Port's brain and lifeline. As long as it had power, the Port was a live beacon.

"Not broken," Ward said. "Not yet."

He cut the chip out with his knife, slicing through the three wires that held it in place. He showed it to the girl, as if shaming her. She watched without reaction as he snapped the chip in half and tossed it.

"If it wasn't broken," the girl asked, "why didn't they come sooner?"

"I don't know." He looked out the window again. This time the figure who drew his attention was a woman in a black suit—black shirt, white tie, red tie bar—with short dark hair and an authoritative grimace that made him think immediately of Agent Compano.

She's dead. I killed her.

Did you, or did MacKenzie? Or Claude?

It doesn't matter. I saw her die.

He drew back, shook the image clear, and looked again. The Agent, who was most definitely not Agent Compano, was speaking with a huge man in tactical gear and the intimidating REC red-on-white designation on his chest above the heart.

He motioned the girl over. She shuffled to the window the same way he had.

"Is that..." she said. "Are those real Agents?"

"Yes."

"Why are Agents here to put out a fire?"

Ward knew it was only a matter of time before she either went catatonic from the mounting shock of the day or sucked it up and decided to fight.

"They're not," Ward said. "We've got to go."

The girl opened her mouth to protest, but someone began shouting outside before she could make a sound. Ward couldn't make out the words, but he knew the tone. Orders. His insides lurched like he'd fallen.

The next words spoken outside were clear. Loud. Final. "Set," the voice yelled, as if through a megaphone. "Fire."

There was no crack of gunfire. There were no shattering windows from a breach assault. There was only a dull hum getting louder. A whooshing that seemed to thin the air in the school, if such a thing was possible.

The light coming through the doors grew brighter. Ward grabbed the girl's wrist and ran, afraid of what he'd see if he turned around.

Fire.

It wasn't a common tactic. The REC preferred prisoners. It preferred interrogation. But not for him, the supposedly dead Terrorist. For him fire, obliteration, was the way go. The

Republic couldn't allow a body to contradict its narrative.

"Where are we going?"

Ward ran on, not letting go of her wrist. He could feel her fighting as he trailed her. Not a lot. Not enough to escape. She was trying to twist enough to see what was coming. He imagined her believing that she would turn and see friendly government employees coming to rescue her, but that's not what was coming.

He slowed, trying to will a voice into his mind to tell him what to do. That voice was gone, however. All he had was himself and the girl. He needed her to cooperate, so he stopped around a corner and let go of her hand. She looked at him, unsure, then moved into the center of the hallway. Ward stayed back, but he could see the glow.

"Fire," she said, choking on the word.

Ward didn't see a need to respond.

"But they're here to rescue me."

"They're here to kill us both."

She backed away from the corner. "Why would they do that?"

"Because they couldn't kill you when they killed your parents."

She turned, her eyes blazing like he knew the front of the school was. They were almost out of time.

"What do we do?"

That was the question, he hadn't figured out how to answer yet. There were only three ways to go. Up, down, and out. Up— Agent Compano's direction of choice—was no good today. They would have started the blaze at the front entrances and then quickly lit the roof. Ward could imagine the fire truck breathing flames from its hoses like a dragon.

Out wouldn't work. That's what they wanted. The fire assault was designed to either burn alive or smoke out. It was a simple tactic, generally reserved for situations where extraction was prohibitively difficult. A zipline of images from the past screamed through Ward's mind. Agent Compano tossing a smoke grenade into an empty ammo crate. The white smoke leaking out its seams.

"Where do the suspects go?" she'd asked.

"Out," Ward had said.

"And if they don't?"

"Collect the bodies," he'd replied.

He wondered how many Agents were out there now. Two? A dozen? Whatever the number, he was certain each of the school's exits was covered by gunners, either local cops, National Police Forces, or Agents. Out would only get them shot.

An explosion rocked the building. Flames darted from beneath a classroom door like a snake's tongue as they ran by. The girl stopped and began to shake. She looked to him for instructions. He had none. Panic trembled in his legs.

The panic gave way to an almost hysterical sensation of irony. The balance of it was so right, he heard himself laugh. Mom. The Tower. Of course he was going to die in flames.

But not the girl, he told himself.

He needed a lifeline. A focus to center him. A line from a novel came to him. A book so high on the censor list even he, a professor with access, shouldn't have read it. He couldn't recall the exact words, but it essentially said: You have to leave something behind when you die, something you touched so your soul has somewhere to go.

The line from *Fahrenheit 451*, a book he only ever got to read because he'd found it here in this school, calmed him. It cooled him. Recalled another memory. The old man.

"Reading opens doors," the old man had said. "Find a book; find an escape."

He'd forgotten that first day entering the school. He'd been ecstatic at what he'd found in the cellar. The books covered the floor like a flood. He's spent days stacking them against the cinderblock walls, trying at first for some measure of organization before giving up and piling them as high as they would go until they concealed all four walls.

Only, one wall hadn't been all cinderblock.

"Let's go," Ward said.

The girl didn't move. Her hands were over her ears. She seemed to be only seconds from dropping to her knees and accepting the fire.

His eyes stung. He pulled the girl to him. For a moment, her face morphed into his mother's. A billow of black smoke tumbled past. In its wake, her face was her own. He grabbed her hand. It was soft and sweaty. He half-dragged her, coughing and hacking, toward the cellar stairs.

The building above them shrieked like it was in pain. They pushed through the door and down the stairs.

"We're going to die," she said, sounding both resigned and terrified of the fact.

Ward didn't have time to calm or reassure her. He flung himself against the back wall. Books flew and tumbled around him. He slid to his knees, got up, and began throwing books aside.

"What are you doing?" the girl asked, her voice now trembling.

Ward dug through the books like a starving man shoveling his way to a banquet, the old homeless man's face hovering in his mind. A familiar face, he thought. Like a man he'd once known, back in those days when he'd been a righteous Citizen. Before he could place it, he hit cinderblock.

The old man's face vanished. Ward let it go. He needed to be in the now or else he'd soon enough be part of the past. He stood back. He'd cleared a third of the wall. He picked a spot and charged back into the books. The girl made noise. Flames licked through the ceiling at random, dropping melted plaster around them. Smoke crept down from the stairs. He dug. The books seemed to be a thousand thick. Paperbacks. Hardcovers. Pamphlets. It would never end, he feared. Then, almost without warning, the pile collapsed.

Behind it, dead-center in the wall, was a door. Metal. Blue. Cool.

Beyond the door was an access tunnel carrying cabling, piping, and whatever else from the main school building to the gymnasium. He'd covered it up those first days living in the cellar and forgotten it. Until now.

He kicked books away from the door's base, wanting to feel bad for the near-sacrilegious act, but wanting not to die more. "Here," he shouted.

The girl joined him on her hands and knees, throwing books aside. A section of the ceiling in the far corner began to sag. The sound of snapping, like bones breaking, chorused from above.

He pushed the door's bar-style latch. It didn't budge. He kicked the door beside where the strike plate should be. Nothing. He took off his backpack and rummaged for his gun, buried beneath the bourbon, junk food, a couple small bottles of water, and other necessities of his homeless life. His fingers found the cool grip. The pistol, a Glock, was light and well balanced, but holding it made him miss the RT40 he was trained on as an REC Agent. That thing fit like it had been made for him.

Not that it mattered. A gun was a tool. Its job was whatever the need of the moment.

He threw the backpack at the girl and aimed at the strike plate. He fired four rounds into the door jam, each explosion louder than the previous, causing him to wince so much that the fourth shot missed high by over a foot. Three would have to do. He stepped back, flexed, and charged the door shoulder first. It burst open with a horrible inhalation sound as the heated air of the cellar rushed into the tunnel. Ward hit the ground hard, the gun skittering from his hand into the tunnel beyond the reach of the cellar's light.

He got to his feet and reached for the girl. She hesitated. The building rumbled and quaked. The ceiling trembled. He grabbed her hand and slingshotted her into the tunnel. He followed, pulling the door closed behind, leaving them in darkness.

CHAPTER 8

The pounding of his heavy breathing, mixed with the girl's wheezing sobs, was all Ward could hear at first. Behind them and above them, the fire growled and hissed and roared.

They found each other's hands.

"Give me my backpack," he told her.

"What?"

"My backpack."

"I," she hesitated. "I dropped it."

"You what?" There was no time to scold her. He needed the backpack. His flashlight was in there. And his whiskey.

He let go of her hand and got on his hands and knees, feeling around for the backpack, irritation and fear and claustrophobia from the fire closing around them making the search sloppy.

"Where are you?" the girl said, voice trembling.

"Shut up a minu—" The side of his face bashed a wall. "Fuck!"

"What was that?"

He rocked back on his ass and felt his face for blood or a broken orbital bone. "Just," he said, his eyes now clamped tight in pain, "stand there. Don't move."

I'm right back where I started, he thought, remembering the tunnel MacKenzie had led him through in that South Philadelphia basement. *Maybe this is all my life's meant to be, crawling through underground pits with girls I've just met.*

He got to his feet, the spinning sensation returning a little.

"We're going to die," the girl stammered to his left. "We're going to burn. We're going to burn." She continued to babble. The stoic girl who had run up the cellar stairs with him before the fire was gone. The determined girl who had fought him this morning was gone. The frightened girl on the edge of keeping it together was back.

"Calm down," Ward said. "Take deep breaths."

He reached his arms ahead and pivoted slowly, trying to find the wall he'd hit. He found the girl. She yelped then clutched at him, clinging to his arm like it was life vest. With his free hand, he continued groping for the wall. Found it. Not a wall at all. A square pole. A support column, most likely.

"I smell smoke."

Ward ignored her. He needed to figure out the direction from which they'd come so he could find a side wall. He needed to find his backpack.

"It's going to get us," the girl said. "The door won't stop it. It's going to burn us."

She was right. The fire would come. But the REC wouldn't. Not into the tunnel, anyway, until they'd searched the ashes for human remains. Only then would they excavate the basement and discover the tunnel.

When she continued babbling, he shouted at her, "Enough!"

Her stammering melted to a whimper then silence.

"I need your help, okay?" he said, trying to remember she was a teenager. She wasn't even old enough to have been through basic training for Citizen's Duty. She wasn't prepared for this. He put his hand over hers. "Can you do that? Can you help me?"

Silence. He imagined her nodding in the dark.

"I don't go here." Her voice was calmer, but not quite in full control yet.

"I get that. My backpack. You dropped it, right? Where? Which direction?"

"I don't know. It's all the same. I'm dizzy."

"Close your eyes," he said. "Now get down on your hands and knees."

He crouched with her so she didn't have to let go of his arm.

"Now, which direction did we come from?"

"I can't see," she said.

"Don't try to see it. Remember it."

"My mom..."

"Your mom is dead," Ward said, harsher than he needed to. His head pounded. His leg throbbed. Sweat was pooling in his boots. He didn't have the time or energy for nice. "Your dad is dead. If we don't get out of here, you'll be dead too. Get it? One big happy dead family, and their dead terrorist friend."

He could hear the kid trying to swallow her tears. He felt bad for her. She didn't ask for this. He dropped it in her lap like he did to everyone he'd ever known.

Pity later. Live now.

"Please," he said, "help me find my..."

"Backpack!" she said.

The tunnel trembled. Rumbled. Shook and sounded like a vengeful earthquake returning to finish its job. Ward could imagine the school's main floor crumbling into the cellar that would never again be his home, finally completing the task the Republic intended when it exiled all those books years ago.

The girl leapt into him, tumbling Ward backwards. He banged his head on the pole again, not hard this time. Not enough to distract him from what was important. The backpack. Next, the flashlight. Then, find the gun.

"Sorry," the girl said.

"It's fine." Ward, the backpack hugged to his chest, stood and rotated the pack until he found one of the side pockets, and his flashlight within. He switched it on and shined the beam around, then on the girl. She was holding her hands sheepishly over her mouth as if embarrassed that they were still alive.

"What is this place?" she asked through her hands.

The tunnel was ten feet or so wide, with a floor of polished concrete. The walls were whitewashed and still bright. Support columns like the one Ward had crashed into sat in the middle of the tunnel about every thirty feet. Above, cabling and conduits ran the length of the ceiling on either side of a line of fluorescent light panels, none of which looked like they would light up anyway.

"Our way out," he said, as confidently as he could.

He panned the flashlight around the tunnel, searching for his gun. The tunnel trembled and groaned again. Dust poured from the ceiling. And ash. They had to move now. He grabbed the girl's arm once more and ran as fast as his limp would let him until, in the distance, near the edge of his vision, another blue door appeared. For a second, he thought they'd run the wrong direction back to the cellar.

"The gym," the girl said. "The way we're going, this leads to the big gym, right?"

"Let's hope so," Ward said, impressed with how quickly she figured out his plan and their direction.

"Won't it be on fire too?"

"Not if we're lucky. If we're really lucky, there won't be more than a few cops keeping watch because it's a separate building."

"Today's the luckiest day of my life," the girl said.

Ward couldn't tell if she was being sarcastic, and before he could ask, she pushed the door.

"It's locked," she said.

Ward gave it a shove.

"I just said it was locked," she said.

Ward ignored her. He balanced himself on his bad leg as best he could and kicked the push bar in the middle of the door.

Nothing.

He backed up a few steps then lunged, smashing his shoulder into the door.

It didn't budge.

"Shoot it again," the girl said.

"I lost my gun."

"You what?"

Ward could hear Agent Compano screaming at him. *You lost your gun? What kind of an Agent loses his gun?*

Or maybe it was MacKenzie yelling. Either way, he wasn't going to offer this kid the opportunity to scold him. He slammed his shoulder into the door once more. It flung open, flinging Ward to the ground.

This time he held onto his flashlight and shone it around. They were in a basement again but not a cinderblock. Painted walls lined with chairs stacked on top of chairs in mute rows. Ahead and to the right, glittering when the flashlight beam hit it, beckoned an *Exit* sign.

"Let's go," the girl said, not waiting for Ward to get up.

"Stay behind me," he said.

She didn't, bounding to the exit before he made it three steps.

"Stairs," she said. "There's light up there, I think."

"Damn it, kid, wait for me."

Again, she didn't.

If he'd been faster, he might have grabbed her and shaken her until she listened, but he was out of breath and his leg hurt. And as much as she reminded him at times of how he imagined MacKenzie might have been at this age—before the training and the purpose of her revolution—he mostly wanted to yell at her to stand still for a minute.

By the time he made it upstairs, she was standing in the middle of an office. The broken pieces of plastic-bronze trophies scattered over the floor signaled it had belonged to the school's athletic coaches. There was only one exit from the room. Its door was long gone, but the way out was more than three-quarters blocked by debris—what looked like the twisted wreck of an industrial sized air conditioning compressor that Ward guessed had come down from a collapsed roof. A block of soft light, evening light, glowed through the top quarter of the doorway that was free of run

He didn't bother telling her to stop this time as she scrambled over the wreckage and through the small aperture at the top.

"Wow," she said from the other side.

"Unless someone's trying to kill you, stay put till I get through."

She didn't answer. He took that as a good sign and approached the doorway. A couple years ago, he'd have been over and through as quickly as the girl. Today, he knew, it would take longer, and it would be more painful.

He switched off the flashlight and put it back in the backpack. Tossed the bag through the door.

"Got it," the girl said.

This time, Ward didn't answer. He climbed.

It was easier going than he thought, though he did get stuck a moment once he was partway through the aperture. The girl didn't notice. She was studying the dark blue sky of late evening floating above the roofless gymnasium.

The remains of the roof covered the floor like so much flotsam. The eastern wall was mostly collapsed, and the whole gym was in shadow cast from the intact, but now slanted, western wall.

The girl handed him his backpack and pointed to a piece of the roof propped against the eastern wall like a ramp.

"I see it," Ward said. "Stay here."

He willed his always aching leg to hold out a bit longer and climbed the ramp, only having trouble where the remains of some machine—probably another compressor—forced him to scramble over it. The view was worth it. Forget the mile or so of clean desert before to the east. There were no police or Agents back here. Their flashing lights could be seen to the south, pulsing through the funnel of smoke billowing into the sky from the main building, but it appeared no one thought they could make it out of the school. And the smoke would be great cover to get away. He hoped.

He waved the girl over. *What the fuck did she say her name is?*

She managed the climb quicker than he had. When she'd joined him, she examined the view over the desert, then turned to the pillar of smoke.

"It's clear," she said, looking for a place to climb down. "Let's go."

"We can't just go running—"

Too late. They were only about ten or twelve feet in the air. She jumped. Hit the ground and rolled and came up like a spring-operated toy. Ward envisioned himself trying it that way, lying on the ground in pain, howling and holding his leg, until the Agents finally made it around and shot him in the face.

He chose instead to swing over the edge, hang from his hands to get his feet as close to the ground as possible, then drop. The pain went through him, ankle to top of the spine, like an electric spike. But he kept silent. Hands pulled at his shoulder to help him up.

"I've got to go home," the girl said when he'd gotten to his feet, the kind of tone Ward knew from his own students as an excuse. They were outside. She wanted to get as far away from him as possible.

So why isn't she running?

"You can't," he said.

"There's no one watching. They're all at the fire."

"There's always someone watching."

He thought she would run. If she did, he'd have to let her go. He hated the way it contorted his insides, but there was no way he could keep up with her at a run, let alone catch her. She'd be killed. REC methods left no doubt. She'd seen him. Taken his photo. Spent a day with him in the school after he assaulted a police officer, likely breaking the woman's skull open, on her behalf. She was as wanted as he was. He simply couldn't let her walk off to her death because of her dumb luck in meeting him.

He made up his mind. This couldn't only be about getting her out of Kingman anymore. He had to get her somewhere far away. Somewhere safe. Somewhere she could start over and not worry about the Tower Terrorist. Where she wouldn't have to look over her shoulder every moment of her life.

The question was how to get her to trust him. She'd stayed with him this long, but he knew that was mostly due to fear. Kids, even college students, seek authority figures when they're scared. It would only last so long, though. He had to get her to believe him. That was first. If she believed him about her parents, she'd be more likely to leave town with him.

"So what do we do?" she asked.

The stupidest thing we can do.

"We go to your house and see if your mom is there."

"Okay," she said somewhat skeptically.

"If she's there and this is all a misunderstanding, you'll never see me again."

"If she's not?"

"Then we need to get the fuck out of town."

She scoured his face, her eyes barely slits. Whatever she was searching for, she seemed to either find it or accept that she wouldn't.

"Good," Ward said. "Now follow what I tell you. We can't go strolling out of here like we're on taking a walk. At some point they'll figure out we weren't incinerated. Or some cop will come around back to take a piss. Or an Eye-D will sweep the area."

"An Eye-Drone? I thought they were only for patrolling the borders."

"You don't really think the Republic lets you go about your life without someone watching, do you? Eye-Ds. Satellites. Informants everywhere. They can control your Port—not just listen or watch through it, but control it—if you don't know how to cut off access."

"Whatever," the girl said, clearly thinking he was at least half paranoid and crazy. "What do we need to do?"

"We go straight east, keep the buildings between them and us. Stay low in the brush. It's basically going to be a crawl. Can you handle that?"

The girl made a face. At first, Ward thought it was about the slow going, but it was confusion not irritation.

"East," he said. "You don't know east?"

"I know what it is, but I'm not a compass."

"For fuck's sake," Ward said, then pointed. "That way. Due east. See the homes there? We go at least three blocks deep into that neighborhood before taking a wide circle back to your house. I'll lead through the desert. You lead once we get to the houses. Keep to yards and alleys. No main streets. By then it should be dark enough to keep us alive. Got it?"

She said she understood.

Ward took point. His plan worked perfectly, though slower than he'd calculated. It was at least an hour before they reached the homes at the edge of the desert, and a rim of burgundy hugging the horizon was all that remained of the day. Behind them, the lights still flashed at the school, and the fire still glowed while black smoke rose like a void against the night. No sirens wailed in their direction, however. He guessed they had around three hours until curfew. Enough, he hoped, to get the girl out of Kingman and somewhere safe for the night.

As they crossed the first block of the neighborhood, Ward

allowed himself to believe he'd orchestrated an almost perfect escape. Then, without a word, the girl skipped into a run and disappeared around a corner leaving Ward standing on the sidewalk, surprised. Confused. Alone.

CHAPTER 9

Books.

The entire school cellar had been full of books. Sam didn't know there were that many books in the entire world. And Hoodie Guy, of course, had been hoarding them. He was dangerous. The most dangerous, and wanted, man in the Republic.

Except he's not wanted, some part of her mind argued as she ran away from him and towards home. *He's dead. They said he died in the Tower.*

No, she wasn't going to let herself get distracted by lies. *His* lies, not the Republic's. So, she ran. It was easy enough to get away from him. He could barely walk, let alone run, with that limp and his alcohol-soaked brain—he couldn't even remember her name!

It was, she reflected, amazing he'd survived this long.

And saved my life. Twice.

She forced herself to stop thinking about him and run. She had to get home. Mom would be there in the kitchen drinking coffee and worrying. Dad would be on the couch. Everything would be okay. Mom would explain the misunderstanding. It was Hoodie Guy—the Tower Terrorist—they were after. In the end, they would give the Vasquez family a big commendation for finding, and surviving, him. They might even offer to take care of Sam's "little thing" and make an exception for her to still enter Citizen's Duty.

This storyline, along with the need to see Mom—and the tingling in her fingertips—made her run faster, but the closer she got to her part of town, the more she worried. Doubted. Feared. What if the police thought she was with him? What if the REC wanted to make her disappear like the guy in the cowboy hat who'd said what happened to the Tower wasn't so bad?

She turned off the lighted streets and into the backyards and unlit lanes of East Kingman, like Hoodie Guy—*his name is Rafael Ward; he's the Tower Terrorist!*—had instructed in the first place. When she reached the Westin's backyard across from her own, she hunkered beside their swing set.

What if he was telling me the truth?

She couldn't help the thought. She couldn't help considering what that would mean. If they'd lied about him dying in the Tower, what else were they lying about? Would they really take her mother to interrogation to protect their lies?

Stop it, stop it, stop, stop it!

She wanted to let herself cry. She realized she'd been holding back her tears since she abandoned the terrorist who'd saved her life. Tears wouldn't help, however. That was a lesson she'd learned years ago when she used to cry at her dad's feet while he snored away on the couch. It was a lesson she'd revisited when Lucas sent her that message which read: *Not my prob, sorry.*

As she watched her house from the Westin's backyard, the television's light flickering and dancing in the family room, she grew angry. At Dad. At Lucas. At Rafael Ward. Had there ever been such a disappointment of men as these three? A drunk, a callous asshole, and the country's greatest terrorist bogey man, who had gone and saved her life and made her doubt everything she knew about history and truth and a Citizen's responsibility.

"Fuck him," she said, surprised she'd said it out loud.

She looked around for a neighbor's light switching on or a face appearing in a window, but she saw none. She shifted attention to her house, trying to sweep away the nagging feeling that she shouldn't have run from her terrorist-hero. Everything seemed okay. Except for the sliding glass door at the back of the family room. It was open almost a foot. Not the first time the back door had been left open a little. But a foot? It reminded her of this morning. Of her open front door moments before Mom was brought out in custody. Before that police woman started shooting her gun.

Fear told Sam to run, to never come back. She didn't give in. not yet. She forced her legs to move. She crept from the swings and climbed the low chain-link fence between the two yards, a simple enough push-and-hop she'd done a thousand times as a little girl, yet tonight it seemed a strenuous exercise, as if her body had forgotten its center of gravity and flexibility.

She crept to her house and waited, making certain no one was watching. When she was satisfied, she shuffled to the back door. The lights, save for the television's strobing glow, were off inside. Other than the general shape of the furniture, she couldn't see much.

"Mom," she said. "Reina?" No response from either.

She slid the door open wider so she could enter. The television, sound muted, hung on the wall to the right. The sectional couch wrapped the wall to her left. She wiped the back of her hand across her cheek, surprised that she was sweating so much, then worked her way around the couch until she was facing Dad's spot in the corner. The relief she felt when she saw him splayed out in his drunken glory was like a bowl of ice cream during a heat wave.

"Dad," she said, not really expecting him to answer. He might belch or twitch, knocking the beer can from his belly but...

There was no beer can. There was no rise and fall of the stained t-shirt stretched over his bloated stomach. The ice cream relief became a chill at her core. She moved closer.

His face was gone. A blackened hole gaped as if his mouth, nose, and right eye had been shoved through his skull and out the back.

Sam was aware of collapsing. She was aware of clinging to her father's leg and weeping with savage abandonment. She became aware, slowly, of shouting, "I'll kill you," though at who this was aimed, she had no clear idea. It was a broad, confusing desire set inside her like hunger.

Eventually, she opened her eyes, unaware they'd been closed. Her left hand, her knuckles, were bleeding, and she could only assume she'd pounded her fist against the floor or the coffee table. She was almost impressed with how much she missed her father considering how long it had been since he'd been Dad and not just some sweaty lump on the couch.

There was a whimper to her right. She turned. Reina was crouched beside her, nuzzling into her thigh.

"Oh, baby," Sam said. She grabbed the dog and pulled her close, inhaling her aroma of wet grass and childhood. She wept.

Eventually, when the heaves ceased, Sam got to her feet. She wiped her eyes and cheeks and began listening to her mind once more. Rafe was right. The police—maybe the REC—had marched into her house and executed her father. They'd taken her mother.

Her first impulse was rescuing Mom, but she knew she wasn't capable of such an act. Rafael Ward, however, was capable. He could help her.

She looked at her father's body once more, settled perfectly in the mold he'd formed over the years in the couch. He'd never even moved when they'd entered the house. He'd been killed without putting up a fight. He'd been unable to protect his wife and his daughter because he was a drunk. It wasn't sad. It was pathetic. And right now, the only person who could help her save Mom was also a drunk.

But I can help him, she thought. *I can help him save her.*

She scrambled to her feet, spooking Reina who darted out the back door. It was okay; she'd be back. Right now, Sam needed to get upstairs and get her things.

It took only a peek into her bedroom—she almost turned on the light but stopped herself, finger an inch from the panel—to see that her father's murderers had been searching for something. The Port maybe. Or evidence of how long she'd actually known Rafe. Whatever it was, they'd tipped over her bureau and flung its drawers about the room. Her bed was on its side, the mattress slashed open. Holes had been smashed in the drywall. The contents of her closet were a mess across the floor and overtop the bureau.

She found a shoulder bag beneath her bureau. Tugged it free

with then dumped a few handfuls of clothes inside, making sure to grab plenty of underwear and bras. Then to the bathroom. The medicine cabinet. Her Lito.

The supply vial was empty.

"Fuck," she said, dropping the bottle in the sink.

Mom had asked to take a few yesterday. A few. Not the whole bottle. She'd had almost a month of halves left. She wanted to scream, but that wouldn't accomplish anything. Instead she had to think. Alternatives. Mia. Maybe she could sneak to Mia's house and get some more. Or Chuck. He'd worked the morning shift and sure as shit would be home on a Saturday night.

Liking the plan, she abandoned the bathroom. Looked down the hall to her parents' room at the back of the house. It too had been ransacked. Broken glass, probably from her mom's vanity mirror, glittered on the floor. And a small wooden box, now not much more than splinters mixed in with the glass. A music box.

She hadn't seen it in years. There'd been a fight—over Dad's drinking probably—when she was about thirteen. She'd thrown the music box at him, breaking the lid. She'd figured it was trash then, but he must have fixed it and saved it all these years. She could hear its song now in her mind. A soft, bouncing melody from Dad's home, his family's home on the other side of The Wall. A song he used to sing to her when she couldn't sleep. She could hear it as well as she could hear his voice singing along in his ancestors' language. *Her* ancestors' language.

Rage hit Sam like a fist.

She inhaled the rage. Let it fill her lungs and pulse in time with her heartbeat. Let it permeate every portion of herself. Let it conjure determination. Force of will. Purpose.

She squeezed this purpose in her fists like clay.

They did this to her. They lied. They broke her music box. They killed Dad. They took Mom.

If they hurt Mom...

What? What would she do if they took her mother away as well? What would she do if Rafe was right and everything was a lie? School and Mom and Dad and terrorists and The Wall and the cams and the homeless and what else? What could one girl do when the entire Republic was a lie?

"I'll do what the Tower Terrorist did," she whispered.

The declaration felt good, despite how horrible she knew it was. It felt right, despite knowing she could never carry out the threat.

She descended the stairs, looking toward the back door to find Reina. Then she could head to—

A hand grabbed at her shoulder from behind.

Not without a fight, she thought.

CHAPTER 10

The house was being watched. It was as clear to Ward, who had crept up between the houses from the backyard to take a look around, as if a sign had been planted in the street with big block letters: STAKEOUT. There were almost no cars lining the curbs like there'd been that morning. There were no kitchen or porch lights on across the street. On the whole block, there was only one bedroom light on, and that was muted by a heavy shade.

The police were in that room, watching. He had no doubt it wasn't REC. They'd never be that obvious.

So he'd kept tight to the wall and returned to the backyard, which appeared to be free of surveillance, and slipped into the house as the girl came down the stairs with a large pocketbook over her shoulder. She was quiet but not stealthy. It was a wonder they hadn't burst into the house to take her.

Because they're waiting for me, he thought.

Which makes you an idiot for coming back for her.

I'm saving her!

He shut down the argument. He'd had it enough times with himself on the way over here, picking up glimpses of the girl as she bounced from backyard to backyard, always a block or so ahead of him. She'd made her choice, he told himself, only to counter that it wasn't about her choice at all. It was his. He was choosing to save her, not responding to a request.

He'd doubted. He'd almost turned back more than once. Seeing her now, however, vulnerable and alone, convinced him his first instinct was the right one. She was in danger because of him. He would get her out of Kingman. If she wanted to leave then, so be it.

He crept through the family room, noting the body on the couch, and reached for her, finger already to his lips to tell her to stay quiet.

She screamed, dropped her bag, and punched him in the clavicle. It was a weak jab, possibly to set up a stronger blow to his jaw. Instead of throwing another punch, her legs wobbled. He grabbed her arms to keep her from falling.

"You," she accused, pulling away.

"Shh," he said. "Do you have a death wish coming back here alone? Want to meet some REC?"

"No, I—" she started, but couldn't finish. Her gaze turned to the family room.

Ward understood the body was her father. He knew she must be on the edge of keeping control, but that couldn't be an excuse for running off. She was lucky the police hadn't come in after her, but if they stayed too long he was sure they'd investigate. He had to hope the body on the couch would be enough to convince her to leave town with him.

"We've got to get her back," she said, her voice wavering a little, but her intent clear. She'd found a strength, maybe in the death of her father, that made her seem again like a young MacKenzie. "My mom, we have to bring her home."

He'd already told her the truth: her mother was dead. Victim of a zealous interrogator, the only kind the REC employed. He wondered if she would hear it clearer now. If it would break her down or build her up. If it would give her the strength to work with him so they could both escape Kingman.

"She's gone," he said, trying to balance harsh truth with sympathy. "And we're in danger."

"Fuck you. You promised to help me get her back. If you back out, I'll—I'll turn you in." She was dangerous. Seething. "I'll kill you."

Ward knew that rage. Knew the irrational determination it brought. Her family might have been killed today, but she'd been suffering for years. And now, for the first time, she had someone to blame. The Republic or the Tower Terrorist. He'd faced a similar choice once. He chose to blame himself. He needed her to blame the Republic.

"They took your mother to question her. To find out if I'd been seen around the house. They might have done it in the car. Maybe at the police station. It didn't last more than five minutes. When they were convinced they knew everything she knew," he paused, watching the girl, trying to predict how she would react, "they put a bullet in her head like your dad."

She wailed. Her fists clenched. He watched his truth and the Republic lies battling in her. He thought she might choose the Republic. Then her eyes narrowed. She stopped hitting him. She stared at the wall over his shoulder. He turned. Her face was on the television. His wasn't. She was wanted. He was, so far as everyone else knew, dead.

"That's not right," she said. "I didn't do anything wrong."

Ward was about to tell her that right and wrong had nothing to do with it when a dog, a knee-high brown and black shepherd-pit mix with matted hair, trotted into the house. The girl dropped to her knees and buried her face in its fur.

"Good girl," she said. "You came back. Good girl."

"What the fuck is this?" Ward said.

The dog lifted its head and growled.

A burst of dizziness rushed up Ward's spine into his head, lodging behind his eyes. The adrenaline of the past couple hours was dissipating. A hangover crept into its place. He tried not to waver, rubbed a knuckle into his temple. He was thirsty.

"This is Reina," the girl said, quieting the dog with a scratch of its chin.

"It's a dog."

"Good," she said, sarcasm obvious and biting. "You know the difference between a dog and trash truck. Your brain isn't complete mush from your booze. Now tell me how we're going to save my mom."

"Why do you have a dog?"

"Reina."

The dizziness faded, but his head throbbed. Thoughts seemed to pop like bubbles as he got close to them. It took a moment to find the conversation again. She was mad at him for forgetting her name again. What was it? She'd just said something.

"Reina, why do you have a dog?"

"I take it back," she said. "You're worse than a freaking mess, and your brain *is* complete mush."

"What are you babbling about?"

"I'm the one babbling? Look, Terrorist," she said, rubbing the dog's head between its ears. It seemed to grin as if saying, *You're going to get it now, bud.*

He cut her off. "No, you look, Reina..."

"Sam," she shouted. "The dog's name is Reina, idiot. I'm Sam. Remember? From this morning? You attacked me. Kidnapped me. Sam, remember?"

"Yes, I remember. Stop shouting."

"You're not acting like you remember."

He felt stupid for the mix up. He wanted to apologize, to prove he was better than that. What came out of his mouth, however, was, "What kind of a name is Reina?"

"La Reina Ave," she said, as if telling him *the sky is blue, dumbass.* "My street. We named her that when we got her. She was this fuzzy little puppy walking around like she owned the world. Reina means Queen in Spanish."

"Queen," Ward repeated.

"Yes, Queen. And my name is Sam. Can you remember that?"

He leveled his sternest you-better-listen gaze at her, ready to tell her it was time to stop playing around and get out of the house. Instead of being cowed into submission, Sam walked right by him to the television and turned the sound on. The perfectly bland newscaster in his perfectly bland navy suit was speaking in a perfectly bland monotone. The image on screen was of Sam's house earlier that day, two police cars out front, lights twirling.

"Once again," the newsman said, "violence has rocked our small town. The murder of the Vasquez family—committed by daughter Samantha, who is missing and believed to have ties to an illegal cult of Believers out of Las Vegas—was completely unexpected on this beautiful Saturday morning, our nineteenth consecutive day without temps rising above eighty-two. More on that in a minute."

The image changed to an ambulance in front of the Kingman Hospital. Two med techs were wheeling a gurney from the vehicle up the ramp into the building. The picture zoomed in on the woman on the gurney. A choking sound came from behind Ward.

"Alissia Vasquez, the wife and mother, died of a gunshot wound on the way to the hospital," the newscaster continued as if still discussing the weather. A headshot of Sam hovered by his head. "We will keep you up to date with any new developments on why the daughter, Samantha Vasquez, turned violent. Anyone with information on the whereabouts of the Vasquez girl is asked to contact the police via the Witness-Report link on your Port. Now for our traffic update, every hour on the fours."

Ward tapped the screen, freezing the newscaster's mouth open, Sam's photo still beside him. She looked at it briefly then hugged her dog once more. It whined as if in agreement.

Ward tried to speak but found his throat tightened up. A memory was coming, like the sun rising over the horizon at dawn. He wiped the back of his hands across his eyes. He fought to keep the memory away. Did his best to shove the burning orb back into the darkness. Too late. He saw her face. His mother. So long gone. So far away executed.

I love you, Raffi, the memory whispered. *Remember us.*

"I'm sorry," he said, the words coming out without forethought.

"No," she said, her voice partially muffled into the dog's fur. "No, they...you. This is your fault."

Her erratic anger, shifting aim with each breath, was exhausting. He told himself that she was just a kid, not equipped to handle this. Who could at her age? Where was he before entering Citizen's Duty? Hoping to make the Republic proud, that's where. Hoping to make his latest foster family regret how they'd treated him. Those teen years were waves of broad spectrum anger and rebellion, misconstrued as keenly focused causes.

Thinking about her this way erased any fear he might have had about her threat. She wasn't going to turn him in. He needed to have patience. Not for himself. For her. Alone, she wouldn't survive to lunch tomorrow. They'd already set her up to be turned in by her friends, classmates, whatever family she had left. Set her up for execution. The news said she was a Believer. What did truth matter once it had been spoken on television?

Keeping his voice even, he said, "You know why."

"Fucking Lucas," she said. "Asshole."

"Who?"

"Nothing. The guy who…forget it."

"Fine, but you've got to see they're not going to let you walk away from this. No one who sees me, who takes a photo of me, can be allowed to live. They'll kill anyone. They'll do anything to protect their truths."

"But it's not the truth."

"What would you believe if you saw that news report?"

She looked at the television, the newscaster's mouth frozen open in a grotesque yawn. Ward waited for her to either accept it or freak out.

"We have to go?" She said it like a question, but they both knew it wasn't one. It was a fact. They needed to go right now.

"Do you have what you need?"

She picked up her bag. "Yes."

"This time do what I say, okay?"

"We will."

We. The dog. The last thing they needed, an uncontrollable yapping machine.

"Reina's coming," she said, as if reading his mind.

"Of course," Ward said, understanding he had to concede this. "We need a car."

"Mom's," she began, and then stopped.

Smart girl, Ward thought. *She's catching on.*

The dog barked. Not loud, but loud enough. Ward immediately feared he would regret having it join them.

"Reina," Sam said. "Quiet."

The dog lowered its muzzle, either in shame or in agreement.

"You said we need a car. What kind?"

She was taking charge. Ward liked that. It meant she had a pragmatic mind under all that teenage bullshit. Maybe the kind of mind that could separate truth and indoctrination.

"Not connected to you or your family," Ward said. For the first time since he'd unplugged he wished he had a Port. He could jump almost any car with the right one. Without a Port what they needed was either an antique that they could hotwire, or a paired Port and car to steal. Not an easy proposition.

"What about a co-worker?" Sam asked.

"What about a Port?"

"I know where he keeps it while working."

"He's on now?"

"At ten," she said. "He's got the curfew shift."

"What time is it?"

"TV says 9:23."

"Good enough. Let's move."

"Are you sure we can do this?"

"Yes," Ward said. It was the only option he could see. If this guy was working the curfew shift, he wouldn't know his car was gone until morning. That might give them enough time to get out of town, get somewhere off grid.

Then I'll get her north into Idaho or Montana. She'll be fine from there. I'll point her toward the Canadian Districts then tell her to keep going, cross from Alaska into Russia. She'll find someone to take her.

If you can get her as far as Montana, his brain countered.

If I can't we're both dead.

His stomach knotted at this thought. He'd managed to stay invisible for so long strictly because he was alone. Their chances of making it to the Quick Price, with a dog no less, were minimal. He didn't want to calculate how slim their chances were of getting through a District border.

Whatever happened next, it wasn't going to be smooth or painless.

More blood was going to be on his hands.

"I'm ready," Sam said.

"Stay low," Ward said. "Stay in shadows and next to walls. Move quick."

He led them out the back door and across the backyard. Over the fence into the neighbor's yard. A car's lights flashed on at the end of the block.

"Run," Ward said.

Reina yipped as they dashed across the street and through at least half a dozen backyards before Ward found a large shed to crouch behind. The neighborhood was quiet and dark.

"Are we safe?" Sam asked.

There was no answer that wouldn't scare her, so Ward kept silent. He'd expected the police to come charging in when they saw it was him with Sam. But a single car? No foot chase? No helicopters?

Either the police in Kingman were amazingly incompetent...

Or the REC knows exactly what they're doing and are following us.

"Rafael," Sam prompted.

"Rafe," he said, knowing there was nothing to do if the REC was on them but keep going until they couldn't go anymore. "Come on."

Together, with Reina close behind, they slipped through Kingman on their way to the Quick Price.

CHAPTER 11

MacKenzie crouched beside a swing set in the backyard adjacent to the target's. The house's back door, a glass slider, gaped open. There was no flickering of a television's light. Instead, a dull glow, as if from a small lamp, illuminated a large couch. A family room. In a quiet house. On a quiet street. No more than twelve hours after the police should have blown through like a storm. Maybe the REC too.

It felt like a setup. Like she should abort and get out of town.

But she couldn't do that, not if Rafe was in there, or if he had been and there was a chance of picking up his trail. More than two years she'd searched for him and this was the closest she'd gotten. Whatever the danger, she was going in. The question was when and how.

She glanced at the horizon across town where the tower of black smoke was visible even against the night sky.

"Is that him?" she'd asked Ker after they'd driven by the fire, as close as they dared with the steady line of police cars and emergency vehicles coming and going. "The fire, is it about him?"

Ker drove them to the nearest truck stop and parked at the back of the lot, behind two tractor trailers then gone to work on his Port. "I'm not finding specifics or names. Just a code and that there's no bodies found yet."

"What code?"

"Open comms have redlighted Codename: M and 'the target.' The target sounds like a local."

"Codename: M? Are you sure?" she'd asked, her heart racing. She hadn't thought about that designation in almost three years, not since she'd done her initial background check on Professor Ward for her congregation in Philly. She'd cleared him in that check, a mistake she didn't realize until they'd reached Paris together. Codename: M had been a double blind, giving Rafe a legit criminal background. Now, they were using it to hide the fact that he was still alive, and that they'd lied to the Republic about what happened at the Tower. Hearing it on open comms meant she was finally close to finding him.

"Know it?" Ker had asked.

"You don't? I thought you were the best?"

Ker, with his usual swagger, had said, "I thought you wanted quick details. Give me ten minutes and I'll have you seeing real-time what President Barclay watches while taking a shit."

She'd told him told him to give her the target's address and directions, then slipped out of the car and onto the streets of Kingman. She'd be damned if she was getting back in that car without finding whatever trace Rafe had left in this desert shithole town.

Prudence said to wait for Curfew to enter the house. Curfew meant no passersby, no car headlights accidentally spotlighting her, and less chance of being spied by a nosy neighbor with their finger on a Witness-Report button.

Operating after Curfew also lowered the chance of civilians being caught in a crossfire, a protocol the Seer insisted on. Collateral damage was to be avoided at all costs. MacKenzie knew once the war came, death would ride shotgun. Until then, she would keep civilians safe if at all possible.

Her patience, however, was evaporating fast. Getting to Kingman had taken two hours longer than she'd hoped. While the programmable vehicle ID box Ker built got them through the Southwest District checkpoint without incident, they'd lost ninety minutes waiting at the single lane border crossing. The longer she waited now, the more likely Rafe would be long gone. Or captured. Or killed.

She was willing to say fuck protocol and enter the house, but the open back door bothered her. Standard police procedure was to close up a house after a raid, and she had no doubt they'd raided the home of the person who'd taken a photo of the Tower

Terrorist. Broken procedure meant a problem. Or a setup. Instinct told her to abort.

The need to find Rafe told her to proceed.

The battle between the two didn't last long. Intel on achieving her objective was likely in the house. Danger was not a reason to abort. She drew her Austrian-made .40 caliber pistol from her belt holster. Checked it. Started for the back door.

"Half past ten," Ker's voice sounded in her right ear.

MacKenzie flinched. She hated the tiny tac-com the Seer had insisted on as part of all ops packages. It looked like a pale lima bean and felt like a child's finger in her ear.

"I'm going to shove your Port up your ass if you do that again," MacKenzie said, ducking her chin to her jacket's zipper where the tac-com's microphone was pinned.

Ker didn't answer. She considered pocketing the tac-com, but like it or not even the General had to follow orders.

"I'm going in," she said.

"Describe what you see."

"No."

"You wouldn't have to if you'd taken a Port."

MacKenzie let silence be her answer. She clipped a green-light from her bag to the underside of her pistol's barrel. She would have preferred the elegance of night-optics, but she hadn't replaced the set she'd lost in Europe, another example of her field prowess suffering as a result of her administration duties as the General. She crept the final few feet to the door and listened one more time. With no hint of movement from inside, she swung inside.

The family room was typical suburbia, except for the body on the couch and the television screen paused mid-scene rather than streaming live. On screen, a newscaster was frozen mid-yawn. Beside his head floated a picture of a girl named Samantha Vasquez.

MacKenzie stayed hunched beside the couch for a few seconds, sweeping the room with her green-light and listening. Convinced she was indeed alone in the house, she examined the victim on the couch. He was an adult male with a large gut and a hole in his face. Mr. Vasquez, she assumed. Executed.

Did you do this, Rafe? MacKenzie asked herself.

She immediately hated the thought. Rafe wasn't a cold-blooded murderer. Yes, he'd destroyed the Tower. She'd never doubted the facts underlying that propaganda. But that was big picture. That was emotional. This was a tactical hit on a civilian. Rafe couldn't do this. That's what made him better than them. Than her.

More important was ascertaining who executed the guy. Cops weren't hit squads. Even under orders, it was doubtful a local officer could have done this. In a town this size, whether they knew the man on the couch or not, they were neighbors.

That meant regional action. Agents had been on scene. Possibly one of the new militarized Agents. The first of those she'd encountered—she called them Reapers—was after a chance identification by a bystander in Rapid City in advance of an ordnance transit op. All protocols for avoiding public engagements and collateral damage had been shot from the start. The Reaper was armored, fast, and tactically sinister. She'd been overmatched from the start.

It had taken only moments for her to realize retreat was the only option, but she was careless. She got herself trapped in a bus station rest room. Standard REC protocol had always been verify, detain, then kill if necessary. The Reaper, however, breached with weapons hot, in full kill mode, while civilians were still on scene. She'd escaped, but the incident cost two civilian lives and landed MacKenzie in Horeb's med unit for three weeks.

She'd managed no significant damage against the Reaper.

All of this reinforced her initial instinct to abort.

If Reapers were on scene, she told herself, *I'd be dead already.*

Not exactly a comforting thought, but it kept her moving forward to the kitchen, keeping to the interior walls and below the window lines. The kitchen was a mess. She imagined a couple cops forcing their way in while the wife was getting her morning coffee. The pot was on its side, dried coffee staining the white countertops, splattering one of the walls, and dripping across the floor.

No, not drips. Tracks. She crept closer. Dog tracks. A family pet staving off the heat by lapping up the coffee throughout the day and then tracking the mess to its water and food bowls in the corner, then back down the hall to the back of the house.

"Nobody home?" Ker's voice asked, deep in MacKenzie's ear.

"Stop fucking doing that. The target, who are they claiming got the photo?"

"No mention of the photo or your man, Ward. Samantha Vasquez, eighteen, they say is part of a cult and killed her mother, Alissia, forty-two, and her father, Javier, forty-six."

MacKenzie considered the photo of the girl, Samantha, on the television. "The daughter didn't kill them," she said. "Any details on her location?"

The tac-com clicked.

"Ker?"

"Give me a moment."

MacKenzie slipped back into the family room then upstairs. When she reached the top, Ker came back on.

"Speed it up, General. Orders just went out on the police bad. No bodies in the fire; presence requested at the target's home."

"Understood. Can you track the Port that took the photo?"

"You need to get out of there."

No shit.

"Track it," she said.

"Registered to the father. Currently offline. Last active a couple hours ago."

"At the fire location?" MacKenzie asked, though she already knew the answer.

"Affirmative. It was there most of the day. Prior to that it was at your current location briefly, after tracking from—you're going to love this—twelve hours at my location."

"Your...the convenient store next to the truck stop? She works there?"

"Yes," Ker said. "And going there is only slightly stupider than staying where you are now. Face it, Ward's gone, and you're almost out of time."

"Understood."

Eighteen-year-old teens didn't have escape plans, MacKenzie decided. If the girl was hiding, it would be somewhere she felt safe. The answer to finding her could still be in the house, and she wasn't leaving without searching for it. There were three bedrooms on the second floor, two at the front and the master at the back, plus a bathroom at the top of the stairs. She started with the bathroom and the empty vial of Lito in the sink prescribed to Samantha. It wasn't due to be refilled for three weeks.

"Get an address for a Doctor Nguyen," MacKenzie said, reading the name on the Lito vial. "She might be heading there."

"Tell me what you see."

"Fuck off and get the address. She's out of Lito. She'll be needing more."

"Copy."

MacKenzie started for the larger of the front bedrooms. It was, as she expected, torn apart. The bureau had been toppled. Clothes had been tossed everywhere. A lamp lay on its side. The bed had been thrown apart. A sewing machine had been smashed, its core sitting beneath the window. As she knelt to look through a pile of clothes, the air in the house changed, the way you can feel a person in an adjacent room. MacKenzie froze.

"Are you upstairs, Miss Vasquez?" a man's voice said. It was loud without having to shout. The question curious but deliberate.

MacKenzie considered her position, careful not to change her weight distribution and risk a creaky floorboard. That the man asking thought she was the daughter was good. It gave her some element of surprise despite how vulnerable she was. All the man had to do was climb to the top few stairs and she'd be visible, with no other exit from the second floor than the windows. Crossing to the stairs or master bedroom would leave her exposed.

"What's happening?" Ker asked.

MacKenzie hazarded a quick shush then locked her attention on the stairs, pistol drawn. Aimed. She calculated it would be a twenty-foot drop from the bedroom windows. She could either fight her way downstairs against an unknown opponent in tight quarters or risk a broken leg outside.

"Or are you Miss Vasquez's new friend?" the voice asked, closer to the stairs.

Whoever it was downstairs, he wasn't going to accept silence as proof the house was empty. The trap was sprung, MacKenzie had ignored her instinct and fallen for it like an amateur. She wanted to scream at herself for being reckless. For being stupid. For losing her touch in the field. She wanted to, but there was no time. She had little doubt the man goading her was an Agent. A difficult enough opponent. But if he was a Reaper...

Misdirection and speed were her best options. She scuttled over the debris on the floor to the window, grabbing the sewing machine.

"Ah, so you are upstairs," the Agent said.

MacKenzie threw the sewing machine through the window and, while the glass still fell, fired three rounds into the street.

She began counting, voices in the street shouting before she reached two. Sirens blared on the street on the count of three. It sounded like the entire Kingman police force out there.

She charged from the room and down the stairs. The house was empty, the Agent, hopefully, out front with everyone else. She fired three more rounds toward the front as she ran out the back door.

The backyard was empty. Her plan seemed to have worked. By now, however, the police and the Agent would have figured out her ruse. They'd be streaming through and around the house to the backyard.

So, the best place to go was out front.

She raced three houses down, then around the fourth before pausing in its front yard to take stock of the situation. She had thirty seconds at best before the street was sealed off. Forty-five before the police were organized enough to start a grid-search and press her against the perimeter.

The closest vehicles were three properties away. A police cruiser and a police roto-cycle, its headlight on. She ran for the cycle, shoving her pistol into her holster as she threw a leg over its saddle.

"Escape route," MacKenzie said into her collar.

A cop, a short female with a pistol in her left hand, turned. "Now," MacKenzie shouted and jammed the cycle's throttle. She was to the end of the street before she heard the first gunshot over the throaty whine of the cycle's electromag rotary engine.

"Are you in a vehicle?"

"Cycle," MacKenzie yelled, leaning the machine hard around the corner, her knee almost scrapping the street.

"Fifty yards," Ker said.

"Then what?" MacKenzie snapped the throttle. The cycle heaved. Its front end lifted while the back tire squealed as it dug into the macadam. Ahead, the street went on as far as she could see, with enough turns and side streets that she should be able to lose her pursuers, if Ker could guide her.

"The Port range," Ker said. "Fifty yards distance from its Port the engine shuts off."

As Ker said this, the engine cut out and the cycle coasted until MacKenzie jumped off, letting it slap against the curb in front of a large brick-faced home. It was all houses and empty front yards ahead. Police sirens behind, an Agent somewhere in pursuit.

MacKenzie found a parked car for cover three houses down. She threw herself over the hood and crouched behind the front wheel, pistol in hand. The street ahead, with twenty-foot tall lamps along the sidewalks, looked like a columned tunnel through the night. A few dozen feet away, the cycle lay on its side like a drive-by victim.

"Get me or give me directions out of here," she said into her collar.

"Working on it," Ker said.

Sirens approached. Headlights switched on up the street. Lighted on the cycle. A car stopped, its high beams preventing identification of the model. The door opened.

MacKenzie exhaled. A barrel-chested Agent in tac gear with riot helmet and face shield exited the car. He fixed his attention on the cycle. If his helmet was equipped with therm optics, he'd locate her in a matter of seconds.

Run! her instinct screamed. It didn't matter that she wasn't facing an Agent. Staying put her at risk of being surrounded.

But if she ran, they would chase. The op would then become about escape, not finding Rafe. She couldn't let that happen. The Agent hadn't seen her yet. She needed to use that advantage. She ignored her instinct again and stood, extending her hands over the car, holding her breath to aim. She would get a single shot. The Agent's gear was likely armored. She lined the pistol's sights on his lower throat, above the jugular notch. The one place experience had taught her no articulated armor could adequately protect.

The Agent saw her. Raised his weapon, a submachine gun model RT136. Medium range. Good stopping power. Adequate accuracy. Devastating at this distance.

MacKenzie squeezed the trigger.

The car's hood and engine compartment exploded before her. She fell back, landing on her elbow, nearly losing her grip on her weapon. She rolled and came up behind the car's trunk, waiting for the salvo that would cut her in half.

It didn't come.

She leaned around the car slowly. The Agent was on one knee, head bowed. Weapon on the ground. Arm dangling.

MacKenzie took a moment to internalize her status. She felt no wounds. No lances of fire or of ice indicating a bullet hole. Satisfied, she approached the Agent. His left hand went to his throat, clawing as if it could remove the bullet that had blown through his neck. Blood streamed from behind his fingers, squirting at odd angles. MacKenzie raised her pistol. The Agent lifted his head. His eyes widened with recognition.

MacKenzie shot him in the face.

The squeal of tires made her spin, weapon raised. A small sedan, not a police car, skidded to a stop in the middle of the street. Its lights shut off. Ker got out.

"You're late," MacKenzie said.

Ker walked by her to the dead Agent. He knelt by the body as if to examine it.

"Problem?" she asked.

He shrugged. "Everybody dies."

She opened the passenger side, expecting Ker to follow. Instead, he tapped the Agent's forehead and neck then patted down the corpse. When he found the Agent's Port, he drew a clear bag with red seams from his pocket and dropped the Port into it, sealing it with a slide clip.

"They'll track us," MacKenzie said when Ker got in the car, deciding to file away the rest of his weirdly ritualistic approach to the body for a later time.

"It's a static bag. Like dropping it to the bottom of the ocean. No signal penetrates."

"That's a hell of a risk."

"It'll be deactivated before it ever comes out of the bag. Big asset here, I'd say. You shouldn't overlook tech." He started the car. "Nothing else in the house?"

MacKenzie pulled the tac-com from her ear. "Not even the dog."

Sirens blared in the distance.

"Dog?"

"Probably went in search of food."

"A pet?"

MacKenzie didn't like Ker's tone. It was different. Off. "Affirmative. Like Fido or whatever. I didn't check the water bowl for a name."

Ker ripped the car through a hard U-turn, running up the curb on the way around, nearly knocking MacKenzie's head against the window.

"What the hell?"

"You should have described what you were seeing. We'd be out of here already."

MacKenzie braced herself for the next turn. The street ahead appeared unoccupied. The car's side mirror showed no one following. "What are you talking about?"

"We're looking for the girl, right?" he asked.

"Yeah."

"The dog is probably hers. She loves it, right?"

"I guess. Does it matter?"

"I know how to find her."

CHAPTER 12

"Five minutes until Curfew," Sam said, pointing at the dashboard clock.

"Like I said five minutes ago, we're fine," Ward replied, as authoritatively as he could, that familiar teacher-blanket wrapping about himself.

He wondered what MacKenzie would think of his plan. Probably not much. She'd have some kind of safe house in mind, a place where they could hide out until a friend or fellow Believer could arrange an extraction. What he was planning, in comparison, was a bad idea wrapped up in a low percentage gamble.

In any case, he drove on, eyes open for the landmark they needed, and tried forcing MacKenzie from his thoughts. Her imagined disapproving glare wasn't helping.

The getaway out of Kingman had actually gone quite well. They'd picked a spot across from the loading dock in the rear of the Quick Price and waited, the dog napping in the back seat. Despite a flare up of sirens a mile or more away, by Ward's estimate, they saw no police while waiting for Sam's co-worker to arrive.

"Is the stuff in the back of the store accessible?" Ward had asked.

"Like in the stockroom? Most of it. Why?"

"Get food and as much water as you can carry."

"Me?"

"You," Ward had said.

He thought she would argue. They sat in silence a moment, then she agreed. It was a start. She was beginning to understand what going on the run meant.

"What kind of food?" she'd asked.

"Snacks. Cans. Anything that won't go bad and can be eaten without being cooked."

"So, camping food."

"Good enough. Be quick, and don't forget the Port."

"I know where he leaves it."

A few minutes later, Sam's co-worker had arrived. She'd gone in, returning quickly with a decently sized plastic bag full of provisions. Ten minutes after that they were outside of Kingman proper, driving Junot's teal four door north on a two-lane street that could have been a dirt road for the amount of dust and desert grit in the headlight beams.

The farther north they drove, the more the road and the desert scenery resembled a dystopian novel more than real life. Ward worried that they wouldn't, in fact, find what he was looking for before Curfew. Not that there was danger of being seen by a passing car or pedestrian out here this late. Eye-Ds, on the other hand, were a worry.

Something bounded across the road.

Ward slammed the breaks and swerved. The car's breaks and tires squealed. Its rear end began to slide. The dog yowled. Ward grabbed the wheel with both hands and fought to keep the car on the road. It was like trying to steer a tractor trailer out of a jackknife.

The car stopped on the side of the road. The dog barked and snarled. Sam didn't seem any happier. In the mirror, Ward saw what had almost made him lose control of the car: a tumbleweed.

"Are you still drunk?" Sam shouted.

Ward laughed. He couldn't help it. The silliness of almost being killed by a tumbleweed was absurd. He let himself wonder, for a moment, what kind of an outlaw he would have been in the Old West. A dime novel Billy the Kid, perhaps? Or a deputized vigilante gone bad?

Such tales were sanitized, however. Their violence filtered. Their characters' hardships never more than they could endure. And it all ended when the reader closed the cover.

"Sorry," he said, his mental detour bringing him back around to the moment and the tumbleweed.

The dog sneezed and sneered.

"Yeah, I think he needs a driving lesson too," Sam said.

"We're almost there," Ward said.

Sam huffed and crossed her arms—the picture of a pissed off teenager—but she didn't protest as Ward put them back on the road. A couple miles farther, the headlights found a squat log cabin with a Spanish-style roof.

"There," Ward said.

"There what?"

The dog whined.

Ward shut off the headlights and pulled onto the side of the road in front of the cabin. A few hundred yards ahead there was another similar cabin. The faint tinkle of lights in the distance showed seven or eight more strewn about.

"Take the Port and get out," Ward said. "Stand right there and don't overthink what I'm doing."

"But—"

"Don't think." He handed her the Port.

Sam and the dog got out. Ward turned the car so it was facing southeast into the desert, away from the cabins. He took off his seatbelt and pushed the gas. The car's tires spit desert in an attempt to gain traction. Caught. The car lurched forward. Ward waited to hear Sam scream but heard nothing. That was good. She was learning, or in shock at apparently being left stranded.

Ward drove as straight as he could until the engine shut off, about fifteen seconds after he'd started. With the car now coasting, he opened the door and jumped.

The landing was harder than he'd hoped but not so bad as it could have been. He managed to keep his bad leg from taking the impact, suffering instead a whanging pain in his left elbow and lightheadedness when he stood.

"What the fuck?" Sam said, too loud, as she and the dog came running.

"I told you to wait over there."

The car found a depression and stopped with a thud and

the crunch of metals and plastics, not loud enough at this distance—a couple hundred yards or so from the closest cabin—to alert anyone, Ward hoped.

Sam, wide eyes reflecting the nearly full moon, said, "Are you insane?"

"Come morning your friend is going to report his car stolen. They're going to find it pretty quick by its ID frequency. They'll track his Port too, but that's not going to be with the car. They're going to have to head a whole different direction for that."

"What are you talking about?"

"That cabin by the road, the guy who lives there drives into Kingman every morning. We're going to stash the Port in his truck. That'll give the police a car facing southeast and a truck thirty some miles southwest. If they're smart they'll think we're going north. If they're smarter they'll think we would know that and go east or west or to Old Mexico or whatever."

"So where are we going?"

"North."

The dog growled in the direction of the car. Sam patted her head.

"North where?" she said. "There's nothing north but the Canyon."

"Yup."

"What?" Sam said, eyes wide. "No. The Canyon? That's crazy." She was shaking her head now. "The whole thing's in a quarantine zone."

That part was true. The Grand Canyon had been placed in quarantine after the Reclamation. During the war it had been a base of operations for an army of Believers. The official story was that the army accidentally nuked itself with an experimental weapon intended to kill millions in Southern California. The fallout was contained to the North Rim area above Flagstaff, but the whole of what was once Grand Canyon National Park was quarantined and remained so today.

Sam was studying Ward's face. "It didn't happen, did it? More bullshit like the news tonight about my parents."

Ward was impressed with how quickly Sam caught on. She'd lived a relatively normal life until today, yet she was unraveling the propaganda machine that was the Republic faster than he had in Paris.

"Something happened in the Canyon," he said. "I don't know what. Experiments maybe, or maybe they found something they don't want going public. It doesn't matter. We're not going that far. There's a spot in the quarantine zone where we can camp out a day or two and figure out what's next."

"But we have to walk there."

"It's about a three-hour hike. We'll need to keep some distance between us so any Eye-Ds don't pick up a big therm signature. Not so far we can't see each other, though, okay?"

Sam agreed to the plan, though it was obvious she didn't like it. Understanding the way the Republic worked was not the same as assimilating to the new paradigm. Ward also knew that such assimilation wasn't a quick process. There would be relapses. Denial. Anger and resentment. All of it pointed toward him. He would have to be ready for it.

"How do you know this guy is going to drive into Kingman in the morning?" Sam asked after they'd stowed Junot's Port beneath an old blanket in the back of the pickup.

"When I came to Kingman, I walked in from the north and found this guy getting into his truck. He saw I was tired and thirsty. He offered me some water and a ride. We talked a little on the way in, going on a good but about how, after so many wars, the white man still owned the land his father's fathers cultivated, and he had to pay to live on it."

And here I am pointing the police right at the poor guy. Ward didn't let himself indulge in the self-loathing he knew he deserved.

"Anyway," he said, "the guy told me he works every day at some shop fixing tractors in town. It's the best distraction I've got."

Sam didn't ask what kind of trouble the man might get in when they found the Port. Ward was thankful for that. He hoped the man would be detained a few hours then set back into his life. He refused to think about alternatives, or the fact that he couldn't remember the man's name.

"Wait, if you came from the north, walking, then—you're

from the prison," Sam said, her face scrunched in an odd mix of accusation and awe.

"Not exactly," Ward said.

"What does that mean?"

"Yes, I came south from the prison, but no I wasn't a prisoner. I visited it after it had been cleansed, about a month after."

"What does *cleansed* mean?"

"I'll explain when we get there," Ward said. He took the bag of supplies Sam had stolen from the Quick Price. "You and your dog go as far that way as you can and still be able to see me. Then we head straight there."

"Reina," Sam said. "Do I need to write it down for you?"

"I got it." Ward pointed just east of due north. "Go."

Sam paced off into the desert, Reina trotting behind, until she seemed barely more than a ghost. There she waited until Ward started them marching in what he was almost positive was the right direction. They hiked over an hour before Ward stopped and waved a water bottle in the air. A few seconds later, Sam waved a bottle of her own over her head, seeming to understand the message. They rested a couple minutes, then went on at least another hour before Ward waved the water bottle in the air again to signal another rest, this time more for his injured leg than for his thirst. He didn't stop them again until they reached the fence.

It was a post and barbed wire barrier, showing more weathering and corrosion than Ward remembered, extending roughly east-west into the desert as far as he could imagine. He tracked it east, checking over his shoulder to be sure Sam and Reina were following, a few minutes to the chain link gate he'd come through two years ago. Wide enough to drive a truck through. Locked with a massive padlock. Topped with a double strip of barbed wire. Like the fence, it was beginning to show some significant deterioration, most obvious in the way it sagged on its hinges, exposing a gap large enough for someone to squeeze through.

"You ready for this?" Ward asked when Sam joined him at the gate.

"To see the prison?"

"Labor Camp."

Sam tilted her head like the dog. "Labor Camp? Come on, they weren't really real back then, right after the Reclamation. Everyone knows about the way Europe and Old Mexico tried encouraging revolutions here..."

She put her hand on the gate. Ward let her work it out for herself, knowing some fictions die harder than others. Knowing what kids were taught from the time they were old enough to speak. She looked at him, then at the gate. Yanked her hand from it as if it was hot.

"Lies about lies, wasn't it?" she said.

"They were real," Ward said. "This was one of three left. The other two are in the Canadian districts. They all do the same thing: slave labor mining. Uranium here, I think. I don't know about up in Canada. What you saw on the news a couple years ago, the prisoner uprising, that was real. Only it wasn't sterile the way they show it. That's why I came here. I needed to see the truth of it."

She watched the darkness and the desert a moment before asking, "What's in there?"

"Death."

CHAPTER 13

The stark desert landscape, even with the aid of the moon, offered only occasional bulges of shapes and shadows as they continued into the night beyond the gate. They moved together now, Ward and Sam almost shoulder to shoulder while Reina bounded around them like they were on a hike through a park. He worried more than once that he'd gotten turned around or was leading them in circles, but when the moon glinted off something substantial in the distance, he knew they were going the right way. The confirmation bolstered his pace even as it opened a cold pit in his stomach.

"It doesn't look like much of a Labor Camp," Sam said when they got closer.

She was right. A single aluminum-roofed trailer, the kind of permanent modular foreman's structure found on a construction site, stood before them as if erected as a joke in the middle of nowhere. Beyond the trailer, only darkness, a thicker black than any they'd previously encountered on the trek.

Ward's hands shook. He began sweating. He felt like he'd walked into a nightmare. Vomit climbed his throat.

Sam's voice pulled him from the spiral he was envisioning— the sight of himself falling into an endless black pit, his brother Daniel burning in the darkness, eyeballs boiling.

"You okay?"

Ward swallowed hard. "Yes," he said, not sure he didn't sound like a frightened child. This was the place where Daniel died. His brother's second death, as Ward had always believed his older brother had been killed in the car accident that took their father's life. Only because of MacKenzie, only because of what he'd done in Europe, had he learned Daniel had survived that crash and been imprisoned here since. Kept alive as a slave to the day the Republic slaughtered him and his fellow prisoners during a mass escape attempt. A secret Ward had only learned that day he'd walked into the Tower with a backpack full of explosives. His goal had been—at least he told himself this at night when the dreams came—to find out where his brother was being held. The explosives were only if he needed to bluff his way out. It was a convenient lie. He'd gone in with rage, and let it consume him when he found the records of the carnage here only a week prior.

But all of that was history. To be remembered, yes. Ward, however, couldn't let it distract him from the task at hand. They were here to hide and rest. To plan how to get Sam somewhere safe.

"See it?" Ward pointed beyond the trailer into the gloom of the desert.

Sam looked. Shook her head. Squinted. Straightened up, her brow creased in curiosity. Ward knew what she was thinking. He'd arrived at night as well. Had wondered if the lone trailer was a sign he was lost. Then his eyes had adjusted. Not to the night but to the intensities of various darknesses. Thirty yards beyond the trailer dropped inky pit of nothing, like a black hole proud of its blackness.

"The quarry," Ward said, pointing. "There's only one road, ramp, up to ground level. All the prisoners lived below at least a quarter mile. They actually took the pit in their little revolution. They controlled it for an hour. Then the Republic firebombed the whole thing. Incinerated it like they'd dropped the sun itself on the prisoners' heads."

A breeze picked up, ambling in across the quarry pit. Sam's wrinkled her nose. Ward knew why. He smelled it too. Over a year since more than two hundred people, prisoners and guards, had been immolated in the pit, and the breeze still brought with it the smell of singed earth. The taste of ash.

"I want to see it," Sam said, her voice uneven.

"I don't think you do."

In fact, what Ward meant was she shouldn't see it. He wished he never had. There was nothing to see. That's what was so horrific. The buildings—bunk houses, showers, guard barracks, latrines, cafeterias—were all gone. Occasional hunks of melted plastic could be found. Splinters of charred wood no larger than pencils lay about. Ash. But nothing reminiscent of life ever having existed in the pit. Save for one scene. Against the hewn rock wall of the quarry, more than a dozen strata down, was the outline of a person, huddled on his or her knees, the void within the outline the only evidence the slave had ever lived.

"I want to see it," she said again. Stern. Determined. The girl of the new paradigm. The one with a chance to survive this ordeal.

Ward thought of the body outline. When he'd found it, he wondered if it was Daniel. If the ashes he tasted, that his boots left prints in, were his brother.

"Tomorrow," he said. "In the light."

Sam examined the trailer as if studying its structural integrity. "Is it safe?"

"It's intact," Ward said. "Runs on a generator and has a cistern on the side. Should be plenty of water for both of us to shower. It's stocked like a dorm. Full toiletries, clothes, a little bit of food. I'm going to take a shower then sleep. We'll figure out the rest in the morning."

"Is it *safe*?"

Can we sleep here, or will they come get us? is what she meant, Ward understood. It was a valid concern. A real fear. One he shared. One he knew he couldn't let her see in him or she wouldn't stay with him. She'd run off and get killed. He couldn't let that happen.

"No one is going to look for us here," he said. "Even the people who built the camp don't want to remember it existed."

She seemed to accept this answer. Ward told her to wait outside while he entered first. He slipped into the trailer, flipping a lever inside by the door to turn on the solar powered generator. A few seconds later a small lamp in the kitchen flickered on, giving enough light to see around the trailer without lighting up their location like a beacon. He did a quick check, finding no indication anyone had been here since he left it two years ago. The clothes and uniforms still hung in the closet. The few cans and bags of food he'd left behind still stocked the kitchen cabinets. There were no footprints in the dust or clean spots on the counters or chairs.

He returned to the door and held it open for Sam and Reina. They came inside cautiously. He let Sam take in the trailer's simple layout. Door off center. Bedroom and bathroom to the left. Kitchen and office with a table and four chairs to the right. A couch against the short wall. Three windows, two facing the pit and one facing the rear from the office.

"There's a shower in the bathroom," he said.

This cut through Sam's hesitation, her eyebrows riding high on her forehead. "Can I go first?"

Ward pointed her to the bathroom and didn't stop himself from laughing when she bleated at the cold water a moment later. He'd done the same his first time. When the water shut off, Sam told him through the bathroom door to leave the trailer so she could exit the small bathroom and get dressed. Again, he didn't argue. Reina went with him. She sniffed around for a place to pee, watching him the whole time.

When Ward and Reina were allowed back in, Sam was in jeans and pastel yellow shirt. Not the best color for anonymity but they could deal with that later. She approached Ward as he came through the door.

"Why did you come here," she said, "you know, before?"

Ward wasn't prepared for the question, or her soft, caring tone. He answered, almost automatically, more honestly than he preferred. "My parents are dead. My brother, they brought him here. I needed to see where he died."

Sam avoided his eyes as if trying to think of something to say. Her mouth opened but instead of speaking, she began breathing heavy, quick. Her hands shook. Ward knew the symptoms. Unknowingly, she'd asked him to offer a parallel for the losses she'd suffered this morning. Her mother taken away. Her father dead on the couch. Now on the run with the Tower Terrorist. It was all hitting her in the emptiness of the devastated Labor Camp. On the very earth of one of the Republic's greatest lies.

The relapse.

She was going to collapse. He put his hands on her shoulders to steady her, to grab her if her legs failed. He tried to calm her, saying, "It's not your fault."

It was as if he'd flipped a switch in her. Her legs straightened. Her hands flexed. She looked him in the eye. No weakness there. No fear there. Strength. Fury. She pushed his hands from her shoulders. Her voice began deep in her chest like a growl.

"No," she said. "It's yours."

He should have expected it. She was right. Whatever chance had put him in her path, it was still him. Always him. Now it was his legs that buckled. The faces, the eyeballs of his nightmares, stormed his vision. Melting. Popping like grapes left too long in a microwave. Responsibility. Guilt. He needed a drink.

"It's all your fault."

Then she was gone. Outside with her dog. Ward found his backpack on the table. Dug out the half-empty bottle of bourbon. Drank. Gagged. Drank again.

Silence clicked in once more.

He brought the bottle with him into the bathroom and took a longer shower than any sane person would in cold water. Afterwards, he rummaged under the sink, tossing rolls of toilet paper and a small first-aid kit over his shoulder, until he found the electric razor he'd used the last time he was here. Shaved his head and face to little more than stubble all around. Took another long drink as if toasting the stranger in the mirror. Told himself to fuck off. His reflection only offered a vacuous stare. He dropped the empty bottle in the trash bin beside the toilet.

When he came out of the bathroom, barefoot and freshly shorn, Sam and Reina were on the couch. Sam looked contrite. Reina yawned.

"Same clothes? Really?" she asked.

Ward didn't know what he did next, if maybe he stumbled on his way from the bathroom. Maybe she just smelled the bourbon. Whatever the case, she popped off the couch.

"Oh no," she said. "You're no good to me sloshed."

"I'm fine," he said.

"Because I've never heard that before."

They watched each other a moment.

Sam huffed and said, "Look, I'll trust you to get me away from," she waved her hand around indicating everything, "but you've got to quit that shit. I'm not going to get shot because you're too drunk to drive or think or shoot straight or whatever."

Ward liked the fight she was showing. It was MacKenzie-like. Something else, too. Concern. The tenor of a daughter of an alcoholic father.

"How old are you?" he asked.

She started to answer. Stopped. Then said, "Twenty."

"No, you'd be in CD."

"I—fine. I'm eighteen. I was supposed to graduate in a couple weeks. Enrollment Day is next month."

"You're not going to make it," Ward said. His words sounded right in his head before he spoke them, but awkward and off topic when they formed on his lips.

"I know."

Another bout of silence.

"You don't look like such a homeless terrorist without the hair and beard," Sam said.

Ward beamed. "Want me to shave your head?"

Sam flipped her middle finger at him but there was no malice behind it. They were okay. Sam headed for the kitchen and sorted out some food. Chips and trail mix and a few candy bars. They ate in silence, Ward at the table. Sam and Reina on the couch. Afterwards, Reina yawned and wandered to the bedroom.

"Go ahead," Ward said, much closer to sober now. "You two take it. I'll be fine on the couch."

"What happens next, in the morning?"

"We hike out of here. Keep heading north until we hit the Canyon. Then west. Once we start seeing civilization, we'll figure out if it's best to get a car or stow away on a truck."

"Seems fairly simple."

"Simple is what keeps you invisible when you're running. If we're lucky, we'll make the Canadian Districts and find an antique car. Gas and no computer. Keep us off the grid a good long time."

"Like real gasoline? Like a bomb on four wheels? I thought they were all gone."

"Up there," Ward said, "people don't always comply with all the rules. It's Republic but not by choice. More like colonies or occupied lands."

"Then what?"

"Does it all need to be planned tonight?" Ward asked. He was tired and wanted her to get off the couch so he could lie down.

"I'd like to know there's a plan."

"Best I can tell you is we try to find some friendly faces to help us out of the Republic altogether."

"Friendly?"

"There's people here and there who would be quite thrilled, I think, to help me out of the country."

"Believers," Sam said.

Reina whined from the bedroom as if the word offended her.

Sam stood. "I don't want to be converted or whatever you do."

Ward wanted to point out the irrationality of her fear. Of Citizens' fear of Believers, as if Faith was contagious by touch. It was everything that was wrong with the Republic, but he didn't have time for a full lesson. "No one wants to convert you."

"Then why are you taking me to some crazy bunch of Canadian Believers?"

"I'm not. I'm saying if we need to, there are people who will help us. People who have as much reason to hate the REC as you. As me."

"Not as much as me."

"You'd be surprised," Ward said.

"Whatever. Just promise you won't try to convert me. Or Reina."

The inclusion of Reina struck Ward funny, like being asked to bring a child's imaginary friend along on vacation. "No one is going to try to convert you or Reina."

"Fine," Sam said. "I'm going to bed. Don't even think about coming over there. Reina is going to keep watch. Right, girl?"

Reina growled from deep in her chest.

Ward waved his arms wide and said, "I am a complete gentleman."

Sam left the bedroom door open, allowing Ward to see Reina curl up beside her in the bed before he propped his backpack and boots beside the couch and dropped onto its cushions.

"Can we leave the light on?" Sam asked. "Is it safe?"

"Sure thing," Ward said. He was comfortable believing no one was going to get within sight of the trailer on foot or by truck. Eye-Ds or helicopters were another issue, but none had found him two years ago. He was willing—or maybe tired enough—to rely on that luck once again.

He shimmied into comfort on the couch, thinking about opening his last bottle of bourbon to help him fall asleep. He was out before he could even reach for his backpack, dreams of children's toys and birds squawking and a woman walking a trio of angry dogs filling his head.

Sam woke, sure that she'd dreamed something important but couldn't remember what it was. Reina snorted and rolled over. The shadow of Rafe, still asleep on the couch, offered only the slightest of rhythmic breathing motion.

She got up as quietly as she could. It was either very late or very early, if there was a difference between the two, and she shivered as she took a drink from a bottle of water. Her hand trembled. She needed her Lito. Though, as she willed the quaking to stop, it occurred to her that her body was reacting far better than should be expected to her lack of medication.

She padded to the couch. Rafe lay on his side, his backpack squeezed between his knees like a pillow. She owed him her life. That much she knew, even if she didn't quite know how to make sense out of the chaos of the last day. Yet everything that had happened was also his fault. He was the reason her parents were dead.

The contradiction was maddening.

I'm an orphan, she thought, the idea surprising her. It felt almost like the air had been drained from her lungs.

Her eyes drifted to Rafe. It was his fault. All of it. She should bash in his skull with the lamp or a chair. Kill him right here and now. End the whole thing. Deliver justice for Mom and Dad. For all the people he'd killed in the Tower and wherever else.

The thought of his brains splattering the couch, however, made her stomach turn, not with nausea but with fear. Could she kill a man like that? Could she become like him so easily?

Better to grab all the food and water and run rather than find out. Get away. She'd figure something out.

Rafe coughed and twisted onto his back like he might wake. He smacked his lips then settled once more into sleep. The backpack was now free, draped over his left leg. Begging her to take it.

He's the best chance I have to survive, she told herself.

Reina whined. Sam turned. Reina was sitting up, her ears perked. Then Sam heard it. A car. She went to the window beside the couch and watched a shape approach against a star-glittered sky that was turning a bit blue at the horizon. It drove around the trailer with purpose, forcing Sam run to the front window beside the door. The dark car had parked a little way from the trailer, barely discernible from the pit behind it. Its doors were closed. She couldn't see anyone inside.

"Someone's out there," she said without taking her eyes from the car.

Rafe murmured unintelligibly then tried to roll over to face the couch. Sam left her post and shook his shoulder.

"Almost there," he mumbled.

"Rafe," Sam said, louder. "There's someone out there."

He was on his feet, backpack in hand, before his eyes had cleared and focused.

"Where? How many?"

"A car. I don't know. It drove up and parked out front."

Ward pulled on his boots then plunged his hands into the backpack. Sam expected him to pull out a gun or two Instead he made a face.

"Fuck."

"What?"

"Stay here."

He went to the front window and then backed away and

looked around the room. Apparently not finding what he wanted, he swept up the remnants of their meal, bags and bottles and a few mini doughnuts, from the table and placed them in the sink. The table he flipped on its side, carefully so it didn't make much noise, and slid the chairs away. He positioned the table between the door and the couch. From a drawer beside the sink he grabbed two handfuls of steak knives.

All of this Sam watched with a mixture of fascination and fear, wondering if he would continue to be this measured and purposed man whom the Republic feared like a boogeyman in a child's story. Or if he would trip over his own feet like the homeless drunk who'd been buying bourbon at a convenient store in the armpit of the Southwest for the last year.

"Stay back here," he said, motioning to the overturned table. He handed her the knives. "Keep Reina quiet and next to you. Anyone who comes through the door that isn't me, you throw a bunch of these at them. Keep one to defend yourself. Got it?"

Sam's hands were shaking. Excitement. Terror. It didn't matter. Whatever was out there was going to come in here. Her best chance for survival was following Rafe's instructions.

"I understand," she said.

"You keep her safe," he said to Reina.

Reina yipped. Sam tried to say something confident and strong. All she came up with was, "I'll throw good."

She wanted to smack herself for such a stupid response. Rafe didn't seem to notice. He crept to the door practically in a crawl and pried it open. She tried to lean so she could see around him. See the car. See what was coming. But without leaving her position behind the table, she could see nothing but Rafe, the door, and a sliver of sky.

He stuck his head out the door a little. Stopped. Began inching back in. Sam was about to ask who was out there when she saw why he was backing up. The muzzle of a gun pressed to temple.

A rumbling voice from outside the door asked, "Who else is inside?"

CHAPTER 14

"Who else?" the voice asked again. Impatient. Grave. Enjoying the moment?

The pistol pressed into Ward's temple like a migraine. "No one," he said.

"The girl, right? And who?" Less throaty. A woman's voice? "Just me and her."

"And her dog." The pistol lowered. "You look like shit," the woman said.

This time there was no attempted disguise.

"MacKenzie?" Ward said, wondering if Sam was right that his brain was too marinated in bourbon to be trustworthy.

She filled the doorway, forcing him to look up at her.

"It's you," he said.

MacKenzie offered a crooked grin. "Need me to rescue you again, eh?"

Relief smothered Ward. Every street corner he'd looked around for her over the last almost three years flooded his mind. Questions overloaded his ability to make words. His limbs buzzed. His eyes swam. He wondered if he was having a heart attack.

A man's voice behind MacKenzie said, "This is the guy?"

A girl's voice behind Ward said, "Should I throw my knives?"

"No, Sam, don't," was all Ward could say before MacKenzie pulled him to his feet and embraced him. The softness of her breasts, the strength of her arms, the solidity of her pistol against his back, he let himself dissolve into all of it.

"So it is him, yes?" the man behind her said.

MacKenzie let go, pulling back in an almost embarrassed

withdrawal.

"Yes," she said. "Rafe, this is my tech operative, Ker. We should get inside."

Ward motioned them in, then introduced Sam. Reina sniffed at MacKenzie and snorted. She trotted to Ker and sniffed at his outstretched hand, then began rubbing his leg like a housecat.

"Reina," Sam said, snapping her finger.

"She's fine," Ker said, rubbing the dog's neck.

Ward wasn't sure what to make of MacKenzie's companion. Tall, thin, and with a Mediterranean complexion, he was immediately likeable, which made Ward immediately suspicious.

Ward placed the table back in the center of the room and suggested they sit. MacKenzie and Sam got the chairs. They sat. MacKenzie watching Sam. Ward watching Ker. Sam watching all of them, her eyes returning every few seconds to Ker who was still petting Reina. Her distrust of Ker—and the way Reina had taken to him—was palpable. Ward wondered if it was more than a little part jealousy.

"What's with the new look," MacKenzie finally said.

Ward's rubbed his head. The stubble felt like sandpaper.

"You should have seen him this morning," Sam said. "He looked like a homeless caveman."

Ward wanted to tell MacKenzie she looked good. Amazing, really. Beautiful. Strong. Healthy. Not at all like the kind of person who would abandon a man with whom she'd shared... what? A moment? An attraction? A crazy week being shot at?

He wanted to say all these things, and none of them. Silence won out.

"Who is the girl?" MacKenzie asked.

Reina, sitting next to Ker, whined. Ward tensed for Sam's outburst, but it didn't come.

"I'm with him," is all Sam said.

MacKenzie raised an eyebrow. Ward didn't know how to read her reaction. He didn't know if he could trust his own judgement when it came to the woman he'd been searching for so long. All he'd hoped for since Santorini was her face to appear. Across a street. On a television. Anywhere. Now she was here, close enough to touch, and he felt like he barely knew her.

"She needs my help," he said when it began to feel like everyone was waiting for him to speak.

Sam made a noise.

Silence returned.

After a moment, Ker pulled a stick of beef jerky from his pocket. "Need a walk, girl?" he asked before taking a bite.

Reina barked an obvious yes. Sam objected, but Ker was to the door, Reina at his heel, before Sam could get up.

"Be back," Ker said, mouth full of beef jerky.

The pair left.

"What are you doing here, Hannah?" Ward asked, receiving the familiar glare for using her first name.

"We've been searching for you for a long time."

"Did you try the beach where you left me?" Ward regretted the way he snapped at her, but she didn't react. He continued, "Who's 'we' anyway? You and the dog walker?"

MacKenzie glanced around, like she was taking in their surroundings for the first time. She leaned back in her chair and said, "Me and the Seer."

"Who?"

"The Seer?" Sam said. "Like *the* Seer?"

MacKenzie nodded.

"You're following a fortune teller now?" Ward couldn't help the jabs. The sarcasm. He wanted to smack himself. Save MacKenzie the effort. Save himself the pain. If she wanted to put him in his place it would be with a closed fist and far harder than he could punch.

"What shithole dumpster have you been living in, Rafe?"

Sam filled in the gaps, telling Ward about the mysterious leader of the rebellion. How he'd risen to infamy within weeks of Ward destroying the Tower. How each time the news said the police or the REC had scored a major victory against his army of Believers, there would be a major theft or attack or bombing to announce that the Seer wasn't done yet. How his terrorists were rumored to have infiltrated every government institution, including the schools.

"We're the terrorists?" MacKenzie said, incredulous.

Sam pointed at Ward. "He blew up the Tower for you and the Seer, didn't he?"

"For her?" Ward said. "For them? No, I didn't do it for anyone else. I'm not a part of anyone's cause."

"You could have been," MacKenzie said.

"This is ridiculous," Ward said, intending to defend his act as his own, but he thought better of it. Such an argument wouldn't help them get away. It wouldn't help get Sam somewhere safe, if there was anywhere truly safe anymore. "Wait," he said. "How did you find us out here?"

"The dog. Ker hacked its ID chip."

Ward was shocked by the simplicity of it. "Stupid," he said.

"You can do that?" Sam asked.

"Yes." Ker had re-entered the trailer without any of them noticing, Reina beside him. "It wasn't that difficult."

"Could the cops find us that way too?"

MacKenzie and Ker looked at each other.

"Jesus," MacKenzie said. "You didn't think of that? They could be on us right now."

Reina lunged between them, teeth bared, a growl rumbling in her chest.

"Reina," Sam said, her voice stern.

Reina seemed to consider Sam's order. She quieted but didn't back down. Ker placed his palm on Reina's head and stroked her left ear.

"Reina," Sam snapped.

Ker pulled his hand from the dog's ear. Reina chirped pleasantly and trotted to Sam. She plopped at Sam's feet.

"I'll re-set her chip," Ker said with a shrug.

"What if they already have a line on us?" Ward asked.

"Then we better go."

"Where? Why are you here? Why now?"

MacKenzie stood. To Ward she said, "Let's take a walk." At the door she told Ker, "Clear the dog's signal then find us a clean route. And keep the kid and her dog here."

"Yes, General," Ker said.

"My name," Sam said, "is Sam."

The way Sam spoke reminded Ward of his mother. They both had strong jaws and dark hair, but that wasn't it exactly. It was her voice. The underlying strength, and insistence, in her words. A font to be leaned upon someday when she was no longer a teenager. If she lived that long.

Ward put the comparison away and motioned Sam to relax. He joined MacKenzie outside, following her to the car. Around them, the sky was brightening, intensifying the blackness of the pit. MacKenzie gave it a disinterested look.

"We should leave the girl here," she said. "There was an Agent at her house. You can bet there's more than one on us. Shit's going to get deep. There's no place for a civilian on the run or in my army."

"Your army, General?" Ward almost couldn't believe what he was hearing. The General part didn't surprise him. But to leave a girl in the middle of the desert and disappear into the sunset? That wasn't like the MacKenzie he knew.

Or is it? he thought. *How well do I really know her?*

She never abandoned you in deep shit.

She needed me. As soon as she didn't she left me unconscious on a beach in the middle of the Mediterranean.

"Yes, I'm the General. Yes, it's my army. Yes, I serve the Seer. He's not some palm reader. He's the prophet we were promised. And he needs you."

"Me?"

"Rafe, I've been looking for you since…for a long time. I've followed every lead personally. Almost been killed. Wherever you've been, whatever you've been doing, come home with me."

"Home," he said, as if unfamiliar with the concept.

He wanted to believe her. He wanted to accept her words as pure and honest, but he'd seen the tattoo that covered her back. The Ten Commandments in a beautiful monastic script. Except for Commandment VI. After the Roman Numerals, the space was blank, as if the commandment *Thou shalt not kill* didn't apply to her. As if she'd been given divine authority to kill for her cause.

Not Sam, Ward determined. *Not her.*

There was enough blood on his hands. He wished, for a

moment, to be a character in a novel. Race Williams: Thrilling Detective, maybe. One mystery down. Book closed. No need for this endless dénouement of dead and soon-to-be-dead faces leering at him from the corners of his vision.

But wishes were for children and fantasies. Picture books and novels. He wouldn't let his feelings for MacKenzie get in the way of Sam's safety. He owed Sam that much for what he'd caused.

"We need you," MacKenzie said.

"Fine," he said, "but we get Sam somewhere safe first. Somewhere she can start over and not remember Kingman or any of us. If you've got an army, you can make her a new identity. She's not a part of this. We're not leaving her on a beach."

MacKenzie leaned against the car's door. "Rafe, I just—"

Ker appeared in the doorway, chewing on something. Sam and Reina joined him.

"We're set," he said between bites. "We should go."

"No REC action?"

"There's a lot of chatter in Phoenix and Vegas, but they seem to have written off Kingman. Probably figured you'd be an idiot to stick around after executing that Agent."

"You killed an Agent?" Sam said.

MacKenzie ignored her. She said to Ker, "Plot us a route around the Canyon then straight to Horeb."

"Horeb?" Ward asked. "Like Mount Horeb where God gave Moses the Ten Commandments?"

"HQ," MacKenzie said. "The Seer established it before he found me. Already had the groundwork laid for the army. Some recruits. I've been adding to it. Kicking them into shape. Horeb is where the revolution starts."

Ward couldn't help but imagine MacKenzie in an Agent Compano role. The trainer. The drill instructor. It was an interesting parallel but not one he had time to explore now.

"Your guy," he said, "is he really a seer?"

"Sort of," MacKenzie said.

"Like Simon was a *sort of* priest?"

At her father's name, MacKenzie made a face. It was a low blow and Ward felt bad for it, but he also felt that he'd earned the right to take a few shots.

"Car good on charge?" she asked Ker.

"Yes."

"Go get the girl and—" She pushed off the car and squinted past Ward's shoulder. "What is that?"

"What?" Ward said. He couldn't see anything other than the now indigo sky.

"Not you. Ker?"

Ker already had a Port in hand and was both aiming it where MacKenzie was pointing and swiping its screen in a frenzy.

"Single helo. RAS model 49. Pilot and two occupants. Could be a regular patrol, but I wouldn't bet on it."

Ward could barely discern the sound of the helicopter's rotors in the distance, like an uneven tapping in the back of his mind. "The chatter was misdirection."

"Cut their comms," MacKenzie said to Ker. She opened the car's trunk and took out a duffel bag and a scoped assault rifle. "Isolate them before—"

"Already on it." Ker was now on his knees, a second Port having appeared seemingly from nowhere. He placed the two units in the dirt and was playing them like some kind of piano. "They're not running standard REC channels. I—wait. I've got the helo's internal comm. They're on blind apprehend orders. All targets found on site."

Ward's thigh muscle began to twitch. Anxiety. Apprehend orders for the Tower Terrorist? That didn't make sense, not after the fire at the school. Blind kill orders he could understand. Preserve the Republic's lie that he was already dead. But blind apprehend orders? Something bigger was at play.

"What do we do?" Sam asked.

"Back inside," Ward said.

"Too late," MacKenzie countered. "Over here behind the car. You too, Rafe."

"Comms and scans locked out," Ker said. "They'll have visual in 30 seconds. On site to drop in fifty."

"Weapon?" MacKenzie asked Ward, loading and checking the assault rifle.

"No."

"What about your gun?" Sam said.

Ward shook his head, not wanting the berating he would get if MacKenzie knew he'd lost his gun.

"Down on this side of the car," she said. "Ker, you too."

Ker waved a finger in the air asking for another moment.

MacKenzie handed Ward the duffel bag. It yanked on Ward's arm, like it was filled with cinderblocks. "Take what you need. Coming in are probably Reapers. Armored. Better trained than you. Shoulder articulation, maybe hip or knee as well if you get an angle, those are your only shots."

"Reapers?"

"I'll draw them to the trailer," MacKenzie continued, ignoring Rafe's inquiry. "Don't engage until you have a shot locked."

Reina began barking.

"Quiet the dog," MacKenzie said to Sam.

"Her name is Reina."

"I don't give a cat's fuzzy ass." MacKenzie sprinted into the trailer.

The helicopter was close now, coming at them in a nose-down, aggressive stance. Ward didn't know aircrafts, but he could imagine a fleet of these coming to firebomb a bunch of slaves trying to win their freedom.

Ker joined them behind the car, crouching so he couldn't be seen from the angle of the helicopter's approach.

"The General is drawing their fire?"

Ward said she was and opened the duffel bag. It was packed with pistols, submachine guns, shotguns, and enough ammunition to keep them in a firefight for the better part of a day. He pushed a few weapons aside and found an RT40. He took it and a fistful of extra magazines. Its weight and balance felt right. Its deadly potential made him want to throw it into the pit behind them.

"Give me a gun," Sam said.

"No," Ward said.

Ker reached into the bag and drew a shotgun and a metallic pistol. He handed the pistol to Sam.

"I said no," Ward said.

"Armed or not, she can die just the same," Ker said.

Something crashed in the trailer. Ward hazarded a look over the car's trunk. MacKenzie had smashed one of the front windows. She broke the other with the butt of her assault rifle. A third crash announced the destruction of the back window. Three shots sounded. Ward dropped back behind the car. His brain told him it was MacKenzie firing, not the Agents in the helicopter. He, Ker, and Sam all peered over the car.

MacKenzie's shots had halted the helicopter's approach thirty or so yards from the trailer, maybe fifty feet in the air. It turned broadside and its panel slid back. Two black forms—the new Agents, Reapers, MacKenzie had mentioned—crouched inside. Lines dropped from the aircraft, like packthread unrolling.

"Hold," Ward said, some remnant of his REC training jumping into the driver's seat of his brain. Telling him that he held rank over a computer tech, a teenager, and a dog.

MacKenzie fired twice more from the trailer. One sparked off the helicopter's door panel. The other appeared to make one of the descending Reapers flinch.

"Shoot them," Sam said.

"Hold," Ward repeated. He understood MacKenzie's plan. Understood how crucial it was to be patient if the Reapers' armor was as good as she thought.

The Reapers detached from their lines, dropping the final few feet to the ground. Ward expected them to split, take flanking approaches to the trailer, but the landscape offered no cover beyond a few shrubs. To Ward's surprise they aligned shoulders, about five feet apart, and advanced at a trot, sleek rifles in attack position.

MacKenzie fired free, detonating plumes of dirt and smoke around the closing Reapers. The helicopter then resumed its nose-down approach. MacKenzie's shots halted. The Reapers were close enough to see in detail. Their armor appeared to be a combination of ballistic textiles and carbon fiber. He doubted their hips and knees would be vulnerable, but maybe the shoulder or neck like MacKenzie had said.

The helicopter flew over their heads, setting Ward's hands

shaking with dread. It had seen them. The ruse wouldn't work.

No comms, some calm part of his mind insisted.

Right. The Reapers on the ground were advancing blind. All they had to worry about from the helicopter was its armament. All they could do was trust MacKenzie to understand the situation.

The helicopter circled over the pit, angling toward the trailer.

"Rafe?" Sam said, eyes wide, close to panic.

"Hold," Ward said.

Ker picked up her unarmed hand and placed it on Reina's neck. She calmed. A shot detonated from the trailer. It occurred to Ward that the Reapers hadn't fired yet. He looked around the car's tire. The Reapers were spreading, one facing the car, the other the trailer.

Another shot from the trailer. This one from the door. The Reapers, neither yet in line with the front of the trailer, halted. Ward watched MacKenzie, now in the trailer's doorway, crouch and aim. She fired once more. The windshield of the helicopter shattered. The aircraft wavered. The closer Reaper turned his back on the car, waiting for his partner to round the trailer's corner. The steady thumping of the helicopter's rotors became a heavy whine. Everyone, even the Reapers, turned.

The helicopter twitched its tail like an angry dog. Its nose dove. Then, like a rock in a pond, it dropped, passing the rim of the pit and out of sight. Seconds passed. Finally, the muffled explosion of its impact at the bottom of the pit, at least a mile deep, set everyone into motion.

MacKenzie ducked back into the trailer. The Reapers advanced.

Ward, his training now in charge, heard himself shout, "Now," as he rolled around the car's tire and took aim.

CHAPTER 15

When the helo went down, MacKenzie scrambled across the trailer's floor. She made it into the shower as the gunfire began. Small and mid-caliber bursts detonated outside. There was, however, no shattering of glass. No sounds of the trailer being ripped apart. The salvos she heard were from Rafe and Ker. The Reapers hadn't yet engaged.

She leaned out of the shower stall. The trailer was empty. She crept to the front window in time to see Ker standing above the car firing two shotgun blasts into a Reaper's back. The attack drove the Reaper to his knee but didn't kill him. He was up before MacKenzie could take aim.

Sound to her left alerted her to danger. She vaulted toward the bedroom as the front door exploded inward. There was no time to wipe away the wood and plastic shards that pelted her face. Her assault rifle, held low in her right hand, was too big to bring up quickly. In one motion she released it, pulling a pistol from her belt and bringing it up to aim. The Reaper breached with a left-right juke. Something whizzed past her. She fired twice. Heard the hollow impact of a bullet on the Reaper's armor. Twisted to the side before leaping behind the bed.

A blast sucked the air from the room. Breath, hearing, vision, all gone. Then, it all returned like a bucket of water thrown hard in her face.

A concussion grenade. The fact that it detonated in the other room while she was behind the bed was the only reason it hadn't knocked her unconscious. She shook her head, willing her double vision to coalesce. Hearing came back in jumps. Outside, someone screamed between salvos.

The Reaper in the trailer, his voice thick as if being mechanically enhanced, said, "Surrender. Death is your choice, not ours."

She listened to his voice bounce off the trailer's tight walls and low ceiling. There was time for a best guess only. She lay flat, stretched her hand beneath the bed, and took a low aim in the direction of the kitchen. Squeezed off four shots.

A muffled groan announced a hit on the Reaper's foot or ankle. No damage, but pain enough to stun. She came up shooting. Leapt around the bed. Hurtled into the kitchen. She caught the crouched Reaper high, getting her hand around his neck briefly before he twisted and used her momentum to send her onto the couch. Her head hit the armrest. Her vision blurred again. She lost her lock on his neck.

As she had earlier, he dropped his rifle. With an awkward motion, he drew from his belt a shock blade, a nasty REC weapon that pulsed plenty of volts into the wound it sliced. A hit to her head, neck, or core could render her unconscious if it was cranked up to full voltage. The way he'd drawn the shock blade, however, told her that all his armor affected his speed and dexterity. She catalogued the weakness and launched her attack before he could approach.

She fired two shots at the Reaper's body armor to distract him then pushed off the couch, aiming her shoulder at his knees. The shock blade bit her thigh as she blew through his legs like bowling pins. He collapsed over her as she hit the ground, but she was already twisting away. She kicked up, her heel catching the descending blade as it aimed for her chest. The shock blade flew from his hand. His other fist caught her jaw. She lost her bearing. He hammered at her back and shoulders with his armored fists. The pain was immense, but it wasn't enough to stop her. She used his armor as leverage, pulling until her arm came free. Her gun hand. She slammed the butt of her pistol against his chest, shoulder, face. A flash blinded her right eye. She dropped the gun. Her fingernails scraped his mask. Caught the edge. Dug beneath. Pulled. She strained so hard she thought her shoulders might explode.

The mask came away like tearing a drumstick from a

chicken's carcass. The Reaper screamed. Her fingers found flesh. Flesh!

She dropped the mask and clawed at his face. Soft. Cabled with something gristly. Her thigh throbbed. Metal touched her cheek. She twisted. Pushed it with her forearm. Another flash outside her peripheral vision. Her thigh now howled in pain. Her fingers dug deeper. Pushed through. The struggle slowed. Her vision cleared.

She rolled off the inert Reaper. His facemask lay beside them. Her fingers were still sunk into his throat. Blood welled and sprayed. Covered her hand to the wrist.

She knew she had to get up. Get outside and help Rafe. But her body needed time. Needed to reset. A single gunshot sounded outside. She got to her feet. Found her pistol. Went for the door. Her leg went numb. She fell, turning to take the impact on her forearms. Noticed a shock blade in the Reaper's motionless hand. No pistol. No time to contemplate why.

She crawled for the door.

At the first shot, Ward's world had gone white. He'd fought the blindness while more shots detonated. Distance was no longer discernable. Explosions went off near and far.

"Get down," someone yelled.

Then two more louder blasts, like cannons, erupted nearby. Shapes began to form before him. Whites and blacks. Yelling. Shades and flashes. The outline of the car. He squeezed his eyes closed. Willed vision to return. When he opened them, it was like he'd walked from darkness into bright light. Flashbulbs pulsed everywhere. He got to his feet, the sound of gunshots now relegated to background noise.

Ker and the Reaper grappled in the space between the car and the trailer. Reina had the Reaper's ankle in her jaws, yanking and shaking. Sam lay on the ground, slowly rolling from her back to her stomach.

The Reaper kicked at Reina, but the dog refused to let go. Ker lost his grip on the Reaper's wrist. The hand came up with a blade, glossy and sinister.

A plunge of silver.

Reina yelped and let go, whimpering backwards from the melee. Sam screamed.

Ward aimed his pistol. Couldn't get a clean shot. Ker, with strength Ward almost couldn't believe from the thin man, grasped the Reaper's arms and forced them to his sides. Squeezed until the blade fell from his hand.

"Shoot him," Ker said.

Ward approached. He could have walked up beside the Reaper and put a bullet in his ear. Could have ended the fight. But Reina's yowling and Sam's screaming stopped him. Visions of eyes melting froze him.

"Now," Ker yelled.

Ward couldn't pull the trigger.

Then Sam was there. Punching the Reaper like a child bashing her fists against her father's thighs. Ker tried to push her back. The Reaper regained leverage. Got his hand free again. Grabbed at Sam's face. Got her hair. Pulled her in.

Ward shoved the gun into the Reaper's neck and pulled the trigger. Whatever armor was there gave way like a paper towel. Blood splattered Ward's face. The Reaper's head lurched forward then slung back. Almost tore from his body. Ker let go. The Reaper slumped to the dirt.

"Help me," Sam screamed. She tore away from the dead Reaper and ran to Reina. In the shadow of the ruined car, she wailed and cradled Reina in her lap.

Ward waited for someone to appear. Someone to help the dog—blood matting the hair around her shoulder, dripping from her paws—who was twitching in Sam's arms.

What is wrong with me?

You're a drunk and a coward.

He looked at the blood that had splattered his hands, his arms, his chest. The Reaper's blood. The man he'd killed to save Sam.

No, I'm not. I can help her. I will help her.

Before he could go to her, MacKenzie crashed out of the trailer. She nearly fell. Propped herself on her assault rifle like a cane. Limped to the dead Reaper in front of Ward.

"Ker," she said. "Report."

Ward turned. Ker was already kneeling beside Sam and Reina, one hand on the shoulder of each. Reina whimpered. Sam sobbed quietly. He whispered something to Sam. Then to Reina. Both calmed.

"Ker," MacKenzie demanded, now halfway to the car.

Ker got up and strode past MacKenzie. He peered into the trailer. "All clear, General," he said. "Working on injuries now." Then he went inside.

MacKenzie was clearly unhappy with Ker's response, but she didn't push the matter. She motioned for Ward to open the car's back door. He did as ordered, relieved to have something to do. He offered MacKenzie his hand to get in. She refused and sat without pulling her legs into the car. Blood covered the side of her pant leg. She covered the wound with her free hand. For a second, Ward was torn between tending to her or to Sam and Reina. The sneer on MacKenzie's face made the decision for him. He went to Sam at the same time Ker exited the trailer with a handful of towels wrapped around what Ward hoped was the first aid kit.

Ker sized up MacKenzie's situation as he approached. Tossed her a towel as he passed, continuing to Sam and Reina. Ward followed. Ker opened the first aid kit, pulled out a thin foil packet and bandages.

"Reina first," Sam said.

Ker said, "Yes," and went to work.

He worked at Reina's shoulder with one hand, the other on Reina's neck, rubbing softly. Reina whined softly. Ward couldn't help but wonder if Ker's pre-revolution life was spent as a dog trainer or veterinarian.

"It's okay, girl. It's okay," he said, over and over. Then he opened the foil packet and dumped a cloud-gray powder onto the wound.

Reina howled, but Sam held her tight while Ker continued repeating his soft, monotonous cadence.

Ward, unable to stop watching, was unaware he'd taken his last bottle of bourbon from his backpack until it touched his lips. He took two long glugs and then put it away. No one appeared to notice.

"Is she going to be alright?" Sam asked.

"She'll limp for some time. You should get her to a vet to watch for any muscle damage, but she'll be fine."

Sam, her hands now crusting with blood, hugged Ker's neck.

He separated himself gently. "What about you?"

"I'm fine," she said.

He handed her some pills from the first aid kit and a bottle of water that had been wrapped in the towels. Then he turned to Ward. His eyes flashed a wolfish blue.

It occurred to Ward that he'd done almost nothing in the last few minutes. Since the fight began, really. He'd thought almost nothing. As if his body and mind had shut down in protest of the situation, acting only in that moment that Sam's life was in danger. Shame made him break from Ker's gaze. The tall man stood.

"You're good," he declared, needing no closer examination to diagnose Ward with the lack of injury that only comes with cowardice.

Ward didn't argue. He sat beside Sam and Reina and stroked the dog's fur.

Ker rounded the car and exchanged words with MacKenzie, nothing Ward could make out clearly. Not that he was listening. Petting Reina was calming him, and he was wholly devoted to the motion, each stroke seeming to brush away a slice of shame, of fear, of failure. Sam, her knee touching Ward's, did the same. Neither looked at each other. That was okay. It was a peaceful moment before what Ward knew was going to be a chaotic future.

The sound of a foil packet tearing open was followed by another exchange between Ker and MacKenzie. A moment later, MacKenzie approached, casting her shadow over the trio on the ground. Her pant leg was torn off at mid-thigh and a bandage covered her leg from her knee to her boot. Ker headed to the trailer again.

"You alright?" Ward asked.

"Shock blades and stun darts," she said, pointing to the Reaper's rifle in the dirt. "For you, they should have come in for annihilation, not capture and interrogation."

Ward knew this. The Reapers' strategy contradicted what had happened at the high school. It contradicted all logic for dealing with the Tower Terrorist, the traitor who should already be dead. There was more happening here, but he couldn't put his finger on it. The more he tried to make sense of it, the more it slipped apart and blew away like a house of cards in a storm.

He put it aside. Focused on the now. On MacKenzie. "You. Are you okay?"

"The shock blade got meat not muscle. Whoever gave their orders really had a hard on for getting us alive." She paused as if considering this last point. "Get whatever you need. We're gone in three. We can't risk staying in case they got a message out before we shut their comms."

She handed over the bourbon bottle Ker had taken, now two-thirds full. Ward could feel Sam disapproving beside him as he took it.

Instead of voicing her displeasure with the booze, she said, "Can I have a gun now?"

"No way," Ward said. "I mean to keep you safe."

"Well I mean to fight. If that's what this is, if that's my life now, then Reina and I are going to fight." She pointed to the General. "Like her."

Ward knew that tenor. Part youth and rebellion. Part MacKenzie. Whether they'd wanted to or not, the Republic had created a willing new recruit for the General's army. A cog in a smaller wheel that hoped to overthrow the big wheel.

Ward also knew from history that cogs didn't often live long enough to see the freedoms they fought for. He hadn't helped Sam escape the Republic's jaws just to hand her over to MacKenzie as front-line fodder.

He also knew that telling a teenager not to do something was the quickest way to ensure she would do it anyway, so he kept his mouth shut while MacKenzie limped to the duffel bag by the car's front tire. He watched silently as she brought it to the back of the car, opened the trunk, and dropped it in. He waited, knowing what was coming, as she sifted through its contents, finally bringing out a pistol. 9mm. Possibly Austrian.

"You'll teach her how to use it," Ward said to MacKenzie, hoping to ease into the idea that the gun was coming with Sam and him, not Sam going with the gun and MacKenzie.

"When we get to Horeb. I'll teach her myself." MacKenzie held out the pistol.

"No. I told you, she's not going to Horeb."

Way to ease into it, dickhead.

Sam stood, Reina struggling to her feet beside her. She took MacKenzie's offering, holding it like she almost knew what she was doing. "Where else are we going to go?"

"North. Out. Away. I don't know," Ward said. "I need to get you away from here."

"She's old enough to decide for herself, Rafe."

Ker approached, a Reaper's facemask hooked over his arm. He closed the trunk. "None of us are going to Horeb."

"What?"

"New orders," Ker said. "Came in last night."

"I didn't get any new orders," MacKenzie said.

"How could you?"

Ward quickly deciphered the conflict. MacKenzie was in charge but was still off grid. Unplugged. Any communication with Horeb would have to come through Ker, a fact Ward imagined MacKenzie hated.

As if confirming Ward's interpretation of the issue, MacKenzie asked through clenched teeth, "Details?"

"The Seer wants the symbol to go south, needs him cleansed and pure before being revealed."

"Symbol?" Ward asked.

"You should have said something earlier," MacKenzie said, ignoring Ward.

"What did it matter if the symbol wasn't to be found?" Ker countered.

"Rafe?" Sam said, clearly confused.

"Hannah..."

"Not now."

"Orders are verified," Ker said. "Time sensitive."

"What symbol?" Ward asked louder, though he didn't really want to know. Didn't want to hear it said aloud. Didn't want

MacKenzie's voice to be the one drawing him back in. To be the one destroying his hope for smuggling Sam away from the coming revolution.

"You, damn it, Rafe," MacKenzie said. "You."

CHAPTER 16

"I'm not a symbol," Ward said.

"The hell you're not," MacKenzie replied. "As soon as you died you became a symbol. The minute you walked into the Tower—"

"Fuck the Tower."

"Guilt," Ker said. "Probably why the Seer wants you purged. Reborn. All guilt, all sins washed away. Your past forgiven."

"Sure, and a bath is going to do what bourbon can't," Ward said. "Who is this guy?"

Ker's face transformed, becoming almost bestial with rage. Then, it was gone, replaced by an aloof tweak of his eyebrow.

"I'll go wherever you go," Sam said to Ward.

At that, Ker grinned. Sam blushed. Ward was surprised by how much he suddenly hated Ker, as if his previous likeability had been shed like a winter coat.

Ker's words, however, kept replaying in Ward's head. *All guilt, all sins washed away.*

Ward looked at Sam. She was still innocent, but the longer she stayed with him, the closer she was to being baptized in the same radicalized fire as the other two.

I'm not going to let that happen, he affirmed to himself. To his mother. What had she said in that dream?

No more fires, baby. Okay? You don't set any more fires, and one day you can see Daddy and me again for real. Maybe even Daniel. Won't that be nice?

All the same, if Ker had a plan to get them out of here and

far away from the hounding claws of the Republic, then he was their ticket. For now.

"Alright," he said. "Guilt. Fine, whatever. Where does your seer want me to go?"

MacKenzie slashed a finger at him. "He's not *my* seer. He's *the* Seer."

"The Seer. Fine." This wasn't the time for theological debate. Warlords and pontiffs were all the same. He had no doubt this one would prove as flawed as any other. An image, a brief flash of a textbook photo quickly into dissolve, came to him. The guillotine upon a stage. The king's head in Robespierre's hand held out to the crowd. *Thus, the revolutionary becomes the tyrant,* Ward remembered a professor saying long ago in grad school. A dangerous assertion for a teacher, but under the guise of a history lesson, one that could slide under the radar if students were open minded enough. "Where does he want this cleansing to take place?"

"South," Ker said. "The message said the temple of the rising sun, within the rock, among the dead. Then to the river to prepare yourself for a second life."

"What does that mean?" Sam asked.

Ward had no idea. "What's with the ambiguity?"

Ker shrugged.

"The Seer speaks for God," MacKenzie said as if that should be explanation enough.

"How far south?" Ward asked.

"Couple days."

"That's Old Mexico," Sam said.

As far south as Mexico City, in fact, Ward calculated. Once a designated global commerce alpha city of near ten million inhabitants, it had declined since the time of the Reclamation, with less than half the population of its height. The construction of The Wall isolating the Republic from Old Mexico had choked the economic life from the entirety of Central and South America.

Ward tried to think of a single church—there were more in Mexico City than he could ever count or name—that stood out as more important than the others. One famous for baptisms or cleansing rituals. Named, perhaps, for John the Baptist. Two or three years ago he might have come up with a list off the top of his head of a dozen or so possibilities. Today he could think of none.

He wanted a drink, but everyone was watching him. He tried to wash his mind clear. The Seer's riddle, if that's what it was, enunciated in Ker's smooth, slightly accented, voice, floated through his mind like bubbles from a child's wand. Eluding him. Laughing at the way he was poking at them rather than snatching them for clues. Overthinking. Trying to recall archaeological sites. Translating cathedral names. Seeking synonyms, pseudonyms, anything. Sun. Moon. River. Ocean. Dead. Alive. Rising. Descending.

"Rising," he said, maybe on to something. "The *rising* sun."

"What about it?" MacKenzie asked.

"Most religions equate the sun with a god, right?" He received blank faces so continued. "The rising sun equals rising god equals the birth of a god. Teotihuacan."

"Teo what?"

"The rising sun among the dead," Ward said, feeling the exhilaration he'd only known recently from a long, hard pull of bourbon. "The Pyramid of the Sun along the Avenue of the Dead in Teotihuacan, about thirty miles from Mexico City. Its name means where the gods are born."

Sam made a face like any student might, simply accepting what the teacher says. MacKenzie nodded, though if she was agreeing, Ward couldn't tell.

"Sounds like the right answer to me," Ker said, rubbing his chin. "Not bad, professor."

Something in Ker's voice struck Ward odd. Wrong. Condescension, perhaps. Figuring out the tall man, he thought, might prove more difficult than the rest of the Seer's puzzle.

"Alright," MacKenzie said. "Gather your shit. Evac in two minutes. That'll be good, yes?"

Ward asked Sam if she could get Reina in the car on her own. She said she could, giving Ward the opportunity to return to the trailer. To steal a moment alone and collect himself. To bring his nerves back to baseline with a quick drink.

Inside, the trailer was a wreck. The table and chairs had been reduced to little more than scrap. The Reaper, facemask torn off, lay on his back in the middle of the floor, arms splayed. Blood arced the body, the walls, the ceiling. Ward's gaze, as though drawn by rope and pulley, was dragged to the man's throat. Rent open, as if by a starving coyote. Next, to the threaded socket holes circumscribing the man's face, the holes via which his facemask had been bolted to his skull. Ward thought he might vomit. What he saw next stopped that impulse.

The Reaper's left eyeball was missing. Not gouged out in the fight, however. There were no viscous threads or oozing nerves. The organ had been gone a long time. In its place was a bird's nest of wires and cables, two thicker leads hanging out, their ends frayed. Matching cords dangled from the facemask's left eye.

Suddenly woozy, Ward struggled to get his backpack off his shoulders. Open it. Find the bourbon. Get the bottle to his lips. The warm fluid burned in the wake of the aborted vomit, but the chills it sent to his arms and legs steadied him. Centered his vision.

That's it, he thought, and took another draught.

"Time, Rafe," MacKenzie called from outside.

Ward shouted his acknowledgement and put away the bottle. His mind now clearer, he let it wander over the journey they were about to begin while he went for the bathroom, filling his bag with a towel, a bar of deodorant, toilet paper, and toothpaste. They needed to somehow escape the Republic, find a river, and do some ritual. Then he would need to figure out how to keep running with Sam when MacKenzie and Ker would want him to come back to the Republic for their revolution. Too much to comprehend, let alone solve, all at once. So, he broke it down. Getting out of the Republic was on MacKenzie. That meant the cleansing ritual was on him. The rest would have to wait.

It was a familiar idea, this cleansing ritual, though not in terms of the correlation of a river and the Pyramid of the Sun. While the pyramid could have some rebirth significance, he knew of no river nearby that offered the same. Elsewhere, sure. Rivers famous for purity rituals were in no short supply.

The Jordan and the Ganges came to mind, but nothing in Old Mexico, not unless he wanted to humor the idea of the Fountain of Youth or El Dorado. The problem, aside from centuries of treasure hunters coming up empty in the search for such places, was that Mesoamerican mythology, and Conquistador misunderstanding of it, was not his area of expertise.

I need a Port, he thought.

You need another drink.

No, I can do this. I can do this on my own.

Determination honed his concentration. A ritual cleansing. Purge. Baptism. Holy fast. Jewish tevilah rights. Too many to pick one. That was the problem. Absolutions were promised by nearly every religion humanity had ever invented. Which one did the Seer want?

A second question accompanied the first. Was the Seer crazy? The supernatural, the divine, the miraculous—they were not real. Participating in the quest for this river was a ridiculous venture.

Then again, there'd been the priest, Adrien Quinque, who'd claimed to be a four-hundred-year-old servant of Ba'el. Plus, the visions Ward had confirming the priest's story when Adrien had touched him. Delusions?

And what about the Vase of Soissons swimming before him in the Mediterranean, closing its lid to trap Ba'el inside. Psychosis?

Or the Beast rising from the sea, the sky and ocean crimson?

Crazy. All of it. But when surrounded by the insane, what option was there but to abide their insanity? To play their game? To solve their riddles?

"Rafe!" There was no mistaking MacKenzie's tone this time.

Ward took a wide berth around the Reaper's body on his way back to the car, questions ready for MacKenzie and Ker. The facemask and eye. The full text of the Seer's orders. Their combined familiarity with Old Mexico. They were arguing about directions when he approached, however.

"Nogales is faster," Ker said. "The borders in Arizona easier to get through. We can be at the Pyramid tomorrow night."

"You going to get in the game here, Rafe?" MacKenzie said.

At first, he thought she meant the argument, but the disdain in her voice indicated she'd seen him freeze when the battle began.

"No, I—" he started, but had no defense.

MacKenzie turned to Ker as if Ward wasn't even there anymore. "And your little car ID trick isn't getting us through The Wall. Payaya City. By Curfew tonight."

"Texas? We have operatives in Texas?"

"Yes."

"Why is this the first I'm hearing of it?"

"Because you're tech," MacKenzie said. "You're support not ops. Get it? Not a decision maker, no matter how much the Seer thinks of your skillset."

Ward couldn't decide if Ker looked like he might cry or laugh. Or maybe drop a grenade at MacKenzie's feet and kill them all. Then, as if there'd never been any other expression on his face, the smooth grin was back.

"Right. Sorry to overstep, General. Here's the thing. I can't guarantee border crossing times into the Central District. And Payaya City, that's got to be a hundred and fifty miles from The Wall. You're adding half a day at least that way."

"Get us into the Central District by Curfew tonight. Payaya before lunch tomorrow. My border runner will arrange the rest."

Ker thought on it a moment, eliciting an infuriated glare from MacKenzie who obviously expected her orders to be followed without question. Just as Ward thought he might have to step between them, Ker relented.

"Who do I message ahead to?"

"You can't. They operate dark, but if this cleansing is that important to the Seer then they're the ones we need. I'll get in touch when we arrive."

"Yes, General," Ker said.

He got in the driver's side without further comment. MacKenzie gave Ward a look that said, *I told you to get in the car.* Ward joined Sam and Reina, who were holding each other like children while their parents fought. He locked his eyes on the side window, not allowing himself to look back as they drove away from the pit.

PART 2: THE FORCED ONES

...efforts should be made to bring them, the children of the errant ones, of the Forced Ones, back in repentance, to draw them near so that they may return to the strength-giving source...
—Mishneh Torah, by Maimonides, c. 1180

President Barclay, if you seek peace and safety for our Citizens, all the Republic's Citizens, come to this border. Bring us the funds. Mr. Barclay, build us this wall!
—Central District Administrator Michelle Richards, 22 March 2054

CHAPTER 17

Payaya City was hot. Ward couldn't even feel the hint of a breeze off the river. It was as if all the heat that Kingman was missing had camped out here for the summer, waiting for them to arrive.

The locals, or they could have been tourists, didn't seem to mind so much. They ambled along the city's River Walk, virtually every one of them wearing a cowboy hat, as if the morning were perfectly pleasant. Many said "howdy" or tipped their hats at Sam and MacKenzie, a touch of Southern Hospitality that struck Ward as mostly perfunctory. Still, it was more neighborly than could be expected on the sidewalks of Philly back in the Atlantic District.

Multicolored umbrellas shaded the rows of riverside cafes and restaurants. Memorable touches like arched bridges over the water carried the impression of European charm combined with American pragmatism. It should have been a nice stroll, relaxing and refreshing. Instead, Ward was panting more than Reina. Sweat soaked his socks so they squished in his boots. Thirst made his head hurt and dried out his tongue until it felt like he'd burned it on a cup of too-hot coffee.

Worse, none of his companions seemed effected. MacKenzie power-walked ahead. Sam was behind her, with Reina next in line. Ker, with a lazy, loping stride, kept a good distance ahead of Ward, who shuffled along, falling farther and farther behind.

He hoped MacKenzie would call for a break and take them into a store or restaurant or anywhere with air conditioning, but they kept on toward the Alamo with the kind of purpose he knew to expect from her. With nothing else to do but walk and sweat, he let his mind wander.

Payaya City had once been called San Antonio. In the first decade following the Reclamation, while the nation's churches were being razed in the Great Cleanse, the ruling party of the new republic ordered a subtler extirpation. All the cities, streets, monuments, and more whose names referenced saints or religion were renamed, their theological histories wiped away. In most cases older Native American names were substituted, such as San Antonio being renamed for the Payaya people who originally settled the area. Or Los Angeles being retitled Tongva City, its larger metro area going by Southland now.

The great irony of the renamings was that the practice of obliterating names from the historical record had religious roots. *Damnatio memoriae* it was called by historians, the "damnation of memory." The phrase itself an afterlife. The Romans did it to traitors. Predating that, the Hebrew army entering Canaan so utterly destroyed the Amalek tribe that no historical record persisted of the Amalekites. The Egyptians annihilated the name of Pharaoh Ahkenaten, who had chosen monotheism over the traditional Egyptian pantheon of gods. Herostratus, an ancient Greek, had his name struck away for setting fire to the Temple of Artemis, one of the no longer celebrated Seven Wonders of the World.

Examples continued from the ancient world to the modern, with even the pre-Republic America changing the name of the tallest mountain in North America from Mount McKinley back to the native Denali after over a hundred years in honor of the twenty-fifth president. The Republic's *damnatio memoriae* was, however, the most sweeping example in recent history.

"What do we do at the Alamo?" Sam asked.

MacKenzie slowed, condensing the group so their conversation wouldn't carry across the River Walk. The look she gave Sam told the girl she had a lot to learn about staying inconspicuous.

"You wait," she said.

"How long?" Ker asked.

"Until the conductor, my runner, arrives."

"Could you be any vaguer?" Ward asked. He wiped the back of his hand across his sweating brow. He wanted a drink, but not enough to put up with the criticism it would bring. Not yet, anyway.

MacKenzie didn't answer. She kept them moving another few minutes before leading them up a set of stairs from the River Walk to the streets of Payaya City. A few minutes later they got a table at a sidewalk café not quite a hundred yards from the entrance to the Alamo. Ward made sure to take a seat that offered a good view as well as kept him in the shade of the tan umbrella above the table. Ker sat opposite Ward, leaving Reina to plop down between the tall man and Sam.

Across the street from the café, tourists packed the original cobblestone road that crossed before the Alamo. The building's entrance—the familiar four-columned and five-windowed limestone veneer that virtually every Republic history text featured in the chapter on the nineteenth century—looked like a postcard. It was one of the few landmarks remaining in the Republic from before the twentieth century. To Ward's knowledge it was the only church standing anywhere on Republic soil. Of course, the thousands of tourists who visited each year had no idea the Alamo began life as a Roman Catholic mission. It stood today, as it had for much of the two centuries before the Reclamation, a symbol of American determination and strength. "Remember the Alamo" remained the unofficial motto of Texas, resurfacing as a battle cry during the War to Reclaim America from the corruption of churches and their religions.

"How do you know he's looking for us to be here?" Ward asked.

A waitress, a dark-haired woman who could have been Sam's cousin or older sister, came by with waters for everyone and took their drink orders. Ward could feel Sam and MacKenzie's eyes on him as a warning. He ordered an iced tea and hoped he might have the chance to pour a little of his bourbon into it when he wasn't being watched like a child.

"This is a drop point," MacKenzie said when the waitress left. "Our people watch it round the clock. When they see me, they'll deliver the message."

"I don't have any data on this location," Ker said.

"How long for your guy to show up?" Ward asked.

"Depends on if he's here or across the border."

"I thought the border was impossible," Sam said. "Like, no one can get across The Wall without authorization."

As much as Ward had tried to bury himself in books and ignorance for the past couple years in Kingman, even he knew about The Wall of Republic Unity. It was, after all, erected because of him. Because he'd destroyed the Tower. The Republic's response was to enact one of the greatest public works in history. In only eleven months, it built a continuous barrier along the Republic's southern border—from the Pacific near Ensenada, through Texas along the Rio Grande, across the beaches of the Gulf of Mexico, and around the Florida peninsula before terminating south of Orlando—to keep vice and crime and drugs and foreign cultures and, of course, Believers buried in Old Mexico.

"We're not going to ask permission," MacKenzie said.

The conversation quieted again when the waitress returned with their drinks and a bowl of water for Reina. Ward drank quickly from his iced tea, the sugar and caffeine giving him an instant buzz. With the buzz came the feeling they were being watched.

He looked around at the other patrons at the café. At the tourists and pedestrians meandering about. At the waitress. None of them struck him as out of place. Still, the feeling stuck with him.

"How are we getting across?" Sam asked when they were alone again.

MacKenzie was locked in on the Alamo and didn't appear to hear her. Sam repeated her question.

"Keep watch," MacKenzie said a moment later. "Keep quiet and stay here."

Then she was out of her chair and crossing the street. She strolled like a tourist, though her head never swiveled like she was interested in the sights. Her trajectory was locked on the Alamo. She took up position beside the rightmost column on the Alamo's façade.

Ward tensed, ready to go when her contact arrived, but the only one who came near her was a coffee cart vendor who rounded the plaza every ten minutes or so. MacKenzie bought a coffee from the vendor on each pass. By her third, Ward was getting antsy. Ker, on the other hand, seemed untroubled, flagging the waitress for a beer and an order of beef enchiladas.

"Something's off," Ward said after Ker's beer arrived.

"Agreed," Ker said.

"I should go see if she's okay."

"She said stay here," Sam said.

"Which means she doesn't want backup," Ker said.

Ward listened without replying. Instinct, and experience, told him to trust MacKenzie, but he couldn't shake the feeling that something was wrong.

"What are you thinking?" Sam asked.

Ward wasn't sure he was thinking, at least not clearly. He needed a drink. He needed his brain to click clear. He watched Ker drink half his beer and place the glass back on the table. Without thinking, he leaned across the table and grabbed the glass. Downed the rest of the beer. It was cool. It was weak. It was enough to feel a little more like himself.

"Nice," Sam said, her disappointment obvious.

"Help yourself," Ker said.

Ward didn't bother apologizing. He was working on that feeling of wrongness, trying to identify it. Trying to remember what it was like to be a trained operative who could trust his impulses.

"I think we're being watched," he said after a moment.

The waitress came back with Ker's enchiladas. A breeze finally came in off the river, floating the aroma of the salsa and the beef to Ward. His stomach grumbled.

"What's mine is yours," Ker said, his overly pleasant tone reminding Ward that he really disliked the man, before ordering three more beers.

The waitress said she'd be right back and headed off to gather their drinks.

"You're not old enough to drink," Ward said to Sam.

"You're not my...forget it," Sam said, sounding exhausted.

Ward knew he should feel bad. He was the reason her father was dead. Her mother too. He owed her safety not smothering. Mostly, though, he wanted to drop the whole conversation and wait for the waitress to bring him a beer. He looked to the Alamo to check on MacKenzie.

She wasn't there.

CHAPTER 18

"She's gone," Ward said.

He jumped up from his chair, bumping the waitress as she returned with their beers. A glass tumbled off her tray and crashed on the flagstone. Heads turned.

I've lost her, he thought, *again.*

She's abandoned you again.

I won't let that happen!

He didn't wait for the others. He grabbed his backpack from beneath the table and crossed the plaza as briskly as he could without drawing attention.

"Police?" Sam asked, suddenly beside Ward, keeping pace. Reina followed, her limp almost gone.

"Cops aren't the issue. This close to the border there's got to be REC activity."

As they neared the Alamo, a man in a dark suit with a large white Texas star on his lapel came through the door.

"No pets, folks."

"We're not going in," Ward said.

"We're not?" Sam said.

"You really should have your dog on a leash, too," the man in the suit said.

"Thanks. We'll do that. Wait here a second," he added to Sam.

He took up position at the last place he'd seen MacKenzie, beside the interior column to the right of the door. He set his back to the column. The Alamo museum was undoubtedly populated with dozens of security cams. MacKenzie wouldn't have set a drop point inside. The location was a starting point, a recognition outpost, for the actual meeting which would take place within sight but out of the public eye.

Almost directly ahead, the line of sight as good from here to the café as it had been from there, he could see Ker finalizing payment of their meal by brushing his Port across the waitress's tablet. To the left, a perfectly manicured lawn edged by trees. To the right, a double gate through the north wall.

"This way," he told Sam.

Reina barked and took the lead as if she knew exactly where to go. Through the gate a sign declared the long barracks and the theater to the left through one of a series of arches. Ahead of them a monstrous tree with limbs like octopus arms reached in all directions. Reina didn't pause. She hurled ahead, around the tree to the left. Ward and Sam followed, nearly knocking down a middle-aged couple—"What's the hurry, partner?" the man said—before Reina stopped in front of the farthest arch.

There MacKenzie stood with her back against the wall. A man with military posture leaned in to her, their noses almost touching. She put her hands on his shoulders. Ward thought she was going to pull him in. Kiss him.

"Rafe," she said, an unfamiliar tone to her voice, as she pushed the man away. She raked her hand through her hair. "This is Oren."

Oren backed away from MacKenzie. He was Ward's height, younger than MacKenzie but older than Sam, broad shouldered, and slightly darker-skinned than Sam. His black hair was tight in military style and he sported a thin beard.

"Hello," Sam said.

Reina rubbed Ward's leg. When Ker joined them, she ambled over to him instead.

"Well," Oren said. "Everyone here, then? Let's talk at the depot. This way."

MacKenzie motioned her approval and took up behind Oren as he led them a few blocks to a shopping district. Crowded and absent of any significant shade, Ward barely noticed the bland twentieth-century three, four, and five story buildings lining the street, as if the developer of this particular lane made sure to align the architecture so that the sun was always overhead. They passed lunch cafés, restaurants of at least half a dozen cuisines, a couple bars, and more all occupying the first floors, finally coming to their destination between a sub shop and a hair salon.

"The depot is a liquor store?" Ward said as they entered.

"Nothing for him," MacKenzie ordered.

Sam voiced her agreement.

"What?" Ward said, trying to protest, but a head shake from MacKenzie shut him down.

"As you wish," Oren said, and made a gesture to the man behind the register then pointed at Ward.

The cashier, wearing an off-white cowboy hat over blond hair, tapped the brim of his hat.

Oren led them into the storeroom, a well-lit labyrinth of multicolored boxes and crates that smelled more than a little of wine and a sharp mash. Ward's mouth watered. They passed two stacks of green label bourbon and a wood cask of some spirit with an unfamiliar name.

Up a short flight of stairs in the back, Oren directed them into to what Ward supposed was once an office or accounting room. It was dark, despite a large half-circle window at the front of the room and quite musty. A long table sat in the farthest corner from the window surrounded by cheap office chairs. The room reminded Ward of photos he'd seen of the Sixth Floor Museum at Dealey Plaza in Dallas. He imagined that room, back when Lee Harvey Oswald was loading his Carcano carbine, smelled much the same—dust, sweat, and old timber.

A man emerged from the shadows beside the table. He wore a black vest over a white Oxford shirt, sleeves rolled to the elbows, and a black bowler hat. To Ward, he looked like a dapper gentleman straight out of the nineteenth century.

"General," the dapper man said with a slight roll of the R and a tap of the brim of his hat the way the cashier downstairs had.

"You remember Lacalle," Oren said to MacKenzie. Ward couldn't tell if it was a last name or a first. "Downstairs was Rivera. Now what exactly—"

MacKenzie, not bothering with introductions, said, "We need to get across."

Oren looked at each of the companions, lingering briefly on Sam, probably because she was clearly not a soldier. He pointed to the table and told everyone to sit. Lacalle held the chair at the head of the table for MacKenzie but she swatted him away and waited until everyone else found a chair before she sat.

Ward ended up between Sam and Oren, who was next to MacKenzie, at the sturdy, cherry wood table. Lacalle and Ker sat opposite them like the pair of gamblers you least want to try cheating.

"We need across tonight, Oren," MacKenzie said.

"Tonight?" Oren said. "Do you know what kind of shit is going down out west? The whole border, I mean the whole thing, is on alert. Patrols have doubled out here in the last twenty-four hours."

"I know."

"For the love of—what did you do, Hannah?"

At the use of MacKenzie's first name, Ward tensed. But the retort he expected didn't come, leaving Ward feeling...angry? Jealous? He felt MacKenzie watching him.

"This is him," she said to Oren.

"Him who?" Oren said. He looked at Ward. Squinted. His eyes widened. "No."

"Yes."

"You shouldn't be here. You need to get to Horeb."

"We need to get across."

"Why?" Oren appeared genuinely confused and concerned with the presence of the Tower Terrorist.

"The Seer's orders."

"Orders." He said the word like it was a nuisance. "Right. This isn't going to be easy. I'm not sure..."

MacKenzie stared: the General demanding her orders be followed.

Oren bobbed his head: a soldier following orders. "Where to once we cross?"

"Near Mexico City."

"You're trying to kill me before we even get to the border, aren't you?"

"What's wrong with Mexico City?" Ward asked.

"You'll see," Oren said. He stood and extended his hand to Ward. "Welcome to Payaya City, Mr. Ward. And thank you."

Ward balked at the gratitude. "Don't do that."

"Rafe doesn't want accolades," MacKenzie said. "Let his presence suffice his commitment."

Ward didn't like her speaking for him, especially not declaring his commitment to a cause not his own. In fact, he didn't like the way things were playing out at all. He felt like a chip, a moveable piece for some goal that was being kept from him.

MacKenzie continued the introductions. Reina barked at her name. There was a moment of silence then Lacalle got up.

"I'll tell her we're coming," he said.

"All of us," Oren said.

"You, sir? You just got back."

"Yes, me. No chances on this one."

"General," Lacalle said, tapping his hat once more before leaving.

"Tell who?" Sam asked.

Before Oren could answer Ker asked, "How long until we're across?"

Oren looked to MacKenzie as if asking permission to answer the question. She tilted her head.

"We've got a run through Eagle Pass," Oren said, hands flat on the table. "Part of the old Railroad. We'll need to hole up until after Curfew, but you'll be in Old Mexico for breakfast."

"Wait," Ward said, remembering a term MacKenzie had used earlier. "You're the conductor. You're talking about the Underground Railroad?"

"Right, you were a teacher." Oren said, amused. "Yes, Eagle Pass crossed quite a few thousand slaves into Old Mexico during the Railroad's original run."

"An underground railroad?" Sam asked. "Like a subway?"

"No, it's a name for the network," Oren said. "Not a real train. Though arguably more important than the invention of the locomotive."

Ward, enjoying the sound of his teacher-voice, added, "It was a system of sympathizers who helped slaves escape from

of the few buildings Ward had seen that rose as high as four or five stories.

Ward sent his mind in search of facts and tidbits about Eagle Pass, anything to keep him from thinking about his bladder. At first, he recalled nothing. Then a sign for a hunting and fishing game shop rolled by the window and the name King Fisher popped into his head. Fisher had been a gunslinger and outlaw who'd set up shop in Eagle Pass at about the same time Billy the Kid was terrorizing New Mexico. A sign on the road to his ranch had read: "This is King Fisher's road. Take the other." Ward hoped the memory, and Fisher's sign, was not a portent of what was to come.

"We'll be stopping up there," Oren said as they crossed Commercial Street.

"Where are we going?" Ward asked.

"You'll see."

And indeed they did see. A couple quick turns had them driving north along a two-lane road, the western shoulder but a few feet wide before abutting a concrete barrier topped with barbed wire. What rose behind that barrier silenced all chatter in the van.

The Wall stood twelve feet high, obliterating all view of what should have been a beautiful vista overlooking the Rio Grande and Old Mexico beyond. Striped in bright hazard yellow and reflective white, the wall was lined with barbed and razor wire along its rampart as well as its base. Soldiers could be seen pacing the top. In less than a minute driving beside the massive barricade, Ward counted three towers and more than twenty spotlights and machine gun turrets.

Even scarier was the death strip between the highway barrier and The Wall. Twenty yards dubbed by the media as Righteous Road, it was a beach of loose sand that would make running difficult and would leave footprints behind any who tried traversing its lines of razor wire, pits, and, rumor had it, land mines.

"We're going across that?" Sam asked, incredulous and afraid.

"Not a chance," Oren said.

You're not kidding, Ward thought.

"Even if we could get to The Wall," Oren continued as if trying to scare them all, "There's therm scanners and fakir beds on both sides for anyone who tries to climb and drop down."

"What beds?" Sam asked.

"Beds of nails," Ker replied beside Ward. At his voice, Reina stuck her head over the seat and nudged him until he rubbed her ears.

"Then why drive us by here?" MacKenzie asked.

"I want to make it clear to them what we're up against. And remind you."

"Consider us all educated. Take us to the safe house."

"Yes sir," Oren said.

A few minutes later, they pulled up in front of a hardware store.

"Here?" Ker asked.

"No," Oren said. "There." He pointed to a small home across the street.

It appeared to be the least safe-looking safe house Ward could imagine. A simple two-story home, dull white with green shutters and accents, at least a hundred and fifty years old. From where he sat, it appeared to be all wood framing and plaster. No places for sentries to hide. No defensive bulwarks. No alcoves, alleys, or other nooks for cover. The house sat a few feet back from the curb, protected by nothing more than a quaint white picket fence. Three windows glared out at them in the van as if complaining that the house had been miscast.

Entering the house did nothing to assuage Ward's suspicions about the building's integrity as a safe house. It was far too much like an old gentry house, the floorplan sectioned and formal. Though the neutral-color walls and stiff furniture spoke of early century decorating, he had no doubt there were generations of wallpaper hiding beneath the paint and countless refinishings shining in the hardwood beneath their feet.

Oren led the group from the front room—once the parlor and now a seating area with a nice cross breeze through the open windows—to the living room. Featuring a stately fireplace opposite a couch and television, this would have been the dining room a hundred or more years ago, Ward guessed, and the room beyond would have been an entertaining hall. The fireplace was easily six feet across and reached another two or three into the room, but for all its majesty, it was the cherrywood mantle that drew Ward's attention. Adorned mostly with picture frames, Ward ignored these in favor of a simple yet stately pewter and black urn. The elegant display spoke of great love for the one who reposed inside.

When Ward's mother was cremated, he was requested to provide his own vessel for retrieving her remains. The Republic did not supply urns for criminals. He'd never been able to get her. If he had, he thought now, this was the urn he'd have chosen for her.

"The dining room and kitchen are through there," Oren said pointing through the doorway beside a massive fireplace. "Stairs to the left off the dining room. The Grossmutter's bedroom is behind the kitchen. She doesn't do stairs well. Master bedroom upstairs is the first on the left. Two more with a shared bathroom down the hall from there to the right."

"Nice place," Ker said.

Lacalle spoke quietly to Oren then tapped his hat in MacKenzie's direction and left out the front door.

"Doesn't say much, does he?" Ker said.

"We're not heading out until after midnight," Oren said. "I suggest you rest now."

"I'm not tired," Sam said.

Her face reddened when the others looked at her as if she'd spoken a secret aloud.

"Neither am I," said Ker.

"Not sure any of us are sleeping now," MacKenzie said.

"Your call," Oren said. "The Grossmutter is out at the baker. I sent Lacalle to get her. He'll then go ahead to prep our run."

"How are we crossing The Wall?" Ward asked.

"Actually, since whatever you and the General did in Arizona has the whole border jumping, our primary and secondary routes are compromised."

"Explain," MacKenzie said.

"The border crossing works with good IDs coming into the

Republic, but it requires great IDs to get out. The problem is, there's a full lockdown in effect right now. No one in or out. Our man at the crossing can't help us. Not that he could on a good day. There's no ID in the world that's going to get him," he pointed to Ward, "or you, General, through those gates."

"Secondary?" The General was all business.

"We've been running the old drug smuggling tunnel, as you know, for almost three years. It works great for munitions and contraband, but it's not suited for people."

"Drug smuggling?" Sam asked.

Ward filled in the gap. "Before the Reclamation, pharm companies had a lot of sway over what was legal and what wasn't. If they didn't manufacture it, they tried to outlaw it. A lot of the illegal stuff came up through the border. They used all kinds of methods, including tunnels. Kind of makes the idea of a wall seem futile when there's tunnels running right underneath."

"Risks?" MacKenzie asked.

"Biggest is suffocating. Besides that, it runs along the floor of the river under a couple feet or so of silt. Their therm scanners would show us like red marbles rolling across a hardwood floor. We only send operatives through when our insiders can shut down the scanners. It's closed circuit. Can't hack it. During a lockdown our people are completely sealed out."

"So we can't try it until the lockdown lifts."

"Correct. Are you sure you don't want to wait?"

"No. Options?"

"One," Oren said. "Untried. Very risky."

"Explain."

"A few years back I did some renovations to the second floor, added another bedroom and such. I found all kinds of documents behind the plaster in the walls. Do you know what this place is, or was?"

No one answered, but Ward thought he knew where Oren's story was going, the same way the hunting and fishing shop had reminded him of Fisher King. That old excitement, the kind that came with discovery.

Oren continued, "It was called California Camp in the

middle of the eighteen-hundreds, back before there was a town here. This house, built thirty years later, was the centerpiece of one of the richest families in the county."

"Wait," Ward said, his mind thumbing through memories of textbooks and lectures. "This is the Hartz House. The mining entrepreneur. You found one of his early mines."

Oren stared, mouth slightly agape, as if Ward had stolen the punch line of his favorite joke.

"You got all that from California Camp?" Ker asked, eyebrows raised.

"Yes," Ward said.

"Turns out he dropped mine shafts all over the area," Oren said, recovering his momentum. "A lot of them went nowhere, but apparently some he didn't dig deep enough. When they were building a supermarket about a mile north of here five or six years ago there was a sinkhole incident. Our people were on it. Did the backfill. Adjusted the blue prints. Gave us access. We've been excavating since."

"Under the river?" MacKenzie said.

"It's deep enough therms won't pick us up."

"What's the catch?" MacKenzie asked.

Ward wanted to say the catch is we have to go underground. We have to break Agent Compano's rule about getting yourself trapped with no escape route. But the look on Oren's face said the catch was actually much worse.

"The tunnel isn't complete yet. We've been digging by hand from both sides. Anything mechanized is either too big or would cause too much vibration."

"Meaning it would either draw attention or risk collapsing the tunnel."

"Correct," Oren said. "We're ready to break through, join the two sides but it's solid bedrock. We've been working on a plan to try a controlled detonation. but the second we set off those charges alarms are going to sound all along The Wall for a mile in each direction. Our plan was to time it with a distraction, some kind of small artillery attack on The Wall itself. It won't leave much time for us, so we'll have to be in range."

"In range as in we have to be in the tunnel ready to run

when the charges blow?" Ker asked.

"Affirmative."

"Prep it," MacKenzie said.

"General," Oren said. "I said we were working on the plan. Our people haven't completed the calculations for the explosives. It has to be precise. There's been no prep for this at all."

"Get your people. This is happening tonight," MacKenzie said.

"Hannah—"

She glared. "General," she corrected.

Ward was surprised by the satisfaction he felt at the way she shut him down.

"General," Oren began again. "If you and I could talk upstairs. In private?"

She stopped him with a look Ward knew well. An uncomfortable silence filled the room.

"Television in there?" Ker said, cutting the silence. He started to the door to the living room before anyone could answer, an energy or granola bar in his hand as if it had always been there.

To Oren MacKenzie said, "Start the preparations. I want an update in two hours. Ready to execute at least four hours before sunrise."

"Yes, sir," Oren said.

"Rafe, go take a shower. Or a nap."

Ward didn't like being ordered about like he was one of her soldiers, but he had to admit he preferred it to the mostly silence he'd received from her since they'd left Arizona.

"Come on, Sam," he said, heading for the stairs. "Let's leave the soldiers to their soldiering."

Sam started to follow, then stopped.

"A bit young for you, Rafe," MacKenzie said.

"What? No, I—"

MacKenzie smirked, roguish and sharp. Sam giggled. Ward felt himself blush.

MacKenzie motioned to Sam. "How about you and I take the master bedroom upstairs? A little time away from the men. That'll be good, yes?"

Sam seemed elated at the invitation and followed MacKenzie

up the stairs, Reina at her heels, leaving Ward and Oren alone. An intense dislike of Oren shot through Ward like he'd been injected with it. Jealousy for the familiarity the man had with MacKenzie. Jealousy. Or was the jealousy about Sam and MacKenzie's new friendship? What did the General care about a teenager anyway?

But the feeling and the questions were fleeting. He had no interest in analysis. Rather, he wanted to pee. Then take a shower. Perhaps the last one he'd be able to take for a while. Or ever.

The same went for his remaining bourbon. Maybe the final few shots he'd ever have. Should he enjoy them now, or wait until they were ready to blow themselves up in a two-hundred-year-old mine shaft?

"And Rafe," MacKenzie's voice came from upstairs.

"Yeah?"

Sam took over. "Stay out of the bottle."

CHAPTER 20

Sam didn't know what to make of MacKenzie, even after their shared chuckle at Rafe's expense. She was easily the most intimidating woman—no, the most intimidating person—Sam had ever known. Strong. Confident. Gorgeous in a violent way that made Sam self-conscious and a bit jealous, especially of the way Oren looked at her.

Or was that Sam's own desire getting in the way? Oren was attractive, though his muscular stoicism was generally more Mia's type than her own.

Thinking of Mia, her best friend, conjured a cold pit in Sam's stomach. Was Mia alright? Had the RFC come for her after all, because of Sam's transgressions rather than Dragon Lady's?

Don't think that. Don't ever think that. She's fine. She's getting ready for Enrollment Day. She's fine.

"Stop," MacKenzie said when they approached the master bedroom. "Wait here."

The redhead limped to the door from the side the same way Rafe had approached the front doors in the old high school. She listened. Swung the door open hard enough for it to smack the wall. Sam watched in awe at MacKenzie's confidence and efficiency—thankful for something else to fixate on than the shitstorm she'd likely brought down on her best friend by getting caught up with Rafe—as she slipped into the room then slid clockwise around its perimeter, right hand by her hip. Checking each of the closets that flanked the closer bed. Around the second bed. Into the bathroom. Returning to the center of the room and dropped to a knee to peer beneath the two beds.

"Good to go," MacKenzie said getting slowly back to her feet, as if only now remembering about her injured leg.

Reina bounded into the room and onto the closer of the beds.

"That one's yours," MacKenzie said, dropping her bag on the other bed.

"Do you always do that?"

"A security sweep? Never seen one?"

Sam shook her head and plopped down beside Reina. She could feel MacKenzie watching her.

"How'd you get caught up in this, Sam?"

They'd already talked in the van about how Rafe helped her escape from the school and the police. She'd told MacKenzie about working at the Quick Price with Mia and about her dead father on the couch. About her mom taken away by the police. They'd talked closely, barely above a whisper, so the others in the van couldn't hear. It was like she couldn't stop spilling her life's story. MacKenzie had sympathized and offered the same blunt response that Rafe had. Mom was dead. The Republic she thought she knew was a lie.

Not knowing what else to add, or what else MacKenzie wanted to hear, she talked about the contest and Hoodie Guy, finishing with, "I need the money."

MacKenzie continued to watch her as if expecting something. Sam didn't know what. She thought over all she'd told MacKenzie. Over what she'd said about needing the money.

"I *needed* the money," she said.

"Now you get it. That life is over. Live in this one. The one that's in trouble. If you can't, you won't make it."

It was blunt but true. Sam knew that. But knowing and accepting are not always the same thing. They don't come as the same speed.

"I still need to see a doctor," Sam said, feeling like her words were on autopilot.

"Are you sick?"

Sam couldn't tell if MacKenzie was being friendly or judging, getting ready to drop her at the first sign of defect. The longer she tried to figure out MacKenzie's aim without offering an answer, the harder it became to speak.

MacKenzie, not really any taller than herself Sam saw, took off her boots and socks and set them at the foot of the bed. Then she stretched toward the ceiling, forcefully, as if trying to detach her arms. This shifted into a slow-motion routine of stretches and movements that were clearly practiced but which seemed almost random.

The next words out of Sam's mouth were a complete surprise. "I'm not trying to steal Rafe from you."

She thought MacKenzie would laugh at her. She almost laughed at herself. But the redhead continued her routine, lingering on movements that must have hurt her injured leg.

"I just wanted you to know," Sam said, as if she couldn't shut off this conversation valve. She wanted to crawl into a hole. Or jump off a roof. Anything to quit babbling like an idiot. "I mean, he likes you."

What is wrong with me! Sam's voice screamed in her head.

The way MacKenzie's eyes dilated told Sam she'd gone too far with that one.

"I'm sorry. I meant, you know, he likes you. It's obvious. I—I'm sorry."

MacKenzie stopped the stretches and dropped onto the floor, landing on outstretched arms that pumped right into pushups. She did ten then said, while in the up position, "He's a good guy."

Ten more pushups.

"I know," Sam said.

"No, I mean *good*. Don't listen to the things they say about him." Ten more pushups.

Sam realized she'd been thinking the same thing about Rafe. *Knowing* it, maybe. He had an agenda, for sure. Everyone did. But he was the only who didn't look at her like she was in the way of that agenda. More like she was his agenda.

She didn't know how to say any of this, or if she should, so she got off the bed and down onto her knees. Stretched out, palms to the floor, and did a pushup. And another. And more. When she got to five, her shoulders began to tingle. At seven, her arms trembled and her shoulders burned. She couldn't finish number eight.

"Not bad," MacKenzie said, and did another ten.

Sam shifted to a cross-legged sitting position. "What about the Tower? Did he really do it?"

MacKenzie also got into a sitting position then leaned back and began doing sit ups. "Yes," she said, one or two words at each rise. "The people in there, they killed his whole family. Most people would have done what he did."

Sam wanted to say she wouldn't have, but the image of her dead father was there, like a reflection on a windshield. Inescapable.

"I would," Sam said. She also began a set of sit ups. These were easier. Her core had always been a part of her track training. Runners didn't work out their arms with pushups. She managed to keep up with MacKenzie's pace, for a few seconds. Then her belly tightened.

Was it fear? She sat up and rubbed her abdomen.

"Then you're the same," MacKenzie said.

"What?"

"As us. You're the same."

"Is that what you want to do? Blow up buildings and kill people?"

MacKenzie kept churning her sit ups, but Sam could plainly see she'd once again said the wrong thing. Pushing it might drive MacKenzie, this powerful woman she couldn't help but admire, to abandon her. But she had to ask. She had to know...something. She couldn't put a name to it. She just needed to know more.

"Are you going to kill people like that?"

MacKenzie stopped her sit ups.

She's going to leave me, Sam thought. It was a stupid thought. A stupid fear. MacKenzie leaving her was the best option. The only one that would end well. The General was death. Sam could see that. It clung to her like perfume. Rafe was her only chance at survival. *Then why do I want to stay with her?*

"I'm pregnant," Sam blurted, the first time she'd ever spoken the words. No more secret. No more "little thing" to be removed from her body like a tumor or an infection. Hearing the words was like taking off a backpack full of an entire year's worth of textbooks.

The relief didn't last. It was swallowed by a terror that sent her heart racing into her throat.

I can't join her army with a baby.

I don't know how to feed a baby.

I can't even take care of myself.

What hit her next wasn't an emotion so much as a revelation: *I have a choice.*

She'd never considered choice before. She'd asked Lucas what to do. When he didn't answer, she'd asked Mia. Once the idea to abort was in her head, she never questioned it. Now, however, she could choose.

Irrationally, surrounded by these killers, herself a fugitive, she wanted the life within her to see the world. Maybe even a better world than the one around her today.

"Sam?" MacKenzie said.

"I'm pregnant," Sam repeated. "That's why I was in the contest. I needed the money to get it taken care of before Enrollment Day. Off chart. The only way I could earn Citizenship. I had to serve so we could get a new Port. So I could get a better job. Take care of Mom and Dad." She was fighting tears. Not tears of weakness. They were of sadness. Regret. Anger. She was angry at herself for being so blinded to think Citizenship and a Port was more important than life itself. "Stupid, right?"

"You're sure?"

"I stole a pregnancy test from work," Sam said. "Two of them, actually."

"You shouldn't be."

"I know."

"No, you don't," MacKenzie said. "Do you know what Lito is, I mean what it really is?"

Sam was startled to find she hadn't been thinking of her medicine. In fact, it had been a day and half since she'd had a dose and felt none the worse. Maybe a little better even, clearer, than before.

"It's a brain wash," MacKenzie said. "A mob control device. That's the whole point, as much as God or Belief. It's about our freedom both from them and from our need for their approval. Keeping you from getting pregnant too young is part of that."

Keeping you from getting pregnant.

"No, that's not what they told me," Sam said, feeling ill. "That's not what they told us."

"They need you to serve, not think. Not know. They need you to be pliable, not protective."

"This doesn't make sense. It...it..."

Sam ran to the bathroom and vomited in the toilet. Each heave brought up doubt and fear until she was shaking. Reina whined at her feet, but MacKenzie never came in to check on her. When she came out of the bathroom, legs weak and eyes still teary, MacKenzie was sitting on the bed, her face emotionless.

"Feel better?" she said.

"I've been on Lito since elementary school," Sam said. "I shouldn't be pregnant."

"No, you shouldn't."

"Will it...hurt the baby?"

"I don't know."

Sam thought those three words were scarier than anything else she'd heard in the last few days.

"How do you know all this?" she asked.

"They said my aptitude was top of the charts for combat and counterintelligence," MacKenzie said, as if discussing the weather. "The shit I saw during my training—and that was just the stuff they cleared us for in basic—I knew something was wrong with the Republic. I knew it in my soul, so I dug where I wasn't supposed to dig. They'd already taught me how."

Sam barely heard the last part. She'd been struck by a single word. "You believe in the soul?"

MacKenzie nodded. "I went AWOL a couple weeks before the end of my Citizen's Duty. Unplugged completely."

Sam became aware she was tapping her belly. Self-consciously, she stopped.

"Lito was invented for blood tracking," MacKenzie said. "Like your dog, with the chip, but in the blood. Completely undetectable except by those who put it there and know the exact chemical makeup. A few parts per million is all. The initial trials were for keeping tabs and prepping assassinations. All it needed was direct injection. A cover operative giving a vaccine or taking a blood test. Whatever. The whispers around it were that larger doses might be the first step toward genetic upgrades. That it could influence muscles, nerves, even signals to and from the brain. No micro-bots or whatever science fiction dreamed of. Straight legit organic interface."

Sam flexed her hands into fists as if that might allow her to feel the Lito that was still in her blood. Or squeeze it out.

"Relax. That's not what you were taking. That first gen stuff was all theory. All for the Republic's domination of its people. Imagine what a team of Agents could do if they were faster and stronger because of that shit rolling in their veins."

"But..."

"But why track you, or why aren't you a super spy?" MacKenzie said, finishing Sam's question. "Because like I said, it was all theory. It didn't work. Except for the birth control part. They kept that and handed off the rest to a different team. Turns out the side effects of a steady dosage are almost as useful as what they originally envisioned. It's non-binding, so there's no withdrawal, but if you can get a person, or a population, to take it persistently, it's like a super benzo without the lethargy, memory loss, or suicide risks. Plus, like I said, it regulates ovulation. The *coups de grâce*, however, is it numbs the desire to disbelieve."

"What does that mean?"

"It's like truth serum in reverse. It makes a person lazy when it comes to debate and logic. The presented information or solution becomes easy to accept. They tried it in the military, but it made us too docile. They went civilian next. You were, what, eleven when they started giving it to you, probably in school, right?"

Sam had been ten but there was no need to quibble over such a point. "You're talking about drugging my whole generation. There's no way. That can't be legal. It can't be true. It doesn't make sense."

"What the Republic does in the name of itself isn't beholden to legality or sense. Your eyes have to be open now after what you've seen, even just these couple days. We're the lucky ones. We can still open our eyes. Opt out. The next generation, they'll have IVs in them before the cord is cut. Lito instead of mother's milk. Think about it. If we don't take down this government now, revolution won't be possible."

It was insane. Lies from a fugitive. A terrorist. But Sam knew that was denial rearing its head in a last-ditch attempt to salvage its own indoctrination. She thought of the news report she'd seen in her house. The lies. Real lies. Not truths that were hard to accept.

They tried it in the military, but it made us too docile, MacKenzie had said a moment ago.

Us. She had been a test subject. A forced Lito junkie on the militarized version of the stuff. A programmed assassin?

MacKenzie got up. Reina bounced off the bed and nudged Sam with her cold nose. Sam rubbed her snout while the General, this scary terrorist woman who had been nicer to her in the last few minutes than her own father had in years, unzipped her sweater and took it off revealing a black vest with side clasps— some kind of body armor, Sam guessed—over a maroon shirt. She took off the vest then pulled her shirt over her head.

She stood, shoulders back, in military-style pocketed pants and a black bra and nothing else. She was the strongest, best proportioned, woman Sam had ever seen. From her stomach to her neck, muscles tensed and relaxed like the pulsing embodiment of power.

No wonder Rafe likes her, Sam thought. She was easily the most attractive woman Sam had ever seen. Not pinup beautiful. Just undeniably attractive, like a gravitational pull. She made Sam feel like a half-formed lump of Play-Doh.

On her left shoulder, where the seam of her shirt would be, was the first tattoo Sam had ever seen. The size of a fist, it looked like a horseshoe with a crooked X in its void.

MacKenzie turned to show her left side.

At first, Sam thought it was a flesh-colored bandage covering her, hip to armpit. She raised her arm. It was no bandage. It was a wound. A rippling pattern that reminded Sam of a burn, narrowest at her hip and armpit, widest at her waist, stretching almost to her belly button like a pointing finger. Like she'd been dragged behind a car for miles.

Mackenzie continued the turn, showing off her back. If the wound was surprising, her back tattoo was astonishing. Two columns of beautiful script, unmatched by any penmanship Sam had ever seen, even with most of the first column obliterated by the scar. She had no idea what it was or what the lack of text beside the VI meant, but it didn't matter. Beauty was beauty.

"What happened?" Sam asked.

MacKenzie put her arm down. "Burst rounds. Outlawed by every nation on the planet. The REC uses them on special occasions. I'm a fairly special occasion. She pulled the waist of her pants down a couple inches to reveal a single pink scar separated from the rest of the damage.

"On my team," MacKenzie said, "they tested the Lito by direct infusion into the bone marrow. Here." She traced the scar with her fingertip.

Sam's stomach fluttered, the way someone who got faint at the sight of blood might react to an open wound. "How? I mean, the FDA and the government…secret birth control; secret testing on people. Citizens. It's insane. How can nobody know?"

"See," MacKenzie said. "A couple days ago, when you were on your Lito, you would have taken what I said as true just because we were in the same room. Now you're questioning."

It made no sense. Or did it make too much sense? Trying to figure it out—to wrap her brain around the proof within the questioning—made Sam's head reel.

"Don't stress on it," MacKenzie said. "Our latest intel says mandatory Lito distribution is still only out west and down south here. Another year or two until implementation back east. Probably the Northeast Metro Corridor first. Nail the core first."

Sam wanted to say something. To show conviction. Strength. Sympathy for MacKenzie's wounds. But what came out of her mouth was, "Do you think now that you're together, you and Rafe will, you know, be together?"

It was the wrong thing to say. She knew it before she said it. She knew it as she was saying it, but she couldn't stop herself.

"He doesn't want me," MacKenzie said. Deadpan. So monotone it seemed rehearsed.

"It's not that bad," Sam said, thinking MacKenzie meant that Rafe didn't want her because of her damaged body.

"Listen to me, Sam. I can keep you safe. You and your baby. We can, in Horeb."

"Horeb," Sam said, liking the way the unfamiliar word felt. She rubbed her belly a moment before feeling silly and putting her hands at her sides.

MacKenzie looked at her like she was important. Like she was more than a girl in need of rescue. "We'll take care of you. We'll give you the best training. We'll help you raise your child. You can both be a part of changing this country. Your kid can grow up free. Isn't that what you want?"

"I think so," Sam said. It was too much to consider at once. She'd only decided moments ago to keep the baby she'd previously wanted to abort. Or, had she decided? She was confused. Tired. She felt like if she didn't stop thinking she would vomit again.

"It's a lot to take in. I'm going to shower and redress my leg. You should get a little sleep. This is going to get harder before it's done." MacKenzie entered the bathroom and closed the door.

Reina looked at Sam and sneezed.

"Yeah," Sam said, rubbing the dog's neck then rubbing her own belly. "I don't know, either."

CHAPTER 21

Ker, with Reina at his feet, was in the living room watching the news scroll on television and munching on a muffin when Ward came downstairs. He felt renewed, somehow lighter, after his shower and brief nap. The few swallows of bourbon helped also, but he'd brushed his teeth so no one would know.

He'd half expected everyone to be in the dining room already, working through dinner, but that room had been empty on his way through, its large table—it looked like some kind of reclaimed wood stained a heavy oak or sienna—set formally for six. He couldn't remember the last time he'd eaten at a properly set table. The sounds of utensils against pots from the kitchen previewed the coming meal, along with the warm smell of fresh baked bread and the spices of cooking meat.

He nodded to Ker. Ker nodded back, the flickering light from the television elongating his face, making it appear snoutish. Ward found his eye drawn from Ker to the urn on the mantle, as if it had blown a slight breeze across the room, cool against his shorn head.

"They're in the front room," Ker said.

Ward's stomach grumbled. Reina snorted.

"Me too," Ker said.

Ward found himself compelled to sit with Ker and talk. It was an odd compulsion. He'd never been one to seek out friends. The closest friend of his adult life had been Ken Hickey, the result of nothing more than officemate assignments at Carroll University.

And look how that turned out, he thought, trying not to feel his hand plunge the Spear of Destiny into his former friend's chest. Not to feel the way Ken's flesh had resisted at first then accepted, almost hungrily drew in, the blade.

"See you," Ward said.

He headed for the front room where Oren, Sam, and MacKenzie were spread out on a large sectional couch in the parlor, a coffee table centered before them. At his appearance in the doorway, their conversation ceased. He rubbed his hand over his head, a new habit he noticed himself developing as he enjoyed the course feel of his shaved head.

"Don't let me interrupt," he said.

"We were just comparing notes on growing up in small desert towns," Oren said.

Sam smiled. "Same boring story."

"I was the same age as Sam when I got pulled into the revolution."

"You were born into it," MacKenzie said, apparently bored with the conversation.

"But I didn't know until I was eighteen," Oren said. "Kept me out of Citizen's Duty too."

"Kind of like what you called Providence, right?" Sam said.

"Close enough."

MacKenzie and Ward exchanged a look. Ward intended his to say, *You should separate them.* Hers was more like, *Kids are idiots.*

Ward sat on the farthest end of the couch, a couple body lengths from Oren, and asked, "What's the plan?"

Before anyone could answer, a woman, her face deeply wrinkled, came in from the dining room, a serving tray held before her. She was at least in her late sixties, barely five feet tall, and wearing a tan shawl over shoulders. She looked like a coat on a stick, but her back was straight, her eyes were wide and lively, and there was a spritely bounce to her walk.

"Baked jalapeño bites," she said, her voice almost girlishly high. "For the guest of honor first, of course." She tottered to Ward, the bites somehow not sliding from the tray.

"No," Ward said. "I'm not—"

"Hungry?" the woman said. "Of course you are. Maybe not like the other one watching the television. He eats like a growing boy. But you, eat. You'll like it."

Ward *was* hungry. What he'd wanted to deny was his label as the guest of honor. The smell of the bites, heady and fresh, pushed him to forget his protest and take one of the breaded bites from the tray.

"Rafe," Oren said. "This is the Grossmutter." He slid closer. "It means –"

Ward was about to tell him he knew what it meant. He'd studied enough German—history, mythology, folklore—to know the term. Before he could speak, though, the Grossmutter shooed Oren aside with the tray then set it on the coffee table.

"We don't whisper to each other, Oren." To Ward she said, "I'm the grandmother."

"My grandmother," Oren said.

There was little, if any, resemblance between the two. The Grossmutter had classic Germanic features, including light skin, a long nose, and thick cheek bones. Oren, however, had more Hispanic features like Sam, his face full of curves rather than angles.

"You are wondering about me and my grandson," the Grossmutter said, no more than the slightest hint of an accent in her S's. "Oren, tend to the meal please. You've heard this story."

Oren got up obediently, casting a look at Sam as he left the room. The Grossmutter sat in Oren's place between Ward and Sam.

"You've heard of the Anusim?" she asked Ward.

He had, though he was a little surprised by her question. "It means 'The Forced Ones.' It refers to the Jews who were forced to convert to Christianity in Europe. Mostly the Sephardi Jews in Spain during the Inquisition. I wasn't aware the General's revolution had Jews."

MacKenzie raised an eyebrow. Sam took a jalapeño bite.

"Many thousand Jews converted. At least a quarter million," the Grossmutter said. "Half that many or more left, dispersing over the course of a century or two. They went east. They went west to the New World. There's a story of the Anusim searching the globe for the last waters of the Temple mikveh. Do you know it?"

Ward shook his head. He knew a mikveh was a bath for

ritual cleansing in Jewish tradition. That much was enough to pique his curiosity given the goal of their orders from the Seer. But he was unfamiliar with any stories about the search for one's water, let alone specifically from the Temple, which he took to mean Solomon's Temple.

Ker, with Reina at his heel, appeared in the doorway as if following the scent of the jalapeño poppers. He chose a seat beside MacKenzie. Reina, limping, went to Sam and rubbed her legs before sitting on the floor beside her.

The Grossmutter continued without acknowledging the new arrivals. "To atone for the sin of hiding their Judaism, in preparation for the Jewish people's return to the Holy Land, a great rabbi sends his three sons into the world to find the vial of water that was hurried away from the Temple, along with the Ark and other treasures, right before its destruction."

"Where's the Temple?" Sam asked.

"Jerusalem," Ward said. "A mikveh is a ritual bath," he added. The Grossmutter's story was beginning to sound familiar, and he wanted the telling to continue without a digression into the full history of the Hebrews from the Old Testament. He hoped it wasn't another version of the Vase of Soissons tale, the quest for a vessel imbued with heavenly powers. Another Pandora's Box or Holy Grail.

"The three brothers travel across land and sea," the Grossmutter said. "But none return. The pilgrimage to the Holy Land is delayed. The Jews of Europe remain scattered. This is my family's story. They settled outside Stuttgart, Germany. One day I was born. I met a boy in school and we fell in love. We got married. And then someone attacked this country."

"Who?" Sam asked.

"You know who. The 2001 attacks. The catalyst for the Republic's very existence. Surely you know that story."

"It's the first story I remember learning in school," Sam said. "The corruption in the big church, whatever it was called, in Rome, and the way it tried to buy the presidency and the way the country finally saw through all the lies of all the churches." She paused. "Is any of that true?"

"Most of it, actually," Ward said.

"Twisted to paint the New Republic Party as heroes," MacKenzie added.

"The revolution against religion wasn't just here," the Grossmutter said. "It came to Europe as well. Not as systematic, not as violent, but scary nonetheless, especially for Jews. We've always been the first target. Quickly there was no differentiation between one Middle Eastern religion and another. *Glaubieren*, they shouted. *Faith-fuckers* is what they were calling us. Masturbators of religion."

Sam blushed.

"My husband and I were told by relatives—Anusim who had settled here in Texas and across the border generations ago—that America was safer. How could we know that the news here had already told of bloodshed in Europe just to make home seem safer? So, we came, two Jews, believing that the question of religious affiliation on the immigration papers was standard bureaucracy. Do you know about the Registries?" the Grossmutter asked Sam.

"The watch lists. They kept an eye on anyone with ties to enemies of the Republic, or America I guess it was still called."

"But they don't teach you who got to decide what 'enemy' meant," Ward said.

"It meant everyone not in the New Republic Party," MacKenzie added.

"I knew about lists," the Grossmutter said. "Lists and yellow stars and trains and gas chambers. My Grossmutter taught us that lesson she learned from the Nazis, but I never thought twice about those immigration forms."

"The Nazis, that's World War II, right?" Sam said.

"Yes. And what they did to Jews, this country did to all Believers."

"They took your husband," Ward said, seeing where the story was going.

"I was afraid and hid. He wasn't and shouted that it wasn't right. He is dead. I am not."

"The urn on the mantle."

"Yes."

"I am sorry."

"I hid for three nights," the Grossmutter said, her voice growing stronger as she told her story. "Across the border. Back then it wasn't much more than a fence. Back then it was for keeping brown people out, not keeping Americans in. I hid and I cried. But I remembered the stories my Grossmutter told me. About how so few fought because they believed surely it would pass. About how so many died. About how she hid. How she soon enough decided to fight. From the forests. From the underground. Every bullet a vengeance. She fought with the Baum Group, if you know them, Rafael."

"I do," Ward said, familiar enough to know it was a resistance movement named for their leader Herbert Baum, and that most of the group was caught and killed by the Nazis. He asked the Grossmutter to continue. Her story was immersive, her telling captivating. She seemed to de-age as she told it.

"What did you do?" Sam asked.

"I took his ashes. I took a nice urn from that place, that office where they stored the remains from the Crematorium. Not a fancy one. Gabriel didn't like fancy. I took them at night, and I burned the building to the ground."

Ward couldn't help but enjoy the old woman's nerve. MacKenzie inched forward on the couch.

"All that for his ashes?" Sam asked. The look on Sam's face was like a child listening to a fairytale, an older, less sanitized version of a story she loved from childhood. Enraptured and terrified.

"For love," the Grossmutter said. "For right. For revolution. Like my Grossmutter, whose title I bear with honor."

"Not for Belief?"

"God watches, but I am not one to whom He speaks. I have no taste for the trappings of His temples and the people who run them. If He is just, then my love awaits in the World to Come. I can hate that long as well. This you understand, yes?"

The question was asked to Sam, but it was out there for all of them. Ward wanted to say no. He knew too many afterlife legends, including the Jewish idea of Olam Ha-Ba, the World to Come, to which the Grossmutter had referred, to think one was truer than the others. In fact, he wasn't even sure he believed in such a thing as a soul at all, but he could feel something buried in his gut grow warm. Threaten to ignite. To return him to the mindset that had walked him into the Tower with enough explosives to demolish three buildings each twice its size. He thought of his mother. His father. His brother most of all. He'd walked into the Tower that day hoping to find the location of the Labor Camp. To rescue his brother. Instead he'd learned about the prisoner revolt and the aftermath. Instead, he'd burned it to the ground.

"Yes," he said. "I understand."

Ker, who Ward had almost forgotten was in the room, broke his silence. "As do I."

"We all understand," MacKenzie said.

The Grossmutter stood. "Enough for now. Let us enjoy a good meal and some moments of peace before we rejoin the fight. Revolution on an empty stomach satisfies no one."

CHAPTER 22

By the time the main dish was served, Ward wasn't sure he could put any more food in his body. His only complaint was that MacKenzie denied the Grossmutter's offer for wine with the meal. When the two-foot carne asada steak was placed on the table, however, he forgave MacKenzie. The smell of the char and the lemon and lime and garlic made his mouth water. He took a small cut. Then another. If he'd ever eaten a more filling, more satisfying meal he couldn't remember it. He wondered if this was the feeling inmates on death row got from their last meal.

"I marinated it myself," the Grossmutter had said when she cut the first piece, not wasting humility on the meal. "Family secret, so don't ask, but there's no store-bought bottles in this house."

When dessert came—a choice between apple and peach pies as well as an assortment of tiny cookies and glazed buns the Grossmutter called *schnecken*—Ward thought he might actually damage himself if he ate much more, so he limited himself to a single plate full, then sat back while Oren and the Grossmutter cleared the table, as she'd refused to allow anyone else to help. Ward lounged uncomfortably, wondering how uncouth it would be if he unbuttoned his pants to breathe a little.

"Going to make it?" MacKenzie asked.

"Maybe," Ward said, looking around the table. Sam's eyes drooped. MacKenzie was breathing heavier than she did after a fight. Only Ker appeared unaffected; though he'd eaten at least as much as Ward, he seemed pleasantly sated and ready for more if it came. "That last cookie might have done me in."

Sam said, "You sure it was the last one and not the ten before it?"

Ward gave her his best annoyed-little-brother sneer and shifted in his chair to find a more comfortable angle for his full belly.

"What's the plan now?" Ker asked.

"Sleep," Oren said, coming in from the kitchen to clear more plates. "You're going to need it."

MacKenzie said, "Not until I can breathe. I don't think I'm ever going to eat again."

From the kitchen, her voice carrying over the sound of the sink water running, the Grossmutter said, "Oren, get the *kartenspielen.*"

"It's okay, Grossmutter," he replied. "We don't need to play."

The Grossmutter appeared in the doorway, her finger up as if to say both, *Don't question me, boy,* and *I don't need to be told what you do and do not need,* at the same time.

Oren ducked into the kitchen, the Grossmutter following him. He returned with a palm-sized red and black patterned box and slapped it onto the table between Ker and Ward. Sam guffawed and leaned across the table to grab it before Ward could see what it was.

"It's been a while," Ker said with a clap of his hands.

The sink shut off. The Grossmutter floated into the room in her spritely way. Reina scampered to her.

"Enjoy," the Grossmutter said. "I'll be in my room for what little sleep old women get."

She patted Reina's head, who whined and padded over to Sam.

"What is it?" Ward asked.

"Playing cards," Sam said.

Her joy was obvious. Childish and contagious. It reminded Ward of the way Daniel used to get over simple things like lollipops or an extra ten minutes playing in the yard.

"What, like real cards?" Ward said.

"I didn't think anyone had them anymore," she said. "I used to play all the time with my dad."

She opened the deck and fanned through the cards. Ward

had never seen an actual deck before. Not that they were illegal. The casinos throughout the Republic simply didn't use real cards or dice anymore. At least not at the low stakes kiosks and tables he preferred. Gambling had never struck him as much of a useful pastime compared to reading a good book, especially one from the Carroll University lockdown storage. Ken Hickey, his former officemate and friend, had been the player, tackling a game of hold 'em player on his Port between classes or at the casino kiosk in The Barrel, their preferred pub.

When he did play, Ward's preferred game was blackjack. It was a simpler game. Elegant. More chance and less skill, meaning better winnings for a rank amateur who rarely bet more than a dollar a hand.

"Does anyone else know how to deal?" Ker asked.

Everyone's attention turned to Sam.

"Me?" she said, putting the deck back on the table. "No, I don't know how to deal. My dad had a deck when I was a girl, that's all. We played fish and—what was it called?—face off or slap war or whatever."

"She only ever taught me to shuffle, not how to deal," Oren said of the Grossmutter.

Ker swept up the deck. "Poker then?"

"Why not?" MacKenzie said, surprising Ward with her interest in such a trivial distraction.

"What are we betting?" Sam asked.

From the stairs, the Grossmutter's voice danced to them. "If you're hungry, there's more snacks in the fridge."

Oren laughed. For the first time he appeared to Ward like a person, not some stock character in a bad spy noir novel. For the first time also, Ward thought Oren was watching Sam more than MacKenzie.

Not that he found Oren's interest in Sam less troublesome than his interest in MacKenzie. But this, at least, wasn't jealousy he felt. It was more protective. Fatherly?

Call it big-brotherly, he thought.

Oren went to the kitchen, calling back, "There's more *schnecken*, or we've got carrots and celery and stuff. Make it fridge stakes? What do you want to bet, veggies or sweets?"

"Grab the veggies," Sam said. "I'll help."

MacKenzie and Ward watched Ker shuffle the deck with a dexterity that bordered on magic, or at least sleight of hand. Sam and Oren returned, hands full, and placed before each player a pile greens, reds, and oranges. Sam took her seat. Oren traded his previous spot at the foot of the table for the Grossmutter's place at the head.

"I was thinking," Sam said, "we could do carrots for one, celery for five, broccoli for ten, and the cherry tomatoes for a hundred each."

"Perfect," Ker responded for the group, and began dealing to his left—Oren, Sam, MacKenzie, then Ward. "Stud, five card, to get us started. Sound good?"

"What's stud?" Sam asked.

"Basic poker. Pairs, straights, same suits. Nothing wild?" Ward said.

"Wild is later," Ker replied. "Carrot to ante."

He pushed a carrot to the middle of the table. The others followed suit. The game was on. The first hands were evenly spread. Ker won three; everyone else won at least one. When he called the change to hold 'em, everyone's veggie piles were roughly equal, though Ker's had a bit more celery than the rest.

They played for hours, each finding brief win streaks before Ker began to dominate. He won just small enough, and lost just often enough, to keep Ward from believing he was cheating. Probably.

"You swear you're not hustling us?" Ward asked at one point after Ker squashed a flush by Oren with a full house.

"Truth?" Ker asked.

"That'd be nice."

"I have no more experience with this game than anyone else my age might."

"It's magic then?" Oren asked.

Sam laughed.

"You believe truth when you hear it," Ker said to Ward, "don't you?"

Ward didn't like the way Ker looked at him, so he shrugged

and focused on his cards. They played on.

More than an hour later, Ward became aware of how quiet MacKenzie had gotten. She sat calmly, thinking her way through each bet, each new card, each permutation of possibility. It was so unlike the cyclone of movement, action and reaction, instinct without forethought, that usually characterized her. She was almost serene.

Almost.

Her eyes spoke of a tempest within. He had no idea if she'd ever gambled before, but he could see the conflagration of addiction in her blood. A fire he knew all too well. One, he noted, he should keep an eye on.

"Two hundred and seventeen," Sam said, pushing her entire pile of veggies into the middle of the table.

For a moment, Ward was lost. Had they skipped his turn? Had he folded and forgotten?

He looked around the table, reacquainting himself with the current game. Oren had folded. MacKenzie's jaw flexed. Sam yawned.

"Rafael Ward," Ker said. "Your turn."

"Right," Ward said. He didn't want to do the work figuring out what each player had and what they might build. Not without a drink first. He pushed all but a few of his veggies into the pot. "You guys can figure out the math."

"It's a raise of three hundred and twenty-one," Ker said.

MacKenzie shoved her full pile forward. "You're an ass."

Ker slid what Ward accepted was the correct number of veggies to call.

Sam showed her cards, a jack and a queen. Ward turned over his and was almost surprised to find he had three nines.

MacKenzie threw her cards on the table. "Dick."

Oren chuckled.

"Close," Ker said and showed his five and eight.

"Another straight?" Oren said, no longer laughing. "Someone check his sleeves."

Ker held up his hands as if he might offer his sleeves, then showed Oren his middle finger. This time MacKenzie laughed. For a moment, Ward felt like he was with old friends. Like this could be any night of a simple life in the years before he'd been recruited by the REC.

"One more?" Ker said. "All or nothing?"

The nostalgia disappeared. Ward was gripped by the desire—no, the need—to beat Ker, like it was his duty to put the tech specialist in his place.

"Yes," Ward said. "But someone else deals."

Ker agreed.

"And we play blackjack."

Ker smiled, big and toothy, like the Big Bad Wolf grinning at Little Red Riding Hood.

"Excellent." Ker collected the cards and held them out for whoever wanted them.

Ward hoped MacKenzie would volunteer, trusting she would keep the game as fair as possible, but it was Oren who grabbed the deck.

"Got it," he said.

Sam got up from the table, Reina at her heel.

"Where are you going?" Oren asked

"No veggies left. I'm going to bed," Sam said.

"Stay," Oren said. "One more hand. Here, play with these." He pushed his remaining carrots to her.

"No, I'm done." She paused. "But I'll watch one more."

"Good," Oren said. He offered his carrots to MacKenzie, who took them. "Now I'm out too. Concentrate on this dealing thing. Hope I get it right."

The three remaining players anteed in. Oren, efficiently enough, dealt each player two cards, one face up and one face down.

MacKenzie shoved her carrots to the center of the table and said, "No time for pussies. All in. Hit me."

Everything would have been different, Ward thought before he could stop himself, *if she'd stayed with me on that beach.*

The idea was such juvenile revisionist bullshit that Ward immediately wanted to drain a bottle of anything strong enough to make himself vomit.

He pushed his remaining veggies in with MacKenzie's. Ker did the same. Oren dealt her a Jack. She flipped her hidden card. Twenty-three. Bust. She tossed her cards at Ker, the action nonchalant but her irritation obvious.

"Looks like I'm with you, Sam," she said.

Oren finished the deal, giving Ward drew an eight and Ker a three.

"Want to make it more interesting?" Ker asked.

"What do you have in mind?" Ward said.

"Truth."

MacKenzie snorted. "How about a duel?"

Reina chirped as if laughing then stretched and yawned.

"Death is nothing compared to the truth," Ker said.

Ward sensed an angle to Ker's proposed bet, but he couldn't figure what it was. He couldn't reconcile how ominous it felt with Ker's easy-going charisma.

"Sure thing, man," Ward said, letting his curiosity outweigh his common sense. "Truth."

Eyes on Ker, Ward rolled over his seven, showing a total of nineteen. He felt good, if not confident. Ker had a three and a Queen showing. If his face-down card was anything other than a seven or an eight, Ward had his victory. And truth, whatever that meant. The only truth he could think of was that he didn't care about the stakes of this hand. He wanted to beat Ker for the sake of beating him.

Ker turned over his card.

A seven.

"For God's sake," MacKenzie said. "The bastard *is* magic."

Oren made it clear with a huff he didn't like MacKenzie's use of God's name in vain. She either didn't notice or didn't care. Ker seemed to enjoy the unspoken exchange for a moment then shifted his attention to Ward.

"Are you ready?" Ker asked.

The night felt suddenly very late. Ward rubbed his palms into his eyes. "For what, a game of truth or dare?"

"The truth is the dare," Ker said. "Why did you destroy the Tower?"

The room grew hot. Ward didn't remember it being hot, but beads of sweat now tickled his brow.

"I don't want—"

"No," Ker said. He seemed like a different person. The charm shed like a winter coat. "We bet. Answer truth."

"Truth?" Ward said, like the word was unfamiliar.

"Truth!"

"I was angry," Ward shouted. He felt as if he'd been badgered for hours on the subject, like he had to tell everything he could to end the interrogation. "They took everyone from me. Everyone. That company, agency, whatever the fuck you want to call it, they did it. I don't give a shit about your beliefs or theirs. It all kills people. All of it." The words kept coming. "I wanted answers, I wanted my brother back, but I didn't go in to destroy it. I didn't do it to be your symbol. I went in for answers, but the only truth in there was that they killed my brother in that Labor Camp."

"You did it because they took your brother from you. You went in ready to do it. That's not anger. That's planning."

"I wasn't going..." Ward couldn't finish. He'd told himself a hundred times he hadn't gone in to do it. To kill all those people. He'd repeated the lie over and over: when he'd logged into the REC mainframe and saw the files, the details about the fire, about the slaughter, he'd lost his mind. He'd taken down the whole thing.

He'd let himself believe the rage did it, but that was a lie. Ker was right. He'd gone into that building for revenge right from the start. Wrestling that confession to the surface, even if it was only to himself, was exhausting. He wanted to lie down. He needed a drink.

"What makes your family worth killing for?" Ker asked. "What makes other families worth dying for yours?"

Ward didn't have an answer. The silence around the table was like smoke, choking and blinding.

"Truth," Ker said with a shrug. He left the table and went upstairs.

After a moment, Oren left. Ward felt like he was in the middle of a contest between Sam and MacKenzie to see who would stay and who would go. Reina whined. Sam shifted in her chair. Maybe to pet her dog. Maybe to leave. It didn't matter. Ward didn't want what was coming soon. The questions. The support. The critique. Whatever it was, he didn't want it.

He wanted a drink.

"Just go," he said. "I'm fine. Go upstairs, both of you."

Sam looked at MacKenzie then said, "Okay." She headed upstairs, Reina limping after her.

"I don't think she knows if she likes you enough to stick around for your bullshit yet," MacKenzie said.

He tried to defend himself, but no words came out of his mouth. She left. He was alone.

Good. Now I can drink, he thought, but he didn't get up.

He sat for more than an hour, feeling like he'd slipped into a void where time didn't matter. Or didn't exist. A place of thinking without thinking.

Or had he slept, passed out with his chin in his hands?

Whatever the case, he finally went into the kitchen for a drink. He found an assortment of wines but no hard liquors. He took the first open, but mostly full, bottle he found and drank half of it in three long swallows. It was good, very sweet with a tart aftertaste, but not nearly enough to slake his thirst. He thought about going upstairs for his backpack, for those two-ounce sample bottles, but he didn't want to risk running into someone who might want to talk. Risk versus reward. He decided sleeping on the couch in the parlor would be best, even if he was mostly sober.

On his way through the living room he stopped before the fireplace. The always-on television flickered its inconsistent light across the mantle. He squinted his way from left to right, down the line of framed photos with the urn in the center. Most of the pictures were faded, some on autostock paper from those pre-digital cameras—the ones that spit the photo out right after you took it. He saw young children in various poses from oblivious play to "Stand still for the camera." One of them could have been the Grossmutter herself, a lifetime ago in a faraway country.

One, however, drew Ward back after he'd reached the end. It was a simple headshot of a handsome young man with bright eyes, a square jaw, and delicate cheekbones. The young man looked familiar. He hadn't on Ward's first glance, but he did now. He switched on the light.

His vision twisted. He reached for the photo, knocking a different frame to the floor.

He knew this man. Had seen him how many times in the last few years? The homeless man who'd directed him to the abandoned high school. The old man on the precipice over the Mediterranean with all that blood, and the Vase of Soissons watching. The friendly man in the bar that night he'd had drinks with Ken Hickey, the last night they'd spent as friends.

"That's Gabriel," the Grossmutter's said, startling Ward. She stood in the doorway as if she'd always been there. "I don't sleep much either."

"No," was all Ward could utter.

"No?"

"Who is this?" Ward asked.

The Grossmutter put out her hand for the photo. "I told you. Gabriel. My husband. You don't seem well."

Ward handed it to her, amazed at how his own hand shook. "Who is he really?"

"Really?" she repeated, rolling the word. Confused. Concerned, but not for Ward. For the man in the photo.

"I know him," Ward said, trying not to shout.

The Grossmutter clutched the photo to her chest. Concern turning to defense. Threatening anger. "The dead deserve to rest."

"What about the living? What about me? I'm not crazy."

The anger came. Then went like a passing shadow on a mostly cloudless day. The Grossmutter's face smoothed. Offering caring, if not understanding. "All answers are found with Him," she pointed to the ceiling.

"And if there is no Him?" Ward said. "No after?" He wondered if this was truly what he believed.

"Then my Gabriel is here." She tapped the photo. "And here." She pointed to the urn. "But," this last with steel in her voice, "you are mistaken."

"I'm sorry," Ward said, his head—his whole being—bowed. "But I know him. His face. I've seen him too many times."

Or am I losing my mind? he thought.

You need a drink.

I need to get away from all of this. Myself and Sam, get us away. Never come back.

"You need sleep," the Grossmutter said. She turned her back. Hobbled toward her bedroom. From somewhere in the darkness her voice returned. "If it is him you've seen then you know what to Believe. And what to do."

Ward's head spun. His thoughts became translucent. He couldn't remember...something. The old woman's husband? Had she said his name? Grabbing for answers made his head hurt. He remembered he was tired. He stumbled into the parlor and flopped onto the couch and waited for sleep to take him.

CHAPTER 23

The supermarket was nice. Shiny, almost slick, tile floors. Vaulted ceiling. Everything in its place. Ward could tell the store's upkeep was a source of pride for whomever ran it.

"Our people," Oren had said. Whatever that meant. Cashiers, shift supervisors, managers, whoever.

Oren led them into the butcher's work area behind saloon-style swinging doors. Three block-top tables were stained dark with the blood of Eagle Pass's fine meats. The smell of iron and copper hung in the humid air.

"Down here," Oren said, opening a door to a stairwell.

Sam, closest to him, hesitated.

"She's fine, Sam," Oren said.

At the Grossmutter's insistence, and with MacKenzie and Oren's prodding, Sam had agreed to leave Reina behind. Still limping, she would have hampered their speed. Then again, Ward had argued, the same could be said for both his and MacKenzie's limps. He didn't like it—he would never be able to keep Sam safe if she had a reason to return to the Republic— but he'd been quickly voted down. Even Ker, who was clearly unhappy with the decision though he voiced his support for it, insisted that Reina would be better off with the Grossmutter and the mission would be better served without her.

"You'll be back soon enough, child," the Grossmutter had said. "Reina will be safe and well-mended when you return. I promise."

Reina had offered an approving nip of a bark. Sam's goodbye had been teary but brief. Ker's had been longer, ending with him hugging Reina's neck and receiving a hearty lick on the cheek.

Ward's flashlight glinted off new tears in Sam's eyes as she nodded her acceptance of Oren's statement and followed him down the stairs.

"Truth is," Oren said when they'd all gathered at the bottom in a small locker room complete with two shower stalls and a top-bottom washer-dryer unit, "we think this was actually intended as a smuggling tunnel before the Civil War."

"The Underground Railroad," Sam said.

Like a good student, Ward couldn't help but think.

"Exactly," Oren said. "They probably hit bedrock and abandoned it."

"Where's the tunnel?" MacKenzie asked.

Oren reached behind the dryer. There was a loud click. He motioned Ker over and the two of them pushed the washer-dryer, which was on casters, into the corner, revealing a square steel plate in the floor with a receded handle. Oren grasped the handle and turned it clockwise then counter-clockwise two rotations. It clicked. He opened the hatch. Climbed into the darkness followed by Sam, Ker, MacKenzie, then Ward.

A ladder in the tunnel wall lowered them twenty or so feet into a crouching tunnel. A sewer line. It smelled, though not as awful as Ward expected. In fact, it was almost sickeningly sweet and strong. For a moment, his equilibrium shifted. The tunnel and the room around him seemed to spin. In that dizziness, he was attacked by the dread he'd felt in Italy, in the sewers beneath the Basilica di San Nicola, when MacKenzie had been swept away. Out to her death, Ward had thought. His failure to keep her safe had made him sick.

That sickness was smothering him now. Not for MacKenzie. For Sam. He recalled how she'd reminded him of Daniel when she held the deck of cards in her hands at the Grossmutter's house. He understood, finally, what he'd seen in her from the start. She was so much like his brother, it was painful to think about the danger he was putting her in. How each step they took brought him closer to failing her. To losing her. To preventing her from having the life Daniel could have had.

Not this time, he thought, battling the urge to vomit. *Not her too.*

Oren climbed back up the ladder and pulled the hatch closed. MacKenzie lit the way for his second descent. He then took the lead, his flashlight finding Lacalle crouched ahead a few minutes later. The quiet man, bowler hat still perched on his head, waved them forward, then took up the rear position of the procession. Soon they'd passed through a hole in the sewer lining into a new tunnel hewn from bedrock. This tunnel dipped hard, and the downslope was slick. Ward lost his footing more than once.

"We're below the river, now," Oren said.

He shone his flashlight on the ceiling above. The dark rock glistened. Ward touched it, expecting his hand to come away wet. Instead, he felt a semi-soft plastic-like coating.

"We've been lining the tunnel with an a-therm coating, like a spray paint," Oren said. "So far it's kept the tunnel from appearing as a void when we run scans. Of course, our handheld units are nothing like what they have on The Wall. If theirs are that much stronger..." He shrugged.

The tunnel soon began to feel like it was narrowing. Ward, his heart galloping, pushed to the front of the line behind Oren, keeping his palms on the walls to his sides. Its width remained consistent, but that fact didn't calm him.

"How much longer?"

Ker, who'd not said much since they'd gone underground, said, "What are you afraid of? Don't like being underground?"

"No, not really. Do you?" Ward said over his shoulder, the change in perspective causing him to bump his shoulder into the wall.

"Drinking again?" Ker said, his standard joviality in full swing, though something sharper hissed beneath the surface of his words.

Ward almost fought back, declaring how long it'd been since his last drink, but he knew any time frame less than weeks or months would only call for more mocking.

"How long, Oren?" MacKenzie asked.

"Just ahead."

As predicted, the tunnel turned hard left then stopped. A new man in a flannel shirt sat with his back against the bedrock wall before them. Over his shoulder three yellow blocks each the size of Port stuck out of the stone. The new man got to his feet—here even Ker could stand—and saluted MacKenzie.

"This is Eduardo," Oren said. "We've got two people set to run the distraction timed with these charges in," he looked to Eduardo, who held up two fingers, "about two minutes. The plan is we back up around that corner and when the charges go we run."

"That's a plan?" Sam said.

"That's what happens when we have to put it all together in one night." Oren glared at MacKenzie.

She didn't flinch.

"Keep your lights on. Go single file. Eduardo and Lacalle will lead. It's like the opposite of what we just came through. The tunnel links into a sewer then a dead end with a ladder. Climb up. Stay there."

There was little else to say except to hope the explosion didn't kill them. Hope the tunnel didn't collapse afterwards. Hope they eventually found their way out to a new country that didn't want them dead.

Eduardo said something to Lacalle, who relayed it to Oren. Eduardo held up his hands and splashed his fingers out four times. Forty seconds, Ward deduced. They backed down the tunnel and huddled together while Eduardo continued the silent countdown.

As Eduardo's final two fingers wavered in a flashlight beam, Ward thought he heard gunfire. The distraction. Ridiculous, of course, this far underground.

Then it rumbled closer. Louder. So loud, Ward feared it was making him dizzy again when the tunnel around him seemed to spin. It took a moment to understand it wasn't spinning. The ground beneath his feet was shaking.

Earthquake! his mind shouted.

Then darkness.

Then a ringing in his head so powerful he thought he must have died, for no sound on earth could be that loud.

Then light.

He was lying on his back, covered in dirt and rubble. He

struggled to his knees. Shapes and silhouettes lurched around him.

The explosion, he understood, his brain feeling like it was trying to run a marathon underwater.

MacKenzie's face appeared before him, haloed by smoke and raining gravel. Her mouth was moving but he couldn't hear anything. Then a hum. A ringing that got louder and louder until he thought it might detonate his head.

She grabbed his arm. Yanked him to his feet.

"Run," her silent mouth said. Screamed, probably.

She ran. Ward followed.

Somewhere after his fourth or fifth stumble to the ground, his hands now bruised and bleeding, the ringing subsided enough that he could hear his own heartbeat hammering. He hazarded a glance behind. There was no one. He couldn't remember if he was last in line. It didn't matter. MacKenzie was his way out. He tried to keep up.

The smoke billowed around him, smelling like sulfur and burnt hair. Blinding him for seconds at a time before thinning enough to see his hands and feet and the occasional glimpse of MacKenzie ahead. When he couldn't see, progress choked to a crawl. Even his flashlight couldn't do more than illuminate the smoke. He bumped walls. Stumbled to his knees. Kept his hands out trying to find…

His feet tangled with someone else's crashing them both to the ground.

"You're bleeding," MacKenzie said, pushing him off her.

Only as she said it did Ward's cheek begin to burn. He wiped his sleeve across his face. It came away with blood.

"Stitches maybe," she said. "Not bad. Come on."

She grabbed his hand this time and pulled him along, his flashlight lost somewhere behind them. Eventually, Ward had no idea how long it took, they found Oren and Sam at the dead end. Eduardo, Lacalle, and Ker had already gone up the ladder. Oren and Sam appeared no worse off than MacKenzie. Some small cuts and bruises and lots of dirt caked in their hair and on their faces.

"All whole?" Oren asked.

MacKenzie said that they were. Ward pressed his hand to his cheek, noticing how much warmer his blood was than the air this far underground.

"You two up next," she said to Oren and Sam.

They went as ordered, followed by Ward. The ladder brought him up through a hole in a tiled floor. Oren and Sam huddled in front of an open stall door like in a—

"A bathroom?" Ward said, looking back at the hole he'd climbed through. Once there would have been a toilet there. He was, however, struck by how clean the room was. The tiles polished, glinting in the dull fluorescent light overhead. Even the hole's edges were rounded and sanded to keep any sharp tile fragments from cutting those climbing out. A soft hint of citrus hung in the air, mingling with wafts of smoke coming up from the hole.

The sound of distant thunder cracked. Again.

"The distraction?" Ward asked.

Oren shushed him.

Ker arrived from somewhere outside the stall. "Eddie and Lacey say we've got a window," he said, apparently having given Eduardo and Lacalle nicknames.

MacKenzie, head poking through the hole, tapped Ward's leg to get him to move aside. Oren and Sam exited the stall.

"Romantic," MacKenzie said when she'd pulled herself from the tunnel.

"Where are we and what's next?" Ward asked. He opened one of the other three stalls—noting the lack of urinals and wondering if they were in the women's restroom or if it was simply ungendered—and took a wad of toilet paper. It was old and flaky but enough to dab at his cheek, just above the bone. The blood was clotting, probably helped by all the smoke and debris that had caked his face.

Oren said, "Piedras Negras."

"Black stones," Ward translated. "Coal?"

MacKenzie spoke before Oren could answer. "Now you speak Spanish?"

"Sort of. Latin more than anything, but I can translate enough vocabulary to get by."

"Isn't Latin that old language for, like, the Bible?" Sam asked, hushing her voice further on the last word.

"Actually," Ward said, about to explain the languages of the Old and New Testaments.

"Quiet," Oren said. "We've got a truck waiting, but don't think because we're in Old Mexico we're free. The REC has carte blanche for excursions within a hundred miles of the border."

"Because the Republic asked nicely," MacKenzie said, heavy on the sarcasm.

"It's the only reason Old Mexico continues to exist. It puts us at a disadvantage short term, but in the long term it gives hope. We're still here. When the revolution comes, Mexico is waiting to play her hand."

"The revolution is going to come from here too?" Sam asked.

"Of course," Ker said. "Why shouldn't Mexicans be allowed to die in this war? Columbians too. Guatemalans. Hondurans. Chileans. Even Rafael here."

"What's that supposed to mean?" Ward asked.

"Nothing," Ker said, like he was trying not to laugh. "Nothing at all."

Ward didn't know what to say. Was Ker making a joke about his mother's South American heritage? Could he know such a thing?

"Enough," MacKenzie said. "What's the plan, Oren?"

Oren moved them all to a narrow foyer inside the bathroom entrance. There was a single window, crusted over so that it was barely clear anymore, to the open door's left. Eduardo and Lacalle's silhouettes were backlit against the window by a dull street lamp a block away.

"Three blocks south, one west," he said. "The truck is silver with a blue stripe. Eduardo and Lacalle will go first. Follow them, one at a time. Ten seconds between. Keep low and dark. We're only about forty yards from the river. If anyone on The Wall turns this way they've got line of sight. The truck is on the south side of the church. Get in. Get down."

Lacalle came inside. He reminded Ward of a bouncer at

a bar. Of Claude, the big Frenchman who'd stood by Simon, MacKenzie's father, in Paris. The kind of person he was grateful to have defending Sam and MacKenzie.

"Still good," Lacalle said.

Oren looked to Mackenzie for orders. She nodded. "Go," he said. Lacalle rejoined Eduardo. There was a pause then they ran.

"I've got the rear," Oren said.

The General took charge. "No. Ker go."

He ran out the door.

"Oren now."

He hesitated.

"Sam's with me," MacKenzie said.

Oren's flexing jaw made it clear he wasn't happy with the order, but he went.

"Rafe."

Ward set his feet. "Get her safe first."

He expected an argument. Instead, MacKenzie grabbed Sam above the elbow and ran. Ward watched them go, their silhouettes growing smaller as he counted to ten.

A salvo of machine gun fire from The Wall detonated so loud it knocked Ward off his feet. He rolled to the left wall and scrambled to his knees. The angle didn't allow a clean view through the window. Through the door he could see only shapes. Explosions of gunfire hitting the street, cars, buildings. For a second, Ward's eye got lost in the architecture. The red tile roofs and the earth tone stuccos that were so similar to Eagle Pass, yet so different.

A thick silhouette caught his attention, dashing down the street a block or two away. It split into two. Both zig-zagging. Ducking. One hurtling across the street as if an invisible hand had grabbed it about the midsection and yanked, folding it unnaturally before dropping it against a car.

Ward's legs pushed him. Churned him to the door in a sort of molasses slow motion.

MacKenzie or Sam? They'd been the last ones out. Which one had been hit? He didn't want to know. He didn't think he could face either.

The gunfire ceased. Someone screamed.

Ward catapulted into full-speed motion. Through the door. Toward the car. The body. The fear that he'd be relieved when he saw who it was.

CHAPTER 24

The body had been torn nearly in two. What remained, made more horrific by the pale street light, was ground beef and ichor. Most of the torso was gone. One hand was missing from the wrist. The clothing, tattered and soaked in blood, was unrecognizable. A boot stood upright on the other side of the street.

Thunder burst and crashed around Ward as he stared, vulnerable and uncaring, in the street.

"Rafe," a voice called.

Shredding metal and shattering glass sounded from somewhere near. Ward barely registered it. Whoever was still alive, Sam or MacKenzie, he knew he would hate her. Better to let the machine guns atop The Wall reunite him with everyone he'd failed.

"Down," the voice screamed. Closer now. So close...

Ward turned. Something hit him in the chest. He lost his feet. Was tumbling. Crashing. Rolling. Waiting for the pain. The oblivion.

"Get up, damn it," MacKenzie yelled, her face inches from his.

She'd tackled him. Knocked the wind from his lungs leaving him able to weave only one word: "Sam?"

"With Oren and Ker. Let's go."

Ward didn't believe it. She was telling him lies to get him moving. He was nothing but a symbol, a tool, for her revolution and her Seer. He turned from her. In the direction of the body. He hadn't meant to look there, to see his failure again, but there it was. Inches from his face. Blood and chunks and tatters. A vest.

"Lacalle?"

"He broke off from us to draw their fire," MacKenzie said. "Now get up or we're next."

He let her pull him up. Lead him away from the body. Storefronts and cars exploding behind them as the Republic tried to obliterate those who'd dared abandon it.

Ward wondered about the citizens of Piedras Negras. Were they being slaughtered in their beds by the relentless large caliber assault? Were they so used to this already that they would hide in cellars and churches until the barrage ceased then go about the rebuild in the same impassive way a bus boy sweeps clear a table for the next guests?

"There. Go," MacKenzie said, pointing to the lee of a concrete and whitewashed stucco church. Pushing Ward to the truck.

Eduardo, in the driver's seat, gave a thumbs-up out the window. Pointed to the back of the truck, its bed covered by a windowless cab. Ward dropped the tailgate and faced the muzzle of a gun.

"Safety first," Oren said, lowering his pistol.

"Make room," MacKenzie yelled.

MacKenzie dove head first. Ker caught her arms and dragged her the rest of the way in. Ward climbed in and rolled to the side. Next to Sam. The relief he felt upon seeing her was similar to what he'd felt when he discovered his brother was still alive. Without thinking, he threw his arms around her and squeezed.

She let him hug her for a second, then she squirmed away, her face full of appreciation and confusion.

"Sorry," Ward said.

"He pushed me away."

Ward didn't ask who. He didn't have to. Lacalle. He'd only worried about Sam or MacKenzie being killed. He'd never thought about it being someone else. Tears made his vision blur. He fought them back.

Before Oren closed the tailgate, Ward locked eyes on the church. Its square towers and steeple featured cross-through windows in the style of the nineteenth century missions that defined old western films. It was, Ward imagined, much like what the Alamo would have looked before the battles for Texas's secession from Mexico.

The last thing he saw was the steeple reaching above the town, surely visible from The Wall. A great stone middle finger shouting *Fuck You* to the Republic. It was a wonder the building was allowed to stand. But Mexico was still a nation of Believers—savages who couldn't organize their own way out of a taco stand, according to Republic news outlets—and Ward assumed the decision had been made in some REC conference to allow the primitives their churches. Their illusions. So long as the Republic had freedom to cross the border at will, what difference could it matter if the fools had a church to got to on Sundays?

For the first time in his life, Ward wanted to cross the threshold of a church for more than its architectural beauty. He wanted to sit in a pew. Open a Bible. Find the words, the scrolling Latin his mother had once prayed. The words that had caused him, eleven-year-old Raffi, to call the authorities on her. To complete his orphaning. He wanted to whisper those words for Lacalle. For Ken Hickey. For his parents. For Daniel. For himself because he felt now, more than ever before, that there would be no one there to say them for him when he finally died.

Stop it, he told himself.

It's the truth and you know it.

I'm going to save Sam. To Hell whatever happens after that.

To Hell? Was he a Believer a now?

Someone spoke Lacalle's name, drawing Ward out of his thoughts.

"We can't leave him there like that," Sam said. "He saved my life."

"That's his job," Oren said.

"General?" Sam said, using MacKenzie's title in her search for an ally.

MacKenzie didn't respond.

"Our people will take care of it," Oren said. Possibly a lie. Ward couldn't tell.

"He saved *me.*"

"He'll be buried?" Ker asked.

Oren said he would, his conviction more believable this time.

"Then have no fear, Sam. He will rest well."

Ker's assertion made Ward think of the *Aeneid*. Of Aeneas's helmsman Palinurus, who was left for dead. His body unburied. Condemning him to wander as a shade along the banks of the Cocytus, the River of Wailing, unable to enter the underworld.

There was something more there. Something he should have recognized. Something about their goal. The Seer's riddle. The pyramid...

His thoughts skipped back to Lacalle in his dapper vest, a moaning shade for eternity. He shivered despite the heat packed in the bed of the truck and wondered if it wasn't better to believe that the pain of death was the end. That regret and glory were equally destined to flicker out with consciousness.

A new idea came to him, the way thirst comes unbidden. He dug into his backpack for his collection of sample whiskeys. Found four. Providence, Simon would have said. He handed the bottles around the truck. Raised his. A salute. The others returned the gesture. No one spoke. That was fine. He didn't need words. Neither did Lacalle. Not anymore.

They drank.

CHAPTER 25

The Pyramid of the Sun rose more than two hundred feet into the night. If the cathedrals of Paris had pinched Ward's heart into a pause with their grandeur and architectural bravado, this structure sucked his breath away with its mass. As if it had its own gravity which his lungs could not withstand. Where a couple years ago in Paris Ward had thought, *Look at what men once could do*, tonight he could only wonder what would ever draw architects to steel and synthetics when the Earth offered such potential in stone.

He'd seen pictures of the Avenue of the Dead, of course, during his studies. Its famous Pyramids of the Sun and Moon and Feathered Serpent. Stunning declarations of what the pre-Aztec Teotihuacanos were capable of a thousand years before Europeans arrived. What rose before him was nothing like those textbook photos: framed, lighted, angled to show majesty and power. No, what stood before him, moonlit better than any professional photographer could manage, was a mirage. A painting the way a desert seems not quite real in the distance. Too much to comprehend at an initial impression.

Curiously, what also drew Ward's attention was the marketplace, now closed due to the late hour—it was almost two in the morning—just off the Avenue. Not present in any photo he'd ever seen of the sight, it was clearly the tourist hub of the town that surrounded the Avenue and its monuments.

"Now what?" Oren said.

"You're asking me?" Ward replied.

MacKenzie said, "Ker?"

"The Seer's instructions seem to be for the professor."

Ward rubbed at the stitches over his cheek bone. They'd stopped a couple hours into their drive from Piedras Negras in some city Ward hadn't cared to notice—Saltillo maybe?—for repairs and resupply. A safe house in the back room of a saloon had provided all they'd needed, including the stitches.

"An improvement," Sam had said jokingly, her first words since taking only a sip of her whiskey in the truck before handing the remainder to Ward.

"Definitely," MacKenzie had added, her level of humor impossible to determine.

Now, after having dropped off Eduardo to prep a depot, a safe house, somewhere in town, they stood on the Avenue of the Dead before the Pyramid of the Sun, the final tourists of the day long gone and the lights along the Avenue burning. The pyramid, built in four massive steps, with stairs rising up the middle, was surrounded by a number of smaller stepped structures. Directly in front sat a low dais, like a waiting platform for those who might ascend to whatever altar waited at the top. Or within. On either side of the dais, a booth, like a large ticketing kiosk, was topped with a light that, as a pair, illuminated the plaza before the pyramid.

"I guess we go inside," Ward said.

Oren raised an eyebrow. "How?"

Ward, who could see no entrance or aperture in the structure, pointed at Ker, directing the others to ask him.

Ker simply shrugged and said, "I told you what the Seer's message read. You're the expert, professor. How do we get in?"

"You read me lines from some crap ass poem," Ward said. "That's all I know. What else do you want?"

"What do you think is in there?" Sam asked.

Ward had gone through annoyed right to pissed off at the way Ker and everyone else kept looking to him for answers. "I don't know. A disco ball inside so you can cleanse me in the glitter."

"Stop," MacKenzie ordered. "We're here. We have a mission. Let's figure it out. Oren, what's the town like? What does it offer?"

"Look around," Oren said. "Same as Mexico City, and we

all but pulled out of there. No point. The only recruits were criminals wanting to legitimize their violent streaks. South of Leon went to absolute shit when The Wall went up."

Ward couldn't argue with that assessment. Their arrival and brief drive through the town revealed buildings in disrepair, potholed streets, vandalized traffic signs, and plenty of small stores that looked like they should be condemned. Homes showed extreme neglect, many with tarps over their roofs or lack of roofs. Even the tourists, no more than a few dozen, whereas all the photos Ward had ever seen of the Avenue of the Dead displayed hundreds, seemed beaten down. As if they'd come here to see a different desolation than they were used to and were disappointed.

Far worse than all of that was the Pyramid of the Moon to their left. Ward had been so focused on the Pyramid of the Sun since their arrival on the Avenue he hadn't looked for the smaller pyramid. All he saw where it should have stood was a hill of rubble and the fields and houses beyond it.

"It's gone," he said.

"What?" MacKenzie asked.

"The Pyramid of the Moon. What happened?"

Oren said, "When we withdrew from Mexico City, I sent a team here to scout for recruits and possible way stations. I thought it might be nicely poetic to set camp in an actual temple. Good irony to shove up the Republic's ass. I had six people in there when it came down."

"Earthquake?"

"Someone talked?" MacKenzie guessed.

"No," Oren said, softly. Then, louder, "Someone didn't deliver on her promise for a truck load of a-therm emitters last year."

"Don't give me that bullshit," MacKenzie fired back. "Your people bungled the drop. I'm not taking the blame for them being tailed to the location."

"You were supposed to be there, Hannah."

Ward tensed, waiting for the requisite assault on the use of her first name.

"The tech was dropped as planned. The Seer needed me

somewhere else. If your people did their jobs..."

"My people? Since when is the Seer factioning us off? Or is it that Mexicans are Mexicans and pawns are pawns." They glared at each other. Oren pointed at Ward. "Or was finding him so important as to take the General away from a supply and munitions drop?"

"Yes. It was." Finality in her tone.

A pause. Finally, Oren said, "It's done. They're gone. Buried in the tunnel underneath that thing."

Oren's words reverberated in Ward's head. A map built itself in his mind, a remnant of a memory. A presentation in a classroom. Snaking lines. Topographical markers. A cross section of a building. A pyramid.

"The tunnel," he said.

"What about it?" Oren said.

"Why did you pick that pyramid?"

"The tunnel," Oren said as if the answer was obvious. "It had been closed to tourists since, I don't know, forever. Nothing down there so no one wanted to pay to see it. It was just sitting there underground. Not huge but enough to set a small depot."

"What about the Pyramid of the Sun? What about its tunnel?"

"I didn't know there was one."

"Exactly."

"Exactly what, Rafe?" MacKenzie asked.

"The message the Seer sent. It said the temple rising among the dead. Where do you bury the dead?"

"Underground," Ker said.

"There's a tunnel under there like the other one."

"And a river?" MacKenzie asked.

"No idea."

"What do you mean no idea? I thought this was your thing."

"European history is my thing. The Classical period. Dark Ages into the Renaissance. Other stuff I picked up, I don't know, collaterally. Some survey courses, comparative studies, that kind of thing."

"I don't need your curriculum vitae. What do you know?"

"Basic Mesoamerican mythology. Intro course level stuff.

The Aztecs, and presumably the Teotihuacanos as well, believed the sun and the moon originated within caves in the earth. Humans also from these caves. That's what the Pyramids of the Sun and Moon were for. Honoring the sun and moon and our origins."

"That's it?" MacKenzie said.

Ker wrinkled his nose and cocked his head.

"How do we get in?" Sam asked.

Ward didn't know. He tried recollecting more about the tunnel, but he was tired. It was after midnight and details were coming in flashes, not scrolls of text. A paper about the discovery of human remains scattered with other artifacts, mostly pottery. The tunnel closed due to instability. In fact, the only reason it was discovered in the first place was—

"A sinkhole," Ward said. "The tunnel itself was sealed, on purpose, two thousand years ago. They discovered it near the end of the last century when a sinkhole opened in front of the pyramid."

"Where?"

Ward crossed the dais. Saw nothing but their own shadows cast up the pyramid.

"What's in these?" He pointed at the kiosks.

"Info booths?" Oren guessed.

"Let's find out."

Ward went for the one on the right. It was locked but the mechanism wasn't much stronger than what might be found on a portable toilet. Ward tore it open, snapping the plastic latch. Inside was exactly what Oren had surmised. Stacks of brochures on a small folding table. Boxes of more on the floor. They tried the other booth. This one with a solid metal door and a heavy padlock.

"Shoot it," MacKenzie said.

"Too loud. I told Eduardo to pay off the local PFs but if we start shooting stuff, they're going to get ornery."

"PFs?" Sam asked.

"The *Policía Federal*. They're not REC but that doesn't mean I want to piss them off."

"Hang on," Ker said.

He went back to the other booth. Boxes flew out the door, splattering their contents on the Avenue of the Dead. The sound of breaking followed. A moment later, the tall man emerged holding one of the metal table legs. Tossed it to Oren. Using the leg as a pry bar, Oren pushed on the padlock. Heaved. His face flushed. The leg began to bend. The amount of force Oren was exerting was more than Ward would have been capable of even when he was on Agent Compano's strict training regimen. Back then, a few sets of twenty pushups were no problem. Now, the only exercise he got was walking. The only lifting he did was bottles.

With a final push, just as Ward thought the leg would snap, the strike plate tore off. Oren crashed into the door. Sam helped him regain his feet.

Ward decided, if he survived whatever happened next, he would start working out again. Starting in the morning.

Oren opened the door. The booth was empty, save for a yellowed tarp on the ground. He kicked it aside, revealing a pit with a yellow-runged ladder set into the wall.

Déjà vu, Ward thought. How many tunnels could a man crawl through before he became buried in one?

"Let's go," MacKenzie said.

"Wait," Ward said. Once he found whatever the Seer wanted them to find below the pyramid, he'd lose his leverage. If he was going to guarantee Sam's safety, he had to do so now—even if they were exposed and in danger—before they entered this rabbit hole. "I need a deal first."

"A deal?" MacKenzie said, as if he'd asked for an ice cream and a nap.

"We go in," he said in his best I'm-the-teacher voice. "I take the bath or whatever the Seer needs. I go back to Horeb with you. Be your little poster boy. But only after this guy," he pointed to Oren, "arranges transport for Sam off this continent."

"You said you were going to take me to Canada," Sam said. "With Reina."

Ward understood her resistance. He was the one who'd opened her eyes to the truth about the Republic. That created a trust. Same as he and MacKenzie. No matter the bond she was building with the General, or the attraction she obviously had for Oren, he was her first lifeline. He needed to break that.

"Sam, I'm never going to escape this war, but you can. Europe. Africa. Wherever. Anywhere you go is better than here. Safer than here."

"Europe? Are you shitting me? Don't you watch the news? They're in the middle of a civil war right now." She was pleading with Ward but looking at Oren and MacKenzie. Whatever she saw in their faces must have told her the truth. "There is no war, is there? Another lie."

"There's trouble everywhere," Ward said. "But not like here. And you don't have to be a part of it."

MacKenzie spoke up. "Enough. Oren will set it up. Get her to the *conservateurs* in Paris. They'll take care of her. New identity. Job. People to watch out for her. That'll be good, yes?"

"Don't talk about me like I'm not here," Sam said. "I'm not going with the conserva-whatevers, or anyone else, without Reina."

"Friends," Ward said. "Museum workers mostly. Her family." He motioned to MacKenzie.

"We run a route through Cadiz, Spain," Oren said. "Easy run from here to there. I can set it for tonight."

Sam was practically screaming in frustration. "You're not listening to me. I'm not leaving."

Oren tugged at her arm. She pulled away.

"I'll go with you," he said. "Reina will meet us in Heroica Veracruz. We've got our own hangar at the airport. All secure."

MacKenzie interrupted. "We need you running site here in Old Mexico."

"It's twenty-four hours round trip. Things will run fine while I'm gone."

"Now that everyone's vacations are planned," Ker said, "can we go down into the dark, scary hole please?"

"Yes, but I'm not leaving until tomorrow. I'm with you," Sam said to Ward, "until this river thing is over."

MacKenzie threw up her hands. Ward didn't bother arguing. Oren messaged to Eduardo to prep the flight for the morning. Waited for the return missive. Informed the General that the depot was prepped, and the flight would be good to go upon their arrival in Heroica Veracruz tomorrow.

"Now?" MacKenzie asked Ward as if all this was his fault.

He nodded, afraid that if he spoke she might hear fear in his voice. Fear of the pit awaiting them in the kiosk. Darkness and no bottom. The mouth of Oblivion itself.

I need to stop reading the Classics, he thought, unable to erase visions of Odysseus, Aeneas, Orpheus, and more descending into the Underworld. Sure they all returned, but they were heroes. He was just a drunk who couldn't do ten pushups if his life depended on it.

MacKenzie clenched her flashlight in her teeth and dropped onto the ladder. Oren followed. Sam next. Only Ker and Ward remained.

"Are you prepared?" Ker asked.

"For what?"

"For what's down there."

Ward's hand moved to his belt beneath his jacket, to the pistol that MacKenzie had given him back in Arizona. He didn't realize he was doing it until his fingertips touched the knurled grip.

"Not that," Ker said. "This." He tapped his finger against his temple and then spun onto the ladder and descended into darkness.

CHAPTER 26

The absence of light was oddly calming. Sure, Ward's mind was running wild with thoughts of dinner plate sized spiders, hell hounds, boogeymen, and booby-trapped pits. But there was also a sense of peace. A calm not completely unlike what could be found in the serenity of a bottle of bourbon.

He breathed the air. Thousands of years old. Mingled with the exhalations of a people so long vanished that scholars didn't even know what they called themselves. Chilly. Musty. Acrid. Old. No longer caring for the rush of those who lived above, or those who were trespassing in what was once hallowed ground.

He clicked on his flashlight and passed the beam around. The others had already moved on from this mid-tunnel drop a few steps from some cave-in blockage. There was only one way to go in the roughly two-person wide tunnel. He shivered in the cool underground air. Worked his jacket from his backpack and put it on. Rushed to catch up, noting the details of the excavation: mostly packed earth over what felt like bedrock with generally smooth walls and a slight downward grade.

After a bit, the tunnel listed to the right. Ward rounded this bend and nearly crashed into Ker. The others flashed their lights at the sound of Ward's arrival, catching him in the eyes more than once. Without a word, Oren restarted their single-file march at barely more than a crawl-pace, their lights often aligning in direction either ahead or above. Like the ribs of a great beast. Ward's mind conjured an image of the Midgard Serpent of Norse mythology.

He almost laughed out loud at the non-sequitur of Germanic

paganism while deep beneath the center of Mesoamerican religion.

"Getting cramped," Oren said from the lead position.

Indeed, a number of steps later, Ward, bringing up the rear, reached the spot Oren had announced. The tunnel narrowed to single file. Soon, however, it widened again, this time to an almost four-person width. Continuing then at intervals, the corridor followed this pattern, widening and wedging. In the bulges, Ward's flashlight glinted off tool marks. Elsewhere the walls appeared natural, with a regular stratification as if carved by water or perhaps magma.

"What did you say, professor?" Ker asked, using his Port for light rather than a flashlight.

Ward, surprised that he'd spoken out loud, felt his thoughts fumble away like a wet bar of soap.

"Not the time to keep your insights to yourself," MacKenzie said.

Ward tried to find the thread of what he'd lost. "This tunnel is almost perfectly centered beneath the Pyramid of the Sun, like they built it on top to commemorate this place. The Egyptians built pyramids to honor kings and give them access to the afterlife. To them, the pyramid was the point, but I don't think that applies here. The people who built this, they sought power in caves, in the earth, not in rising above it. There was a series of caves, seven I think, that were supposed to be the earth's womb from which humans were born. I remember at least one study suggesting that the caves were magma tunnels."

"What about the river?" MacKenzie asked.

"I don't remember anything about a river beneath the pyramids."

"Not bad so far, professor," Ker said.

Professor. It was a title Ward used to take pride in. It was a role he'd dreamed about returning to.

When he heard the word from Ker, it curdled in his gut. It felt like a slap in the face. A taunt.

"You can stop calling me that," Ward said, trying not to let Ker know he'd found a soft spot.

"Just picking your brain," Ker said, sounding both defiant

and disinterested at the same time. "If anyone here is an expert, it's you, right?" He turned his Port over in his hands. "Onward we go," he said, pushing his way to the front to take the lead.

They stopped again in a squared off portion of the tunnel. An intersection, branches running off in opposite directions, roughly north and south, Ward calculated.

"One of these, or do we keep going?" Oren asked.

Ker looked up each of the branches but did not shine a light in either. "Keep going."

"What's down them?" MacKenzie said.

"Nothing."

"How do you know? Have you been here before, Ker? Is that why the Seer sent you?"

"Be my guest," Ker said, waving his arms wide indicating he would wait until she'd checked both tunnels to see they were as empty as he said.

MacKenzie said to Ward, "You check down that one. Thirty seconds then turn around. Got it?"

She started up the north branch without waiting for an answer. Ward went down the south one, counting the seconds.

He made it to seventeen before he couldn't go any farther. It was a dead end.

Or was it?

He got up close to the wall and slid his hand down it. Plaster. Expertly disguised as stone. He rapped his knuckles on the wall. It sounded solid. Or at least very thick. Too thick, he estimated, for them to dig through. Probably the entrance to a tomb. Walling up a niche or an entire chamber was common in the catacombs of Europe. Why not here?

Ward arrived back at the intersection before MacKenzie.

"Dead end," he said.

"Here too," MacKenzie's voice announced a moment before her flashlight beam and then she came into view.

"Where's the river?" Sam asked.

"We have to move on," Ker said.

Oren moved closer to Ker. "Why?"

"The Seer ordered this," MacKenzie declared, ending the debate.

To Ward, it sounded like she was having doubts, but Oren straightened up.

"To Canaan," Oren said.

MacKenzie motioned them onward.

Ward hadn't heard this mantra before. It worried him. It reminded him too much of Adrien and Gaustad and the other followers of Ba'el. If he'd learned anything from history, it was that absolutes and calls to crusade resulted only in death. And coming from MacKenzie, it was even more troubling. For all her zeal, she was practical. Or had been. Not one to run headlong into a pillar of fire because scripture said so. Her approval of a saying like this—invoking the genocide of the Canaanites by the arriving Hebrews in the Old Testament—portended dangerous change.

The tunnel widened and narrowed at intervals as they continued deeper beneath the Pyramid of the Sun. Finally, they came to the end. Four chambers splayed out in a cloverleaf pattern, like chapels in a Medieval cathedral. Each one roughly aligning, Ward estimated, with one of the cardinal directions.

"*Sanctum Sanctorum,*" Ker said, barely above a whisper.

"The Holy of Holies," Ward translated, the name referring to the inner sanctuary of Solomon's Temple in Jerusalem where the Ark of the Covenant was kept. It was a correlation with the Grossmutter's story of the search for the mivkeh water that Ward couldn't ignore. He filed it away in case. "Is that what this is?"

"It can be any holiest place in a temple," Ker said. "Doesn't matter what religion. I guess this could be such a place for the Teotihuacanos who built the pyramid."

He moved into the cloverleaf, looking at his Port's screen the way people do when following walking directions. When he reached roughly the center, he popped a stylus from its top corner. From the opposite bottom corner, he popped another stylus. These he arranged across each other on the ground so that their four ends pointed each into one of the chapels, as Ward was now thinking of them.

"Where's the river?" Oren asked, approaching Ker.

"You're in the way," Ker said.

MacKenzie bobbed her head indicating Oren should retreat. When he was out of the way, Ker tapped a pattern on the screen of his Port. The device hummed for a second then went silent. Another second and the styli began emitting a pinkish light. Not directed like a flashlight. More like an emanation. A glow that made Ward a little queasy at first the way it highlighted the natural lines and strata of the walls, giving the room a feeling of motion.

The light shifted from pink to green. Gradually, new lines appeared on the walls. Curves and right angles that nature didn't know how to make. The light rolled through a range of yellows then continued changing from one hue to another.

Ward had seen this before. Historians using isolated wavelengths from outside the visible color spectrum—infrareds, ultraviolet, and more—to reveal truths about history's greatest artistic achievements. The first draft sketch of DaVinci's *Mona Lisa* hiding beneath the oils. The golds and greens of the Lemnian Athena statue, long weathered away. The nanometals of the Ulfberht sword.

The images coalescing before Ward were more breathtaking than any of those textbook experiences. Each of the chapels revealed a series of whirls and lines and arches that were unmistakably hand painted. Cave art. Wall art. Mesoamerican graffiti?

Whatever it was, it wasn't supposed to be there.

The lights settled into an odd blue-ish red haze. The images consolidated. Ward spun round and round, trying to make sense of the murals in each chapel. A woman. A pair of dogs. A tree. An odd still life.

The still life held him. A bright colorful bird alighted on the edge of a pitcher of water, a golden branch in its beak.

The pitcher.

He was dimly aware of someone asking Ker what the images were.

"Ask him," Ker said. "He's the genius expert."

But Ward couldn't answer. The bird, the branch, the pitcher. They appeared to be moving before him. The pitcher tipping over. The bird screeching. Shrill and purposeful.

He could hear it.

Couldn't he?

"She's beautiful," Sam said from somewhere too distant. But Ward couldn't escape the pitcher.

"Is that what I think it is?" MacKenzie said, suddenly very close to Ward's ear.

The Vase of Soissons. The prison into which El cast his adversary Ba'el so that His chosen people could thrive, if Adrien Quinque's version of Biblical history was to be believed. The vessel which Ward cast into the sea, nearly drowning in the process, in order to save MacKenzie's life.

"Can't be," Ward said. And then it wasn't the Vase at all. It was just a pitcher.

Fear told Ward that if he continued to stare the pitcher might once more become the Vase. He forced himself to look away. Forced himself to move to the next chapel, clockwise around the clover. He approached Sam, who was still before painting of the woman she'd called beautiful. The woman was radiant in reds and blues and greens and browns flowing throughout her robes. Her central adornment was a multi-tiered necklace reminiscent of the Egyptian Pharaohs, with an ornately painted pendant in the center of her chest. Her headdress, however, was the most striking feature. Gold and lapis lazuli coils wrapped tightly beside each ear like oversized headphones. She had the mien of royalty. Of someone more important than revolutions and theological semantics.

Needing to see all the chapels, as if there were going to be a test later, Ward crossed to the east cloverleaf. Two dogs, a white one above a black one, facing opposite directions. Yet too large to be dogs, though there was nothing else in the mural to give a sense of scale. Just a dizzying background which appeared to offer of a sun setting into a sunrise. It reminded him of a something. Maybe many somethings. A Greek riddle from the Sphinx about the sun and the moon. A story of life and death. A legend from Central America about guardians and betrayers. Nothing firm to grasp. To elucidate the painter's intention.

Ward entered the last chapel. The tree. Ker snorted. Ward ignored it and let himself get lost in the picture.

His first thought was of Yggdrasil, the World Tree of Norse mythology, but it didn't fit. It was too symmetrical. Too layered, as if its branches were pointing in the same cardinal directions the chapels represented. And, like the branch in the bird's beak and the headdress on the woman, it was gold. Trunk, branches, and leaves, all shimmering gold.

"Rafe," MacKenzie said, again closer than Ward had thought. "That looked like the Vase, didn't it? I mean, it doesn't now, but it did. I swear it did."

Ward thought he heard Ker clapping, but when he looked, the tech specialist's arms were crossed and his face was blank.

"What vase?" Sam asked.

"You're projecting is all," Ward said to MacKenzie, afraid to face the necessary conclusions if it was true.

"You're in denial," MacKenzie said.

"Alcoholics do that." Sam's wide eyes indicated she hadn't meant to say that out loud. Seeing the others turn to her, however, seemed to solidify her resolve. "Well, it's true," she said.

Oren, rocking impatiently, said, "I'm going to check on the entrance. Maybe you'll find the river before I get back."

Ward turned from chapel to chapel, searching for a clue to why they—him and his companions, as well as the four paintings—were there beneath the Pyramid of the Sun. He was missing a piece of it, like he was looking at fragments of authentic images mixed together by an amateur trying to pass them off as legitimate to the era and location. Like the artist couldn't make up their mind because...

Where are you? he demanded of the missing voice in his head. His own. Ba'el's. It didn't matter. The silence was gnawing away his ability to think. Leaving him able only to see the ambiguity of the murals. Their variedness. His hand went to his breast pocket. To his heart.

"Son of a bitch," he said, the answer darting through his mind like an angry bee. Zipping from place to place. Daring him to catch it. To hold it in his hand and suffer the sting for the honey. He swiped at it. "They're nonspecific."

"What do you see, professor?" Ker said.

"Nothing," Ward said. "Everything. I don't know."

The bee kept barely out of reach, its buzzing hinting at something. He started talking. To no one. To everyone. Reasoning it out loud while the buzz filled his head.

"They're all something and nothing. Specific and vague. The tree here is like the Norse World Tree, but almost every mythology uses a similar motif. World Tree. Tree of Life. The Bodhi Tree. The Iusaaset Acacia in Egypt. The Banyan Tree in Hinduism. You can't confine it to one belief system. Then there's the pitcher and the bird. Where there's a Tree of Life there's some kind of Water of Life. Fountain of Youth..." It all fell into place. "You've got be kidding me!"

"What?"

"The Grossmutter," he said. "Her story about her family. The brothers seeking the water from the mikveh in the Temple. It's a Water of Life story."

Blank faces all around.

"We're standing here in Teotihuacan, in the center of Quetzalcoatl's realm. The feathered serpent. And that bird," Ward pointed back to the south chapel, "is a parrot or a quetzal or whatever you need it to be to make the picture work. Call it a dove of many colors or a phoenix or any other religiously important bird-symbol." He looked at Ker but received no indication of success or failure. "That's what this is, isn't it? You're testing me."

"Me?" Ker said like a child caught beside a shattered glass.

"I don't have time for this shit," MacKenzie said.

Ker tapped at his Port's screen. "None of us do, but we follow orders like good knights, don't we?"

"What's the test?" Ward asked. "The question? You've been baiting me with it since we got here. What is it?"

"Her," Ker said. He strolled to the west chapel. The woman with the headdress.

"Her necklace could be Egyptian," Ward said, continuing his analysis as he followed. "Her robes could be Classical or even older. Homeric, I'd say. All of these are more European than indigenous here. Her features, however, narrow nose, high cheekbones, prominent chin—she could almost be native to the

Americas. Or Middle Eastern. Northwest Levant. Coming back to the Mediterranean perhaps...but her eyes...almost Asian. No, that's wrong too. She's like the rest. Many and none. An amalgam."

And then Ward knew. He ignored the woman's features. Ignored her necklace and her robes. He looked at her face and he knew. He recognized her. Not all of her, exactly. Just her head. He'd seen it before. A different piece. A different painting maybe. Or statue.

"Iberian," he said, snapping his fingers.

"Is it, Professor Ward?" Ker said.

"Wait, no," Ward said, confusion clouding the breakthrough he thought he'd made. "That wouldn't make sense."

"Someone better start making sense," MacKenzie said.

"Ask him," Ward replied, frustrated with being relied on when Ker obviously knew more than he was telling.

"I'm asking you."

"Well, I have no idea."

"Bullshit."

"I don't know everything," Ward said. He was nearly screaming. "Is that okay with you? It's his fucking game. Order him to tell."

"What's Iberian?" Sam asked, jutting in to the briefest pause in the exchange.

"The southwest corner, the peninsula, of Europe," Ward said, trying to lower his voice. To be the teacher answering a legitimate question. "Spain, essentially."

"I thought you knew all this history shit," MacKenzie said.

"I didn't memorize all of it on the off chance I'd one day be a fugitive who needed to identify a painting underneath a pyramid from two-and-a-half millennia before I was born. This is a bit before my main teaching era."

"I've had enough," MacKenzie said. "Ker, give me your Port. I want to see the message about this river."

Ker didn't move. "Do you see it yet, professor?"

"Now," MacKenzie demanded, a pistol in her hand.

Ker, without acknowledging her, handed the Port to Ward. "You'll need this," he said.

Ward took the Port. It was a custom one-off model that was definitely not Republic approved. Its screen displayed a list of academic applications with which he was familiar, each one a scan for a particular medium. Metals. Stone. Organic compounds. Ceramics. The fifth one down, highlighted, was paints. Ward turned to the mural and activated the scan, aiming the Port slowly from her head to the floor of the chapel. The Port's screen flashed red then green.

"Impossible," Ward said.

"Damn it, Rafe. What is it?" MacKenzie said.

"Egg tempera and hematite," Ward said. "Gold leaf. Wrong style. Wrong age."

"Wrong for what?"

"For pre-Colombian America. It's twenty-four hundred years old, give or take, but it uses both Egyptian and Greek style and materials, along with what seems to be Phoenician characteristics. These methods and materials weren't used here when this painting was made. They weren't known. They couldn't have been. She was painted two thousand years prior to Columbus. Fifteen hundred years prior to the Norse at Vinland. Who is she, Ker?"

"The sister of three brothers," Ker said.

"Knock off your bullshit and give us an answer," MacKenzie said.

"Did you really think," Ker said, "your history book timelines are infallible? That the Teotihuacanos decided to build pyramids here like in Egypt because human nature leads inexorably to triangles? I truly thought you were smarter than that."

"I don't understand. I thought we were coming down here for an underground river," Sam said.

MacKenzie seemed ready to shoot someone—anyone—to get answers. "What the fuck does this have to do with the cleansing ritual the Seer wants?"

"The Seer, yes," Ker said. He bounded to the mural and pointed to the pendant on the mural-woman's necklace. "This is the river we need. The river you need."

Ward approached, the details of the pendant becoming

clearer the nearer he got. It wasn't simply a decoration. It was a design. A flat disc, circumscribed in blue. Embossed, like a three-dimensional painting. Or a raised-relief map. He reached, intending to touch it. Let his fingertips recognize what his mind couldn't quite grasp. Ker grabbed his wrist. Ward tried to pull away, but the lanky tech held it tight.

"The other thing, professor, is you need to be quicker. Drink more or drink less. Whatever you need to do to keep your mind sharp. Do that and you'll put it all together in time."

"Put what together?"

"*La Dama de Elche's* ashes. That's your key. Keep the Port. You'll need the scan."

"Elche?" The name was familiar to Ward, but he couldn't identify it. Once again, the answer seemed lost in a buzzing in his head.

"Where's the fucking river?" MacKenzie shouted.

"Doesn't matter," came the answer from up the tunnel. A second later, the bobbing beam of a flashlight came into view. Then Oren, running, pistol in hand. "There's a bunch of PFs massing outside the entrance."

The buzzing coalesced in Ward's mind. He saw the woman's head. A statue. A marble bust. "That's it!" he said victoriously

"Not now," MacKenzie said, a pistol in each hand. "Time to go."

She took off at a jog, passing Oren without pause. Without fear. Sam tried to follow, but Ward grabbed her.

"Stay with me," he said. "Behind me." He hoped he sounded half as confident as MacKenzie looked charging toward whatever awaited them. He hoped his bravado would be enough to keep Sam alive until they could get her on Oren's plane.

The plane, he was beginning to fear, that would take her right where Ker wanted them to go.

CHAPTER 27

"Fourteen cops out there," MacKenzie said, climbing back down the ladder. "They look like teenagers wearing paramilitary costumes."

"Don't underestimate them," Oren said. "They start young here. How tight is their formation?"

"Perimeter only, like they're waiting for orders or a support team to arrive. Can't say there aren't more of them, though, up the streets. Behind the market would be the most likely placement."

"No Agents?" Ward asked.

"We're in Old Mexico," Sam said.

"They don't stop at the border," MacKenzie said.

"What's our objective?" Oren asked.

"Escape," Ward said.

"Which will be easier if we kill them all."

No one spoke for a moment. Ker seemed to be sniffing the darkness.

Eventually, the tech specialist said, "We should go now."

"Agreed," MacKenzie said. "Oren first. Draw them to the right around the platform in front of the pyramid. I'll go next, to the left. Rafe, go up third and roll right. Spread wider than Oren. Give them three targets. Ker, when they're divided, you go up and set up shop in the middle of the platform. That'll be good, yes?"

"What about me?" Sam asked. The fear in her voice was clear. It was also overshadowed by a hunger Ward recognized. She wanted to fight, but she had no idea what that really meant. The skirmish at the Labor Camp trailer was nothing compared to the potential slaughter waiting for them above.

"Come up with me," MacKenzie said.

"No, she stays behind me," Ward insisted.

"Do I get a say in this?" Sam asked.

MacKenzie and Ward, at the same time, said, "No."

"General," Ker said, "You and Oren are in the most danger going up first. The good professor has the farthest to go. She should come up with me after the forces above are divided."

"Right," MacKenzie said. "With you, then, Ker. Here." She offered Sam a pistol from her backpack.

Everything was going so fast, decisions being made that he couldn't control, that Ward felt sick. The plan, he was sure, was flawed. The shade from his dream, Aeneas, flashbulbed before him. Reminding him of the warning in his dream. Of the one hunting him. Of the one he will hunt. Whatever that meant.

Sam took the pistol. Ward tried to protest.

"No way," he said. "She's a noncombatant."

"She'll die a noncombatant," Ker said.

Sam held the gun in her right hand, aimed at the ground. "I'm not a child."

Oren said, "Unarmed is suicide, and you know it."

The truth of what they said was so obvious, Ward had to relent. Whether she went up with him or with Ker, or if she stayed down here in the tunnel, she couldn't be without the means to protect herself.

"Protect her," Ward said to Ker.

"With my life," Ker said.

Oren took hold of Sam's hand and pressed the safety. "It's live. Just point and shoot. Two hands on the grip."

Sam flipped the safety on then off again. She looked confident and scared. Ward worried her confidence was for the battle and her fear was of the gun.

"Weapons ready," MacKenzie said.

The metallic clicks of soldiers loading and checking their weapons filled the tunnel.

"To Canaan," Oren said, and began his climb.

MacKenzie started up the ladder before he disappeared. Gunfire erupted above. Short bursts then longer, like exploding

Morse code. Each one felt like a thumb jabbed in Ward's temple.

"Ready?" he asked Sam. "Stay low. Stay behind Ker. Don't shoot unless you have to. It makes you a target."

"Got it," Sam said.

Ward's stomach twisted and sank.

"Go on, professor," Ker said. "I've got her back."

The guns above thundered. Sam nudged Ward's shoulder. He didn't turn to look at her. If he did, he might lose his nerve. He grabbed the first rung and pulled. At the top, he fired two shots into the air then heaved himself out of the pit. He scrambled from the kiosk to his right. It took two tries to get to his feet, the first ending with him stumbling back down when the dirt beside the kiosk exploded.

He found Oren crouched behind the right corner of the platform. Ward ran to him, head down, sliding feet first when he arrived.

Endless volleys of gunfire. Then shouting. Ward hazarded a look. The kiosk was decimated, leaning awkwardly to the side. He caught sight of movement behind the center of the platform.

"Down," Oren yelled.

Ward dropped to a knee. Lunged right. Stone erupted where he'd been, pelting his clothes. His cheek burned. A new wound below his stitches. No time to worry about it. He tucked, rolled, and vaulted to his feet. Gun still in hand. Firing as fast as his finger would squeeze. Not looking for targets. Just buying time to collect the scene.

Most of the PFs had gathered in the market's open square and were trying to flank MacKenzie's position to the left. A small contingent was advancing on Oren and him. One, an assault rifle to his shoulder, broke off at the far side of the platform and was trying to get an approach angle.

Ward aimed. Squeezed twice. Misses, both. The recoil drove his hands too high to attempt a third, but the PF dropped his rifle from the sighted position and hunched his head. Oren crossed over Ward, shooting as he went. The PF tumbled. Tried to stand. Oren fired once more, his gun so close to Ward's head that his vision flashed white. When it cleared, the PF was on the ground.

"Go," Oren said.

Ward ran for the far corner of the pyramid. Halfway there, an explosion louder than small arms fire went off behind him. He dropped to his stomach. Rolled in the direction he'd been running, then popped back to his feet. He reached the cover of the pyramid's corner, impressed with his speed and reflexes so far. Considering how poorly he'd reacted to battle back at the Labor Camp, he took the fact that he was still alive as a sign of improvement.

When he looked up the market was on fire, lighting the Avenue of the Dead like a torch. To the left of the conflagration, a shadow waited. Not a Reaper. This figure was larger. More ominous. Ward remembered the armored figure he'd seen at the high school. Unique then, with no frame of reference. Now, it was clear this was no standard trooper. A commander, perhaps?

Whoever it was, it moved away from the flames to a boxy, military-looking off-road vehicle parked dangerously close to the blaze. The vehicle's headlights flashed on. Ward braced for the vehicle to drive headlong into the fray. Instead, it turned a slow arc and drove away.

Movement caught Ward's attention. He turned, aiming. It was Oren rushing to his position.

"The General?" Oren asked after he'd scrambled around the corner.

"Did you see that?" Ward asked, pointing to where the off-road vehicle had been.

Oren shook his head. No one spoke. The gunfire had expired. Only it wasn't real silence. The sounds of pain, of people dying, moaned like the wind.

"There," Oren said, pointing.

MacKenzie approached from the south, a pistol in each hand. As if enjoying the moonlit night, she strolled the square between pyramid and burning marketplace, putting bullets into every PF that remained. The ones writhing and wailing in pain. The ones already silent in death. The ones that ran, fleeing before her like grasshoppers before a wheat harvester. She put a bullet in the head of every one of them. Nonchalant, robotic, efficient. There was no return fire.

"Everyone okay?" MacKenzie shouted when she'd finished her chore.

"Good to go," Oren said.

Ward, doing his best to not think about the simple efficiency of MacKenzie's actions, asked, "Where's Sam?"

"Evac now," MacKenzie said, meeting them before the platform.

Oren already has his Port in hand. "On it."

"You didn't have to kill them all," Ward said. He didn't mean to. The words came out, and with them came a measure of horror at what MacKenzie had done.

She glared at him. He tried to find Sam. Sirens started in the distance, reminding Ward of Paris. Of the car chase from the Pantheon with MacKenzie. Of a time when she didn't scare him.

"Where's Ker?" MacKenzie said.

"Here," Ker said, coming out of what was left of the booth with Sam.

"Were you hiding down there, you fuck?" MacKenzie said.

"You okay?" Ward asked Sam.

Sam, eyes wide, didn't answer. At first, Ward thought she'd kept Ker with her in the tunnel, afraid to come up. Then he saw the way her arm was bent, as if being held behind her back. Ward started toward them.

"This isn't going to work if you don't play along, professor," Ker said. "The plane to Cadiz is great, but I need you on it."

"You need?"

"Truck is on the way," Oren said. "Safe house is set. I had— what are you doing?"

Oren had seen the way Ker was holding Sam. All three now closed on the pair, Oren taking a line between Ward and MacKenzie, who still held her pistols in her hands.

"With or without your friend here, you're getting on that plane," Ker said.

He moved so fast his arm was a blur. No one reacted. There was no time.

No one but Oren.

One second, he was beside Ward. The next he was diving at

MacKenzie. Tackling her. Hitting the ground.

Only after did Ward's mind register the single gunshot.

Sam, her face splashed with blood, screamed. MacKenzie shoved Oren from her, twisting to a knee, pistols aimed at Ker. Oren clutched at his stomach. Ker held Sam by the throat, the gun MacKenzie had given to Sam to her temple.

"The rules change, professor," Ker said. "It's not ideal, but we're still in play. I need you to make it to the river by three midnights from now. If you don't, the girl is going to eat the whole pomegranate. Get it? You've got all the clues you need now. Three midnights."

"Do you want to die, Ker?" MacKenzie said.

"Oh, I think you're more afraid of that journey than I."

Oren, on the ground, moaned and rolled to her side, his body clenched like a fist. The dirt around him darkened with his blood.

"Everything you need is in that Port, professor. Follow *la Dama de Elche's* ashes to Ameles and hopefully you won't disappoint poor Sam here. But don't worry; it won't be as easy as it sounds."

"Take me," Ward said. "Whatever game you want to play, I'll play it."

MacKenzie crossed in front of him. "Let her go or I'll put a bullet in your eye."

"Are you that good a shot?"

"Do you want to find out?"

The sirens were close now. Lights bounced above them, settling on Ker. Behind him, Ward heard the hum of a vehicle. Eduardo with the truck, he hoped.

"Nowhere to go, traitor," MacKenzie said.

Ker laughed. "If you knew how ignorant that sounds."

"Just take me," Ward shouted.

"Oh no," Ker said. "Then we'd never know if you're as smart as you think you are. Back up, General, or I'll shoot Oren in the head. You've got a chance to save him now. Want to lose it?"

MacKenzie held her ground.

"Plenty of bullets for you and the professor, too," Ker said. "Not the way I want it to go, but I'll find someone else if you insist on both of you dying here."

Ward closed his eyes. If he was going to get Ker, if he was going to save Sam, he would have to play whatever game this was. He rebuilt the murals beneath the pyramid in his mind. Could he figure out the riddle? The map? Would it matter? Would Ker kill Sam anyway?

Dying tomorrow is better than dying today.

Do you want to die?

I don't want Sam to die.

He opened his eyes and said, "Put them down, Hannah."

She didn't lower the guns.

"Help me save Oren. We'll get Sam. If you don't, we're all going to die right here. Aren't we, Ker?"

"Close enough to truth," Ker said.

"I'm going to cut your throat," MacKenzie said to Ker as she tossed her guns.

"Like that Reaper?" Ker said, still charismatic. Still like he was selling an upgrade to leather seats in a new car. "Turn around and face the pyramid."

Ward and MacKenzie did as told.

"What's his game?" she whispered.

"He's your friend," Ward said.

They both flinched at the gunshot. MacKenzie recovered first, dropping to a crouch. Ward turned. Ker had shot Eduardo through the truck's windshield. He was now shoving Sam through the driver's door into the passenger side. Mackenzie dove for a gun, grabbing it on a belly slide and coming up to her knee shooting.

Too late. The truck was rounding the still-burning market. From the north the first police car pulled into view, its lights forcing Ward to look away. At Oren. Bleeding and moaning. He knelt and tried to find the wound, to stop the blood.

More gunshots.

This time it was MacKenzie running at the police car, emptying her pistol into the police officer inside. She pulled the driver out while the car was still rolling. Got in and sped to Ward, showering him and Oren with dirt and gravel as the car skidded to a stop.

"Get him in the back," she said, already reloading her gun. Then she was out and on the car's hood shooting at the police cars coming into view.

Ward managed Oren into the back of the car. Searched for the wound. Found it and pressed his hand over it, feeling the warm blood trying to push through his fingers. Gunfire tempted his attention, but he forced himself not to look out the window. He knew what he'd see. MacKenzie putting bullet holes in every police car that came into sight, her teeth clenched in brutal concentration.

He wondered what happened to the woman he knew. The one who'd wanted to save lives. He wondered if she'd ever existed at all.

Her tattoo, the missing Sixth Commandment, as if *Thou Shall Not Kill* did not apply to her, God's General, said she'd always been this cruel. But he didn't believe it. He couldn't. Not if they were going to save Sam.

He found the wound. Pressed his palm over it. Pushed as hard as he could. Oren screamed. He didn't let up. The scream strangled to a choked whistle. Then nothing. Oren ceased struggling.

Then Mackenzie was in the car and they were speeding off.

CHAPTER 28

"Where's the safe house? Oren, where is it?"

Ward wasn't sure how long MacKenzie had been shouting the question. It felt like a voice in a dream, that faraway, drowsy voice that nears as consciousness interrupts.

"He can't," Ward said.

The car swerved so hard Ward was certain they would roll over. He had to dig his fingers into the synthetic leather of the back seat to keep leverage on Oren's wound. He could feel the man's pulse, the push of his blood, slowing beneath his fingers.

"He can or we're all dead," MacKenzie countered.

Ward clenched his eyes. He wondered, inexplicably and inappropriately given their situation, if car chases were less terrifying when they still ran on gasoline. Loud engines growling, drowning out the noise of squealing tie rod ends and wailing shock mounts. Veiling the sounds of gunshots.

The car lurched as if running up the curb. Or a body. Ward's eyes popped open to find Oren's hand pushing a Port across the seat against Ward's knuckles. His lips stretched like he was trying to say, "Here," but no sound came. His eyes rolled back. His hand went limp.

Ward shifted so he could operate the Port. A message from yesterday from Eduardo, in Spanish, opened: *Florería Calle Subestación.*

"Florist Street Substation," Ward translated.

"Where?"

"I don't know. Florist Street."

The car jerked, sending Ward's head into the armrest. He almost lost his hand on Oren's chest.

"Where's Florist Street?" MacKenzie said.

"I'm not a map."

"The Port. Open the Port's fucking map."

Ward swiped out of the messaging program, not allowing himself time to feel stupid, and typed "Florist Street" as best he could in the shifting, shimmying car. The map zoomed out, showing Wichita Falls in Texas.

"Twenty hours," Ward read.

"What the fuck are you doing back there? I've got four on us and road blocks everywhere. There's no twenty hours."

"Shit, wrong city. Sorry. Doing the best I can."

"Do better."

It was a simple command. One Ward feared he couldn't fulfill. He forced himself to breathe. To hold the inhale like he'd been taught when taking slow aim with a rifle. To calm his trembling hands and throbbing leg. He counted to three. Time slowed. His throat itched. The dry air, maybe. Or the need for a drink. Didn't matter. He pushed it aside. He thought about his heartbeat. Willed it to slow.

The threads of his mind untangled. Thoughts elongated into rational understanding. Cause and Effect. Positional relationships. Spanish, he remembered from college, was a postnominal adjective language. Descriptors came after the nouns they modified. It wasn't the Florist Street Substation. It was the florist on Substation Street. He pushed the erroneous entry off screen. Typed the correct one.

"East then south. Get on Camino Real. Then two lefts. It's a long straight shot. Neighborhoods after. Getting us out of sight after that is up to you."

"Better," was all MacKenzie said.

She piloted the car through Ward's directions. Oren's breathing, already shallow, slowed to no more than a few inhales a minute. Ward tried not to count them. Tried not to think about someone else dying because of him. The man's blood literally on his hands.

Ker's hands, he told himself.

And what are you going to do about it?

I'm going to find Ker. Save Sam. Then I'm going to let

MacKenzie be MacKenzie.

"Here?" MacKenzie asked as they crossed a street called *Aztecas.*

"There's an alley to the left," Ward said, bracing for the tire-screeching turn. "Right, then over the street before right again into another alley. Big circle around. Lose them there and maybe we can find—there!"

A row of garage doors presented a chance.

"Do two more crosses then get us into one of those garages," Ward said.

"Jump out at the second crossing and open one."

"If I take my hand off his chest, I don't think he'll make it."

"For fuck's sake. Hold on."

MacKenzie threw the car into a spin, dropping the gear shift and locking it into reverse. The motion and sudden stop left Ward fighting to keep his hand on Oren's wound. To keep his own stomach from giving up its contents. The car squealed backwards, with MacKenzie hanging out the driver's window shooting at the two police cars chasing them. Her third shot hit home. The lead police car's front tire exploded. It ground hard to the right, smashing into the brick building lining the alley. The chase car hit it full speed from behind, the resulting eruption of plastic and fiberglass chunks was oddly quiet, like a movie explosion with the sound muted.

"Get me to those garages," MacKenzie said, spinning the car back into drive.

Ward directed her through a couple more turns until they stopped in front of a green garage door. MacKenzie jumped from the car and smashed at the padlock with her boot. Again. Twice more and the latch tore from the metal door. She threw it up, casters rattling like a train, revealing a sunglasses storeroom. Five display cases and the walls lined with pegboards filled with hundreds more sunglasses. The kind of garage-front retailer that was common on boardwalks and in densely populated markets. MacKenzie got in the car and drove into the store, crushing everything, until the car was all the way inside.

Oren convulsed. Before Ward could speak, MacKenzie was out of the car once more. Closing the garage door. Turning on the fluorescent lights hanging from the ceiling.

"Where are we?" she asked.

Ward kicked open the car door. "Across the alley is a florist. That's all Ed's message said. I guess the safe house is inside. I saw a *Farmacia*, a pharmacy, half a block north."

"Can you get him to the florist?"

Ward wanted to say yes, but Oren had to weigh almost two hundred and twenty pounds. Even Agent Rafael Ward, fresh from Agent Compano's training regimen, would have had trouble carrying him that far. Before he could answer, the sirens of three or four police cars whipped by, their lights flickering beneath the garage door.

When they'd passed, MacKenzie said, as if reading Ward's mind, "We'll get him there together, then you go the pharmacy and get what we need."

They waited as long as they dared before making the dash to the florist, Ward's elbows hooked under Oren's shoulders so he could keep pressure on the wound, with MacKenzie carrying his legs. He was heavier than he appeared. Solid muscle acting now as dead weight. More than once Ward thought he would lose his grip. By the time they stood before the store—another garage door beneath an unlit neon marquee that announced *Floreria del Angel*, the Angel's Flowers—Ward was sweating, and his arms were beginning to tremble.

"Turn," MacKenzie said.

They pivoted so MacKenzie was closest to the door. She smashed its padlock the way she had the other. Two kicks this time, and they were in. They placed Oren on the first counter, beside the register, an actual old-time cash register. MacKenzie moved off for a security sweep. In her absence, Ward listened to Oren's breaths, becoming aware of his own inhaling the aroma of the shop. It was like fancy hotel soap in a moldy locker room.

There was a crash in the back of the store. MacKenzie returned.

"He did good," she said.

She lifted Oren's legs. Ward grabbed his shoulders. Together they carried him to the back of the store. An attic drop-door swung lazily above the remains of a plastic and cardboard display stand. Pieces of purple and white vases scattered on the floor. Ward tried not to think of the Vase of Soissons as the remains crunched beneath his boots.

Getting Oren into the attic wasn't easy. Ward pulled his shoulders from the top while MacKenzie, perched on a construction of a stepstool and a glass display case, pushed. Somehow, they got him up and onto the attic floor without losing too much more blood. A fact that Ward worried was simply an indication of how little blood remained in Oren's body.

"Jackpot," MacKenzie said, the first to her feet.

From his crouch beside Oren, Ward followed MacKenzie's investigation of the attic with his eyes. The safe house, it turned out, was a perfect waystation for fugitives on the run. A number of bunks lined the left wall. An arsenal of small arms, along with a couple shoulder-mounted rocket launchers, stacked the right wall. The entire front portion of the attic, like a galley kitchen straddling two blacked out and barred windows, appeared to be a fully functional emergency clinic.

They worked Oren onto a gurney, Ward holding pressure to Oren's wound, in the clinic beside a small table with a full-sized tablet computer on top labeled *Procedimientos.* Procedures.

With his free hand, Ward powered on the tablet and did a search for his best translation of "gunshot wound." The screen offered a close-up of a scalpel incision through dark flesh.

"Make it translate to English," MacKenzie said.

"Can you do this?"

"Translate it, then find bandages and some kind of pain killer. I'll take care of—"

A phone rang. Not an electronic facsimile. A real bell. They froze like children caught in the act.

It rang again.

"There," MacKenzie said, pointing to the bunks. A black, square phone box hung on the wall between the first two bunks. "Go," she said, placing her hand over Oren's chest for when Ward released. "You speak better Spanish than me."

Ward slipped his hand from Oren's wound and grabbed a towel from a nearby bench on his way to the phone. He wiped the blood from his hands as best he could and then lifted the receiver.

"*Estado? Necesariamente?*" the voice in the other end said.

At first, Ward didn't know what to say. Slowly, his mind reworked the two words into English forms he thought made sense. "Status? Um, injured. Oren. Gunshot. We need medical assistance."

"Name?" the voice asked, suspicious of the unfamiliar person who'd answered.

Ward almost gave his name, stopping himself on the first syllable. "The General is here," he corrected. "Oren needs help. Shot in the chest."

"*El General?*" the voice said, using the masculine, though Ward doubted it was mistaken identity. "*Si.* Understood. Help is four minutes. Can you stabilize?"

"I don't know," Ward said. He felt weak. As if his legs might give out. It was the dissipation of adrenaline, part of his mind knew. He could feel MacKenzie watching him. Feel Oren's life reaching for help. Hear Sam calling from somewhere far away. It was all he could do to remain standing. To say again, "I don't know."

CHAPTER 29

The amphibious plane, decked in yellows and oranges, looked like a city bus with a bar welded across the roof to serve as wings. Like misshapen shoulders, two propeller-and-engine lugs rose above the wing line. It made Ward think of a pregnant cat floating beside the dock.

It also made his heart pound and his head spin as if he'd been twirling pirouettes.

"You've got to be joking," he said.

MacKenzie didn't seem much happier at their transport. "Graciela said it's their fastest one. Best pilot. Nothing inside but fuel tanks and two smuggling holds."

Graciela was the contact Ward had spoken to on the phone in the attic safe house. She'd arrived with four others, all in khaki fatigues, in under four minutes. Two of her companions had set to Oren with practiced hands right away. A third had tended to MacKenzie's wound while the fourth collected Oren's Port and their weapons. MacKenzie didn't object, so neither did Ward.

"The plane waits in Veracruz," Graciela had said, her accent thick but without the stutter of discomfort. She was a stern woman some ten years older than Ward, with a build that reminded him of a gymnast. "Only you two now?"

"No, change of plans," MacKenzie had said. "We need a crossing back into the Republic. We've had a security breach. The Seer needs to be briefed."

"I'm not going back," Ward had said. "We need to find Sam."

"Oren is the conductor, General. Without his orders, there are no crossings."

"What if he dies?"

"A new conductor will be chosen."

"Then choose an acting conductor. A temporary."

"No."

MacKenzie had looked like she would argue. Or challenge Graciela to a duel. Instead, she said, "Fine. Get me a secure comm line."

Graciela had made a teacher's face. "No," she'd said, as if that one word should have reprimanded MacKenzie with, *You should know better than to ask that.*

"Fuck," MacKenzie had said. She kicked a bunk, the sound echoing like a dropped frying pan. Paced the attic, stopping and starting as if making up her mind then changing it a number of times.

Ward considered offering Ker's Port for the communication, but he didn't think MacKenzie would accept it as secure. He also didn't want Graciela's man confiscating the only tangible clue he had for finding Sam.

"When you get back," MacKenzie said to Graciela, "send a message to the Seer. Tell him the op is ongoing. We're on our way to Cadiz."

Graciela had accompanied them down into the garage to a waiting van. "*Vaya con dios, El General,*" she'd said at their parting.

If Ward had found the absence of his name in Graciela's wish for God's accompaniment on their journey ominous, he found the plane they faced downright terrifying. And it must have showed.

"We're going to have to get you over your fear of flying at some point," MacKenzie said, pointing at his hands, clenched so hard his knuckles were ashen.

"It's not fear," Ward said. "It's the pressure."

"In that case," the pilot, a man in a tan cowboy hat whose name Ward didn't catch, said, his accent more native Spanish than Mexican. "I think you're going to enjoy this flight."

"Why?"

"Low and slow," the pilot said, pointing to the propellers. "No pressurized cabin." He patted Ward on the shoulder and climbed inside.

Ward groaned.

On board, huge riveted fuel tanks on either side gave the impression of walking through a corrugated steel press that might begin squeezing them at any moment. The narrow aisle between the tanks, barely shoulder width, led to an open hatch in the floor.

"Cannot have either of you in the cockpit," the pilot said from behind them. "Too recognizable. Orders say you're the cargo. Sorry." He entered the cockpit. Closed the door. Locked it with a clang.

Ward, in front of MacKenzie and with no room to maneuver around each other, entered the hold first. Mackenzie watched him get situated, a frown growing on her face.

"This is going to be tight," she said.

Ward did his best to let her in, but there was no way they could situate without touching. MacKenzie proposed facing each other rather than back to back, bags in their laps, her left leg tight against Ward's right. She offered an attempt at a reassuring smile. It felt more like condolences at a funeral.

The takeoff wasn't too bad, but the way the plane dipped and twisted on its way to cruising altitude, made Ward's head pulse and swim like an attack of vertigo. Even MacKenzie kept her hands pressed against the sides of the hold. Once they leveled out, the flight was relatively smooth, though cold and uncomfortably tight.

"Tell me about the painting under the pyramid," MacKenzie said.

Ward didn't have any answers yet, and told her as much. "I need more time to sift through it all. Let's talk after we're there."

MacKenzie agreed, though it seemed to Ward she was unhappy with his decision to withhold what he knew so far.

As the hours went by, they became more and more uncomfortable, their arms and legs pressing against each other awkwardly. Some hours into the flight, at least halfway, Ward hoped, he tried shifting his tingling leg to alleviate the pressure on his tingling ass.

"Knock it off," MacKenzie said, backhanding his elbow away.

Ward tried to say something smart, something stinging while still being playful, but he was cold. Hungry. Thirsty. The first thing that came out was, "You shouldn't have killed them all."

"What?"

Too late. It wasn't going away now, so he went for it. "The PFs, the way you walked through there shooting them. Even the ones who were running away. You were like...like..."

"Like an Agent?" MacKenzie said.

Her eyes cut into him. It should have shut him up. Should have put him in his place no matter how short a time he was employed by the REC.

Instead, he said, "It wasn't right."

"Neither was the Tower," MacKenzie said. "But it needed to be done. That's a truth. It needed to be done and you did it."

"Forbear, ye nations," Ward said, the words from the *Odyssey* spilling from his mouth as if he was reading it from a book in his lap, "from mutual slaughter; peace descends to spare."

"What's that supposed to mean?"

"It means death only brings death. There's no end to the cycle."

"You want to be a coward, fine. But don't tell me I'm wrong. I'm not the one making policy about killing children because of what their parents believe. I'm not the hypocrite trying to silence whoever disagrees with me. There's only two sides. Mine and theirs. Which one are you on?"

"You want absolutes? Yours is the side that celebrates a God who killed the firstborn children of an entire nation because its leader wouldn't obey."

"We find your friend," MacKenzie said, "then you're coming back with me."

Ward tried to remember that feeling he'd had in Paris when they'd gotten separated in the Metro. When he'd missed her, recognizing for the first time there was more between them than physical attraction. He tried to remember the way he'd sought her out across every street and around every corner while fleeing west after the Tower. Tried to want to look into her green eyes.

But he couldn't. Not now. He was afraid he'd see himself in the mirror of those eyes.

There's still time to win her back, he told himself.

She has her army now. You're just a pawn.

Not yet, I'm not. Not yet.

It was enough to keep his hopes up. He dug a water bottle from his backpack and offered her the first sip. She took it. Drank. Handed it back. It was a start.

At first, Sam thought she was in the trunk of a car. The jolting and shimmying in the cramped space, longer than it was tall, bore that out.

She'd hidden in the trunk of Mia's car once. The new one her parents had bought her at the start of the school year. She'd climbed in while it sat in Mia's driveway, holding the lid down without letting it latch, then messaged to say she was waiting outside. Out came Mia, looking for Sam.

"Hey!" Sam had shouted, popping up from the trunk. She'd tried to leap out, but her foot had caught the taillight. She'd flopped to the macadam face first.

It was a good memory, even with the embarrassment and the bloody nose. It should have made Sam chuckle. But being trapped and having no idea what had happened to her best friend in these last few days sapped the humor from the moment. Suddenly itchy all over, she thrashed about, bashing her knees and elbows against solid metal. No soft, hollow smacks like in a car's trunk.

Taillights! she thought.

She twisted around and around looking for the red glow of light coming through the translucent lenses but found nothing. No red. No light. Panic trembled through her, chopping her breathing into spurts. Her hands sought something, anything that wasn't solid, smooth, cool metal. All around. Like a steel box.

Like a coffin.

She screamed for help but heard only her own voice bounce back. She screamed again until her breath failed and her ears and throat hurt.

Get it together. What would Rafe do?

"He'd have MacKenzie save him," she said and snickered. It felt good to laugh. Better than any size dose of Lito. Thinking of the drug made her want a prod.

No, it made her remember what it was like to want a prod. She found she didn't want one at all. Not anymore.

Never again, she told herself. The thought felt better than the laughter. It centered her. She concentrated on her breathing. Slowing it like they'd been taught in school during lockdown drills.

Your best weapon is your mind, she recited, the automated preamble to the instructions repeated once a week since elementary school until she could almost remember it as her own voice.

Run. Hide. Fight. Only engage a shooter as a last resort. Wait for the authorities to rescue you.

"What if you're so well hidden you don't even know where you are?" she asked the darkness.

Slowly she resolved to make sense out of her situation. She started at the end of the box above her head and worked her hands across its surface, searching for a blemish, a hinge, a latch, anything. The wall on her left. By her feet. Beneath. On her right.

A hole! No more than two fingers high but a foot or so long. Then another. A third, the three spaced evenly along the long wall at the top corner. Like air holes. Not a comforting thought, but it was better than finding nothing. She stuck her fingers through the center hole, contorting her body to get the farthest reach possible.

The box bounced like a car crossing half a dozen train tracks. Dropped. Sam slammed into the roof. More train tracks. Their severity lessening with each rumble before leveling like...

I'm on a plane.

It was a satisfying yet terrifying realization. She tried to remember how she'd gotten here. Ker had grabbed her while they were still in the tunnel. Twisted her arm and taken her gun. Forced her up the ladder only after the sounds of battle had ceased. Held her like a shield. Shot Oren. Shot Eduardo. Shoved her into the truck.

"I won't kill you if I don't have to," he'd said as he got in. He'd had a small black object in his hand. He'd stabbed at her with it. She remembered it was cold and sharp against her neck. Then nothing.

Only now did she become aware of the aching in her neck. Her fingers sought the spot, feeling two tender raised welts. A stun baton of some sort.

She resumed her examination of the box through the air holes, finding nothing identifying or helpful in either the foot or middle holes. She tried the one by her head. There. An imperfection. No, an embossed design. A symbol. A letter!

She traced it carefully, her finger finding another to its right. Then more. She traced them as far as she could reach. Then she went over them again, this time sounding them out.

"KGC," she said. "Imr? Imre? Imp? Imports. KGC Imports. Good. I guess."

But it wasn't good. It was information with no context. She was on a plane in a box labeled KGC Imports. How did that help? Was the K for Ker? Was she being sold? Delivered? Was she already dead?

Too many questions. No answers. Nothing to do but wait.

She thought of the child growing inside her. It was the first time she'd enunciated the word *child* in her mind, not *it* or *her little thing*. The first time she'd thought about it ceasing to exist. She shivered. Realized she'd been cold the whole time. She curled up, hands going to her belly. She thought about praying to whoever MacKenzie prayed to, but she didn't know how. And she didn't believe it would do any good other than to pass the time. She laughed. It turned to crying. This too passed the time, so she gave herself to it, weeping with abandon.

PART 3: THE LADY

Thou shalt have no other gods before me.
—Book of Exodus, 20:3

Near unto the blessed shore,
"Asperges me," I heard so sweetly sung,
Remember it I cannot, much less write it.
—Purgatorio, by Dante Alighieri, c. 1308

CHAPTER 30

The landing was not pleasant. Ward had almost forgotten they were in an amphibious plane until the pilot's voice announced, "Splash down in two."

Ward had thought that when Graciela said Cadiz, she'd meant an airport somewhere in the province. But a water landing indicated they were likely arriving in or near the city of Cadiz. Founded by the Phoenicians as Gadir over three thousand years ago, the little city on a promontory was the oldest continually inhabited city in Spain. Some legends had it that Hercules founded it after slaying the giant Geryon—Medusa's grandson—as part of his tenth labor. It was also the launching site of two of Columbus's journeys to the New World and was one of the cities on Ward's hope-to-visit-one-day list.

The imminent landing, however—right up there with take-offs for things he hated about flying—kept his excitement in check. He braced as best he could, but the landing was like being inside a rock someone had skipped across a turbulent river.

"That was fun," he said once their momentum slowed.

MacKenzie began the process of disentangling their limbs. "You mind?" she said when Ward's knee jabbed her thigh.

"So you are talking to me?"

"Grow up, Rafe. We've got an op. Let's get it done."

Ward pushed his back straight, making sure his foot pressed hard into her side. "Sam isn't an op. She's a kid who doesn't deserve any of this."

MacKenzie shoved his leg away. "Since when is life about deserve? You don't deserve what you've been through. You don't deserve me or that beach. And I sure as hell didn't deserve…

Forget it. I need you focused. I need you to be you, not a drunk or some weepy big brother. Can you do that?"

"Was that an apology?" Ward asked, the moment feeling like familiar banter.

"Don't push it."

He was happy not to. He was even happier when they climbed out of the smuggler's hold and were able to exit the aircraft. They'd docked among sailboats and small fishing ships at the north end of Cadiz, according to the signs. Despite being the only plane among the marine vessels, no one seemed to be paying them or their plane any attention.

"From Graciela," their pilot said, handing over an envelope before they set off.

"Any word on Oren?" MacKenzie asked, taking the gift.

The pilot shook his head and retreated into the airplane. MacKenzie opened the envelope then tossed it to Ward. He looked, then looked again. It had to be thirty thousand euros in hundred-euro bills.

"Should have us covered," MacKenzie said.

The twenty-minute walk into the heart of the city, which reminded him of Bari, Italy, was pleasant enough, if lacking in conversation between the pair. In the late afternoon sun, the whitewashed limestone buildings with their red clay roofs made Cadiz look like a city of burning candles. And domes. Whitewashed domes and gold domes as far as he could see, as if law required any building over four stories to be domed.

This is where I want to go, he thought, *when the rest of my life—this violent part of my life—is over. This is where I want to read and teach and sleep and die.*

In the distance, he could make out a pair of towers reaching above the city roofline. Rocco and neoclassical combined in unique oblong cupolas. He assumed he was looking at the eighteenth-century Cadiz Cathedral, also called the Cathedral of the Americas because it was funded almost entirely by merchant trade between Spain and America. He could imagine viewing the whole of the ancient world from those towers, Europe, Africa, the Mediterranean, and the Atlantic, like an ancient Greek map showing the world as flat disc.

The image was so stark it startled Ward. The answer was there in that tableau. In what they'd seen beneath the Pyramid of the Sun. Or maybe in something Ker had said while they were down there...

"There," MacKenzie said, interrupting Ward's momentum. She pointed to a public restroom beside a small outdoor marketplace. "I'll get a Port. You get the food."

"I have Ker's Port," Ward said.

"You trust it?" she asked.

"I can disable the tracking."

"Get the food. I'll be back."

She left for the restroom. Ward wandered the market, trying to recall where his thoughts had been going before the interruption but found nothing. His stomach grumbled. He gave in and browsed the food stands, choosing an assortment of meatballs, breads, and a fish he didn't recognize. On top of these, he piled garlic roasted prawns, then picked up four bottles of water. The last stand in the row offered wine and beer. His mouth watered and his head hurt. If MacKenzie was going to give him shit for having a drink, so be it. He grabbed two bottles of dark beer, barely managing to pay for them without spilling his plate of food.

He set up at a high-top table without chairs and swiped into the Port's settings menu. It was bare. Almost like the device had been reset to do one thing one: scan the murals beneath the Pyramid of the Sun. He reconfigured the Port's ID parameters, essentially setting it up like a newly purchased device for the European internet, making sure to keep Ker's scan program active. This done, he reached for a beer. The bottle was cold and already sweating. He lifted it. Stopped.

The feeling of being watched, the same feeling he'd had in Payaya City, hit him like a sudden gust off the sea. As in Payaya City, he couldn't find the source. No one was out of place. No one was whispering into a microphone on their collar. No one was loitering at a corner or behind a food stand.

I'm becoming paranoid.

"For fuck's sake," MacKenzie said, coming up behind him, "can't you do anything sober?"

"It's a couple beers, not a keg," Ward said, feeling like a teenager caught sneaking a sip of booze. "Maybe it'll relax you a bit."

"Not as much as you're hoping," she said.

Her answer confused Ward. Was she angry or simply giving him shit? He must have made face because she gave him that crooked grin he'd missed so much. Sinister. Playful. He imagined it could easily mean she was about to steal your wallet as drag you to bed.

"No," he said, getting what she'd meant. "I didn't mean…"

"That's why you never get any."

He had no response, and that quick, she was back to business.

"So we need to find this Lady of Leaches or whatever her name is, right?" She opened a beer and took a sip. "This is good."

Ward reached for his. MacKenzie snatched it away.

"We're on an op," she said. "I need you sober."

He held back his frustration, refusing to give her the satisfaction of an outburst. He ate two meatballs, *albondigas*. They were flavorless. He chased them with water. Also flavorless.

"Lady of Elche," he said. "Elche is a city on the east coast, probably four hundred miles from here, but I don't think that's where we're going."

MacKenzie popped a prawn into her mouth. "Where then?"

Ward did a search for "Lady of Elche" on his Port. The first image stopped him. "Son of a bitch," he said.

"What? No Leech Lady?" The grin again. It was almost like here, an ocean away from her army and her revolution, the General was gone. Only MacKenzie remained. But for how long?

Ward rotated the Port so she could see. "Not exactly."

MacKenzie dropped the crouton she'd been lifting to her mouth. "Wait, isn't that…"

"Yup," Ward said. He zoomed in on the photo, a limestone bust of a woman so unique it couldn't be a coincidence. The woman in the mural beneath the Pyramid of the Sun, the woman with the odd headdress and the vibrant multicolored robes was looking at him from the Port screen. "Meet *la Dama de Elche. The Lady of Elche.*"

"One's a copy then, right?" MacKenzie asked.

"Seems so, but if that's true then twenty-four hundred years ago people were traveling between Europe and South America."

"Or maybe she was the one traveling."

"Maybe," Ward said, not willing to explore that theory yet. "At least we know where we're going."

"Not Elche though? It's another game, running your riddles place to place."

"Those were your riddles in Paris, and this is Ker's game. You brought him. This is on you more than me."

MacKenzie took a long swallow of her beer. Watching her drink made Ward's mouth go dry and his tongue feel like it was stuffed with cotton.

"But his hard-on is for you," she said. "Besides, being right all the time is only attractive in women."

"Then you should give it a try," Ward said.

"Fuck you," she said, popping a prawn into her mouth. "Where's our lady?"

"Madrid. How do you want to get there?"

"You don't really think I have any idea where we are or where Madrid is, do you? I mean, other than being next door to France."

"Middle of the country next door to France is a good start."

"See, even without your special professor knowledge I was able to pick up some stuff while I was over here after—" she stopped, obviously hesitant to bring up the beach at Santorini where she'd left Ward unconscious. "While networking the *conservateurs* with my people back home."

Ward let it go. He could imagine it hadn't been an easy time for her, dealing with her father's death. Probably his funeral.

"What about Ker?" he said, changing the subject. "Who is he? Where'd he come from?"

"The Seer brought him in while I was running an op. He came with great references from someone the Seer knows for his tech skills. From over here somewhere."

"*Conservateur?*"

"No, an Eastern European faction. My people are straight up the middle. Northern Italy through the British Sequester. I've got nothing here in Spain or east of Stuttgart," MacKenzie said.

"The Seer insisted God approved of him."

"Maybe we should ask which god is talking to the Seer, then," Ward said.

It was a dangerous quip, and he held his breath a moment waiting for MacKenzie's rebuke. Or her attack. Thankfully, she didn't appear to be in the mood for a theological debate.

"How do you want to get there, car, train, or bus?" he asked.

She appeared grateful for the return of the conversation to logistics. "How long is the drive?"

"Five or six hours."

"Too long for a stolen car during the day. Too likely it'll be missed. I'm betting you don't have any kind of ID that'll rent us one or get us on a train."

"I've got my REC credential," Ward said, thinking of the ID card he'd been given upon completion of his training with Agent Compano; the card he'd used to enter the Tower with his bag of explosives that day. "Too conspicuous?"

"I'd say so. Alright, let's do a bus. What about Ker's deadline?"

"He said three midnights. Tonight will be the first." Ward searched bus station locations and scheduling on the Port. "We can get a bus in three hours. It'll get us in to Madrid around five tomorrow morning."

"Giving us two days to figure all this out and get Ker."

Get Ker, Ward noted. *Not save Sam.*

For now, he decided, they were the same goal. He would deal with the discrepancy later, if he had to.

They finished their food then made their way to the bus station a couple miles south, passing the time until their bus boarded at the adjacent café. MacKenzie sat with her back to the wall and trained her vision on the red and yellow lights across the walkway indicating when busses were ready to board. Ward read from the Port, adding to his limited familiarity of *The Lady of Elche*. The bust was indeed twenty-four hundred years old and was found outside the Spanish city of Elche just before the turn of the twentieth century. Studies indicated that it was originally a complete polychrome statue, perhaps with the Lady seated upon a throne or in similar posture.

He imagined the mural beneath the Pyramid of the Sun

coming to life and sitting regally upon a throne of reds and browns and yellows.

Ker's words came back to him: *The sister of three brothers.*

"The Water of Life," he mumbled.

"What?"

"Nothing. A Spanish folktale I'm remembering."

"You know what the last one of those led us to."

"Yeah," Ward said, then fell silent, replaying the tale in his mind.

"Come on, out with it. And," she added, "do the voices."

"There's a lot of versions," Ward said, ignoring her request, "and I don't know them all. In fact, the story the Grossmutter told us about her family, the three brothers and the water from the Temple, is a lot like it. I'd bet probably a Hebraic folktale adopted from or possibly originating in the Levant. The version I know goes like this. There was once an old king with three sons and a daughter. The king was in failing health and the oldest son decided he would go on a quest to find the Water of Life which could heal his father. Legend said the Water of Life could be found across the mountains and through the Valley of Singing Rocks, but that within the Valley you had to walk straight ahead, not looking up or down or back or to the sides or you would never return."

"Why?" MacKenzie asked.

Ward shrugged. "Because it's a fairy tale. The only problem was no one knew where the Valley of Singing Rocks was. The oldest brother set out anyway, and when he'd crossed the mountains a great colorful bird came to him."

"Like in the mural under the pyramid."

"Yes. It tells him the way to Valley, leading the quest for three days, all the while warning the brother to look straight ahead at all times. When they finally come to the Valley, the bird flies off and the oldest brother begins crossing the rocks, so many of them it's like a mountain has fallen apart right there and he's crossing its remains. Partway across he hears the sweetest song he's ever heard. He can't help it. He turns to see who is singing and is instantly sucked beneath the earth, trapped forever in the underworld as a minion of death or the afterlife or some such thing. When he doesn't return, the next brother sets off on the quest, then the youngest, both coming to the same fate as the older brother."

"And the sister has to save the day."

"She does. She keeps her vision straight ahead through the Valley of Singing Rocks, and when she exits the bird returns and leads her to a glade where waits the Water of Life, a perfect, clear pool. Beside the water stands a tall pitcher of many colors. She fills the pitcher and returns to the Valley where she spills a little of the Water onto the rocks three times. With each spill one of her brothers appears until they are all together again. The four of them return home and their father drinks the rest of the water and is healed. He rules a hundred more years, but the bird returns each winter for the brothers because they are not entirely free. Part of them belongs to the earth now, the underworld, and they must return to their new home during the coldest six months of the year. Every year. Forever. And that's why the kingdom has winter."

"What does all that have to do with Ker and his river?"

"No clue," Ward said. "But it's similar to the Greek myth of Persephone. That's what he meant about the pomegranate, I think. Hades fell in love with Persephone while she was gathering flowers and kidnapped her to his underworld kingdom. He knew that if she ate anything from the underworld she'd be his forever, but he could only trick her into eating six pomegranate seeds. So, six months every year she has to live with Hades. That's why there's winter. I have to guess he's either trying to reenact these mythologies or he's insane. Maybe the ashes will tell us."

"What do we do with them?"

"Again, no idea."

"Like Paris," MacKenzie said.

"Like Paris."

The placard for their bus turned yellow meaning it was time to board.

As they gathered their things, MacKenzie said, "I'm not going on a quest for another vase."

"Fair enough."

They boarded quickly, MacKenzie choosing a pair of seats two rows from the front. Ward could imagine her calculating the difference between the anonymity of the back and the quick escape offered by the front. She took the window seat, turning so that her profile wasn't visible from the outside.

When they got underway ten minutes later, MacKenzie was already falling asleep. Ward watched the lights of Cadiz over her as they pulled away from the bus station. Their route took them east across a mile-long bridge to the mainland. Then north. Doubt kept him awake. Was Madrid correct? Had he missed a clue? Was Sam going to die because he couldn't figure out the fucking game Ker was playing?

If he were a Believer like MacKenzie—*like Mom*, he thought—he might have asked for a sign. Proof that Providence was on their side. The only signs, however, were the ones whipping by outside the bus window.

Then he saw them.

The first sign on the side of the road read: *Excavación Tartessos 12.9 km.*

The second read: *Guadalete.*

Fucking Providence!

He wanted to wake MacKenzie and tell her, but the details were still unformed. Part of his theory had been proven correct by the signs, but not all of it. He let her sleep. He let himself begin to drift off, hoping that his sleeping mind could work out the specifics that eluded him.

CHAPTER 31

The *Museo Arqueológico Nacional* in Madrid cast its shadow over the small gathering of tourists waiting for its doors to open for the day. The museum was a powerful, two-story neoclassical building, its façade presenting tall windows and columns in a matter of fact manner. A wide staircase led to the main entrance, flanked by two sphinxes, breasts bared and pointing at onlookers as if watching them. It wasn't as grandiose as Paris, but Ward was impressed nonetheless.

Madrid itself, he mused, at least here in the city center, offered a similar comparison to Paris. Neoclassical architecture framed the streets, with aging limestone on the upper floors and storefronts faced with neon marquees and steel facades. The collective hum of electric traffic and the aroma of spices surrounded them. Same but different all around, Ward observed. The speed of the day was comparable with France's capital, as well. Pedestrians massed forward at a steady if unhurried pace. Like Paris, like Cadiz, like every memory Ward had of Europe, the air tasted freer than any breath taken in the Republic.

Unlike Paris, there was more of a uniformity of faces in feature and complexion. A tone darker but far closer to Ward's than to McKenzie's fair, freckled cast.

The ticketing booth grill rolled up with a *rat-a-tat-a-tat* sound. The doors opened. The crowd moved forward as if it couldn't decide between staying a mass and forming a line.

"Let's go see what she looks like," Ward said, impatient to see *The Lady of Elche.*

"We can't just walk in there like we're on vacation," MacKenzie said.

"Why not? We're not running from anyone. No one knows we're here."

"Except Ker."

"The worst thing that happens if he spots us is we confirm what he already knows, that we're following his bread crumbs. If we're going to outthink him, we need to see whatever it is he wants us to see about this statue. If you want to case the place first," he paused, flinching at his choice of words, like a bad crime novel, *case the joint*, "be my guest. I'm going in."

He got in the ticket line to the right of the northern sphinx, wondering if he was being too cavalier. MacKenzie was right. Just because no one knew they were in Madrid didn't mean they were free and clear to bounce around like tourists on holiday. He was still the Tower Terrorist, even if he was believed dead. Surely his face had been streamed around Europe on the news feeds almost as much as in the Republic.

He hunched into his jacket, doing his best to keep from looking at the girl in the ticket booth straight on. People recognized mug-shot style full-faces better than profiles. He kept his eyes down as he placed cash on the counter and held up two fingers.

The tickets collected, he turned to give one to MacKenzie. His gaze rowed over her shoulder to a set of tall green double doors across the street. His eyes followed the lines of the door up to the balconied second floor window above. A dark mass filled the double panes. At first, he thought it was a large man in robes and a hood. As his eyes adjusted to the light and distance, focusing like a camera finding the center of the frame, he saw it was the armored soldier from outside the high school in Arizona. The one that had watched the gunfight on the Avenue of the Dead. The ominous shade who was both Reaper and more.

Closer than he'd yet been to the figure, he could see details previously obscured by distance, smoke, and battle. Where Reapers' masks covered their faces, this soldier appeared to be wearing a single unit, three-quarter helmet covering his entire head and face save for the right cheek, eye, and forehead. It reminded Ward of the Phantom of the Opera's mask.

It hadn't been that long ago a day like this, stepping into a grand old building in search of an ancient relic with MacKenzie beside him, would have been like living the pages of an adrenaline-soaked novel. Like he was Philip Marlowe, Childe Harold, and Aeneas on collision course with victory and, perhaps, MacKenzie's bed.

Now, seeing the mysterious masked figure once more made him feel like Oedipus. Too smart for his own good. So smart he should be able to see the coming end, but failing time and again to do so. Trapped by misguided oaths and angry fates until it's too late, all the while missing what's right in front of him.

What am I missing?

What's right in front of you?

I don't fucking know!

"What is it?" MacKenzie said.

The window was now empty. The figure was gone. The curtains weren't even fluttering. Ward wondered if he wasn't starting to lose his mind. If all he'd done, seen, and drank had eroded his sensibilities.

"Nothing," he said. "Let's go in."

The entrance hall stopped Ward cold. It was nothing like the exterior. The floor was marble and modern. The ceiling looked like dark hardwood flooring. Lights ran like sunrays the length of the hall, guiding tourists between three massive block pillars that might have once housed ticketing booths or information kiosks.

Ward followed the crowd, driven by an irrational need to get as deep into the building as possible. MacKenzie grabbed his arm as he passed through the pillars. She pointed. Ward followed her finger to a very tall, slightly beer-bellied man in a blue suit crossing the hall before them. Ward could feel MacKenzie relax beside him, as if she'd exhaled an illness. The blue suits of the *conservateurs*, as they were called in Paris, were a uniform of friends. Allies of Simon, MacKenzie's father. A network of Believers devoted to protecting humanity's arts and history.

"Are they the same here as in Paris?" Ward asked.

"Can't say. Some maybe, but there's no central body I know of."

"I thought you made connections."

"Like I said, there's no central body in Spain. No one to call. Oren's contacts here aren't part of the movement. They're just business, and I don't know them anyway." She seemed to be sizing up the blue-suited man as he followed a crowd down the hall. "I think it's a darker blue, too. Almost navy."

"Blue is blue," Ward said. "He works here, right? We're tourists. Let's ask."

MacKenzie raised an eyebrow as if she hadn't considered something so simple. Ward wasn't surprised. To ask for help, to draw attention to herself when unnecessary, went against everything that made MacKenzie who she was. What surprised him was how quickly she agreed, taking off down the hall at nearly a sprint in the direction the blue-suited man had gone. Ward, startled and quickly left behind, went after her, the paintings on the walls—mostly Renaissance, best he could tell by the styles—zipping by without time for him to examine or identify.

He found the blue-suited man in a room devoted to Michelangelo Caravaggio. He was speaking with a short, dark-skinned woman in a hijab before the room's centerpiece: the *Medusa*, the smaller and earlier of the two the Old Master painted of the Gorgon.

The woman's traditional Islamic veil gave Ward pause, as it had the first time he'd seen one in person, not long after he'd gotten off the island of Santorini. While he'd learned it wasn't uncommon in Europe, especially in the south, it would have been a death sentence in the Republic. The distraction lasted barely a second or two before he noticed MacKenzie waiting behind the woman, twirling her hair in a manner so out of character that he almost asked what she was doing.

The woman in the hijab nodded thankfully to whatever the blue-suited man told her and left the room. MacKenzie then pushed her chest out and approached the blue-suited man, batting her eyes up at him.

"*Excusez-moi*," MacKenzie said, in almost flawless French. "*Où est la Dame de Elche?*"

The man shook his head and answered in Spanish that his

French was poor. He then asked if MacKenzie had inquired about the location of *la Dama de Elche.*

"Yes, Elche," MacKenzie said, faking a French accent. "The statue. Where can I find it?"

"Ah, Inglés," the man said. "I speak it more than French. The statue *de Elche* is in our protohistory area. We stand here," he drew an imaginary map of the museum in his palm and pointed the way, going over it twice to be sure MacKenzie understood. "I apologize for the crude map. My Port I forgot at home. It's a long day already with my boss angry at me for having to be recoded to enter."

MacKenzie took the man's hand and pulled him close enough, almost, to kiss. Ward was sure if she was wearing a low-cut top, the man would be staring down her chest unabashedly.

"I hope he's not too mean to you," she said, almost too soft for Ward to hear.

"No, please. I am happy to help."

"Then I'll be sure to find you when I need my next map."

She dropped his hand, spun on her heel, and sashayed out of the room. Ward, after a moment of disbelief, followed.

"What was that?" he asked, catching her in the hall.

"What?"

"*That.* And French. You speak French now?"

"That was good work, and yes, I speak French. You're not the only one with a brain here."

"I didn't mean—I mean, I did…What do you think? Is he one of your *conservateurs?*"

"I don't think so, but then things wouldn't work so well if they were obvious. Either way, he'll make a good backup plan."

"How?"

"We'll worry about that if we need to. Let's go see our Lady."

The direction the blue-suited man had given proved excellent and within moments they were standing before *The Lady of Elche.* Cased in a four-walled block of glass, she was exactly the woman in the mural beneath the Pyramid of the Sun. Except that she'd been blanched of all color. An impressive piece. Ward could easily imagine, at her current height atop the marble dais inside the case, a full-size statue of the Lady sitting upon a throne.

"What do you see?" Ward asked.

"A stone bust of a lady with interesting headphones."

Ward crouched a bit before the bust. Then moved to each of the front corners. No matter his angle, the Lady's colorless eyes followed him.

"What are we supposed to do?" MacKenzie asked. "Light it on fire and wait for the ash?"

"I don't know," Ward said. "It's got to be a marker of some kind. That is, unless it's some crackpot shit Ker came up with to buy time and drive us crazy."

"Or both."

"Let's think it through. It wouldn't make sense to send us here unless it's a trap or..." He thought of the two street signs he'd seen from the bus.

"Or what?" she asked.

"Or there's something here we need. It wouldn't make sense to bring us here for an ambush. Ker had the drop on us in Mexico. He could have killed us then."

"Okay, what is it we need? How do we make ash out of marble?"

"Limestone, actually, I think," Ward said.

"I don't need the geology of it. Can we burn it and make ashes or not?"

Ward waved her off. "Let me think."

MacKenzie approached the case, tapping her finger against it. "The sister of three brothers."

Ward's thought process was shattered by her words. Ker's words. They were important. But why? How? He needed time to think. He needed quiet. He needed a drink.

"What about back here?" MacKenzie said from the backside of the glass display case. "There's a hole."

Ward, conscious of the way a few other tourists were watching them poke around so close to the exhibit, joined her at the back. Just below the Lady's neck was a melon shaped hole.

"Of course," he said. "They used to use busts like this as memorials. They'd burn incense on days important to the dead or use them as urns." The Grossmutter's story, so similar to the tales of the Water of Life, rattled through his brain. Three brothers in all versions. One with a sister. One without. Vases. Urns.

"What are you thinking?" MacKenzie asked.

Ward wasn't sure how to explain what he was thinking. It was stupid. Probably a bit crazy.

"Never mind," she said. "Keep doing your thing. I'm going to scout the rest of the museum, get the full layout. While you're brainstorming, though, see if you can find Alfonso."

"Who?"

"Our blue-suiter."

"I didn't hear you get his name."

"Name tag, Rafe. Keep it simple, and keep an eye on him. I'll find you in thirty minutes."

Ward didn't like the glint in her eye. It meant she had a plan that would almost certainly supersede whatever he came up with, a plan that would almost certainly end in running, shooting, or both.

CHAPTER 32

MacKenzie caught up with Ward as he was buying coffee near the museum entrance. He sensed her approach from behind, a ball of energy resonating like a tuning fork.

"Black?"

"Always," she said, taking the offered cup. She found an available table in the café while Ward dumped a load of sugar into his coffee at the condiments stand. "What did you find?" she asked when he sat.

"He does rounds," Ward said. "Mostly the main hallway, then sometimes into the Egyptian room. He answers questions and picks up trash. Seems more like an usher than one of your *conservateurs*."

"Probably," Mackenzie said.

"So, if he's no help, what do we do?"

"Get a couple sandwiches then head out."

"We're leaving?"

"You want to come back tonight, right?" she said.

Ward almost asked how she knew, but it was fairly obvious. He needed to get a closer look at the statue, which wasn't going to happen while the museum was open for business.

"Good," she said, taking his silence as affirmation. "I arranged a safe house for the day, plus possibly a reentry here tonight."

Ward accepted her answer without comment. If she wasn't offering more details, he wasn't going to press. He didn't want to spend the day seeking flaws in her plan. He decided to trust her, and to allow himself to finish his coffee in relative calm. When they were done, he bought two sandwiches—Iberians they were called, with thin sliced ham and vegetables on baguettes—to go. Outside, MacKenzie gave Ward an address and told him to find a route on his Port. He did as ordered then fell into step behind her.

Projected at a forty-five-minute walk, there was plenty of time for Ward to work on Ker's riddle along the way, especially with MacKenzie a few paces ahead and showing no sign she wanted to talk. She strolled the streets of Madrid like a queen afraid of nothing. Vigilant. Disciplined. Aware. Beautiful.

Ward watched her for the first block, enjoying her confidence. The sway of her ass. The feeling that he was meant to be here, with her in the lead. Then he turned his mind back to the stories of the three brothers, both the Water of Life and the Grossmutter's. He went over them again and again, but whatever connected them to what they'd seen beneath the Pyramid of the Sun, to *The Lady of Elche*, eluded him.

Needing a different approach, he tried Ker's words. Ameles, the man had said. The River Ameles. *The Lady* had to be a marker to find it. But how do you find a mythical river with a statue of a dead woman?

Dead woman!

Yes. A step. Not the answer, but a step. The second sign had said Guadalete. The River Lete, or Lethe. He had an idea now. One that pointed them four hundred miles back the way they came, but an idea nonetheless.

One step forward, he thought, *four hundred miles back.*

He wanted to talk it out with MacKenzie, but she was marching ahead. In the end, the headache that rolled from the bridge of his nose to his left temple made him let it go once more. For now.

They walked by a single-steepled church with dark stone in the Mudéjar style—a remnant of Spain's Muslim dominated past. Thankful for the distraction, Ward slowed enough to get a good look at the splendid building. A statue of a saint over the doors named it as in honor of San Fermin, the saint connected with the Running of the Bulls in Pamplona in northern Spain.

"Come up with anything, professor?" MacKenzie said, waiting at the corner.

Ward hurried caught up. "It's got to be the Lady. Ker wants us to find a river, but what river? And where along the river? It could be hundreds of miles long. The answer has to be with the statue. I just can't figure how."

"Maybe some quiet time will help. It should be around the corner."

"What should? Where are we going?" The map had shown only a large square building at the address MacKenzie had given him. An office or an apartment building.

"Come on," she said.

Their destination was, in fact, a five-story apartment building with similar balconied windows as near the museum. Fairly average for what they'd seen of the city.

MacKenzie climbed the stairs and examined the call box to the left of the front door. "Downstairs," she said. "Apartment A."

"Where are we?"

"Improvised safe house for the day. At least until the museum closes, I hope."

"You hope?"

"We'll deal with whatever we have to deal with when it comes up."

She tried the door. It opened—not a good sign for a safe house, Ward noted. The entryway was a small landing with stairs running up and down. They went down and through a heavy fire door. Apartment A was the first door on the left, beside apartment B, with C and D on the opposite wall. A laundry room without doors lay ahead.

"Knock?" Ward asked.

MacKenzie took a small tool from her bag and knelt before the door, working at the lock. A few seconds later the door swung open. The apartment was small, with a couch almost right in front of the door. An end table and coffee table, along with a television, which was powered off, completed the living room. The kitchen was ahead with bedrooms, and bathroom presumably down the hallway beside the it.

"Seriously," Ward said, closing the door behind them. "Whose place is this?"

When Mackenzie finished her security sweep she went into the kitchen and said, "Alfonso's."

"Alfo—the usher?"

"Here it is," MacKenzie said, holding up a Port.

"What are we doing here?"

"He made the mistake of telling me he'd left his Port at home, so I stole his wallet and got his address. I figure we can use this to scan back in to the museum later."

MacKenzie opened the refrigerator. From his angle on the couch, Ward could see a couple bottles of wine standing up in the fridge's door shelf. MacKenzie brought out a carafe of iced water and brought it, along with their sandwiches, to the couch and sat.

"We can't do anything until tonight," she said. "And if Ker is watching for us, then someplace off the grid is the best place to hole up for the day."

It made sense, but it also made Ward nervous. They had no control over this apartment. No surveillance around the property. The whole setup was out of character for MacKenzie. Then again, maybe that was the point. Maybe being out of character was what she hoped would make the place safe.

If so, it wasn't working for him. Neither was the powered off television, its black reflective screen staring at him like an expectant void.

Like an abyss, he thought, remembering the line from Nietzsche.

If you gaze long into it...

I need a drink.

They ate in silence for a few minutes until MacKenzie apparently had enough sitting still. She began pacing the apartment while Ward stayed on the couch, taking occasional bites of his sandwich. It was good, but what he wanted was one of the bottles of wine he could see in the cabinet next to the fridge.

"The answer is in the ash," MacKenzie said after a lap around the apartment, "which is inside the statue."

"Best I can figure," Ward said.

She went on another lap. This time he heard closet doors opening. He got up and padded to the kitchen. Opened the refrigerator as quietly and as quickly as he could and took out a bottle of red wine. He didn't waste time reading the label. He took a long drink. It was cool and fruity, not what he would have preferred, but it mellowed his overactive brain. He took a couple more quick swallows, finding a nice calm in their aftermath, and returned the bottle to the fridge, then hurried back to the couch before MacKenzie returned.

"He knows we're here," she said, coming out of the bedroom hallway.

Ward didn't want to talk about this part of it. Ker knowing they were in Madrid, because this was exactly where he'd lead them, meant Sam was in greater danger. If they could get off this set course and put Ker on edge, he'd need Sam as insurance, but as long as they followed his path, she was nothing more than a carrot on the stick before them.

Then again, deviating from Ker's path might prompt him to hurt Sam in an attempt to get them back on course.

"Eat," he told MacKenzie, if only for the hope that she wouldn't say out loud what he was thinking.

Thankfully, she picked up her sandwich and began munching, though she remained standing, rocking back and forth beside the couch.

"What is she to you?" MacKenzie asked between bites. "Sam, I mean."

"She's a good kid," Ward answered.

"That's not what I asked."

MacKenzie did another lap. Her sandwich was gone when she returned to the living room. Ward knew she was going to ask about Sam again. It was a conversation he didn't want to have. He got out his Port.

"Got something?" she asked.

"Maybe," he lied, hoping she would leave him be.

She spent the next little while going through the apartment's rooms again and again while Ward reviewed maps of Europe and tried to come up with new search words or phrases to reveal whatever he hadn't thought of yet.

"What if," MacKenzie said on one of her passes through the living room, "it's more about…"

The heavy fire door outside the apartment banged shut. MacKenzie sprang toward the apartment door as it opened.

She had Alfonso by the arm before he'd fully entered the apartment, slinging him inside. He smashed into the couch, knocking Ward to the floor. When he got to his feet, MacKenzie was on Alfonso, bending him over the back of the couch. The big guy struggled, surely stronger than MacKenzie, but she had leverage. Then she had her gun. It pushed into the soft flesh under Alfonso's chin. His head angled back so far Ward thought he might go over the couch.

The Spaniard let out one cry before MacKenzie got a hand over his mouth. His eyes watered. He blubbered. Ward wondered if she hadn't just attacked a large child. MacKenzie had no such qualms. She punched him in the chest then returned her hand to his mouth. He wheezed but held still.

"You're not going to scream again, right?" she said.

He shook his head.

She removed her hand. "Say something."

"*Que quieres?*"

"English."

"What do you want? I give whatever you want."

"Do you remember me?"

Alfonso's eyes widened. "The Lady," he whispered.

"Yes. You drew a very good map. What are you doing home?"

"Lunchtime," he said. Tears flowed but he kept from further whimpering.

"Shit. Rafe, there's duct tape in the drawer next to the sink in the kitchen."

"Wait, what are we doing?" Ward said.

She gave him a look that was all the General. Orders. Follow them or be punished. Ward followed them.

"*Conservateur*, yes or no?" MacKenzie asked Alfonso.

Alfonso made a face. "*Ujier*. Usher. I am usher."

She slapped his cheek. Hard. "Do you know the *conservateurs*?"

"For painting repair? Sculpture?"

MacKenzie punched him in the ribs. He sucked air then bawled until she stuck the gun in his face.

"Hannah," Ward said, as loud as he dared.

She ignored him. Jabbed her knee into Alfonso's thigh. He cried out.

"*Conservateur?*" she demanded.

Alfonso shook his head as if afraid to open his mouth to speak.

"General," Ward said, louder than was prudent.

She raised her fist.

"He's just a guy," Ward said.

Just a big, Spanish version of Sam, in the wrong place at the wrong time.

"He's an asset."

Alfonso wept. "I know nothing. I am Usher. Usher."

"Shut up," MacKenzie said. She punched him in the jaw. He went limp, his eyes tweaking back in his head. "What's security like at the museum after closing? Are there alarms on the exhibits?"

"Stop," Ward said, approaching them. "What the fuck is wrong with you? This is torture."

"The revolution will do whatever is necessary. If you can't get on board—"

Alfonso pleaded with MacKenzie to stop.

"This isn't the revolution," Ward shouted. "This is about Sam. Saving her life."

MacKenzie punched Alfonso's ribs. He wheezed and tried to double over in pain but couldn't. She raised her fist to strike again.

Ward grabbed her arm. She twisted. Shoved Alfonso over the couch, her leg catching Ward in the thigh with a hard kick. He stumbled. She had his arm. The world spun as she leveraged him around. She tried to flip him, but he pulled free. He saw the jab coming at the last second and turned, taking it on the shoulder rather than the jaw. Her hand grabbed at his throat.

"Look at us," Ward managed to say before her fingers closed. She pulled his face to hers. "Whatever it takes," she growled.

"Then what makes us better than them?" Ward managed.

She squeezed. Flashbulbs went off in Ward's vision. Then she released him.

His legs gave out. On his knees, he shook his head to clear his vision. It only made him dizzy. The sound of paper tearing filled the room. His vision cleared enough to see Alfonso bent over the couch, MacKenzie wrapping his hands in duct tape. She tore off another strip and wrapped his legs.

Ward didn't watch the rest. He got unsteadily to his feet. Stumbled into the bathroom. Closed the door. Turned the faucet on cold. Watched the water rise in the basin.

What had just happened? What had MacKenzie become? Was she really willing to torture an innocent man for information, a Spaniard with no connection whatsoever to the Republic or her revolution?

I have to leave, he told himself.

And do what? How far will you get without her?

How far will she make me go if I stay?

The bathroom door opened. Ward turned, ready to protect himself. MacKenzie filled the doorway as if her presence, her strength, was twice the size of her physical body. She reached for him, slowly to show she was no threat. She put her hands on his shoulders. Pulled him forward. Toward her. Mouth to mouth. Strong. Soft. Demanding. Needing.

Then it was over. They watched each other, neither moving. Neither breathing.

Ward's mind glazed. He wanted to ask what she was doing, how she could think this was appropriate with a hostage tied up in the living room, but he couldn't remember how to make words. He tried and tried until he could force sound from his mouth.

"What are you doing?"

She kissed him again. Pulled him from the bathroom. Down the hall into the bedroom. Before they were through the door his jacket was on the floor. Hers hanging from her arm. They moved in unison to the bed, his hoodie dropping, her shirt lifting off. Her hands sought his shoulders, his stomach, his back with her nails. He wanted to stop her probing, embarrassed at the contrast between her strength and his soft flesh, but his hands wouldn't leave her. His fingers ran the lines of her muscled neck, shoulder, back. He imagined them tracing the letters of her magnificent tattoo. They found her waist and—

He stopped. He couldn't help it. When his fingers touched the scarred skin, it was like the background music cut out, and everyone in the room looked to see why.

"I'm not perfect," she whispered, her tongue working from his ear to his neck.

She could have meant her damaged flesh. She could have meant what happened in the living room. It didn't matter. He would forgive her anything. That was his commitment to her. His burden. As sure as he knew hers was that she'd always leave.

"It's okay," he said.

They fell onto the bed, everything else tumbling away.

CHAPTER 33

"I looked for you for a long time," Ward said when they were sweaty and sated in Alfonso's bed. It was probably, he reflected in the long silence that followed, the stupidest thing he could have said.

After a few moments, MacKenzie said, "And I've been looking for you since."

"You didn't have to leave."

"Too much left loose in Paris."

Ward thought she would go on, but she didn't. He should have let it drop, but with her he couldn't.

"Maybe if you'd stayed I could have helped."

"Stayed? For what? Walks on the beach and a candlelit dinner? Come on, Rafe. That's not us."

It was more apology than he ever thought he'd get. It was probably true, too. Still, he couldn't help pushing. "Maybe if you'd explained that much, I wouldn't have done what I did."

"The Tower? You're blaming me now?" She rolled away from him and sat up, not bothering to cover herself with the sheet. "That was a great thing you did. The defining moment in the revolution. Without it, we wouldn't be as close as we are. If you can't own it, fine, but don't bitch about it or cop out and blame me. I never forced a damn thing on you."

"Except to go to Paris."

"You would have followed me into a bucket of shit if I'd asked. For fuck's sake, Rafe, you stare at my ass like it's Renaissance painting. What? You didn't think I noticed. Women always notice."

He had no comeback for that, not that she waited for one.

She was up and into the bathroom in seconds. He listened to her shower. Watched her come out of the bathroom and pick up her clothes. Heard her go into the kitchen, opening and closing the refrigerator. He stayed in bed in through all of it, eventually falling into a restless sleep.

It was a little after midnight when Ward woke. After a quick shower, he found MacKenzie waiting on the couch. Alfonso, still tied up, was passed out beside her.

She slapped his cheek, gently, until he woke, eyes wide. She put her finger to her lips. He nodded.

"You want to call the cops," MacKenzie told him, "be my guest. But wait until after dinner tomorrow. If you don't, I know where you live."

"Sí, no police," Alfonso said, his voice hoarse. "I promise."

She cut him loose with a knife from her pocket. He repeated his promise. She ordered him to go over what he knew about the museum's layout and security. When he stuttered, she menaced him with a glare, but she didn't hit him again. Ward chose to believe the lack of violence was because he'd made his point earlier.

When they'd gotten all the intel their hostage had to offer, MacKenzie repeated her threat, and then dropped a ten-thousand-euro bundle on the coffee table. Alfonso started to cry.

"Let's go," MacKenzie said to Ward.

They didn't speak on their way back to the museum. Had things been different, Ward mused, it might have been a nice walk. The tension between them, however, along with the odd feeling of being out so late without a curfew, kept him on edge. There were no dark or deserted sidewalks like he was used to late at night in the Republic. No places to hide. They had no choice but to try to blend in with those coming and going from pubs and parties and wherever else.

When they arrived at the museum, they found the employee entrance right where Alfonso had said it would be, off the alley along the south wall of the building. Next, his Port, as promised, got them inside without sounding an alarm. They hurried through the museum, pausing once for a janitor— an old man in a light blue apron pushing a cleaning cart from room to room—to move out of their path before they made it to the protohistory exhibit where the final test of Alfonso's honesty waited: the freestanding glass cases surrounding the Lady of Elche.

It was linked, he'd told them, to motion and pressure sensors, which activated after closing time. The solution to this problem was that the sensors throughout the museum were switched off on rotating two-hour intervals each night so the janitorial crew could clean without fear of setting off the alarms. The protohistory exhibit's sensors were scheduled to be off from midnight to two, giving them almost an hour to get what they needed from the statue.

"What do you think," Ward said as they entered the exhibit room, "ten minutes until a janitor comes back around?"

"Get what we need in three," MacKenzie said.

Ward had expected her to say one. He counted three as a win. He crept to the statue, MacKenzie at his back. Without the overhead and floor-mounted spotlights illuminating it, the Lady looked more like a corpse than a statue.

"Thoughts on how we get it out?" he asked.

"You're shitting me, right?" she said. "Professor Knows Everything isn't prepared for this?"

Ward couldn't tell if she was annoyed or playing with him.

"Forget it," she said.

She approached the display like a lioness stalking prey. Ward expected her to make a full lap around the statue, but when she got to the back, she stopped. She examined it for a couple seconds.

"Thoughts?" Ward said.

Instead of answering, MacKenzie backed away from the display. Ward expected her to suggest a way to cut the glass, either the back or the lid. Instead, she ran at the case and leapt like she was trying to break open a door with her shoulder. The impact sounded like a bottle smashing someone's skull. Ward jumped back as the case tottered forward, seemed to resist, then tumbled toward him. MacKenzie, somehow, twisting off and away as it hit the ground and shattered across the floor like marbles dumped from a bag.

The crash echoed for what seemed like minutes. When silence returned, the Lady lay decapitated in the mess of broken glass, her head staring at the far wall.

"What did you do?" Ward said, choking down shock at the destroyed artifact.

"Got us in the case," MacKenzie said, getting to her feet and brushing broken glass from herself. "Now figure it out so we can get out of here."

Ward wondered if he would ever go back to studying history rather than destroying it, but he didn't allow himself to dwell on the question. They'd made their presence known. He had to act fast. He knelt beside the Lady's broken body. With a heave he turned it over. The hole in her back was empty.

"Get back," MacKenzie shouted.

Ward fell away from the Lady, but it wasn't to him she was speaking. Her gun was pointed at two janitors, the old man from earlier and a short woman with her hair in a tight bun, who'd come running into the room.

"Against the wall," she said.

The old man trembled. The woman began to cry. MacKenzie waved her gun indicating she wanted the pair to sit with their backs against the wall. They seemed to understand and followed her instructions.

"Don't shoot them," Ward said.

"Thanks for your faith," MacKenzie replied. "Tie them up."

"Little busy," he said, examining the hole in the back of the statue. He needed to do something, but what? He feared it was so obvious that any distraction would make him miss it.

"Two of them. Two hands. One gun. Do the math. Tie them up." It was the General speaking, and she expected her order to be followed.

Ward left the Lady and went to MacKenzie. With her f hand, she took the duct tape from Alfonso's apartment ou her bag. He used it to bind the janitors' hands and feet. Put duct tape into his backpack and returned to the broken rem of the Lady.

"Figure it out?"

"No," Ward said. Not knowing what else to do, he stuck his finger in the hole in the Lady's back and ran it along the smooth walls of the aperture. He withdrew his hand to find a layer of dust on his finger.

Or, as he'd surmised earlier, ash.

Keep the Port, Ker had said. *You'll need the scan.*

He took out the Port—Ker's Port—and opened the scanning program and let it work on the ash.

"What are you doing?" MacKenzie asked.

"Ker didn't mean we would need the scan from the Pyramid. He meant we would need the scanning program to—yes!" He almost laughed when he saw the results.

MacKenzie twirled her finger in a *keep going* gesture.

"Guadalete," he said, the whole thing fitting together now like portions of a lecture brought together at the end of the class period. "On the bus from Cadiz, we passed a sign for an archaeological excavation at Tartessos, then we crossed the Guadalete—the River Lete, or Lethe. Translated, it's the River of Forgetfulness or the River of Oblivion. The thing is, nothing in Greek mythology has only one name. It was also called the River Ameles. I can't believe I didn't remember that"

"Follow the ashes to Ameles. That's what Ker said, right? He wants us to find a mythological river?"

"The river we crossed on the bus is real. It's one of, I don't know, half a dozen or more in the world called Lethe, which is one of the rivers of the underworld."

"Styx," MacKenzie said. "Give a coin to the boatman to get across the river."

"Yes," Ward said, appreciating this new, more intellectually rounded MacKenzie. "There's five rivers of the underworld. The Styx is one of them. There's also the Acheron—"

"Do I give a shit about the others?"

But not too intellectual yet, Ward thought.

"Lethe means forgetfulness," Ward said. "The shades, or spirits, have to drink from the River Lethe to erase the memory of their earthly lives before they can cross the border and enter the underworld."

"Tartessos."

"Close. Tartarus is the underworld," Ward corrected. "Tartessos was a nation in Iberia, here in Spain, during roughly the First Temple period, the time of the Grossmutter's story. The Tartessians were incredible artists and traded with the Phoenicians. Could be they influenced the Phoenicians, or maybe the Phoenicians influenced them, bringing Mediterranean or Middle Eastern ideals here to Spain. Whatever the relationship, Tartessos was thought to be a myth, like El Dorado, until the last hundred years when archaeologists began finding actual traces of them all over southwest Spain. And the ash here is human. Twenty-four hundred years old, give or take a minute. Better yet, it's female."

"How the hell can you know that?"

"DNA is amazing. What seems like a speck of dust is an entire world under a microscope. DNA can sometimes survive in trace amounts, even in ash," Ward explained. "I actually consulted on the team that enhanced the ability to pull mitochondrial DNA from miniscule or cremated remains. They needed someone to externally verify ages while—" he saw the way MacKenzie was glaring at him. "Sorry. There's soil mixed in with the ash here. Ker's program runs a kind of geospectral analysis, and it's showing two distinct regional origins for the soil. One is unique to the area in and around Mexico City."

"Teotihuacan. The Pyramid of the Sun."

"Exactly. The other is local, ranging the whole southern coast of Spain with specific markers near Elche, Granada, Cadiz. There's traces of tin in the soil that match Tartessian artifacts at over ninety-eight percent. Right here." He brought up a map of Spain, then zoomed in on a city called Arcos del la Frontera, through which the Guadalete flowed. He held up the Port so MacKenzie could see.

"And the tin is the marker?"

"Has to be. I'd bet Ker's endgame is in an old tin mine or some other cave system around Arcos de la Frontera."

"Alright. Let's get out of here before the police come in and find us playing detective."

Ward stopped their exit from the room to whisper apologies

to the terrified, bound janitors, as well as assurance that they wouldn't be hurt. He then followed MacKenzie to the employee entrance they'd used to enter the museum. At the door, she paused. Ward went to open it, but she stopped him with a hand to his chest. Hard.

"Do you hear that?" she said.

She drew a pistol and placed her ear to the door. "Cars. Voices."

"Could be nothing," Ward said.

"It's never nothing."

Ward knew what was coming next. He gripped his gun, his hand already sweaty. MacKenzie looked at him to make sure he was ready. He nodded. She breathed deep twice, held the second one, and shoved the door open.

The flashing lights atop the police cars filling the alley blinded Ward, forcing him close his eyes and back away. No sirens sounded but there was plenty of yelling. Police screaming in Spanish. MacKenzie yelling back. From behind them, the sound of boots on marble. The police had entered the museum. They'd be pinched between the two contingents in a matter of seconds. He forced his eyes open, fought through the bursts of yellows, red, and whites in his vision to count at least ten police cars and twice that many officers in the alley, ranged in a firing line should the suspects decide to fight.

"Put your gun down," Ward said to MacKenzie. It was the only way he could see this ending without massive bloodshed. With these odds, even she couldn't blast her way out. But she wasn't listening.

"Fucking Alfonso," she said. She drew her second pistol and chose a target with each.

CHAPTER 34

"Of course they're in the museum," the voice said. Patient. Teacher-like. The kind of level voice a therapist might employ. Or a salesperson.

Then again, there might have been no voice at all. Sam, still in the box, was hot. The kind of sweat-soaked overheating that gave chills. She was hungry, thirsty, angry, tired. Most of all, she was unsure how much of what she was seeing and hearing was real. Heatstroke, if that's what this was, could cause hallucinations. Everyone who lived in the Arizona desert knew that.

She tried to center herself, give her somersaulting brain a focal point. They'd taken her off the plane hours ago. It had been daylight then, from what she could see through the three air holes. Possibly sunrise or sunset. The cut-out by her head had offered a constricted view of green fields when they unloaded her. A turn and distant white-capped mountains had presented in the other direction. Through the process, the men in matching windbreakers and hats carrying the box hadn't spoken. Simply shuttled her into the back of a white box truck, like loading a casket into a hearse. The side of the truck, the quick glimpse she got, had showed a wolf or an angry dog illustration beside the name KGC Importing.

The voice had joined her in the back of the truck for a brief period some hours ago after a stop for recharging. How long ago she couldn't tell. She counted the passage of time by the intervals between sweating and shivering. The gaps between the cramps that crumpled her into a ball then left just as quick, but always threatened the next bout.

"Don't worry," the voice had said. "We'll be there soon enough."

"Where?"

"Soon," the voice had repeated but said no more.

Another few bouts of cramps and the truck stopped again. The voice exited. Somewhere in that next interval of silence, she'd gone through multiple fits of screaming and crying. No one came for her. She'd stopped looking for an escape. Stopped trying to guess where they were going. Stopped being afraid. There was no point. Instead she let anger regulate her temperature. Keep her patient. Seek an opportunity.

Like now.

"No, I don't care until they leave Madrid," the voice—Sam now recognized it as Ker's—said. "Police aren't our problem. They'll figure it out. Believe me, this isn't going to fall apart because of city cops."

Another pause. A telephone conversation, Sam surmised.

"Yes, let me know, but be ready in case they actually figure it out on the first try. You'll need to get here before them."

The sound of a key in a lock grated through the box. Sam clenched her teeth. Bit her tongue by accident. Yelped.

The box opened.

Low lighting saved her from the blindness that might otherwise assault her fresh out of confinement. She tried to stand. Couldn't get her tingling legs to cooperate. Settled for propping herself up. She was in a small garage or warehouse. Nothing special or distinguishing about it. Just a plain, as-you-might-draw-it-generically, room. A little way from the box, Ker stood beside a metal chair.

"Fuck you," Sam tried to shout, but all she managed was a hoarse squawk and a cough.

"Thirsty?"

He produced a bottle of yellow fluid. Tossed it to her. It landed in the box at her feet. She tried standing again, refusing to touch the bottle despite the way her throat puckered and her teeth itched. She managed to get to her knees. Looked around for a weapon. An escape. There was nothing but Ker and the chair and two roll-down doors, surely locked, a good fifty feet behind Ker. The lack of obvious options only fueled her want for revenge on this bastard who'd kidnapped her, who'd fooled Reina into liking him.

"I'm going to kill you."

"I'd prefer not to speak hyperbole if you don't mind," Ker said. "Please drink the juice. If not for me at least do it for the one you're carrying."

"How," Sam said, the only word she could produce. Had MacKenzie told him? Did she look pregnant? She was surprised to find her hands across her belly.

"Drink the juice. Some food will be brought shortly."

"Why are you doing this?"

"Motivation."

He came close, boots clacking on the concrete floor. Sam tensed.

"Relax. I don't want to hurt you any more than necessary."

Sam got her legs under her, rose, clenched her fists. "Then why'd you fucking stun me in the neck?"

"Save your energy. I told you I don't want to hurt you any more than necessary, but I will if I need to. What I'm after is far more important than one girl's life."

"What are you after?" She hated the way his voice, smooth and confident, soothed her despite his threats.

"A second chance, let's say. Try to relax. Have faith." He sniggered. "Your professor will do what he needs to do. Then you'll be free."

Sam's stomach rumbled. She picked up the bottle. Drank. It was orange juice, cold and fresh. She guzzled the whole thing.

"Slow down or you'll get cramps."

"Get me more and I'll cooperate."

Ker moved, faster than she expected, around the box to right beside her. She could feel his breath. Hot. Pungent like wine. She tried to turn but he grabbed her arm below the elbow, twisting it behind her back. She yelped. Tried to pull away.

"Hold still or this might get messy."

He forced her to bend at the waist, as if leaning her over a table. Bent her arm more, pointing her hand to the ceiling. The pain in her shoulder and back was unlike anything she'd ever felt.

Worse, however, was the sound of a tool being taken from a metal tray or toolbox. A ratchet, maybe. Or pliers.

Sam twisted, a heavy, slow horror pumping through her veins, until she could see the gardening shears in Ker's hand, its blades open like a hungry maw.

"What are you doing?" Sam shouted.

"Stop squirming."

"You said you didn't want to hurt me."

"No more than I have to."

She felt the cold first. The cold of metal, of unsympathetic steel, against her naked flesh. She had a moment to wonder why it didn't hurt before the burning came. Then the pain. So much pain it seemed her whole body was screaming. She could taste it. See it swirling around her. Hear it screaming back at her, re-echoing, surpassing. Deafening.

Then darkness.

The standstill persisted for minutes. Or perhaps it was only seconds. Whatever the case, Ward's hand, the one holding his gun, trembled. He didn't want to die now, not so close to finding Sam.

The first motion was, of course, MacKenzie's. She trod into the alley, the invincible queen. "Get ready to run."

Shouting resumed from the police. Orders to surrender. Drop weapons. Get on the ground. Ward silenced the part of his brain that heard them.

"Look around," he pleaded with MacKenzie. "Put your gun down. We're not in the Republic. They don't know us. We're just thieves who broke into a museum. We can figure out how to get away. You start shooting, this is all over."

She held firm.

"For God's sake, Hannah, listen to me."

"Since when do you care about His sake?"

"I care about you."

"You have a plan for after they arrest us?"

"Since when do you and I need a plan?"

MacKenzie's left hand lowered to her side. "Okay, Rafe. Get Spanishing at them. Keep us from getting shot." She lowered her other arm. Dropped both guns.

Ward didn't have time to react. Didn't have time to speak. They were smothered by rushing police officers like children blanketed to put out a fire. Ward's arm twisted painfully under his body as he was shoved to the ground. His cheek then his nose mashed the sidewalk. He couldn't tell if it was blood or tears he felt on his face as they cuffed him, actual metal handcuffs rather than the thermoplast ties used in the Republic. Rolled him onto his back. MacKenzie was already up, hands behind her back, when Ward was dragged to his feet.

Side-by-side they were half-walked, half-carried to waiting police cars on the corner. MacKenzie was shoved into the back of one, her temple scraped and bleeding. Ward was spun toward another car. Slammed onto its hood, his stitched cheek taking the brunt of the impact.

"This wasn't the plan," MacKenzie said before they closed her in.

Ward tried to keep MacKenzie's car in view as it took off in the direction of Alfonso's apartment building. Only when it had gone was he jostled into the back of the car on which he had been held. It smelled like fresh bread and cooked pork. There was little leg room and his shoulder burned from the angle of his cuffed hands behind his back.

He shifted in his seat to get alleviate the pressure on his shoulder. A dark shape slid in front of the right-side window. A man in a black suit, the kind of boxier cut suit Agents wore to allow room for their weapons underneath. Though he could hear the man talking to some of the police, the conversation was muffled. After a short time, a police officer handed Ward's backpack to the man in the suit. The door swung open. Ward was yanked out and marched to an unmarked black sedan on the edge of the police perimeter. Jammed into the back seat. His backpack tossed in at his feet.

Again, Ward had to try to adjust to keep from being in constant pain. If he could only hook a foot in the backpack's strap, he could pull it near. There had to be a tool inside he could use to unlock the cuffs. But getting the backpack up to the seat, let alone to his hands, seemed impossible. The driver's door opened and the man in the black suit—broad shouldered, tight collar, and short gray-streaked hair—slid into the car.

"Where are we going?" Ward asked.

The man started the car, indifferent as if he hadn't heard Ward's question.

Ward tried again in Spanish. Still no response. The man navigated them into traffic in the opposite direction MacKenzie's car had gone. They drove a few miles, making three turns, then pulled into an underground parking garage beneath a modern hotel that did nothing for Ward to landmark where they were. Four levels down then to the back, as far from stairs or an elevator as possible. The driver backed them into a space between two white vans.

"Get out," he said, flattening the second word in a Middle Eastern accent. Israeli, sort of, but not quite.

Ward laughed, a shaky, panicky kind of chortle. He couldn't help it. If the total collapse of his plan to figure out an escape with MacKenzie while they were driven to the local police station wasn't enough, here he was being told to get out of a car with his hands cuffed behind his back. He couldn't open the door. Couldn't even scratch his fucking nose.

The black-suited man neither laughed nor got out to help. He kept his head perfectly straight and repeated the order. As if someone else had been listening, the left door opened. Large, hairy-knuckled hands hauled him from the car. Slammed him against the van. Hard enough to make a point, but not hard enough to knock the wind from him.

The man, in a similarly tailored black suit as the driver of the car, looked like a barrel with arms. He could have been REC. He was definitely military and mean.

And something else. Ward almost didn't notice it at first, but the man's left ear wasn't an ear at all. What he'd thought was a tactical comm device in the man's ear was, in fact, an ear-shaped mechanism, the interior of which mimicked the tragus and ear canal. The rest of the ear seemed natural enough, except that it wasn't. Ward couldn't put his finger on what was off about it other than to simply feel like it was somehow uncanny or wrong.

"There," the man said, pointing at an empty parking space across the aisle, lit by an overhead fluorescent bar.

"How about taking off the cuffs?" Ward asked.

It seemed worth a shot but neither the ear-man nor the driver, who'd gotten out and now stood in front of the car with arms folded, said a word. Gauging the futility of running and the absolute idiocy of trying to fight with his hands cuffed behind his back, Ward went where instructed, setting his feet in the center of the parking space.

"I almost couldn't believe it the first time I saw you," a voice said, uneven, as if being heard through a vent.

A shape separated from the darkness. Ward watched in fascinated horror as the proportions and features of the speaker seemed to shimmer and shift like a nightmare beast. It stopped, as if posing, at the border between gloom and light.

"But it really is you, Rafael."

Silence, broken only by the sound of the thing's heavy breathing, thick and labored.

It moved.

What stepped into the light was the armored soldier Ward had seen in the window outside the museum. The one he'd seen in Mexico. The one from outside the high school in Arizona. Only up close, it didn't look like a soldier. It didn't look like a person. It reminded Ward of a robotic supervillain from one of his brother's comic books.

It came closer, its chest heaving with each breath.

The carbon fiber and steel mask, its trim and wiring displayed like a gothic badge, was reminiscent of a car's engine compartment. Or a cybernetic octopus suctioned to the thing's face.

Small cables ran from the chin to beneath the body armor. The one visible eye was wide and alert. Not threatening, but not inviting either. The eye drew him in. So bloodshot it was nearly all red, split by lightning cracks of gold. The gold. He knew it. It had watched him for months, once, a lifetime ago. Every minutia of his movements. His thoughts. His following of orders.

The name coalesced in his mind, shaped on his tongue, but he couldn't speak it. Not yet. He needed time to accept what he was seeing.

Instead, his voice barely croaking past his lips, he said, "But you're dead."

CHAPTER 35

"You look like shit," Agent Compano said, her coppery voice coming from somewhere within the tentacled mask, a sickening parody of the first words MacKenzie had said at the devastated Labor Camp.

Ward tried to respond but couldn't escape her eye. His last vision of her had been her other eye oozing down her cheek on a train in Italy. Gasping on the floor. Body shredded. His mind clicked to the Tower. The dream. The flames. The eyes popping. His gut seized. He sucked a breath to steady his system.

"How?" he finally forced himself to say.

"It wasn't easy," Compano said. The metallic glint to her voice Ward now thought was servos moving her jaw. She tapped her breast. "The lungs aren't even mine. On the plus side my Port is fully integrated." This time she touched the mask over what should have been her left eye. "I can aim like a motherfucker. Want me to shoot your eyelashes off?"

Ward couldn't tell if she was serious or keeping him off balance. She'd never been cruel, but who knew what this kind of physical damage could to a person's psyche?

"What do you want?"

"Officially, Horeb."

"Horeb?" Ward asked, surprised.

"Oh, did you think it was all about you? Both the General and her friend you're so diligently chasing rank higher on most lists than little old you."

"The REC—"

"Don't be so black and white." She strained a bit on the "W" in white, as if the movements to make the sound were forcing the mechanism over her face into uncomfortable positions. "The REC isn't the only player at the table. Besides, you're dead. Even I don't have clearance to know otherwise. If I bring you to the wrong people, I'll be the one with a bullet in my head."

"Which they?" Ward asked, confused. Wondering on whose behalf she was *officially* here.

"They left me in that train. Did you know that? Four bullets in me. Want to guess which one was yours?"

Ward knew there was no way anyone could determine which bullet had been his, but if she told him the eye was his shot ...

"Some of your girlfriend's—let's call them compatriots— arrived on scene before the REC cleanup team," Agent Compano continued. "I couldn't move. I had to watch them checking everyone for vitals with my only eye. My ears were good, though. I heard everything they said. They'd been watching your girlfriend for some time."

"Stop calling her that."

"You too. They were looking for both of you. They found me. They saved me, in a manner of speaking. Four months in a bed. Many more relearning how to use my limbs. How to let my mind process through all this equipment. Then they delivered me back to my employers."

Ward had so many questions he didn't know where to start. Who had saved her? *Conservateurs?* Unlikely, unless it was for interrogation. But then why heal her? Why give her back to the REC? Why explain any of this to him?

"You should have died on that train, not me."

"You didn't die," Ward said, shifting his thoughts to the possibility of some other faction in this whole mess. Some group with an agenda that...well, if that was a cabal with an objective outside the Believer-atheist dichotomy, he wasn't sure he wanted to know about it.

"You should have died many times, Rafael. You and your General. You know, when they told me you'd been killed in the Tower, I think I knew better. Somewhere in the midst of the surgeries and the pain and the rehab, I knew. There's something about you two. Like someone is watching out for you. I bet you could do almost anything together. The REC wants her. Her army. Her headquarters. They're not afraid of you anymore. She's the boogeyman now."

"You're no longer REC, are you?"

"I died on that train, but I've been studying during my resurrection. My new friends, the ones who saved me for this," she passed her hand over her torso like a game show host, "they encourage education. One thing I know is your General's revolution will come. No doubt. And I'm sure you and she will be on the winning side. Someone or something will make sure of it."

"You sound like a Believer," Ward said. *Or crazy,* he added to himself, not sure which word was a more accurate description for those with Faith.

"There are more heavens and earths than you know in your philosophy."

The quote was inaccurate, but Ward recognized it from *Hamlet*. He couldn't help but think it almost fit better this way. "You know Shakespeare now?"

"I always did. Tell me, why'd you do it, Rafael? Why destroy the Tower?"

Again, that question. Ker and Sam and MacKenzie all trying to get at why he did it. Wasn't it obvious? Wasn't it just as apparent that he didn't want to talk about it?

"They deserved it."

"Who deserved it?"

"The REC. The Republic."

"The evil government."

"Yes." The questioning made Ward angry. It seemed like a test. A pop quiz on material that should have been self-evident.

"And you hurt them for what they did to you."

"Yes."

"Did you?"

"Did I what?"

"Hurt them, Rafael. Did you hurt them? By killing fathers, mothers, sisters, brothers? Did you hurt them? All those Agents. All those office staffers. The temps, the janitors, the prisoners in the lower levels. Who in that building hurt you? How many of them weren't even REC?"

"Following orders is no excuse. Working for them is no excuse."

"Like you followed orders. Like you worked for them, as if you had a choice in that."

"Yes, I followed orders." Ward struggled against his handcuffs. "But there was always a choice. I was afraid to make it until it was too late, and I was punished for it. No, I was punished first, before you'd ever recruited me. That building, no matter who was in it, was a symbol for that twisted government. An arm strangling everyone. I took off the arm."

"You maimed for revenge." Her voice was softer, the servos thus louder, as if she was considering his argument. "An arm for a death?"

"For deaths," Ward said. "For so many deaths."

Silence for a breath. Two. Then, "Is the Republic evil, Professor Ward? Its government? Its people? Can you define evil?"

"It's...it does horrible things," was the best Ward could come up with. It was a shitty answer, but it was accurate.

"In the name of Satan?"

"When did you become an academic?"

"In the name of who?"

"In the name of horrible things for the sake of horrible things, damn it."

"Be careful, my friend. You don't want to get caught spouting that kind of talk."

"What are you getting at?"

"Do you believe," Agent Compano asked, "that the people making decisions for this Republic do so because they are evil? Because they want the world to burn while they wring their hands? Or because they think they're acting in the best interest of the country?"

"It doesn't matter. It's not about intentions. It's about actions."

"Then what makes you better than them?"

Ward staggered as if she'd slapped him across the jaw. He had no answer. No philosophical quip to explain why murder was an acceptable response to murder.

As if erasing the entire dialogue about the Tower, Agent Compano said, "I've got an offer for you."

"From who?"

"The REC."

"I thought you didn't work for them anymore."

"Oh, I'm REC. Infiltration. The whole program. All mine."

"What does that mean?"

"Black ops, Rafael. A whole section of covert soldiers in development since before you were recruited."

"Reapers," Ward said, using MacKenzie's name for the armored Agents who'd assaulted them at the Labor Camp."

"Reapers. I like that. But we're off target here a bit. You're a special problem. Orders were for you to disappear in Arizona. Then the General showed up. Her and her friend. That complicated matters. Luckily, you ran to Old Mexico. Then, even better, here to Spain. The REC doesn't operate internationally anymore, not after Gaustad's little fiasco over here. Officially, I'm on leave. Only the Secretary knows where I am and what I'm doing. Speaking of secrets, do you want to hear one? Your General's friend had a different agenda than you. It's not easy playing both sides of the deck when the house is watching."

"You're a double agent?" Ward said, concerned about her use of a gambling metaphor, as if she knew about the poker game at the Grossmutter's house. At least as disturbing was her apparent interest in Ker.

"I'm awake and aware. Once you left the Republic, you opened up all the wild cards."

"What does that mean? Whose side are you on? Are your friends there," Ward motioned to the two men in black suits, "REC, or are they part of something else?"

"The offer is this," she said, as if he hadn't spoken. "Surrender. Full amnesty. Relocation anywhere in the world that isn't the Americas. The Republic has no imperialist designs. Its position is the rest of the world can go fuck itself, and it can do so quite pleasantly with you inside whatever other borders you want."

"But MacKenzie..." Ward began, leading to the catch.

"Like I said, they want the General. They want Horeb. They'll give you the world for these two little things."

"You keep saying *they*, not *us*."

"You have two eyes and are still blind," Agent Compano

said. "The world isn't black and white. It's not right and wrong, us and them. There are others with their hands in the pot."

"The ones who rescued you from the train," Ward said, imagining some sort of anti-*conservateurs*.

"This offer is the Republic's. Will you accept it?"

"Is it real? Will they really let me go?"

Agent Compano ran a finger down her cheek and across what should have been her mouth. On another woman, it might have been a sensual motion. "Do I look like a Believer?"

Of course not. That was the answer to both questions. It was as Ward expected from the REC. What he couldn't figure was what to make of this new Agent Compano. She was offering truth to gain his trust. But it wasn't the whole truth, that was clear.

"Tell them to go fuck themselves," he said.

Agent Compano bowed, servos clicking and whirring, as if to say, *As you wish.* "Offer number two."

"From your friends on the train?"

"Yes."

"And I'm supposed to trust them?"

"You're supposed to listen to the offer. It goes like this. The General is not their priority. Her friend is."

"What does Ker have to do with this?" Ward asked.

"My friends want him. They'll even help rescue the girl. All you have to do is lead them to him."

"What's the catch this time?"

"They would like to speak with you as well. Just talk."

"There's more," he said.

"Of course. I can't go home empty handed," she said. "I need the General."

He should say yes. Get himself out of this parking garage, out of these handcuffs. There was no way for the REC, or anyone else, to bind him to such a pledge. No way for them to keep him from running. He could, maybe, rescue MacKenzie from the police before the REC could get to her. Together they could find Sam, of that he was sure. It was Agent Compano's interest in Ker that worried him. What if Ker was a bigger threat than they thought? What if he had his own throng of followers, too many for two people to defeat?

"You may not both survive this time," she said.

"I'm already dead. Like you."

Agent Compano—no, she was no longer an Agent; she was just Compano now—didn't react. Ward grew self-conscious under her gaze, her eyes. One mechanical. One souped with blood. Quickly, before his courage wavered, he pieced together as many scenarios as he could. When the sound of her jaw mechanics announced her intent to speak, he stopped her.

"I tell you what," he said. "I've got a deal for you."

CHAPTER 36

Compano's men uncuffed Ward on her orders. They left him the sedan and its linked Port. They left him his backpack. They left him a 100ml bottle of Destilerías y Crianza whisky in the passenger seat.

They left.

He sat for a time in the car—his shoulder tingling, his leg aching, his hip stinging—and replayed his discussion with Compano. Over and over. Her offers. His counteroffer.

The deal wasn't perfect. It left him open to being double-crossed so many different ways he didn't bother trying to count them. But it gave him room to maneuver as well. Most important, it was the best opportunity he could see for saving Sam. What he still couldn't figure was if Compano could arrange to have him taken from police custody and brought to the parking garage, why couldn't she do the same with MacKenzie? Why the subterfuge? The deals? Why not take what she wanted, for the REC and for her new friends?

He needed a drink. He needed clarity to convince him that he'd made the right choice. To help him stop envisioning, over and over, Compano's shocking science fiction appearance. He picked up the bottle of Spanish whisky from the seat beside him and twisted off the cap. It smelled piney and flat. Cheap. But good enough to do the job.

Don't, he told himself.

It's a small bottle. Barely a sip or two. Maybe enough to calm you and let you think straight.

Okay. Last one. Then I'm done drinking.

He swallowed the whisky in a breath, letting the chill shoot through his extremities first. Then he leaned his head back as the tingling warmth spread.

He exhaled. Felt alive. Strong. Smart.

So smart I haven't wondered how Compano knew to leave me a bottle of whisky.

There was no snarky reply from his mind this time. No dialogue to debate the options: either Compano knew of his taste for spirits from her time as his training Agent, or she'd been watching him drink his bourbon in Arizona for the last two years.

"Stupid," he said. "Stupid, stupid."

He tossed the bottle out the window and watched it skitter across the ground.

Whether Compano had been watching him or not, whether she knew what he was planning or not, he needed to get MacKenzie out of police custody. That was step one. A plan for step one popped into his head fully formed. Formulating step two could wait.

He dug into the backpack for his REC credential. Holding it felt odd, like studying a photo of an ex-girlfriend many years later. Seeing what you never allowed yourself to notice then. The way love controlled you. Blinded you. Left you alone and afraid at night, in the dark.

He put the card in his pocket and used the Port to locate the closest police station, the most likely location where MacKenzie was being held. It wasn't far. He examined the area around the police station as well. Compano taught him to know the layout. Find the exits. Consider the best and worst-case scenarios. When he was satisfied, he started the car and exited the parking garage.

Just off the Gran Via, one of Madrid's key arteries, now awash in morning sunlight, Calle de Leganitos was a narrow one-way street with cars parked on either side. The Police Station Centro Leganitos waited halfway down the west side of the street. A nondescript stone façade beside a garage entrance, it seemed to dawdle beneath four stories of brick face populated with sixteen evenly spaced windows, air conditioners casting short shadows down the brick. The entrance was a single glass door. A uniformed officer lounged in a chair to the right.

Ward parked seven or eight car lengths up the street and got out of the car. He did his best to brush flat his jacket and run his hands through his hair. He slung his backpack over his shoulder and palmed his REC credential.

"I can do this," he whispered.

He took a heavy breath, enjoying the mixture of Madrid's spicy aroma and the aftertaste of the whisky. Exhaled the doubt. He needed MacKenzie. Sam needed her. All the rest could wait.

The seated sentry, a man in his late twenties with a bored expression, didn't seem to notice or care about the card Ward held forward like a shield.

Inside, the air was warm and stale. Sweat dampened his armpits before he'd gone five steps. He wondered if he should have left his jacket in the car, but he knew it was more presentable than his hoodie—stashed in the backpack—or the grimy shirt he wore underneath. He wiped the back of his hand across his forehead and proceeded through what he guessed was a check-in area staffed by a bald desk sergeant who was sifting through stacks of forms and papers. No seemed to pay Ward any mind. Figuring the best plan was to simply act as though he belonged there, he marched with purpose, peering through every window and door for MacKenzie.

When he'd cleared the first floor, he entered a stairwell in the back of the station. Instinct told him holding cells would be in the basement. Compano's training, and his experiences since he met MacKenzie, told him to avoid basements and tunnels. But if she was down there...

He went down. The door exiting the stairs at the first landing was locked. Breaking down a door inside a police station was foolish even as a last resort, so he continued to the next level down, the bottom. This door was unlocked. He opened it slowly, prepared to offer an excuse about being lost if an officer was standing guard, but the door revealed an empty brick hallway with an antique-looking boiler at the far end.

She wasn't down here.

Ward listened for company in the stairwell. Heard nothing. Went back up, passing the main level, to the second floor. This door, like the cellar's, was unlocked. He pushed it open, nearly hitting a woman who was reaching for the door.

"*Hola. A quién estás buscando?*" she asked, wanting to know who he was looking for, her voice free of suspicion.

Ward held up his ID card. "*Busco una prisionera. Pelirroja. Americana.*" He made no attempt to imitate a native accent. Being a visiting REC Agent come for the recently apprehended American prisoner was his best play.

"*La Americana,*" the woman said. "*Sí. Sala de interrogación 4. REC? Guau, ella debe de meterse en líos.*" She pointed the way, seeming genuinely happy to have an REC Agent in her station, expressing how much trouble the prisoner must be in.

Interrogation Room 4 was at the far end of the floor, the front of the building. Ward took note of the red LED lit above the door, indicating, he assumed, that the room was being watched by a live camera. He also saw an exit sign down the hall to the right. A stairwell he'd missed on his way in.

He rubbed more sweat from his forehead with his sleeve, wondering if he shouldn't have had that drink. Too late to change it now, he did the only thing he could. Slid the bolt unlocking the door. Slipped inside without opening it all the way.

"Jesus, Rafe, what are you doing here?" MacKenzie said before Ward could pull the door shut behind him.

He shushed her, taking a quick second to find the camera over the door. "I'm REC." He showed his credential.

She seemed to understand the plan in an instant. "I'm not talking to you, you fucking liar."

She seemed unharmed, sitting in a metal folding chair pulled up to a stark wood table. Her hands were twisted behind her back. It was every clichéd interrogation room in every cheap novel he'd ever read.

"I don't know how much they understand so keep your voice low," Ward said, keeping his back to the door.

"How did you get away?" she asked.

"Tell you later."

"You shouldn't be here."

"That's how you thank me for rescuing you?"

"Oh, for fuck's sake, knock off the pouting," she said. "I would have gotten away when they transferred me."

"I don't think you would have."

"No faith?" MacKenzie said.

"There's other people here. They want you."

"Agents, like real Agents?"

"I don't know," Ward said, giving the best truth he could. He needed her to understand. And to believe. "They're dangerous, though."

MacKenzie watched him a moment. "They let you go so you could break me out, didn't they?"

"Yes."

"You dealt me to save the girl."

"No," Ward said. "I told them what they wanted to hear so they would let me go."

Again, she watched him.

"Do you really think I'm going to give you up now, after everything?"

"Get me out of these cuffs," she said.

"I don't have a key."

"You are, without a doubt, the worst savior I've ever heard of. Give me a paperclip or a knife or something."

"It'll have to wait until we're out of here," Ward said.

"Fine." She stood. "They took my backpack."

"Where is it?" Ward took her arm above the elbow.

She shrugged. Nearly pulled her arm from free. "No idea."

"Then it stays."

"You really want to do this unarmed?"

"You really think I came in here with nothing in my bag?"

She didn't answer. He led her from the room. The officers had all shifted, turning their chairs or sitting on desks, to watch the fabled REC Agent take custody his prisoner.

"*Gracias,*" Ward said to the crowd, feeling stupid as he did, but certain leaving without saying anything would have been more awkward.

The stairwell he'd seen to the right did, in fact, lead back downstairs, putting them on the first floor beside the desk sergeant. Ward waved his REC credential. The desk sergeant bobbed his head and waved as a phone buried in the paperwork began to ring.

"*Gracias,*" Ward said. He led Mackenzie outside as quickly as he could without appearing suspicious.

As he had on Ward's way in, the sentry paid no attention to them.

"Will this work?" Ward asked as he slipped a paperclip into MacKenzie's hand.

"From the guy at the desk?" she said.

"Quickly, before they catch on."

When they reached the car, MacKenzie brought her hands from behind her back, the handcuff bracelets closed around her right fist like a pair of chromed brass knuckles.

"I'll drive," she said.

"*¡Alto!*" a man shouted.

Ward turned. He couldn't help it. The desk sergeant and the sentry were crossing the street, quickly but still at a walk. Neither had drawn a weapon.

"I think they wants their prisoner back," MacKenzie said.

Ward, closer by a step to the car, pulled open the driver's door and jumped in, struggling out of his backpack as he started the car. MacKenzie scrambled over the car's hood and into the passenger side.

"I said I would drive," she said.

Ward let the squealing tires be his response as he pulled into the street, smashing through the bumper of the car parked in front of them. "Port's in my pocket."

"Got one," MacKenzie said, holding the Port that went with the car. The one Compano had left him. The one Compano could surely track.

Sirens started behind them as Ward took a hard left, angling them onto a parallel street going back the way they'd come.

"Where are we going?" MacKenzie said.

"I'm supposed to hand you over at the Gate of Toledo, to the south."

The street dead ended. Ward forced the car right, harder than it was designed to handle. He nearly lost his grip on the wheel. MacKenzie braced herself against her door.

"So we're going north?" she said.

"Find the Metro line."

"Fuck, I don't know what any of this means," she said, her swipes at the Port sounding like slaps. "Here it is, I think. Right then left. When I say, cut up onto the sidewalk and get ready to ditch. We'll need to run."

"Got it."

"No, I mean *run*. Can you?"

Ward knew she meant his leg, his limp, but it felt like she also meant his general physical shape. "I'll run."

"Good. Faster. We've got two coming up our ass."

Ward had already seen them in the rear view and pushed the accelerator to the floor. If they could make the Metro, they had a chance. The police would search the trains all night, but they probably wouldn't send officers into the tunnels on foot. That would be their escape.

"Wait," MacKenzie said. "There's a bus stop a quarter mile more."

"Buses? No, the Metro—"

"Do it. Faster!"

The divided six-lane thoroughfare, bordered on the right by tall, nondescript buildings behind a narrow sidewalk, opened on the left to a plaza of concrete, grass, trees, a fountain, and a marble monument Ward didn't have the time or interest to examine.

The bus stop was on the right curb, a three-quarters enclosed glass shelter with a couple benches inside. It was empty of people but at least a dozen loitered around it. There were also no buses.

"Fuck," MacKenzie said. "New plan: hit the bus stop."

"What?"

MacKenzie leaned across and slammed her hand on the car's horn, blaring their approach to the startled pedestrians along plaza. "Sidewalk. Aim for the bust stop. Ditch when I say."

Ward swerved the car onto the sidewalk, sending at least two people diving into the fountain for fear that he would continue into the plaza.

"Now," MacKenzie said.

"Wait," Ward shouted, but she was already opening her door. "San Marcos," he shouted. "San Marcos!" Then she was gone.

Ward opened the door and rolled. For a fraction of a second, he wondered if gravity had forgotten him. Wondered if he truly was floating above the sidewalk.

Gravity wrenched him to the ground. The impact was jarring, but it didn't hurt at first, except for his teeth, which slammed shut with the force of a sledge hammer.

Then he was rolling, sliding, scraping, bouncing across the sidewalk. The sound of the car crashing came from too many directions, as if every car in Madrid chose that moment to smash into a wall or light pole or each other. His head continued to spin even after his body came to a stop. Another crash sounded somewhere to his right.

No, not a crash. Gunshots.

Ward got to his feet unsteadily, searching for the gun beneath his jacket. The gun that wasn't there. The police had taken his pistol. By the time he accepted this fact, that he was defenseless, the only sound he could discern was the sirens. All around. Somehow from inside his skull. He tried to shake his head clear. He looked for cover. For MacKenzie. There was no one near. No place to hide but the marble-bowled fountain.

Police cars swarmed the far corner of the intersection. Police officers filled the plaza, guns drawn. Searching.

Ward limped into the crowd that was forming, watching the chaos. The officers on scene didn't glance his direction. They were closing on someone across the plaza. He had no doubt it was MacKenzie. What worried him wasn't that he couldn't see her but that he couldn't hear her. The gunfire had ceased for the moment, but he was aware that the shots he'd heard couldn't have been hers. Her weapons were back at the police station.

The crowd got him close to the nucleus of the police swarm, but not close enough. He broke ranks so he could see around the parked cars. The legs and feet of two or three people stuck out from behind the tire of the silver car. Officers or MacKenzie, he couldn't tell.

Three police officers in semi-tac gear, two with shotguns,

charged. Ward flexed, ready to fly to MacKenzie's rescue. The advance halted as quickly as it had begun, however. Other than some shouting, there was no commotion. After a quick sweep, the tac officers dragged two of their brethren from the car and waved for a medic.

Another officer moved into the middle of the street, arms up in the universal symbol meaning *I have no idea*.

MacKenzie was gone.

Police cars emptied. Officers on foot began scanning the crowd, heads swiveling, bobbing, eyes wide in disbelief that they could have lost a surrounded suspect. A handful of officers, led by a lanky man with a wide mustache and medals on his chest, aimed their attention on the bystanders behind Ward.

Ward tried to blend back in to the crowd, but he knew he would stand out to even the most casual inspection. Torn jeans. Arm cocked across his chest due to the sharp pain in his elbow. Throbbing in his bad leg. He wiped his sleeve across his face and came away with blood from his chin. He was a mess.

Worse, as the officers approached the crowd, it began to disperse. Ward needed to get to cover, but there was little of it in the plaza. His best bet was to make the far side where traffic continued to roll. He took up behind a small cadre of teenagers, one flipping a green ball into the air. They crossed the plaza quickly, getting Ward almost to the street.

"*Alto*," a man commanded.

The teens spun. Saw Ward. Saw who was behind him. Without a word, they split up and ran.

Ward turned. A police officer, roughly the same height and build as himself, brandished a telescoping baton. The officer scrutinized him up and down then lifted a whistle to his mouth. Out of options, Ward charged.

He feigned left, as if to go around the officer, then went right at him. Low. His leg and hip howled in pain as he cut beneath the officer's baton. He came up under its arc with an uppercut to the officer's throat. The whistle dropped. Ward grabbed the hand that held the baton. Its tip was forked. A stun baton. If it hit him, he'd be electrocuted into unconsciousness. He dug his heel into the grass and spun, flipping the officer over his shoulder. The man hit the ground hard. His eyes rolled into his skull.

Ward looked back. The police were setting a perimeter near the fountain. They hadn't seen the altercation. Neither had the crowd of bystanders. Yet. As soon as one did, however, there would be Ports in hands all around. Recording from all angles. He needed to keep from being identified on one of those feeds. He grabbed the officer's pistol from its hip holster. Scooped up the baton from the sidewalk. Yanked up his hood. Kept his head bowed. Ran.

He turned corners at random, running through the pain. Running even when it drew attention. Running toward MacKenzie, hoping she'd heard his message before she leapt from the car.

CHAPTER 37

Circling back would have been suicide. The police had the intersection locked down and were sending officers onto the roofs of the surrounding buildings for better sightlines. The Metro would surely be swarming with police by now.

What did Rafe shout before I jumped? MacKenzie thought. *Sand acres? Sandman? Fuck!*

She continued north, hoping Rafe would figure out a way around the police blockade, stopping a few blocks from where they'd jumped out of the car. The brunt of the impact had left her shoulder aching. She'd also twisted her ankle while scrambling beneath a car to get away before the police had surrounded the corner. She limped into a small general store beneath a bright display declaring *Bodeguita*.

In the back, she found a rack of painkillers and bandages. Here, she examined the Port she'd taken from the car. Its screen was cracked down the middle, but it worked. She pulled up a local map and asked the Port to translate to English before searching for "sand acres" and "some acres." No results appeared.

"Come on, Rafe," she whispered. "Where did you tell me to go?"

It's Rafe, she thought. *Go with the obvious.*

She filtered the map to show only museums and churches, and scanned the nearby results. The answer stood out like a blinking beacon. Three blocks away was the Church of San Marcos.

Knew I could count on you.

She closed the map and looked up the Spanish word for "painkillers" on the Port. She pocketed a box of extra strength pills with a skilled hand, wanting to avoid going anywhere near the security cams at the checkout counter, and left the store.

Her progress to the church was slow, each step firing bolts of pain up her ankle to her knee then lower back.

If this is how you feel all the time, Rafe, she thought, *no wonder you drink.*

She almost missed the church. It was lodged between exceptionally modern buildings, including the only skyscraper MacKenzie had thus far seen in Madrid. In contrast, the church was probably a couple hundred years old. Rafe would know the exact age, she knew, and found comfort in that knowing. She found comfort in the building as well, its squared features offering a calming effect, as if its center tower, replete with rectangular column façades, had called her here to sit and relax and wait.

She opened the gate in the white fence separating the church from the sidewalk and entered the courtyard. The building's exterior curved like an invitation for embrace, forming a concave atrium of sorts, which offered a good deal of shade. She tried the front door but, finding it locked, chose to sit in the deepest, shaded corner of the atrium. She took a handful of pain pills and pulled up her hood and tried to remember the name of the city Rafe had said was their destination. The one with the tin mines.

Arcos de la Frontera, she recalled. *I'll give you an hour, Rafe, then you'll have to find me there.*

Blocks away, the sirens ceased. There was a temporary moment of calm. Then the police came. In twos and threes, peering into crowds, knocking on doors. Searching. Looking everywhere but at MacKenzie, who did her best impression of a sleeping homeless woman.

In contrast to the trained and forceful response of the police at the plaza, these canvassing officers were casual. Polite. Ineffective. It struck her that it wasn't just the police. It was an overarching attitude she'd noticed here in Spain. An atmosphere that allowed everyone to move at their own pace, without hurry or worry. It was the kind of pace that sounded good in theory but that she thought might drive her insane if she had to accomplish anything, like start a war.

A pace for the future, a long way off when she was no longer the General and the people of the Republic no longer needed her.

She bowed her head lower when a line of tourists speaking a language she didn't recognize stopped to take photos of the church. A family with a toddler on a leash. A pair of silver, wrinkled folks. An array of groups and couples in their twenties doing the normal things people her own age did when they weren't building a revolution.

None seemed to notice her. She was nothing more than a huddled figure they would likely edit out of their souvenir photos.

When they were gone, she adjusted her hood for a wider view of the street. Rafe wouldn't come strolling up the sidewalk. He was smarter than that. He'd watch the site somewhere half a block away. Thinking of him brought back the way he'd looked at her in Alfonso's apartment, with her hand around his throat.

Look at us, he'd said.

Us.

Like they were a couple on holiday, not a pair of fugitives who'd been on the run almost since they'd met. The MacKenzie he'd known wasn't the General. The MacKenzie he'd known wasn't responsible for bringing the war that would save the people of the Republic. But neither of those facts changed the way he'd looked at her. Not fear. Concern. And contempt. And pity. Even after they'd fucked, those emotions tainted the way he'd looked at her. When had she changed so thoroughly?

She'd returned to the Republic a week after the Tower had come down. The first test for her new Mexico-to-Spain contact, Oren, who'd promised he could shuttle anyone or anything across the Atlantic. Philadelphia was her first stop. Center Square was still a pile of rubble. The air still smelled of sulfur and death. She remembered her first emotion vividly. Pride. Her friend Rafe had done this. Had struck the first blow in the revolution she'd already decided the nation needed. No more chipping away. No more small victories. Seeing the twisted corpse of the Tower only enhanced her need to start the war.

She'd wanted to see faces like hers in Philly. Eyes lit with the need for vengeance against the oppressive Republic.

Instead she saw a hand-painted banner flapping in the breeze over the entrance of an office building across the street, declaring: *Philly & NY Our Towers Will Stand Forever.* She saw an endless procession of mourners approaching the fence that had been erected around the site, kissing their fingers then touching chain links. She heard them muttering about killing the fuckers who did this. A young girl, maybe fourteen, let go of her father's hand to press her face against the fence.

"When I grow up," the girl had said, "I'm going to stop people like this from hurting us."

The father had hugged her.

MacKenzie had to fight to keep from screaming, *THEY did this to you, not Rafe. He tried to save you. He died to save you.*

Even then, however, she'd felt—she'd known—he didn't die in the Tower. That narrative was too convenient for the Republic. It was the only way for it to claim a victory from this first strike in the revolution.

Is he here, waiting for me? she'd thought. *Will he let me apologize for leaving him?*

The awareness of a man standing beside her had wiped away her thoughts of Rafe. He was large, this man beside her, in both size and presence.

"Hell of a thing," he'd said, his voice deep yet barely above a whisper.

She'd known immediately he was a compatriot. A collaborator. It wasn't just the use of banned language. There was more. A manner, an aura almost, that made her feel both at ease and fervid.

"Language like that," she'd said, "will get you in trouble."

"Not with you, I think."

He'd put forth his hand, the swirling line of a tattoo peeking from his sleeve, wrapping his wrist. As if compelled, she shook his hand. He hadn't offered a name. Later, after they'd negotiated a careful conversation designed not to reveal too much until each was convinced the other was who, or what, they seemed, he'd told her to call him the Seer.

"That's a dangerous way to introduce yourself," she'd said.

"It is my name."

Sensing they'd overstayed their welcome at the site, that others had begun to notice them, like a blemish on a freshly painted wall, MacKenzie had offered a quick goodbye.

"Not yet," the man had said. "I need to know first, you are the MacKenzie I've been looking for? The one the REC is after? The one who knew the Tower Terrorist? The one who has grown a cabal reaching from Europe into the heart of this Republic?"

The man's brazen, public display of sedition had shocked her. She'd offered neither confirmation nor contradiction.

He'd continued, "The difference between a disaffected populace and a revolution is twofold. First, the people need to be awakened. Your friend has set the first alarm going here. The second is simply an army. And an army needs a general. Come to the police depot in Trenton tomorrow night. Two-thirty. You'll see."

He'd whisked into the crowd before she could ask any questions. It didn't matter. She'd already made up her mind to go. What she saw that night was exactly what she knew the nation needed. Organized, dedicated, and resolute, the Seer's people had looted the depot's entire stock, killed the guards, and set the building afire in under ten minutes, without a single alarm going off. And those, the Seer had told her, were untrained soldiers. If she could take over and turn them into an army...

"Why me?" she'd asked.

"The Lord chose you," the Seer had said. "He set me to find you. All that's left is for you to accept His covenant."

She had accepted. Of course, she had. Did that make her a different woman than Rafe had first met?

No.

Liar, she told herself. She'd changed. So had he. Questioning herself now, reevaluating herself now, would only lead to hesitation. Hesitation could only lead to death.

"After," she told herself.

Yes, she could talk to Rafe after. Figure themselves out after. For now, Rafe's allotted hour had expired, and she needed to determine her next action. She checked the pistol she'd taken from one of the officers at the crash, leaving both unconscious but alive.

Rafe would be proud of that.

Nine bullets. No extra magazines. She stood, taking stock of herself and her surroundings. Her leg ached where she'd been stabbed back in Arizona, but Graciela's medic had done a good job limiting it to discomfort. Her ankle throbbed, lancing pain up her leg when she stepped, bad but not a serious injury. The street was free of police. Pedestrians were sparse.

Determining she was good to go, she exited through the fence gate. She looked up and down the street once more for Rafe. He was nowhere to be seen. But another man was. A man at the corner watching her intently.

CHAPTER 38

Ward stood at the corner, in the shadow of a four-story, plain-faced building with haphazard window placement. Up the block, on the other side of the street, was the domed late baroque or rococo style Church of San Marcos. With square towers and a triple portico, its façade was adorned with Classical style reliefs. It recalled to Ward the cathedrals of Paris, though on a far smaller and less ostentatious scale. It wasn't a hot morning, but he was sweating. He'd been sweating a lot. With the running, the adrenaline, and the fear, this was no surprise, but he feared there was more to it. Maybe it wasn't only being out of shape as he neared his mid-thirties. Maybe he was becoming ill or one of his wounds had become infected.

Or maybe, with only a couple small drinks in the last few days, I'm starting to feel symptoms of withdraw.

He put a stop to that line of thought. The only thing that mattered was finding Sam. To do that, he needed MacKenzie. He'd been certain she would be waiting for him here, like a girl on prom night expecting her corsage.

She wasn't. That left three options. First, she'd been arrested or killed. He dismissed this one right away. The police were still canvassing, though with less tenacity and in a smaller radius than in the first few minutes after the crash.

Second, she hadn't heard him shout the name of the church before she jumped from the car. Or, she didn't understand or couldn't find it. He thought these unlikely.

Last, she was inside the church.

Or, she doesn't want to be found, he thought.

By them, sure, but it's you. She has to be trying to find you.

Unless she's done with my quest to save Sam.
No, he wasn't buying that. He would go into the church and find her there, waiting.

"Or I'll find her at Arcos," he said, remembering that he'd told her the name of the city they needed to travel to next.

"Arcos de la Frontera? Das ist auch unser Ziel. Fahren Sie mit dem Bus oder dem Zug?"

Ward looked up to see a pair of tall men in bright shirts watching him. It took a moment for him to understand that one of them, the blonde one, had spoken to him. Another second or two to recognize he'd spoken in German, a language Ward could understand well enough, if slowly, but had no experience speaking.

Arcos de la Frontera? the man had said, Ward was fairly certain. *That's our destination as well. Are you going by train or bus?*

While Ward was finishing the translation in his head, the blonde one asked in German if he was okay. The other man, even taller with a mop of curly brown hair, smiled in a *you poor thing* kind of way.

Ward stumbled through an attempt to say he was fine.

"English?" the blonde one said.

Ward nodded.

"Are you lost?"

"I've lost my friend," Ward said, giving the first narrative that came to mind. "We were supposed to take the bus to Arcos."

"Ah, we go by train tonight," the blonde said. The other whispered into his ear. "Tobias doesn't like to speak in English. He thinks his accent is ugly." Tobias frowned. "He says you appear ill. May we assist you?"

Ward constructed a smile. "Too much walking is all. My feet hurt a little."

The German gave a knowing bob of his head. "Good shoes are most important. You should consider a new pair. Tobias and I had to buy new shoes on our first trip here, how many years ago was that, Tobias?" Tobias held up four fingers. "Four years, yes. We too were unprepared for the miles on our feet. May we help with finding your friend?"

Ward declined their offer and wished the men well. He wondered how many years it would take for the Republic to be such an open place where strangers could worry for other strangers on the street. How long before any Citizen's interest in another would be concern rather than suspicion? A generation after the fall of the current government? Two?

He watched the men walk off, their hands linking. When he looked back up the street, there was MacKenzie emerging from the lee of the church, a spot that had been invisible to him from his angle. Her attention was farther up the block, on the other corner. On a man in a black-on-black suit with gray-streaked hair. One of Compano's men, the one who'd driven him to the underground parking garage. MacKenzie saw Ward and made for his location, passing the German couple, who turned in unison to watch her approach Ward as if they knew she was the one he was seeking.

"We've got to go," she said as she neared.

"Smile and wave."

"What?"

Ward waved to the Germans who were grinning and waving back with the enthusiasm of small children. The blonde gave the A-OK sign. Ward returned a thumbs-up.

"What was that?" MacKenzie asked.

"Nothing."

"Good. We're being watched."

Ward stared over her shoulder directly at the man, hoping he'd notice and take the hint.

"Don't look," MacKenzie said.

The man got the message and wandered off. "There's no one there," Ward said.

MacKenzie scanned the street. "He was there. I don't think he was REC, but who knows over here? You see anyone following?"

Ward said no.

"Alright. Let's get out of here. Eyes open."

They found breakfast at a take-away window, a crusty bread

dish covered in a tomato and olive oil spread called *tostada con tomate y aceite*. Coffee they picked up shortly after at a sidewalk cart across the street from a Metro entrance. Two police officers stood watch. The same at a bus stop a block and a half later.

"Stealing a car is too risky this time of day," MacKenzie said, licking the tomato spread from her finger as they watched a pair of officers chat beside the bus stop. "The owner could call it in at any minute. Then we're stuck in a locked down vehicle in the middle of a freeway. No thanks."

"Same issue as before with trains and planes. What about another bus?" Ward asked.

"The depot to get us to Arcos is three streets over that way. Right in the middle of the all this police activity. Got any college-level ideas on getting in? A diversion perhaps?" MacKenzie said.

"No," said Ward, the idea of repeating their diversion tactic at The Wall made his legs go a little weak. He thought a moment. "Let's ride right into the depot." He finished his coffee, a strong, powerful blend that had needed a number of sugar cubes.

"That's ballsy. And stupid."

"No, listen. We find a bus stop whose line runs in, one that's far enough outside the police perimeter that it won't be under surveillance."

"Because they're only going to be watching for us trying to get onto a bus at the depot, no ride in and do a transfer," she finished.

"Hopefully," he said.

"Like I said, ballsy and stupid. Let's do it."

Ward layered all the bus stops in Madrid onto his Port's map. Added to this a series of colored lines indicating their routes. Then began deleting them one at a time until he found what they needed. A route from a planetarium another kilometer or so south of their current position.

The plan worked, though not perfectly. There was a single police officer at the bus stop outside the planetarium, but he was young and much more interested in the college-aged girls coming and going than on his duty. Ward and MacKenzie waited across the street for the bus then slipped on board while the officer was pretending to interrogate two girls with brilliant colored tattoos showcased by their sleeveless shirts. Another tier of freedom taken for granted in Europe that would have resulted in arrest and possibly execution in the Republic where body art, common as an identifying feature between Believers, was illegal regardless of subject matter.

"Get on the bus to Toledo at the depot," Ward explained the plan. "An hour and a half there, then change buses and on to Arcos de la Frontera, which is practically all the way back to Cadiz."

"Of course. Fucking Ker. How long to Arcos from Toledo?"

"Another five and half hours according to this. That puts us there around six tonight."

"With six hours until Ker's deadline. That's cutting it close."

She was right. It would be cutting it very close. Six hours, give or take, to figure out where the mine was, get inside, and find Ker and his hostage. A flat tire or a delay because of the manhunt for them here in Madrid and they could well miss the deadline.

"We'll make it," he told her, as much to hear himself say it as to convince her they would succeed.

And for the next few hours he believed it. The transfer was smooth. The bus was waved in to the depot by a young officer whose glazed-over eyes spoke of trying to pay attention to all of the hundreds, if not thousands, of passengers in and out of the depot in a single day. He watched the passengers in the window while another officer, presumably, did the same on the other side of the bus. Ward, in the window seat, feigned sleep, his head back and cocked toward the interior of the bus. A half hour later they were on their way to Toledo on a bus piloted by a man whose gut obliterated the view of his thighs. The officer who waved them out didn't even offer a pretending-to-do-my-duty glance.

In Toledo, they changed buses again, experiencing the city only long enough to inhale the aroma of bakeries. They took seats near the front, MacKenzie wanting the aisle, a couple rows ahead of a group of women in vivid red Flamenco style dresses. They were on their way to Arcos at half past noon. There was no banter between them. No questions about last night or the last couple years they'd been apart. The red tile roofs of Toledo quickly gave way to the greens and yellows of the countryside. The Flamenco women's chatter, like melodic white noise, cleared Ward's mind, allowing him to intersperse his thoughts with the clues Ker had left. There was a thread teasing him, almost within his grasp, but the roll of the road and the sounds of the bus kept calling Ward to sleep.

He woke to the fading memory of a dream that didn't seem to want the light of day. He rubbed his eyes and let it go. MacKenzie was looking over him. He could feel coffee and morning breath mingling in his mouth, so rather than speak he gave a quick smirk then turned to see what she was looking at. His first thought, as Arcos de la Frontera was winding into view, was that he was seeing white seafoam cresting a dark wave.

The bus wound through the sandstone mountains, revealing and occluding the city at intervals, faster than he thought was prudent given the width of the road. As they emerged through the valley, the cliff-built town and the river below it, like toy houses glued along a steep set of stairs, slid into the window frame. If Cadiz had been a town of candles aflame, then Arcos de la Frontera was a place for sunlight itself to gather, reflecting off the whitewash in a blinding display.

The bus did not climb the heights of Arcos to the medieval sandstone castle that overlooked the town like a brooding overseer. The driver, instead, opened the door for the passengers to disembark at the lowest reaches of the city. The Guadalete flowed beneath a bridge nearby and meandered off to the horizon, the sound of its waters as serene as the Flamenco women's voices.

The bucolic landscape and river of the lowland created an even starker contrast with Arcos above. Every building, it seemed, was in agreement. Whitewash, black shutters, and the occasional spotting of red flowers beneath the windows. It was all so uniform that Ward wondered if it was illegal to decorate a home or business in any other fashion.

"Follow the ashes, right?" MacKenzie said.

He continued scanning the city above. The ashes simply weren't specific enough to point them to a location. A tin mine, he'd initially thought. Sure. Where? Which one? His gut now told him the ashes were just to get them to this city, to the general area of their goal. There had to be another clue that would point the way from here.

His gaze kept coming back to a sandstone square-columned steeple rising above the lower levels of the city. A church. Lighter stone than the castle way above, but out of place against the whitewashed city. Like a marker.

"Maybe," he said, trailing off as he used his Port to identify the church. "*Iglesia de San Pedro*. The Church of Saint Peter."

"What's that have to do with the ashes?"

"It has to do with the rock."

"Peter," MacKenzie said, then recited the dialogue from the Book of Matthew. "On this rock I will build my church."

"Remember what Ker said first. 'The temple of the rising sun, within the rock, among the dead.' Somewhere in that church. Ossuaries, maybe, in the crypts below."

"These fucking riddles. I'm going to cut his tongue out so he can't say a damn thing before I kill him."

This time Ward didn't object to her tendency toward violence. They made their way to the church, a twenty-minute walk up streets that often enough turned into steps to keep them rising ever up the cliff into which Arcos was built. The church's baroque façade was ornately scrolled and, save for the steeple, could have been a fortress rather than a place of worship. Inside, the nave acted as a focal point for the ribbed cross vault, its lines like thick veins in a strained arm. Gold adorned much of the interior, as did satin in reds and yellows.

As they'd done before, examining churches in France and Italy, they split up. MacKenzie went in search of the crypt entrance while Ward sought anything else that might connect to the riddle. He went for the transepts first, avoiding the central aisle between the pews despite the way it seemed to call to him. To draw him toward a life-sized effigy of Jesus Christ hanging on a cross in the apse beside the ancient altar, one of the oldest, he recalled, in this region of Spain.

"What are you looking at?" MacKenzie asked before Ward knew she was beside him.

"Nothing." He tried to mask his flinch as part of a natural turn in her direction. What had he been looking at? He'd zoned for some reason, while staring at a glass sarcophagus beside the altar within the massive gilded apse. Inside were the remains—possibly just the head, if he remembered correctly—of a venerated saint whose name he could not recall.

"The crypts aren't open to tourists," MacKenzie said. "I think I found where they are, but something doesn't feel…What about that?"

She was pointing at a small box, no bigger than a shoe box, set atop the sarcophagus. Ward did a double take. Had the box been there when they'd entered? Surely, he would have seen it. He glanced around the church. It was bare of tourists and clergy.

"You feel it too?" MacKenzie asked.

"Like a setup. Like we're being watched."

"Exactly."

There was nothing to be done about it. The test had been laid before them and they'd followed its lead this far. They separated, approaching the sarcophagus from different angles, Ward hugging the right wall around the pulpit, MacKenzie up the middle aisle. They reconvened before the sarcophagus. The box, made of a red wood and carved to give the impression of rope lined corners, was beautiful. It was also clearly not supposed to be there. Had it been placed atop the sarcophagus earlier, surely it would have been witnessed and removed. That meant…

"There *is* someone here," MacKenzie said, giving voice to Ward's concern before he could speak. "They waited to put the thing there until we were inside."

Ward slid the box from the sarcophagus. The exterior lid was adorned with a silver plate and an embossment of what appeared to be an apple. There was no lock or latch.

There was only one thing to do.

Ward opened the box.

CHAPTER 39

Ward could feel Jesus watching him.

The effigy of Christianity's namesake hung on his cross in the opposite corner of the apse, head bowed beneath his crown of thorns. Yet Ward could feel the eyes mocking him.

Or maybe it was MacKenzie's impatience. With this rescue operation. With Ker's puzzles. Ward's wrong guesses. The impending deadline. She had taken to Sam, that much was clear. How or why or when didn't matter. It gave Ward hope to see MacKenzie so intent on rescuing her. Intent on saving rather than destroying. She hadn't even asked for a gun since they'd left the police station in Madrid.

That was another potential worry. Ward had only the one pistol and a few magazines, a knife in his pocket, and the two-thousand-year old counterfeit Spear of Destiny. Not the best arsenal for the remainder of this quest, which Ward knew wouldn't end without conflict. That is, unless she'd picked up a gun and hadn't mentioned it.

"What is it?" MacKenzie asked.

She'd planted herself back from Ward, defensively, body turned to see anyone who approached. No one had. The church was eerily silent, save for the soft creak of the box as it opened.

The interior was once a lavish purple plush. Now, it was darkened and crusted with blood from the slender right hand, hacked off above the wrist, inside. A folded piece of paper, also stained, sat atop the hand.

"Sam," Ward said, reflexively, almost dropping the box.

MacKenzie left her post to see. "The fuck," she blurted. "I'm going to pull his lungs out through his fucking throat."

"Sam," was all Ward could say, over and over. He fought to keep from crying. He fought to keep the hand from morphing before his eyes into some twisted vision of those nightmare eyeballs bursting in the Tower's flames.

He must have handed MacKenzie the box. Must have sat on the cool stone floor. When awareness returned, she was holding the note.

"You okay?" she asked.

"No."

"Drink. You have water?"

He did. They shared a bottle, each taking a few sips. When he got to his feet she handed him the note.

I had hoped for better from you, professor. But I'm a sport. Maybe this last hint will get you where you need to be before Sam becomes a permanent resident of Paradise.

Ker

"How is her hand a hint?" Ward said, his throat tight.

"I think it's these." MacKenzie opened her hand. In her palm were six tiny crimson berries.

"What..."

His attention shifted from the berries to the box on the floor beside MacKenzie. The silver label. The apple. Except it wasn't an apple. And they weren't berries. He took one. Everything swam before him like skywritten shapes. Maps. Myths. The murals beneath the Pyramid of the Sun. Persephone. The Lady of Elche. The three brothers. Images. Sounds. Smells. Even tastes. Grouping. Aligning. Splitting. Converging. Falling away.

All the things Ker had said.

All the things he hadn't.

There it is.

"Pomegranate," he said through gritted teeth. He brandished the seed to MacKenzie like young Arthur showing off the sword he'd pulled from the stone. "Motherfucking pomegranate."

"That's it. Now make it make sense and tell me where we're going."

"He said if we don't get there on time Sam will eat the

pomegranate. The Persephone myth."

"So you said. What does it mean?"

"This is a pomegranate seed, and this..." He got out the Port and called up the scan results from the ashes in the Lady of Elche. "I saw the tin and homed in on Arcos. It made sense but here, remember what I said?" He pointed to the list of organic compounds found in the ashes. The third one down was pomegranate.

"I'm with you but..." She twirled her hand in the air as if to say, *Keep moving with the explanation so we don't waste any more time on this history-mythology goose chase.*

"He's a smart bastard. Really thought this through. Even the paintings under the pyramid. I don't know. Maybe he painted them himself to fuck with me. The Water of Life. The Vase of Soissons. He did his homework on us. He seems to know how I think. Maybe he twisted his clues and his test to keep it always ahead of me."

"Why? Why you? Why Sam and me?"

"I'm not so sure you and Sam have a part in it other than being ways to me."

"Then why you?"

"We're only going to get that answer if you don't kill him when we get there."

"Where, Rafe?"

"Granada," he said, the whole of Ker's test now laid bare to him. He went back into the Port's map. "About three hours away."

"You're sure?"

"Yes."

"Find me a hotel nearby with a pool."

"Wait, what?"

"I'll explain once we're on the road. Then you can explain your professor stuff. For now, find the hotel."

He found one a block away. They hurried as best they could with Ward's perpetual limp and MacKenzie's leg wound to a nicely kept contemporary three-story hotel with balconies and a wraparound terrace. MacKenzie told Ward to wait in the parking lot. He did as instructed, chiding himself for letting

MacKenzie convince him to leave the box behind in the church. "There's no doctor that can reattach that," she'd argued about Sam's amputated hand. "It's better here in a house of God than with us in a hot car for the next three hours."

Logical, sure, but it didn't feel right. There was nothing to be done about it now, though. Time was against them.

MacKenzie returned with a Port in her hand, tapping away at the screen.

"Where'd you get that?" Ward asked.

"Tourists leave their shit on their chairs when they swim in hotel pools. You ready?"

A red convertible with a white top one row over beeped, its lights flashing twice. The car, a Jaguar, reminded Ward of the yellow sports car he never bought with the professor's salary he no longer had. Its front end seemed to grin, saying, *I'm fast, I know it, and you can't wait to get in me.*

Ward began calculating how far they could get before the car's owner would find his Port missing and call the local police. All the way to Granada? Halfway?

"Stop it," MacKenzie said.

"What?"

"I can see your damn brain drawing the map and checking speed and distance. Just stop. The guy's in his fifties, probably divorced and remembering when he could still get it up if this car is any indication. When he's done his laps, he'll wander around the hotel asking if anyone has seen his Port. Then he'll go up to room thinking he left it there. Then he'll walk into town to wherever he had breakfast or lunch or hit on some café waitress his daughter's age. He won't think to go to his car because he can't drive it without the Port his dick-medicine-befuddled brain can't find."

"What if he does call it in to the police before we get there, and they shut us down on the motorway?"

"We'll improvise."

She hopped between two parked cars and catapulted herself into the driver's seat before Ward could consider getting in first. He slid in the other side. It took a few seconds to get comfortable—disappointingly difficult to do—and they were off. He read her the directions from his Port, enjoying the powerful thrum of the Jag's engine. Republic Motors cars didn't sound like that.

"He'll be waiting for us," MacKenzie said.

Of that, Ward had no doubt. Ker was always going to be at the end of the line waiting for them. What worried him was who else would be there with Ker.

"Someone had to be in that church," he said, "when we arrived to clear out the other tourists and keep them out. To place the box on top of the sarcophagus when we weren't looking."

"Someone who was already driving to Granada before we made it to the hotel to get this car," MacKenzie said, confirming that they were on the same page. "Now out with it, the rest of whatever you think is going on here."

"It's Granada," Ward insisted. "Ker never said river. He said Ameles, which is another name for Lethe."

"The River Lethe in the Underworld. We already covered that."

"Right. Except they're not just names for the river. Maybe it's the idea in the ancient world that the deity and the object are not separate entities. Whatever the case, Ameles is also the plain through which the river flows in the Underworld. The River Lethe, the Lethean Plains, and that's not all. Lethe, the minor goddess, barely attested in the surviving literature. They all share the name. Could be the river's name came first. Could be the name of the goddess. I don't know. She's the daughter of Eris, goddess of strife and discord."

"So Ker says to find Ameles meaning the River Lethe, but the trick is he wants us to figure out that he means the place not the river."

"People have been looking for the place, the Underworld, forever. No, I think he meant find the goddess, which might be more difficult."

"Are we going to the Lethe or not?"

"Exactly."

"Rafe, I will beat your ass without taking my hands from the wheel."

Ward understood her frustration. He wasn't explaining it well, convoluting it even to his own ear. He tried again. "If you're an ancient pagan and you want to worship the goddess Lethe, namesake of one of the five rivers of the Underworld, where would you honor her?"

"In the Underworld. Right there at the river. But we're in Spain. Why aren't we in Greece for this? It's Greek mythology. Greek gods and rivers."

"The Greeks thought they were the center of the world. Guys like Hecataeus and Anaximander before him drew maps of the world like a disk twenty-six hundred years ago. Like the pendant on the painting of the Lady under the pyramid. I think that was a Hecataean map she wore. The blue ocean surrounding a great landmass and the Mediterranean, with Greece in the center, at the heart of the thing. His map, a complete one with labels and…"

"And what?"

"A key. Like a key on a map not a key to a door. That's what he meant when he said her ashes were the key. This whole region, according to Hecataeus, was Tartessos. Aristotle wrote about a Tartessos River that traversed Iberia from the Pyrenes to the Pillars of Hercules. That's the Spanish-French border to the Straits of Gibraltar. But there is no such river. At least not above ground. If there was, however, if it ran underground let's say, in the rock like Ker said, it would run right through Granada."

He took a moment to digest all he'd said. And what he was about to say. Yes, it worked. It fit. It clicked. Better than any mug of bourbon could click his mind clear. Solid. Settled. Peaceful.

MacKenzie was watching him, her eyes shifting from the road to him and back again, waiting, letting him work it out.

"And why not in Spain anyway? To the Greek mind, the rivers of the Underworld would just as logically be here, at the edge of the earth, as they would in Greece itself."

MacKenzie didn't argue. She trusted him, it seemed. Snuggled deep in the Jag's bucket seats, he felt a chill. Here he was once more, the teacher. MacKenzie his student. Together hurtling toward insanity. He couldn't decide if he felt sick or exhilarated. Or if it mattered. His personal emotions were insignificant to rescuing Sam. He steeled himself for that outcome. Maybe the first step toward redemption for a man who didn't believe in it, in a world which couldn't decide on its existence. Save Sam and maybe there would be peace in his future. Forget paradise. Forget hell and purgatory. Just peace until oblivion.

"So where's this underground river?" she asked. "Where's Ker?"

Ward looked at her. Really looked. One hand on the steering wheel, her left leg bent up and leaned against the door. Her jaw set. Eyes firm on the road. The cuts and scrapes on her face enhancing her beauty. There was nothing soft about her. Even in bed she'd been a force. Not in a bad way. Not in a way that he didn't love. Not in a way he was foolish enough to think he could ever tame.

"The Abbey of Sacromonte," he said. The words, spoken aloud, confirmed his conclusion. Made it the truth.

"The endgame or another breadcrumb?" she asked. "I'm not sure we'll have time for the latter."

Ward tapped his finger against his temple. He was certain of the *where*. The *why* was getting clearer. Like a shape in the distance, barely discernable from the horizon. The closer they got, the clearer it would become.

"No, I think the abbey is the endgame. Too much converges there. Granada itself, the name means pomegranate. The Greeks called it the Fruit of the Dead. You've got the Persephone myth. Then there's the myth of Adonis, which ends with his blood soaking the soil, in turn birthing the pomegranate into the world. I'm going to do some more research while we drive, see if I can find more. Maybe something that will give us an advantage. If I'm right, once we enter the catacombs we'll find symbols or other clues linking the place specifically to Lethe."

"If?"

"I'm right," he said. Solid. Convincing. For all the good that would do for Sam, who'd lost her right hand and who knew what else.

Because of me.

Why? What's Ker's obsession with you?

I don't know, he thought. *I didn't do anything to him.*

MacKenzie pushed the Jag to the legal speed limit but didn't exceed it. At times, Ward thought she might slam her foot on the accelerator and push the car to whatever its maximum speed was. She seemed to almost vibrate with impatience at the prudent limits that would keep them as inconspicuous as they could be in a red sports car.

Ward wondered if it would almost be better if they were caught. End it here. Before he did what he was going to have to do.

Sam was cold. She'd lost a lot of blood. She was pretty certain she also had a fever. She knew her chance to get back at the asshole who chopped off her hand was fading with each bead of blood dripping from the rag wrapped around the stump of her arm. She knew her baby—there was no time for the "little thing" euphemism anymore—was in danger.

But mostly she wanted sleep. Maybe, if her captors were generous, to be moved from the concrete floor to a bed with a blanket.

"She's going to die," the big voice said.

There were at least two people in the room with her. The big voice came from the big man. His hair was bright and hurt her head when she looked at him. There might have been more than two people, but she didn't trust her eyes anymore. Everything blurred.

"And?" the mean voice said. The one who'd taken her hand. Her right hand. The hand that put on her makeup. The hand that tied her shoes. The hand that shot a gun. The hand she masturbated with. An odd thought considering the circumstances, but it made her angry.

She tried to sit up. Pushed with her right hand out of habit. The stump ground into concrete. She howled in pain. Cried. Her nose ran into her mouth. It was sweet, almost syrupy.

That's gross, a part of her brain told her, but she was hurt and thirsty and too tired to spit.

"He won't cooperate if she's dead," the big voice said.

"She only has to seem alive, Garm. Get him deep enough to

set his feet in the water. Nothing else changes. And since when are you squeamish about collateral damage?"

"I'm worried for our brother. For delays."

"He's waited this long, and if it can't be our good professor, we've got backups."

The big voice said something else, but Sam's hearing was now garbled the way her vision was. She was going to pass out. Or die. Her head hit the ground. Cold. Felt good. If only they'd bring her a blanket, she'd be happy to take whichever darkness came for her.

PART 4: DESCENT

We long ago resolved to serve neither the Romans nor anyone other than God...We were the first to revolt, and shall be the last to cease the struggle.
—Eleazar ben Ya'ir, c. 73

Alas! life is obstinate, and clings closest where it is most hated.
Frankenstein, by Mary Shelley, 1818

Aye, aye! and I'll chase him round Good Hope, and round the Horn, and round the Norway Maelstrom, and round perdition's flames before I give him up.
—Moby Dick, by Herman Melville, 1851

CHAPTER 40

They entered the neighborhood of Sacromonte via a narrow road, walled on both sides, with steep hills of green rising to their left. At times, the wall on the right morphed into the walls of buildings, homes mostly, in dirty whitewash that gleamed here but would have appeared grotesquely out of place in Cadiz. Once home to the Nasrid Dynasty, the last remaining Berber Dynasty in Spain, which ruled until the end of the fifteenth century, Sacromonte was now squeezed between the great hilltop Moorish citadel Alhambra to the south and the Abbey set atop the caved hills to the north.

"We walk from here," Ward said at a split in the road. He pointed up a narrow lane to the left. "The road is gated ahead for deliveries and official traffic only."

The sun had set more than an hour prior, leaving a little over two hours to meet Ker's deadline. The hill they ascended promised to consume at least thirty minutes of that time. The tree-lined walking path, lighted at intervals and surely packed with tourists during the day, was steep and cut a sharp left before joining with the winding road that had been gated below.

"*Calle Siete Ceustas,*" Ward said, reading a sign posted at the next curve.

"Yeah?"

"It means the Road of the Seven Slopes."

MacKenzie watched him, offering no indication that she understood why that was important.

"Rome was the City of the Seven Hills," he continued, "but it wasn't unique in that. Athens too. More important, both Jerusalem and Mecca were known as cities upon seven hills."

"Judaism and Islam."

"Not to mention the seven plagues, the seven heads of the beast, the seven archangels, the seventh son in Galician mythology being damned as a werewolf, or the seventh son of the seventh son, you get it, right? Better yet, it's the number of gates to the Underworld in Sumerian mythology."

"Sumer, as in Mesopotamia."

"As in Ba'el."

Ward wondered if she felt the same chill he did crawl from his spine down his legs and up his neck.

"Plus," he said, getting them moving again and pointing to another sign across the street, "we're climbing Valparaíso Hill. The hill over Paradise Valley."

"Paradise. Elysium."

Ward wasn't surprised she knew that one—the plains of the Greek Underworld where heroes, warriors of renown, went to spend eternity. "Bordered in mythology by the River Lethe."

"Providence."

"Providence," Ward muttered.

The path grew steeper with each curve. By the time they left the Road of the Seven Slopes for another designated walking path, Ward was sweating and limping. Each step felt like the kind of noogie his brother Daniel used to give when they were kids, only the knuckling pain began in his ankle, then surged to his knee, before spending a little time squeezing his groin muscles the way you might wring out a wet washcloth. Even MacKenzie limped.

He thought of Sam with a bag over her head. Her body wracked with feverish chills from infection due to her untreated wounds. He thought of what was coming and what he'd have to do to save her.

He wondered if MacKenzie would ever understand.

Understand or forgive?

You might get one but not both.

I can live with that.

He pushed on, taking the lead until the Abbey came into view the way photos slide across a Port screen. The moon, full a few nights earlier, was a spotlight on the sandstone and clay-colored brick dominating the hilltop. The Abbey's design was simple, multi-windowed and multi-tiered, reminding Ward more of a medieval warehouse than a monastery. Three arches, the middle one gated, beckoned them into a courtyard of small cobblestones. Ward passed through the leftmost arch, MacKenzie the right. The courtyard was bounded on the left by the three-floored wall of the lowest tier of the Abbey. Its ground level windows were caged. The windows of the top two floors were gated with faux-balconies. A single door of weathered bronze barred entrance into the Abbey from the courtyard. Ahead the courtyard dissolved into the Road of the Seven Slopes as it completed its winding way up the hill to terminate here at the Abbey. No cars were parked here or could be seen off to the left beyond the Abbey wall in what Ward assumed was a private parking lot.

The Valley of Paradise plunged down from the courtyard to the right, then swooped up the far hill higher than the tallest reach of the Abbey. A simple view. A breathtaking view. A refreshing view that reminded Ward, the way the ocean can remind a person, how insignificant most human struggles are. Relationships and careers and the rest.

But not life itself. Not death.

It was time to find Sam.

They circled back through and to the right around the arches to the Abbey's entrance.

"Is that a David Star?" MacKenzie asked, pointing over the door. "I thought this was a Christian Abbey."

"It's a hexagram, a six-sided star. It's found in so many religions I can't guess who used it first. Hinduism. Jainism. Islam. Judaism. Freemasonry. It's actually somewhat common in Eastern Orthodox imagery. I've read that the ancient Romans used it as a symbol for the six points of knowledge. The Babylonians used it."

"Ba'el again."

"Maybe. I don't know," Ward said. "They built this place because some treasure hunters found the supposed remains of Saint Caecilius in a cave here in the hillside along with the bones and ashes of some other saints."

"The Lady of Elche's ashes."

"Wouldn't discount the possibility. The actual oven where they cremated the saints and made the ashes is in the catacombs below the Abbey."

MacKenzie's face scrunched up. Ward remembered how she'd balked at the prospect of opening up what they thought was Adrien Quinque's coffin in Bari, Italy.

"You're fine with blood and war, but ancient burials and ash creep you out?"

"Let's just find a way in," she said.

Ward tried the door. It was locked, as expected after hours. But Ker knew they were coming. It didn't make sense to keep them from the end, from the river or whatever else he had in store for them. Ward banged on the door. It opened a few inches, revealing only darkness inside.

"*Que?*" a voice asked.

"Ker," Ward said.

The door opened all the way. A round faced, round bellied monk in black waved them inside. He held two candleholders in his left hand. He offered one to MacKenzie.

"*Abajo,*" the monk said. He motioned down the hall then scurried off and disappeared, the sound of a heavy door closing following soon after.

"I thought it would be empty like the church," MacKenzie said, setting the candle down and taking out a flashlight.

"Maybe he couldn't buy this place out. Or his influence only covers so much. We can ask when we find him." Ward did his best to concentrate. To not get caught examining their surroundings. White stone. White plaster. Gold adornments. Sconces and portrait frames and intricate carpet runners and more.

They followed signs for the Santa Cuevas, the Holy Caves, deeper into the Abbey, the air taking on the stiffness of century old wet laundry. Soon they stood before the imposing iron and wood doors to the catacombs, set behind an already open wrought iron gate. Enter and they were fully committed to Ker's game.

Ward stopped MacKenzie from opening the doors.

"What?"

"Give me a second," he said, returning to the hall. Empty but for a single door on one side.

"What are you doing?"

"Making sure."

He opened the first door. Inside was a small chapel with an oblong window high on the back wall. Ward didn't bother examining the accoutrements. He closed the door but didn't latch it.

"We good?" MacKenzie asked.

"Let's go."

MacKenzie drew a pistol. Ward should have known not to be surprised by that. It had probably come from a police officer in Madrid, same as the one tucked in his own belt. It gave him pause, enough for her to reach the doors. To grab the ornate handle.

Steady, he commanded himself.

From his jacket pocket he took the stun baton he'd picked up in the plaza in Madrid. Flicked it open. MacKenzie paused. Before she could turn he jabbed the baton's prongs into her neck.

She stiffened. Shook. Dropped.

Ward let go the baton. Twisted to get a hand beneath her skull so she didn't smash it on the stone floor. Fell with her.

He laid beside her a few seconds then rolled over and made sure she was breathing.

He took her gun, a Swiss-made 9mm, and lifted her by the shoulders. Dragged her to the chapel. Set her inside. Bound her legs and hands with what was left of Alfonso's duct tape. Dug into his backpack for the pad of paper he kept there. His fingers found something else. The Spear of Destiny wrapped in a blue shirt. He slid it from the pack like a piece of fragile pottery. Unwrapped it. Watched his distorted reflection in its steel.

Balance. Symmetry. Providence. Whatever it was called, he knew what to do next. He got the pad and wrote the note. Placed it and the Spear beside MacKenzie and kissed her cheek.

"I'm sorry," he whispered, standing. "I'll take understanding if that's the best you can do. This is the best I can do to save Sam. And you."

He closed the door behind him, panic hissing through his core at the sound of the latch. There was no turning back now. He'd placed his bet. Ker had made his. It was time for everyone show their cards.

CHAPTER 41

The doors to the Holy Caves swung open silently, presenting Ward with stairs leading down through painted walls into the rock itself. He drew his pistol and flashlight for the descent. At the bottom, a low tunnel built of cobblestones as much as hewn from the earth pointed the way. The criss-crossing bricks of the tunnel floor seemed to shimmer like a too-busy carpet that induced vertigo. He kept his eyes ahead, locked on a flickering light at the terminus, so focused that he didn't notice the two men at the end until they were close enough to touch him.

He leapt back, gun up, and nearly tripped over his own feet. His back hit the wall. Instinct kept him from shooting. He looked again. The two men were wax effigies in ancient robes, their faces an attempt at serenity, he guessed, though Ward found them much creepier.

"Sorry," he muttered to one of the effigies, not bothering to examine either closely enough to find out which saints or early Christian martyrs they were.

Instead, he took in the room. Lit by sconced bulbs designed to look like candles, the room reminded him of the clover-leaf chamber, albeit with more chapels, beneath the Pyramid of the Sun. Some of the walls were natural bedrock, others plastered over, and four great columns seemed to pride themselves in holding the room in the hill's belly.

Ward walked by each chapel, glancing through their black iron gates. An effigy, an altar, a painting, an encased relic, and more. He saw them but didn't. His legs and hands trembled with adrenaline and anticipation, pushing him to keep moving. Save for one.

Behind its grill smiled a four-foot tall oven, reminding Ward of a shallow brick pizzeria oven, set into the back wall. According to legend it was the oven used to cremate the remains of saints. The connection to the Lady of Elche was too obvious to ignore. He was in the right place. But what next? There were two exits from the room. Was he supposed to take one? Was there another clue here at the oven? Or elsewhere in the chamber?

He paced the room, trying to work out the details. Having MacKenzie to bounce ideas off would have made it easier, but he'd made the right call with her. If she would heed his letter when she woke, he'd gladly suffer her wrath somewhere down the line.

Even if it comes to violence down here, to killing? Will I believe it was the right call when the gunfire begins?

He waited for his brain to respond in the typical back-and-forth dialogue he'd gotten used to since his sentinel abandoned him after the loss of the Vase of Soissons, but it didn't come. Instead, he heard the ghost of a voice, softly, like a breeze at first.

No more fires, baby, the voice whispered. His mother's voice.

Even Ker? he asked the voice, the dream.

Silence in the Holy Caves.

He almost asked what he should do if it came down to a choice—Ker or Sam—but he feared the answer. He feared contemplating if his choice was really between Sam in this life and seeing his parents again, his brother again, in an afterlife as the dream version of his mother had implied.

I don't believe in the afterlife, he thought.

Again, his internal dialogue refused to respond.

"Fuck it," he said. "I can do this on my own."

But he couldn't. He needed another shot of clarity, like he'd gotten in Madrid from the bottle of whisky Compano left for him. A gulp or two would be plenty, if only...

He dug into the backpack, shoving aside the junk food, the water bottles, the loaded magazines. There, at the bottom, partially stuck in a rolled sock, was a two-ounce sample size bottle. Willett Rye.

Before any part of his mind could protest, he pulled off the cap and poured the amber liquid into his mouth. Barely a sip. He held it a moment, letting it roll about his tongue before swallowing. It was acute and intense, with hints of oak and vanilla and cocoa. It was good.

He dropped the empty bottle back into his bag to avoid leaving a marker that he'd been here. Let himself pace the chapels as his mind wandered. He was searching for Lethe. The river. The plains that bordered Elysium. The goddess. One of them. Any of them. It occurred to him the irony of the symbolism. The three faces of Lethe. The three bodies of the Catholic Trinity. Paganism and monotheism alike coming to the same spirituality. Belief was Belief.

It would make an intriguing lecture, if he were to ever find that academic life again, in a country that allowed such education. Truth be told, he was happy Ker's test, and the accompanying mythology, led to a triad. He'd had enough of the El and Ba'el binary to last a lifetime.

He'd hardly noticed that he'd approached the grill before the oven. That he'd placed his hands on the stone, cool and smooth, around it. That his finger was tracing a shallow imperfection. Etching. Graffiti. Triangle.

Like Lethe. Out of one, three. Only this triangle was missing the bottom. Was pointing to the ceiling like an arrow. Or a…

"Lambda," he said, naming the Greek letter. The first letter in the word Lethe.

He scoured the walls for another. There. Barely visible on the edge of a floor tile before one of the gated exits from the room. He went through the unlocked gate, flashlight beam bouncing before him, charging recklessly. There was no time for anything else. Ker's deadline was approaching, and Ward had no idea how deep into the catacombs he had to go.

Sam had been slipping in an out of consciousness. The last thing she remembered was being in the back of a truck. Like in Mexico. A pickup. Now, she was lying on cold ground. Her fingers and toes were cold. Her eyes were closed. She didn't want to open them yet.

Nearby, the mean voice and the big voice were arguing.

Sam tried spreading and clenching her fingers and toes to

warm them. Some didn't respond. Some set her hand aflame.

She screamed.

She'd forgotten her hand was gone. She could still feel it. The fingers pulsing on fire like they'd been prodded a thousand times at once. The wrist a tight blunt ache that felt like it might go on forever.

A hand covered her mouth. Heavy. Smelling of sweat and fried foods.

"Do that again and I'll take the other hand," the mean voice said.

Sam opened her eyes. She knew the mean voice. Ker. His face snarled inches from hers.

"What about the—" the big voice said. The one Ker had called Garm.

"Not until he's here," Ker said. "Not until everything is in place. Let him prove how smart he is then."

"Too much," Garm said. "You're risking too much."

"Tell that to our brother."

Ker stood, leaving Sam on the ground. Above her was darkness. For some reason she thought it might be the darkness of a cave. She tried to get a better look around. Her vision blurred.

I'm going to black out again, she thought. *Good. My hand hurts.*

The pain flared. Her vision flickered. Then winked out.

Ward had worked his way through all of the touristed tunnels, a lambda offering him direction at each crossroads. He'd passed through a few red velvet ropes, some draped chains, and five metal gates, all unlocked and swinging open. Twice he'd had to climb through rubble-laden passages, the holes likely traveled by archaeologists no more than a handful of times over the years. The tunnels were growing progressively lower and narrower.

Fear for Sam kept claustrophobia at bay, but the downslope of the tunnels was hard to ignore. He must be halfway down the hill he and MacKenzie had spent a half hour traipsing up. How many millions of tons of earth slept above him?

As if he'd crossed a demarcation line from one world to

another, the walls ceased displaying hand-cut roughness and offered an odd pattern. Where before the stone cutters who'd built the tunnel had paid no mind to the flatness of the wall, leaving jutted hunks and deep depression where the hardness of the stone dictated, now the walls showed an attempt at uniformity. And plaster. Rectangles of plaster some four feet wide and a couple feet high checkered the walls. Behind the plaster, visible in those places where it had cracked and wilted away, dark niches resided.

Ossuary niches. The remains of ancient Christians placed in each recess after having been buried elsewhere for decomposition, leaving only bones. The niche would then be plastered over, and often the name of the interred carved before the plaster hardened.

Ward couldn't help running his hand over the plasters that were still intact, feeling the names and epitaphs of those slumbering therein. He couldn't make out any of the letters or words—time had not been kind to them—but it didn't matter. For a few moments he was simply a visitor to history's stories. A scholar on location.

From somewhere ahead a noise whispered. Louder. Then louder still. Like heavy breathing. Or running water. He switched off the flashlight and gripped his pistol.

No more killing, he told himself.

Then why the gun?

Because I don't want to die either.

He proceeded deeper into the earth, letting his fingers on the plaster guide him. The blackness was so complete, so disorienting, he had to close his eyes to keep from getting dizzy. The present melted away, leaving only the past. A memory of a work study in his second year of graduate school, excavating a Norse longhouse, possibly a mead hall, in southwest Newfoundland along the Gulf of Saint Lawrence. It was Ward's first trip into the Canadian Districts. His first taste of the crisp salt air of the North.

He'd been working a three-person team with a girl named Rox and her ex, who'd insisted she be called Winter. Ward hadn't thought about them in years. Best he could figure, Rox and

Winter had signed up for the trip together then broken up right before it began. Rox then used Ward to stoke Winter's jealousy, slipping her fingers up his sleeve every time she leaned in to see his brush work. Making sure Winter was watching when she bent over, the top few buttons of her shirt open. And, of course, climbing into Ward's tent at night. Not that he'd minded being her tool of vengeance. At least not until Winter had gotten her own.

They'd been extracting a piece of timber, a lintel, when their professor had noticed a fragment of something speared on a protuberant splinter. Halting the extraction for the possibility that it was organic, he'd ordered Ward and Winter to carefully gather the sample.

"Watch it with that," Ward had said, thinking only that Winter's choice of a sharp probe was inappropriate.

"You're in the way," Winter had said. She'd slipped. Put her hand forward to brace herself. But it was orchestrated. Obvious. The probe pushed through the fleshy pad of Ward's thumb like a knife into a melon.

The incursion of that instrument into Ward's finger replayed as his hand pushed through a brittle slab of plaster. His knee cracked the wall. Pain shot through his hand. He snatched it back.

"Fucker," he said, his voice returning at the slightest echo.

He switched on the flashlight, keeping it tight against his body to limit its glow. A splinter was sticking up from his palm. He pulled it out. A drop of blood welled like a red eye. He wiped it off and peered into the niche. A few bone fragments fractured at biting angles were scattered within, covered in a layer of dust.

I've been stabbed by the dead, he thought, comically.

He shut off the light. Held still a moment. Listened.

He heard nothing. Felt no coming presence. In an odd sort of calm, he felt nothing at all save for the air he breathed and the throbbing in his hand. The air, he realized, was cooler now. The water was close. He pressed on, eyes now open, until the softest inkling of depth perception presented itself. A light waited ahead. He readied his gun and crept forward.

Sam saw him coming. Neither Ker nor Garm seemed to be keeping an eye on the tunnel. They were engaged in conversation to the side, their feet inches from the water in which she'd been forced to kneel.

They thought she was unconscious. Slumped in a kneeling position, ankles bound. The positioning reminded her of a presentation in school on how to find neighbors who were secretly be Believers, kneeling in prayer in the dark of their basements. The water, splashing her thighs at a swift and regular pace, was cold. When the spray touched her hand it hurt, like the water was boiling.

Stump, she told herself. *There is no hand. It's a stump.*

They'd taken her bandages, leaving the stump, now crusted over, bare. She held it in her lap and ground her teeth, determined not to reveal that she was awake.

Her stomach clenched and gurgled. It had been far too many hours since she'd eaten. Days. Almost as many since she'd had anything to drink. The water around her was so clean and crisp, it was all she could do to keep from leaning over and taking a sip.

But that would give her away.

Not yet.

Her eyes barely open more than slits, she sought a weapon. A stick. A rock. Anything in the water or by its edge she could use when the time came. Ker and Garm were still discussing something. Not paying attention to her. She turned her head just enough to widen her search.

Movement brought her attention back to center. He was there, pressed into the shadow by the mouth of the tunnel. Rafe. He'd come for her after all. She looked for MacKenzie, flitting her eyes this way and that, but couldn't find her.

The disappointment was harsh but the fear, like a robust chunk of meat swallowed down the wrong pipe, was worse. She'd thought MacKenzie was her friend. She knew MacKenzie was her best chance at escape.

I'm going to die, she thought. *I'm going to die thirsty, kneeling in a river.*

She wanted to laugh, but her strength was dwindling. Her

life fading. Her baby's life was probably already lost. All of it for nothing.

Not without a fight, she told herself.

She tried to stay awake—needed to stay awake—for whatever Rafe had planned. He would need her help. But there was no rock. No stick. And the light was shrinking to a point.

CHAPTER 42

The tunnel opened into an underground river scene Ward could imagine as a screen saver. A packed sand beach, dotted with rocks and small boulders, stretched ahead beneath endless thin stalactites like the filtering baleen of a great whale. Torches were set at intervals atop pikes by the river's edge, showing the green-black gleam of the languid water. The walls of the cave—wavy sedimentary layers of reds and creams and browns—sparkled with feldspar and quartz.

What Ward at first thought were stalagmites rising from the sand on the opposite shore, revealed themselves to be piles of bat guano when a number of the winged mammals detached from the ceiling in a startled mass. They burst to the water of a single mind, refused to cross it, then reset themselves within the darkness. It wasn't difficult to imagine them as the shades of the dead flitting about the river's edge, waiting permission to pass into the Underworld. It wasn't a stretch to imagine this place as Lethe, Ameles, the port at which the living joined the dead.

Ward pressed tight to the wall, as deep as he could within the tunnel to remain invisible among the niches, plastered and open, around him. To the right, almost beyond his line of sight, the water lapped at Sam's slumped form. Of anyone else, he could see or hear nothing save for the river's murmur passing right to left.

Or could he?

Barely discernable, rumbling and with a less steady cadence, Ward became aware of a voice. He couldn't make out the words, but it was there. A conversation hidden by the drone of what he'd now accepted as the River Lethe, the deep voice followed by a silence Ward interpreted as another person speaking. Then the deep voice again.

Two people. Two lives to be threatened but not taken. A point definitively settled.

"Fine," the deep voice—glinted with a Scandinavian accent, perhaps Finnish—said, now close and coming closer. "I'll get him, but I think we should use the girl."

Ward scrambled backward in an awkward crab-crawl, trying to find the blackest point of the tunnel. The owner of the voice appeared. Tall, broad, like a blonde Viking in business casual, he filled the tunnel entrance, peering into it so intently that Ward thought for sure he'd be seen.

"If he doesn't show we will," said Ker's voice from behind the blonde man. "For now, we wait. What do you want, him to show up behind us while we're caught in the moment? Lose Cadejo and ourselves as well, with no one remaining to find second bodies for us?"

Cadejo. Ward knew that name. His mind tripped back to the murals beneath the Pyramid of the Sun. The bird. The water. The dogs...

"It's been so long now is all." The big man entered the tunnel a few steps, arresting Ward's thoughts. He reached into an open niche and removed a large bag, carrying it in his arms like a gift. Or a body. "Every minute waiting is a chance it won't work."

Ker said a word Ward didn't understand. The blonde exited the tunnel and made for Sam with the thing in his arms. Ward's mind screamed about what was happening. Cried out for him to wait, to think it through. To understand what he was about to barrel into.

Fear took hold. Not for himself. For Sam. The tunnel behind him was empty. He was all alone. He was Sam's last chance.

He stood, knees flexed, one heel propped against the tunnel wall like a runner ready to sprint. He aimed his pistol at the only target he could see: the blonde Viking.

He fingered the trigger. Held his breath. Braced for the more important second move. Squeezed.

It took MacKenzie more than a few minutes to extricate herself from the duct tape. Her heart pounded the entire time, her stomach twisting over what had happened to Rafe. Every second she wasted trying to escape what should have been simple bonds was a second of peril he wasn't equipped to deal with. Not anymore. The bourbon, or whatever the hell he drank, was thick in his veins, and his head, no matter how much he wanted to deny it. His instincts and reaction times were both impeded. She couldn't forget the way the pistol had trembled in his hand outside the museum in Madrid.

How could you let them surprise you like that? she admonished herself.

Finally, the duct tape tore from her wrists, pulling flesh with it. The pain was deserved. She'd allowed Ker, or whoever, to get in behind them as they were about to enter the catacombs. That was the last thing she remembered. Her hand went to the back of her neck. Found the two round lesions she knew she'd find. She'd been stunned. Up close.

She ripped the tape from her ankles. Swiped the note that had been teasing her—sitting just out of reach in a slice of moonlight from the window behind her, folded in half so that she could read *Hannah* scrawled on its cover—from the floor and got to her feet. She prepared herself for Ker's taunt. A ransom demand. A photo of Ward's disemboweled corpse. Anything but what she read when she opened it.

Her body locked in disbelief. Only her eyes moved, scanning the lines again and again. Looking for the clue that would declare it a joke. Part of Ker's test. A hallucination. Only when her eyes locked on the Spear, recognizing it as the relic she'd left with Rafe on the beach at Santorini, did she comprehend what had happened.

Rafe had betrayed her.

There was more to it, of course. There had to be. But she could only process this one fact. Wrath was all she had. She flipped over an altar that sat against the side wall, scattering a small portrait, a candelabra, and whatever else had been upon it. The door to the little room ripped nearly from its hinges at her kick. The resulting crash echoed the various dooms she was swearing for Rafe and Ker and everyone who'd ever crossed her.

Only, it didn't stop echoing.

She halted a few steps into the corridor. Listened. She heard footsteps, boots on the stone floor. At least three people coming her direction. She sought a point of advantage. A place to ambush. The chapel was useless now that she'd destroyed its door, all potential surprise lost in its wreckage. The door to the catacombs, too far. The other end of the hall, also too far. The footsteps were too close.

The window.

The idea of escape, of retreat, was like rotted vegetables in her mouth. But the prospect of a confrontation in this hallway, outnumbered and still lagging some from the effects of the stun, was worse than a bad taste.

She didn't bother with stealth. On the move, she slid one-kneed and grabbed the candelabra. Flung it through the window, paying no mind to the shrieking of exploding glass. She leapt, grabbing the ledge with her right hand, ignoring the shards and shavings of glass plunging into her flesh, and wrenched herself up and through the window.

There was nothing to stop her fall. The landing drove the breath from her lungs, replacing it with a squeezing pain. Unable to get to her feet, she clambered behind a nearby tree. Scanned her surroundings. She was outside, in a yard populated with a sparse number of similar trees. A wall, too far and too high to scale with no breath, rounded the yard. Probably the wall that circumscribed the Abbey. There was no other cover. No other escape. Her eyes locked on the window.

No one appeared. No alarms sounded; no guns fired. There was only the distant chirping of birds and moonlight.

And the insistence, like a drum beat, in her head that she'd missed something.

Read the note again, it said.

She was surprised to find it gripped in her fist. She opened it. Crumpled and torn, Rafe's message remained intact. She read it. His apology. His explanation of the deal he had to accept. His intel that the REC was splintering somehow. His appeal for her to return to her army.

Then she read it a third time, focusing on the final lines, letting herself hear his voice, his inflections and emotions, say the words:

I understand now why you left me on that beach. I'm sorry for blaming you. Be careful and please don't follow me.
R

Her anger abated but didn't depart. It would never depart; of that she was certain. But she understood.

For the first time in years, she knelt and prayed. She asked God to watch over her friend. Then she stood. Spat. Wiped her bloody hand on her thigh, and began the trek to Paris. To her *conservateurs.* And, eventually, to home.

CHAPTER 43

The Viking crashed like a felled tree, both the sight and sound of it, when Ward's bullet entered his leg below the knee. The bag he'd been carrying hurled from his hands, clattering along the sand to near where Sam still knelt inert.

The man twisted, a pistol coming up in his massive hand. Ward fired again. Missed, exploding the beach beyond the man's head. The resulting shower of rocks caused the man's return fire to miscue high.

The bats swarmed on the other side of the river, their screeching pulling Ward's vision from his target. Less than a second. More than enough. His next shot missed. It was a wonder his first shot had found its mark at all. But he was on the man now. He kicked the gun from his hand, heard it skitter and splash into the water. Danced from the Viking's swiping arm. Backed away, pistol trained on his victim. Eyes darting every direction for adversary number two.

"Cutting it a little close, professor," Ker said. He stood by the river's edge, a pistol aimed at Sam's head. Not far from them lay the bag the blonde had dropped, looking like a burlap coffee sack large enough for his own weight in grounds.

"Let her go," Ward said, "and you can do whatever you want with me."

"That was the plan. Then you had to go and shoot my brother."

Movement to Ward's left made him back up a step and turn, making sure to keep both men in front of him. The bigger man had gotten to a knee. Ward leveled his gun on him. On Ker's brother. A piece of information Ker shouldn't have let slip. It gave a bargaining chip.

Ker's brother held steady under the watchful muzzle of Ward's gun. Stoic. Showing no sign of pain at the bullet wound that might end up costing him his leg. No gasping or howling. Not even a grimace.

He'll live, Ward thought, impressed by the man's pain tolerance.

"Where's the General?" Ker asked.

"I sent her away."

Ker stared, his eyes narrowing.

"I hit her with a stun baton and tied her up so she wouldn't get hurt down here," Ward said. "This is about us not her."

Ker laughed. "You did, didn't you?"

"I told you, Kerberos," the blonde said. "Stop the game and let's do this."

"Kerberos," Ward repeated. He said it again, feeling almost like he was in a trance. Information bombarded him. Pages, videos, stories, photos, memories of mythologies from every stage of his life. The Pyramid of the Sun. The murals. Cadejo. "Fucking Cadejo," he said when the deluge began to coalesce.

"Now the professor gets it," Ker said.

"You think you're Kerberos," Ward said, using the Greek hard *K* pronunciation of *Cerberus* that the brother had used, "the three-headed dog who guards the underworld?"

"Three heads. Always three heads. You humans and your twisting of truths. It's brothers, professor. Three brothers."

"Kerberos," Ker's brother said, clearly trying to end the conversation.

"Enough," Ker said. "Both of you. Garm, sit back down and shut up before you bleed to death and we have to use the girl anyway. And you, Rafael, dear professor—"

Ward laughed. He couldn't help it. The standoff playing out here was too much to take seriously. Like a derivative Western film mashed together with a ridiculous mythological premise.

"Garm now? Kerberos, Cadejo, and Garm." He couldn't believe he was saying the names out loud. Garm, the hound who guarded Hel, the Old Norse language idea which gave rise to the English word and Western concept of Hell. Kerberos, guardian of Tartarus. And Cadejo, the Central American dog spirit who guided the dead to the underworld. Like the mural, Cadejo came in two forms. Black to take the souls of the wicked and white to take the souls of the virtuous. "What's the game, Ker? Really? Your little fantasy isn't going to play. What do you want with me and Sam?"

"Fantasy," Ker said, as if the idea insulted him. "Did you not listen to that old woman's story? Did you not find the ashes of our sister? How can you be so astute yet so obtuse?"

"The sister of three brothers," Ward said, repeating what Ker had declared about the mural beneath the Pyramid of the Sun. The Lady of Elche. For a moment he let himself consider believing. Why not? After all, look at what he'd gone through because of Adrien Quinque's madness.

Does it matter, Rafael, if you believe it to be real? Or does it only matter if those who will kill you believe it to be so? Simon, MacKenzie's father, had said.

The pieces of the puzzle began clicking into place. Like after a long, strong drink. The burn then the chill. The unification of body and mind in the pursuit of a single goal. With bourbon it was escape. With this, Ker's test and Sam's life, it was the understanding.

Three brothers trapped ever in the earth, the Underworld, according to the stories. Three dogs offered by mythologies guarding the passage in and, more importantly, back out.

"You never considered who was in the Tower," Ker said, returning Ward to the standoff. "All your brains and smarts and books. You never thought it through that far, did you?"

"I…" Ward began, but he had no more defense.

"The prisoners beneath that monstrosity, like a perverted obelisk. The prisoners, professor. Like our brother Cadejo, being held, tortured, murdered not by the REC. By you."

The words were a punch to Ward's throat. A name. Somehow the difference between feeling guilt and being guilty. The name of a victim. He couldn't breathe. If Sam weren't in danger he might have dropped his gun and submitted to whatever vengeance Ker wanted.

But if he wanted me dead, Ward thought, *he could have done that anytime.*

He wants something else.
What's worse than death?
"Lethe," Ward said.
"What's this," Ker said, his glee sounding almost like madness. "Is he getting it, Garm? Is he?"
Garm shifted but didn't speak.
"The souls that throng the flood," Ward recited, the words of the epic poem the *Aeneid* coming back to him despite the years since his eyes had crossed it, "are those to whom, by Fate a second body is o'wd."
"Not my favorite translation," Ker said. "Certainly not so poetic as the Latin, but it does the job."
"You think you can resurrect your brother?" Ward said, his willingness to believe strained almost too far to continue. "Bring him to life in my body?"
"It's time to believe, my friend. It's long past time with all you've seen and done. Did you think your El and Ba'el had a monopoly on theological truths? If two can exist, why not four? Why not forty?"
"You're not a god," Ward said, hating how he sounded like he was trying to convince himself. Somewhere—maybe in the back of his mind; maybe deep in the tunnel from which he'd come—he heard a noise that reminded him of the *clack, cla-clack, clack* he'd heard in the sewers beneath Bari.
"As if you could fathom what a god truly is," Garm said, his teeth bared like a hound's.
"Thou shalt have no other gods before me," Ker said. The first commandment. The first line of MacKenzie's tattoo. "Doesn't make much sense if there are no other gods around to be placed before big bad El, does it?"
"Gods don't die."
"We were here long before the gods of worship," Ker said, angry. Resolute. As if intensity could make truth. "We were here before men and cities and lies. We are of the rock and the mud and the river. There is nothing older than that. Then came your *gods*," he sneered this last word. "For you. Because of you. From you. I don't care. Their time is ended. The enemy of my enemy and all that. The General's war is our war. I don't give a shit for

one life or a thousand, or if it ends with civilization standing or burning. I only care for victory."

There it was again. The sound in the tunnel. A metronome ticked in Ward's head, counting off Ker's words. Letting him talk. Pacing the seconds. He needed more. Just a little more.

"How does it work?"

"There he is," Ker said, a smile erupting across his face. "The professor, curious to learn. Isn't that the best way, Garm?"

Garm grunted and swapped hands over his wound.

"Did you know Vergilius sought me out when he wrote his *Aeneid*? No, don't jeer. I'll tell you the same as I told him. I want you to understand it all. I want you to end knowing the exact result of your wanton vendetta. The dead submerges in the river. So long as there remain heart, liver, and lungs of flesh, even charred slivers of each, the transference works. The dead submerges and the second body drinks of the river. The drinking is what does it, vacating the soul, the memory, the identity from the second body, leaving it a hollow vessel. Then the dead, like osmosis, slips inside and we on the shore speak the words. That's it, but don't worry. You won't feel anything other than tired, professor. Confused perhaps. Then nothing. Nothing at all, forever."

Ward understood the theory. Transmigration of the soul from one body to another. It sounded insane, but Ker believed it. That belief, Ward hoped, would give him the few moments he needed.

"And you'll spend eternity seeing my face when you embrace your brother," Ward said.

Ker flinched. His pistol lowered a couple inches. As Ward expected, he hadn't considered this. Ward rocked onto the balls of his feet. He listened, ignoring Ker's voice. What he wanted to hear would be coming from the tunnel. The slightest scrape of a boot on rock. The faintest echo of breathing.

"Promise you'll let Sam go," Ward said. "She needs a doctor."

"She'll need a mortician if you don't cooperate. Into the river, now."

"Let her go or your brother stays in a bag forever." Ward put his gun to his temple.

"Oh, come on," Ker said. "Are you not paying attention? I want you, but she'll do fine. Go ahead. Kill yourself."

Ward exhaled, made sure to slump his shoulders in defeat. Lowered his gun.

"That's better." Ker waved his pistol to the water. "Get in."

It was the move Ward had been waiting for. He swung right, firing as many shots as he could over Ker's head. Planted his foot. Turned. Pain shot up his leg. He did all he could to ignore it. Flexed to spring forward, to put himself between Sam and Ker's gun. Felt more than saw Garm limping at him. Ker resetting his aim. The bats screaming downstream to escape the havoc.

Then, with shouts and gunfire, Compano's two men from Madrid burst from the tunnel.

Ward dove for Sam.

CHAPTER 44

Someone was knocking on a faraway door.
   Tap. Tap-tap-tap. Tap-tap. Tap.
   Getting closer. And closer. And...
   Sam was cold. Tired. Her hand hurt, a Tingling agony. She wanted to go back to sleep.
   Tap-tap. Tap. Tap-tap...
   Gunshots, Sam's mind yelled.
   Her eyes popped open. At first all she saw was water. Then her thighs. She was kneeling in the water. Her lap. Her hands.
   Hand.
   The one that hurt wasn't even there.
   Memory was worse than the pain. All of it at once, then gone again, as if her brain was a television with a bad feed.
   Someone shouted her name.
   She looked up. Saw Rafe coming at her, arms wide, like he was flying. Then, a shadow behind him. The man who'd cut off her hand. Ker.
   Rage. Determination. She remembered these from home. From when she'd seen her father. Shot. Dead. She forced her legs to move. To try to stand.
   The flying Rafe hit her in the chest. She went over into the water. A new pain, a beehive of anguish, erupted in her handless arm. Made her gasp. Choke on the river.
   I could stop this, she thought. *I could end the pain with a couple more drinks.*
   Rage and determination screamed at her. Refused to let her give up. She needed to get out of the water. She needed a

weapon. Her fingers found something cold beneath the water.

Ward hit the water hard, like falling onto a glass table that holds a moment before shattering. At first, he couldn't tell if it was pain exploding through his body or simply the shock of the cold. As everything went dark beneath the surface, he worried that he'd missed Ker's shoulder as he dove and had been shot.

He rolled, keeping his mouth clamped shut, trying to not inhale when the water burned his nose. No, he didn't think he'd been shot. He surfaced to find one of Compano's men, the one with the fake ear, grappling with Garm. The big blonde had produced a knife—in a smaller man's hand it might be a sword—and plunged it into the black suit's lapel.

Gunfire from somewhere nearby caused Garm to jump back, leaving the blade in the falling man's chest. He fled, limping and loping like a wounded dog, from the light, disappearing from view downstream.

On his hands and knees, Ward tried to find Sam in the water. He tried to shout her name, but his mouth wouldn't open, as if it was terrified of swallowing the river.

"Stop," a metallic voice said.

Ward, arms still submerged in hopes of finding Sam, sought the voice. First, he saw Ker getting to his feet in the knee-deep water. Then he saw Compano in the mouth of the tunnel, darkness against darkness.

"I'd like to talk to that one," Compano said, pointing to Ker who was being held under the aim of her remaining soldier. She moved from the tunnel to stand beside Cadejo's bag. She didn't appear to notice her other man, Garm's blade protruding from his chest like a monument.

"Help me," Ward said to Compano, to her soldier in the black suit. The water was too shallow for Sam to remain under this long. "She hasn't come up. Help me." He began groping the rocky river bed once more, ready to dive into the water. Ready to use every ounce of air in his lungs to search the coldest depths of Ker's fucking River Lethe.

"Where's the General?"

Before Ward could answer, before he could open his mouth

to question her callousness, Sam exploded from the river behind Ker. She leapt onto his back, wrapping a handless forearm around his neck. Grabbing at his face, fingers raking his mouth open in a horrific gape. Over backwards they went, splashing back into the water.

Neither came up. The surface calmed. Two seconds. Four. Ten.

Ker burst forth as if he'd been vomited up, landing on his hands and knees in a half foot of water. Gasping.

"What," he wheezed, his eyes wide and glassy. Panicked as if he had just woken from a nightmare. "Who…"

Sam rose purposefully from the water behind him. A gun, Garm's gun, in her hand.

"Wait," was all Ward had time to say.

Sam put the gun to the back of Ker's head and pulled the trigger over and over until it clicked empty. Until there was nothing recognizable as human atop Ker's neck.

Ward, covered now in Ker's blood, brains, and flecks of skull, could only watch as the pistol fell from Sam's hand. Her eyes rolled back in her head, and she fell, unconscious, arms wide, back into the water.

"Where is the General?" Compano asked, repeating her earlier question.

Sam was being tended to by Compano's remaining black-suited soldier, the one who'd driven Ward to the parking garage in Madrid. She was in shock but would probably live, he'd said.

Probably.

Then he'd said, "The baby, I don't know."

"Baby?" Ward asked.

The soldier had held out his Port, the screen showing a double-columned list of medical terms. At the bottom, the word *Positive* shone in bold red. Two lives in one body. Ward felt like he'd just been told of Daniel's second death again.

He'd been unsure how he was going to play the aftermath of the deal he'd struck with Compano. Until he saw that Port. The results on the screen had locked him in to the course of action he'd wanted from the start: get Sam as far from the Republic as possible.

"She didn't come," Ward said, unwilling to look directly at Compano's eye.

"Hannah MacKenzie ran out on a fight? I find that hard to believe."

"She decided the revolution was more important than a girl."

"Is that so?"

The servos in Compano's mask whirred ever so slightly. Ward imagined a knowing smile somewhere beneath the carbon fiber, cables, and metals that comprised her face. A smile he'd rarely seen when she was his commander, but one that had offered some warmth back then.

There was no warmth in her words or demeanor now. "We had a deal."

"We still do."

"She was the deal."

"No," Ward said. "I told you that after you helped me get Sam back you could have the General. I never said I'd give her to you." He put out his hands, palms up. "Go get her."

The soldier approached. "She's stable for now. If she wakes, give her this." He handed Ward a pill bottle. "One only. Not with that water." He pointed to the river. "I'll go to the surface to call in assistance and cleanup."

Ward thanked him for helping Sam. Watched him trot up the tunnel until he was swallowed by the darkness.

"Was she worth it?" Compano asked.

"Sam?"

Compano nodded, like a mountain bowing its peak. "Your girlfriend is never going to forgive you."

Ward wondered how much Compano really knew. Decided it didn't matter. "You still win, either way. You've got us."

"I've got you. I lost Ker. The girl is nothing."

"Wherever you're going to take us, she's valuable," Ward said, hoping Compano would fulfill her part of the bargain, to bring him and Sam somewhere safe and faraway from the Republic and the revolution. "Unless you have an endless supply of recruits."

"Do you think pregnant teenagers are in demand?"

"I think people willing to believe whatever you believe are in demand."

"Are you ready to find out what it is I believe? What it is me and my people know?"

Ward looked at Sam lying on the sand. Her chest rising and falling at long intervals. He'd failed her. He'd cost her a chance at a peaceful life. Cost her a hand. Maybe a baby. She might blame him. She might not. The same questions that would linger about MacKenzie.

What concerned him, however, was anger and regret. What she'd done to Ker, the way she'd executed him. That could stain a person. It could follow a mother and her child forever. He found himself hoping that the river might be mystical enough to let her forget that one act.

He turned back to Compano. This time he locked onto her eye. Heard the servos in her mask twitch.

"I'm ready," he said.

PART 5: THE LONG OBLIVION

The souls that throng the flood
Are those to whom, by fate, a second body is o'wd:
In Lethe's lake they long oblivion taste.
—The Aeneid, by Virgil, c. 29 BCE

EPILOGUE

"Morning, Sam," Rafael Ward said. "Doc's not here yet?" Sam didn't answer, of course. She was still unconscious.

Coma, Ward thought, uncomfortable with the ominous diagnosis. *She's in a coma.*

He patted Sam's hand—her remaining hand—and sat on the gurney beside her. The infirmary was quiet, save for the steady beeping of the machine that monitored and fed her. It was the first morning he'd arrived to find her the only patient. The first morning he'd arrived to find her doctor, Rivka, absent.

He looked over his friend. Except for the odd carbon fiber and alloy cuff on the stump of her right wrist, she appeared perfectly healthy. She could have been sleeping, her chest rising and falling with the machine's beeps, her eyes fluttering like she was dreaming.

"I think I'm starting to like your new 'do," he said of her shaved head. It gave her a seriousness, a worldliness that belied her youth. At the same time, it softened her face, hinting at a cherublike quality. "What do you think? Want to wake up so we can get the hell out of here?"

The machine beeped on.

They'd been here, in this underground military base, less than a week, but he was already finding it difficult to ignore the machine's relentless beeping. Each day it seemed to drill deeper into his brain. He worried that if he didn't get a drink soon, he might smash the thing. But a drink was one of the two things Compano had explicitly prohibited.

The other was leaving. Not that Ward was going anywhere

with Sam attached to that machine. Her coma was a better jailor than a thousand guards and an electric fence.

Ward suspected that Compano's order denying him alcohol was for no reason other than her own cruel amusement. Nearly a week without a drink. This morning wasn't his breaking point, but it was coming soon.

He got off the gurney and paced the infirmary, trying to focus on the room rather than the beeping. It was a high-ceilinged cave, carved of the same khaki-colored stone as the rest of the base. Functional and bland and not the least bit comfortable or interesting.

He'd asked everyone who would talk to him about the base, trying to find out where it was and why it was built of ancient tunnels rather than modern structure. Most of the people here avoided him the way he imagined lepers were shunned in antiquity. Those that allowed him to ask his questions offered few answers, usually directing him to Control, a room he'd as yet been unable to find in the base's confusing system of tunnels and caves.

So, he'd taken to wandering, as much as he was allowed, cataloguing the base's features in an attempt to diagnose its location. The tunnels were hand cut through, he was fairly sure, mostly limestone. Remnants of mosaic tiles and faint traces of paint pointed to at least partial domestic use in the ancient past. And then there were the varied accents and languages Ward overhead. Taken together, the clues had led him to a theory: they were somewhere in the Middle East or North Africa, within the borders of what had once been the Roman Empire.

The problem was, now that he'd figured out their general location, he was bored out of his mind. All he had to look forward to was sitting with Sam each morning, and hoping that Rivka—the only person here who talked to him like he was a human being—would join them for a chat.

As if thinking of the doctor has conjured her, Rivka entered the infirmary, wearing scrubs rather than her standard fatigues. She was about MacKenzie's age, with an intense casualness about her, as if everything was so important there was no sense in rushing for any of it.

"I can't stay long," she said in her husky, probably Israeli, accent.

"Trouble?" Ward asked.

Rivka felt Sam's forehead while checking the readout on the beeping machine. She placed her hand on Sam's right wrist and nodded as if confirming what she saw on the machine.

Ward watched her routine without interrupting. He hadn't expected her to answer his question. While she was open with details about medicine and Sam's condition, and even the occasional anecdote about her childhood, she'd made it clear that operations and infrastructure were restricted subjects.

"Did you pass along my request to bring Sam to the surface once in a while?" Ward said. "You said fresh air would be good for her."

As if he hadn't spoken, Rivka said, "Have you considered the surgery for your leg?"

"Not yet."

"Bar-Ilan insists it'll take away your pain," she said of the base's surgeon, a man Ward had only seen a few times in passing.

Ward shrugged. He liked Rivka. It was obvious she cared about Sam. She was also one of the few people here without some kind of modification, like Compano's man in Spain with the mechanical ear. He'd seen soldiers with exoskeletons on their hands or arms, cybernetic threading around their mouths, glowing disks in their necks, and one who an implant jutting from his hip like he'd been impaled. Ward had no idea what that one did.

The modifications bothered him, and Rivka knew it. He couldn't put his finger on exactly why, but the thought of them, the thought of whatever mod Bar-Ilan had in mind for his leg, made him queasy.

"I need a comm link out of here," he said, bringing up a subject he knew annoyed Rivka.

"I told you, Control is in charge of all comms."

"Then I need to talk to Compano."

"She's not here."

Ward's first thought was: *Maybe I can get a drink.*

Then: *Who's in charge?*

"She left?" he said. "For how long? Why are we still here?"

"A couple days ago. We all follow orders. Hers are in your country."

"Then get me a comm to her," Ward said. "If she's in the Republic, maybe she can arrange for Reina to be brought here. Her dog, that's good for people in comas, right? Maybe Reina can help Sam come out of it."

"You have to ask Control."

"Control isn't a person. I don't even know where it is. You're a doctor. Help me. Help Sam!"

"Don't you think," Rivka started. She shook her head. Began again. "There are almost a thousand people within the mountain."

The change in subject threw Ward. Rivka had never offered specific logistical details before.

"We have about seven hundred soldiers," she went on. "Plus families. That's another almost three hundred people. Over a hundred of them are children, too young to serve."

"Why are you telling me this?"

"We have cooks, electricians, plumbers. We have masons, mechanics, pilots, a blacksmith. We have eight nurses, almost twenty med techs, and two doctors. What we don't have is a teacher."

"A teacher," Ward repeated. "Wait, are you asking me...you want me to teach a hundred kids?"

The idea rippled through Ward like first day jitters. Then it thrilled him, warming him like a shot of strong whiskey.

"We need someone," Rivka said. "It would be good for you as well as them."

"Would Control approve it?"

Rivka gave him a patient, almost condescending look. Like she was waiting for him to pick up on something. To offer something.

What do I have to offer...

"A trade," he said. There was a flash of approval in the doctor's eyes. "I teach in exchange for a comm link."

She smiled. Small. Crooked. Too much like MacKenzie.

"Yeah," he said, trying not to sound too eager, "Can you tell them?"

Rivka put her hand on Sam's forehead again. "I'll tell them," she said. "I have to go."

She marched out of the infirmary, leaving Ward to imagine teaching again. Telling stories. Being free to tell *all* the stories, not just the ones the Republic approved. For the first time since he arrived here—for the first time since the Tower—he felt optimistic. He felt like celebrating.

He wanted a damn drink.

I should have asked for a bottle of Scotch in the deal.

He returned to Sam's bedside. "What do you think, kid?" he asked her. "Should I teach?"

The machine beeped its plodding rhythm.

"Should I—"

The infirmary door swung open hard. A soldier entered.

"You have a link," the soldier said, his accent likely Egyptian.

That was fast, Ward thought.

He patted Sam's hand and said, "I'll be back."

"This way," the soldier said, leading Ward out of the infirmary.

"Where are we going?" Ward asked.

"Control."

Ward followed the soldier to a set of narrow hand-cut stairs he'd not previously seen. The steps led down to a mosaic platform decorated in rolling waves and sunbursts. The tiles were easily two thousand years old. Ward barely glanced at them.

"Who's the comm from?" he asked the soldier.

"The Republic."

MacKenzie!

It was a quick thought. Fleeting. MacKenzie would never risk a potentially traceable link to talk to him. Not after what he'd done.

Besides, Rivka had said Compano was back in the Republic. It had to be her linking in to check on him. Good. She had questions to answer.

The soldier took him to another flight of stairs. Ward's leg began to ache halfway down. His knee threatened to lock up at the bottom—*maybe I should consider Bar-Ilan's surgery*—but he pushed on, following the soldier through a confusing series of twisting, seemingly abandoned, tunnels.

Finally, they turned a corner and stood before a simple wooden door painted with red block letters: CONTROL.

The door opened and an officer—the number of bars on his collar left no doubt of his advanced rank—filled the entrance. He dismissed the soldier who'd brought Ward here.

"Come," he said, his accent similar to Rivka's.

The cave-room was small and cold. And filled with computers. The only ones Ward had seen in the base. Every inch of wall space was covered by them, their screens all currently switched off, like black mirrors. A large array jutted from the left, cutting the room in half.

"Orders are just you in the room for the link," the officer said. "Push the white button in the middle when you're finished to lock out the connection."

He left, closing the door with a thud. Ward looked around once more and then stepped behind the array. He steeled himself for Compano's inhuman visage and pushed the button.

The largest screen in the room, directly in front of the array, dissolved from black to white to a bright silhouette. The silhouette became a face.

"Mr. Ward, it is you," a young man with a soldier's jaw said. "Thank God."

"Who are you?" Ward asked, confused.

"I have the Seer. He needs to speak with you. Time is short." He backed away from the feed.

A new shape filled the screen. The image focused, dissolving contrasts until a powerful man with thick creases around his mouth and across his forehead appeared. His eyes were deep. They drew Ward in. He knew those eyes. He'd seen them a thousand times in his dreams. He'd watched them die again and again.

Ward's chest seized. He couldn't breathe.

"Hi Raffi," the Seer said, his voice as sweet as a memory could be.

There was only one word Ward could say. One word that, when spoken, would make this real. He licked his lips. Swallowed. Spoke.

"Daniel?"

ABOUT THE AUTHOR

Michael Pogach is an American author. He's written over three novels. At least two of them—*The Spider in the Laurel* and *The Long Oblivion*—have been published. His other work includes the "dirty and intense" chapbook *Zero to Sixty*, and contributions to anthologies such as *Tales from the Combat Zone (Workers Write! #8)* and the *CAM Charity Anthology (Horror & Science Fiction #1)*. He lives in Pennsylvania with his wife and daughter and an empty space in his garage for his next motorcycle project.

michaelpogach.com
@michaelpogach
facebook.com/MichaelPogachAuthor
instagram.com/michaelpogach

Curious about other Crossroad Press books?
Stop by our site:
http://store.crossroadpress.com
We offer quality writing
in digital, audio, and print formats.

Enter the code FIRSTBOOK
to get 20% off your first order from our store!
Stop by today!

CPSIA information can be obtained
at www.ICGtesting.com
Printed in the USA
BVHW092124261118
534071BV00019B/521/P

9 781948 929455